Death & Taxxis

Chris Graham

Gray Home Ink

Published by Gray Home Ink, in the United States of America

Gray Home Ink
PO Box 175
Derby, CT USA 06418

https://GrayHomeInk.com

Cover Image and Design by Nikki Blanchard

https://WitchNikki.com

ISBN: 979-8-9863672-0-0

Library of Congress Control Number:
2022910437

Dedicated to my Seashell, for hearing this story two thousand times before ever reading it once.

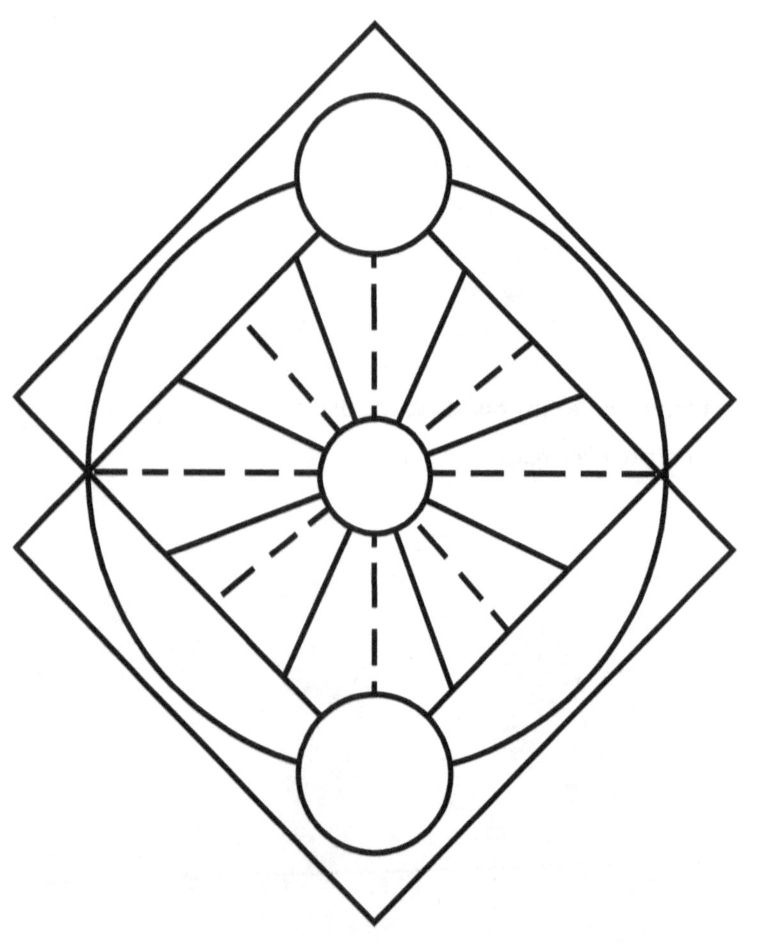

Chapter | One

The end of the world started with a dream. A witch had been watching, hearing secrets from the dreams of others. This is not uncommon as witches do not sleep because they cannot sleep. When they close their eyes, they see the well from which all dreams come. Here, there are more dreams to see than any single person ever could, more than all the witches that have ever been could see, if all they ever did was watch. Behind a witch's eyelids was an eternal spring that bubbled up visions, gossamer echoes from the source of all magic. The witch that started the end of the world just so happened to be watching them at the exact right moment. There was something comforting about the way they drifted by like clouds, shapeless ambiance, the distant sounds of the stream like a gentle song. That's when she saw it.

She did not see it with her eyes; she was aware that an object that had been just there, only a moment ago, had wholly and suddenly gone away. This drew all of her attention like a spider in a web, and she focused there, where it had been just a moment ago. Her magic left her reflexively and sent a strand of her power after it, as thin as a spider's web. That web pierced the space where the dream had been and became rigid, tight as a fishing line that had hooked something. It was holding the invisible vision in place.

She had seen something here. Her magic was holding on to an object she could not perceive with her senses; there was strong magic here. The witch used more fingers, and more strands came out of her, wrapping themselves around the dream to reveal its shape. Only one thing required such magic to keep hidden, a precious secret. The Witch used a portion of her cunning to slip into the dream unseen. As soon as her crux passed over into the dream, its energetic form became solid. The sound of her heels clicked on the grey-blue floor of an empty classroom as she looked around. There were dozens of desks, all arranged in rows, and a larger one sitting at the head of the class. The witch carefully placed several black feathers on the floor behind that teacher's desk.

They were arranged in a strange shape within a rough circle, and when she was done, she stood up to examine her work. Satisfied, the witch wiggled her fingers in a way that could have been an elaborate dance but, in this case, was a magical method. In moments the circle began to fill with a dark and terrible fluid that looked like chunky oil. From that oil rose a shape, a monstrous form of feathers with more eyes than anything needed. All of them red. It had too many hands, wings, and a massive beak as slick and black as obsidian. It nearly filled the space before the witch made magic by twisting her fingers. There was a cap on them to the first knuckle in caps. They looked like thimbles with ornate carvings on them, and they had a faint glow when her magic flowed through them.

When her finger manipulations were done, light spilled in thin wisps like spider webs from her fingertips. They moved on their own and crept along the floor until they reached the creature. It did not fight back, and the threads began to encase the mass of feathers and eyes and muscles, condensing the form down and into shape. When it was done, there was a man where once there was something else entirely. He was tall, and his eyes were as grey as a stormy sea. The thread made him a human body complete with clothes, right down to the shoes. The thing in a man's body stretched lazily, looking at his hands bemused for a moment, then he examined the rest of himself and strangely canted his head.

"I don't like when I have to wear these," he said.

"Your true form is not fit for the places where humans thrive. You would not fit through the doors," she said.

"My talons?" he asked.

She only had to wiggle just one of those capped fingers to create the blades he asked for. The glittering handles grew out of his clothing, building themselves up layer by layer. It took only a breath to create several weapons, knives already strapped and holstered in various places around his body. A single but massive sword sat on his hip, and he laid his hand on it with a familiar motion. The witch smiled, and though she was wearing a black mask that shrouded her entire head, it was clearly a smile. The mask was made of many short threads, closely crowded together. When she moved her face, the mask moved with her features but made it impossible to know who wore it.

"May I ask, why does everything sound so strange here?" he asked.

"This is a dream. Dreams are prone to strange physical fluctuations," she said.

"Why do you dream of a high school? You never struck me as the sort," he said.

"This is not my dream," she said.

"You always say the most interesting things, Master," he said.

They were standing in a darkened high school classroom, dozens of single unit desks carefully arranged in front of a chalkboard. There was even a child at each desk, all frozen in motion with opaque skin and faceless heads. Her partner was now staring at one very closely, curling over like a reed to look at the mostly clear face. He reached out to touch it, and his hand passed through the form of the child so quickly that it startled him. The complete form of that faceless child atomized like smoke in the thick air and was gone from the chair.

"This mask you wear. It reminds me of a pin screen. Do you know this toy? They were huge in the nineties. I was many birds in those times. The pinscreen was a good shiny. When you wear it on your face, I can't tell that it is you," he said.

"That is the point," she said.

"Then it is working well," he said plainly.

"Enough. Can you sense the core of this dream?" she asked.

He closed his two visible eyes, and unseen appendages beneath the skin began to move and contort as things were set in motion. The skin around his eyes bulged for a moment as though hands beneath his flesh were at work, changing his eyeballs like lightbulbs. When the creature opened the holes on his face again, the eyes inside were different. A bright orange. He turned slowly, squinting here and there as if looking off through walls.

"I can easily see where the core of this dream is. However, I'm not sure if this is a human," he said.

"Show me," she said.

The two of them stepped out of the classroom door and into the unlit hallway. Lockers were flanking them on both sides of them, the shape was right, but they were devoid of weight or color. Made of the same material that the classroom had been made of but slightly opaquer. The color was stronger even further down the hall to the left. To the right was a darker space; the ceiling sagged so far that it nearly touched the floor. As the two of them watched, the roof in that section of the hallway slowly collapsed and blended like fluid until it was gone. All that was left was a sheer wall of cloudy white material, flat as a board, and everything beyond was swallowed up. The ceiling began to sag in the classroom they had just left.

Her partner made a face, and she smiled.

"I do not like this place," he said.

"Dream spaces are confusing for everyone. You have only just begun to see its eccentricities," she said.

"Forgive me, Master Kingmaker, but why are we here?" he asked.

"This is someone else's dream, a distant point in it specifically, where the stability is weakest. That makes it the easiest place to sneak in undetected," she said.

"I see. But pretend that I had no idea what that means?" Jackdaw asked.

"These places have the lowest concentration of magic. The

closer we get to the person having this dream, the more tangible things become. These parts are unstable." she said.

"That's cool, but I meant why here? Why would we want to sneak into a dream?" he asked.

"Some dreams are special. Some have visions of the future, and some hold secrets. This one is more still. You see, something drew me to this place. Something dangerous." she said.

Every time she answered a question for him, his eyes took on more of a noticeable glow. They were nearly glowing like a firefly in the night, and he seemed pleased. Though he said nothing, nor did he smile, his face was still emotionless.

"What is it?" she said.

"Something is close," Jackdaw said.

The classroom behind them started to collapse on cue, the room folded into itself like egg whites. There was a sudden movement from the far corner, and both of them looked up. A faint shape was moving toward the door rapidly; it was hard to distinguish from the shadows. She lost sight of it as it reached the door and melted into the hallway's darkness, escaping the room's demise. Jackdaw stepped in front of his Master, his hand moving to the sword at his hip. It was almost as long as his body and wider than two hands. Before he could draw it, her hand touched his shoulder gently.

"Calm down. Here, there are many ways to hide your presence, and I know them all," she said.

"I see; excuse my ignorance, Master," he said.

Jackdaw stepped away from her and straightened up. His eyes scanned the hallway.

"You can relax. They have likely gone on," she said.

"How can you tell?" Jackdaw asked.

"Because this hallway is likely the next to collapse," she said.

The ceiling above their head started to sag like marshmallows, and the two moved on. The sound of the hallway collapsing behind them was quiet but heavy. The hall they were standing in was very different from the previous one. This one was entirely in color, and teenagers' opaque effigies were moving here and looking through their lockers arbitrarily and adjusted clothes and hair, all made from the same fluid clouds they had just seen. These teens had skin tones and coloration; more muscular shapes, but they still lacked faces.

"Why don't these... beings have eyes?" Jackdaw asked.

"That question makes sense coming from you. These beings are only a supporting cast of faceless shapes. They are made of the same stuff as the walls and floor. They follow the same rules," she said.

Jackdaw only nodded. The two of them picked through the dense crowd of faceless teens. Not bothering to dodge the slow and methodical movements they repeated like animatronics at an amusement park. The two of them cleared a broad swath down the hall as they walked on. Once they rounded the corner for the next hallway, everything was different. The space had taken on the weight of steel and stone, the slick of polished floors. The effigy was so good here that it was hard to distinguish from reality. The sound of their footsteps echoed off down the hall to precede them. The faceless characters around them were all perfectly formed humans with cloudy faces like they had been blurred for television.

"We must be close; the dream is so vivid here. Can you sense the dreamer?" she asked.

Jackdaw closed his eyes for a moment. When he opened

them, he pointed further down the hall.

"The core of this place is further down that way. However, there is something else near… powerful… not of this dream," Jackdaw said.

"Where?" she asked.

"Just there," he said.

Jackdaw pressed his hand to the wall immediately to his left and closed his eyes.

"Yes, I am sure of it," he said.

"Show me," she said.

Jackdaw held out his arm, and she placed her hand on top of it. As soon as he did, he was stricken by the formidable power of her magic as it entered him. The discomfort was temporary, like a needle's prick, and then he couldn't feel anything. She removed her hand from his forearm, but her magic did not pull away; it stayed with him, tethered with a thin strand of her magic. It was more delicate than hair and almost invisible; it disappeared into his forearm and connected to her pointer finger. A thimble on the end of her finger glowed with a gentle light as her magic flowed through it and now him. She nodded, and Jackdaw touched his hand to the wall again when she was through.

"You said this would act like the real thing, yes?" He said.

Kingmaker nodded, and, in a flash, Jackdaw had drawn his sword and cut the wall in a wide clean motion. Where his blade passed through left a deep depression in the wall, blackened around the edged as if it had been oozing oil, it fell away before them like the walls of a sandcastle. Jackdaw put his blade away, looking pleased with himself. A single blow was enough to crumble the wall, and he created his own door to the outside.

"A door," Jackdaw said, patting his sword.

"Go," she said.

Jackdaw answered with a single nod, then he exited his self-made door with purpose, stepping out into the central courtyard. There was more supporting cast here than any other part of the dream, and they were so realistic it was hard to tell them from real. They did not vanish from a slight bump, and he knocked more than a few of them down as he stalked through the courtyard.

"You cannot hide from me. I always find what I'm looking for," he teased.

He was ever so slightly growing larger with each step until he was the size of a pro athlete. The school's courtyard was primarily a green space around a central oak tree. The tree was massive and hung over the school and the courtyard alike. The tree had been burned heavily on one side and was nearly split in half as if a lightning bolt hit it. There were still small fires burning in the high branches, dancing as bright and green as pine needles. He had never seen such a fire in his life. The fire moved strangely. It was much faster than a normal fire, and it skittered through the branches. It was crawling slowly but certainly with the sort of mobility that only came from living things. The sight of it made him freeze. He did not know why, but he knew that this fire was dangerous. There was tension from the iridescent thread hanging from his forearm. He was not to investigate the fire.

He turned back toward the door he made, and his master shook her head. Jackdaw started to walk away from the tree when the sound of a sneeze made him freeze in place again. His hand fell to his hip, and the blade tore through the crowd around him in a near-complete circle in a flash. The teenage effigies vanished in a puff of smoke as the sword cut them all through the chest.

The suddenly clear area left only Jackdaw and a small female with her body curled into her knees. She must have leaped down there to avoid his blade. The girl looked at him with dark sunglasses over an obviously fake nose. She seemed to scream. It took a few moments to reach him in this air. There was no time to celebrate, though; work was to be done. His sword rolled over the back of his left hand, and he swung his shoulders to flip it up and over his head. Higher than he needed, but the look was so critical that he couldn't keep the smile off his face.

"Shiny," he whispered.

His voice was enough to cover the sound of the descending blade in the thick air of the dream. The girl spoke, and the hunter struck, her words barely preceding the blade.

"**Be still,**" she said.

Her words were strange. They were distorted when they reached his ear. Heavy with power. Every part of him was helpless to obey, and he froze on the spot. The edge of his blade a heartbeat from her throat. Jackdaw made a low sound like a bird might make when agitated. The girl did not even look afraid; she looked up at him inquisitively. Not a bit of fear in her. She had the second most peculiar eyes he had ever seen; there was only living flame where there should have been iris. This one could speak.

"You must be powerful to keep me here with such small words," Jackdaw mumbled.

"**And silent,**" she said.

Her voice was so heavy with magic that it did not sound human; it sounded like a distant screaming. Thunder. Rain and a dozen voices repeating her words in languages he could not hope to understand. She spoke to his muscles. Her words danced in his cells and told him to keep still. To keep silent. Jackdaw would have seethed in his anger, but he could no longer move or speak. He did his best to keep his eyes on the girl as she came closer to him to investigate. He flexed against her magic, but he could barely keep his lungs working. It felt like being encased in iron. He looked at her intensely, taking in every detail of her face. He said nothing; he stood precisely where he had been, carefully breathing against his unmoving body. He continuously struggled against her magic, but he was held in the strong spellwork of a powerful being. Had he the ability, he would ask her what she was.

"What kind of thing are you?" the girl asked.

Her voice was normal now. She was young, short, and looking him over through sunglasses even though it was night. The girl looked him over carefully and flinched as though she had been shocked. Then she kneeled and looked him in his orange eyes. She walked around him and back again before she spoke again.

"You are an interesting Other, aren't you? I've never sensed core magic like this before. Such turmoil, poor thing," she whispered.

She started to walk away, then she stopped and turned back to him.

"Whatever you are, I'm not going to hurt you. But I will leave you here. Something called me here, and I have to find it… I think it's in danger," she said.

Jackdaw wanted to protest, but he could not. Instead, he felt the tension on the nearly invisible thread on his forearm tighten. Something was pulling against it and applying pressure to the magic holding him. The line on his forearm started to vibrate, and the potent spell holding him still a moment ago lost its stability and cracked like glass. Jackdaw pushed against it with all of his might and the weight of his big body, and the spell fell away in splinters. The girl didn't even look back. She smartly tried to run, but Jackdaw's body was already in motion, and he threw himself forward, completing that swing of his sword. He caught her back leg with the belly of his sword, and she lost her balance, putting her hands forward to catch herself. Perhaps that is why she did not see the other woman's approach.

"Shit!" she said.

Someone else appeared before the girl could catch herself, and like a snare, she was caught. The woman held her only by the face in a monstrously strong hand. It didn't seem large enough to reach, but it closed like a vice grip around her mouth. The moving pin screen mask had the desired effect, and the girl started to squirm under her grip. Try as she might, she could not break free. Jackdaw ripped her from the young woman away from the death grip of his master and held her down in front of him. He leveled his massive sword across her chest to keep her still.

"You are already dead, do not fight it," Jackdaw said.

"This one has power," Kingmaker said.

Kingmaker held up her hand, and dark inky threads started to slither from each finger's tips, crawling along the girl's face and towards her sunglasses. She stiffened. Kingmaker laughed a dark, dry cackle. The leg that had been severed did not bleed; instead, it leaked a smoke-like substance slowly. Magic. This was a dream, and this person was projected here, much like they were. Once the threads reached her sunglasses, they pulled them down up and off her face.

"High-density magic stretched thin like filaments. That's clever, but I've seen that before," the young woman said.

"Tell me why you are here, and I promise that we will not kill you," Kingmaker said.

"Threatening me in the Aether? Funny stuff, no power can kill someone in a dream," The girl said.

"Oh?" Kingmaker asked.

With no hesitation, the threads that came from Kingmaker's fingertips began to rush at the girl's face like snakes. They started to pierce the skin of her eyelids one by one, moving on their own to begin the grim process of sewing her eyes shut. The girl was screaming now, screaming for her life, while Kingmaker laughed.

"You see, it's not all that impressive. All I have done is disable a simple spell. A small component of the natural barrier that protects your mind from the Aether," Kingmaker said.

"Please, don't," the girl said.

Her voice was so small in comparison to the screaming. The threads continued to work on the girls' eyes, and the screams returned, but just for a moment, there was real fear. Kingmaker kneeled so close that she could feel the girls screaming against her face.

"Isn't it amazing how much you can do by plucking just one thread? That spell is only one of many that protect your body from the sensory information of your aethereal projection. Do you know what that means?" Offrey said.

She was speaking against the near-constant screaming of the poor soul before her. The witch even held a hand to her ear, feigning as though she could not hear them even though she was very close.

"No? You will feel everything that your projection feels,

right in your nervous system," Kingmaker teased.

The threads began to crawl under her skin, eliciting more screams and laughter from Kingmaker.

"There, you see. It can't harm you physically, but they say it may still kill you if it's bad enough. Tell me just before you feel like you're about to die?" Kingmaker asked.

"No**w**, plea**se**….**Kill me!**" the girl screamed.

"Don't be stupid. Your magic won't work on m-" Kingmaker started.

Jackdaw drew his blade and removed the head from the young woman's neck in a single swipe. The edge passed harmlessly by Kingmaker's face, and the screaming stopped immediately. Her aethereal form melted away like one of the supporting casts or the destroyed wall. Once she was gone, Jackdaw blinked and slowly put his sword away.

"I've never encountered a speaker like her before," he said.

"This one was smart," she said.

"I will not fail you again," Jackdaw said.

"See that you do not," she said.

"Yes, Master," Jackdaw said.

"Keep your words; they are as empty as your bones," Kingmaker said.

The pressure around them changed suddenly as if all of the heavy air was drained away. The sounds were clear now, and the supporting cast was lively.

"What is happening now?" Jackdaw asked.

"The dreamer is coming," Kingmaker said.

She smiled through her mask, and the two of them slipped off to a corner and out of sight.

"Is that our target?" Jackdaw asked quietly.

"Where?" she asked.

He directed her back to the dangerous fire that had grown considerably larger since the last time he looked. She shook her head.

"As far as I know, fire cannot dream," she said.

"That is a fair point, but-" Jackdaw started.

"You use magic every moment but know nothing of where it comes from? I have no time or patience for fools," she said.

"Come, master. You must tell me. My mind cannot contend with curiosity," he said.

He started to fidget nervously. It would not have been a problem, but his form had taken on quite a bit of mass, and it was starting to become noisy. Kingmaker sighed.

"The Aether is what occupies the subatomic space between our cells and the vastness between the planets; it is the infinite beyond where all magic is born. We are standing in it right now," she said.

He had the courtesy to look stunned by its magnitude, even if he didn't understand it. He fidgeted some more. This time because he was excited. A low coo came from his chest like a bird.

"How can something like me be here?" He asked.

"I have called you here from the waking world to use your eyes. You see, there is a secret here, a big one. I intend to see it for myself," she said.

"See what?" he asked.

"Whatever someone would put themselves through this much trouble to hide," she said.

They both fell silent just a moment before the sound of running came. Shortly after, someone ran out of the hole that

Jackdaw had made earlier and into the courtyard. It was a young man. At first, he was indistinguishable from the supporting cast, he was wearing a brightly colored hoodie, and the hood covered most of his face. The boy was fast, cutting sharply from left to right with an almost unfollowable pattern. He was doing it purposefully, shuffling himself in and out of the crowd of dream children because of what was chasing him. A massive feline burst through a solid wall, destroying even more of the school as it exited because of a large pair of thick horns on its head. They pulsed with dangerous magic. Jackdaw fidgeted with excitement. Kingmaker shook her head. He could not help himself; he had never seen such a large animal before. It was a lion blessed with many rows of eyes and three pairs of legs. These additions made it a formidable runner and moved hundreds of feet in a single stroke. Its long green body was unguilting like a house cat as it stalked the crowd. Orange eyes searched the dream children for their prey with quick and precise movements. It had two sets of eyes, one on top of the other, and each group had a smaller interior eye for a total of eight. They allowed the beast to search two places simultaneously and move as fast as a car at highway speeds.

"Shiny…" Jackdaw whispered.

"That is a Slide Lion," she whispered.

"Why does it have horns?" Jackdaw asked.

"They are ancient Wildings, like sabretooth tigers. The horns allow it to invoke powerful magic and vanish from sight," she said.

"I was speaking of the boy," Jackdaw said.

Kingmaker turned sharply toward the young man, nearly shoving Jackdaw aside to look at him. Sure enough, there they were just under that hoodie, just under his hairline. Two horns. Kingmaker was smiling so vast that it was evident through her pinboard mask. Jackdaw tilted his head. She couldn't help the laughing that fell out of here.

"Of course. How could I have been so stupid," she said.

"You know this devil?" Jackdaw asked.

"I did. A lifetime ago," she said.

Her voice was distant. Her mind wandered through memories of a childhood that she had long since repressed. Her shoulders began to shake. Jackdaw reached for her in concern, but she was not sad; she was happy. Kingmaker was laughing. Loudly. Heedless of the boy and his harrowing battle with the wild beast. Jackdaw pulled her back behind their cover before orange eyes could discover them, and he started to fidget.

"Master. That boy is the source of this dream," he said.

"He is supposed to be dead," she whispered.

"He looks like he has never been dead," Jackdaw said.

"Jackdaw, sometimes you say brilliant things," Kingmaker said.

His master was radiating a sort of joy he had never seen in her before, and for a moment, Jackdaw did not know how to proceed. She reached out and touched his shoulder.

"There is nothing more to see here," she said

"But master, we have not even seen… his face," he said.

Kingmaker touched the high school walls and glanced past the ongoing battle of the young man and the Lion. The mascot of this place was familiar. When she looked back at the young man, the tide had turned against the lion. Jackdaw was watching excitedly.

"She was hiding him right under our noses," she said.

"Hiding who? What must I do next?" Jackdaw asked.

"Find him in the waking world," Kingmaker said.

"And once I find him?" Jackdaw asked, his voice distant.

"Then you and I will kill him," she said.

The sounds of the battle were still going on, and jackdaw was watching with even wider eyes.

"Are you listening to me?" she asked.

"Of course. It's just, I've never seen a human do these things," Jackdaw said distantly.

"Do not obsess," she said.

Jackdaw did not answer. His face was slack, and he was staring now. Kingmaker sighed heavily.

"Corvid," she whispered.

Jackdaw turned toward her sharply. His eyes only showed his shock for a moment before he nodded his head.

"Please, any name but that, Master," he said.

"**Wake up**," she said.

Her voice boiled with the strength of her magic, and Jackdaw's body faded away under her hand like a cloud. Once he was gone, Kingmaker removed her mask, tossing it to the grass at her side. She stepped out from behind the cover of the wall and started to walk toward the young man. He was still standing, his hood down and horns glowing with magic, burning with green fire. She couldn't help but stare at him. He looked so different now. The last time she had seen him had been nearly ten years ago, he was a child then, and now he was a young man. Only a few years younger than her, if she remembered correctly. He looked solid and well-fed; the old witch had been keeping him comfortable all this time. His eyes mirrored the flame. She opened her mouth to speak his name and confirm her suspicions, but she could not make the words; something else was on her tongue. It was liquid, hot enough to burn her tongue, and she recoiled immediately, but it was too late; it had already entered her mouth.

The bittersweet flavor of brewed leaves, mixed with just a touch of cream and honey, a taste she knew. It drowned her words and filled her lungs in moments, and her aethereal body crumpled to the ground. The tea was starting to spill out of her nose, and she could not take a breath; her body had lost its strength. Kingmaker started to fade. The flutter of a silk scarf danced through her field of vision, and the woman who wore it kneeled over her. The old witch closed her eyelids for her, and her aethereal body lost its ability to remain stable and fell away. Her mind was released, and her spell protections carried it through the Aether and back to her body. It was not dissimilar to waking up from a dream, but her eyes were not closed. Her mind wandered further than any average mind could hope, and when it could wander no more, she returned it to her body. It was as easy as coming out of deep thought.

Chapter | Two

The real world greeted her with the light of the morning sun. It was bright and alive, hungry for her to see its glow, and the merest tingle on her skin always made her frown. She tried to pull the covers to protect her from it, but it was no use; there was nothing that could stop her from seeing that light. Not her blankets or her arms, not even being born blind. She could see because all things radiate energy somehow, even inanimate objects. There was nothing she couldn't see in ways far beyond normal eyes. In a way, she was thankful for the relentless consistency of the sun, it kept her honest, and she was always up before the roosters, which kept her sharp. She did not look away; she faced right into the distant flower of the sun. Her phone started to ring before she could enjoy herself, and she sighed heavily.

"What is it?" she said into the receiver.

"Offrey! Thank O'do you answered, I thought-" a young woman started.

"You will address me as Magistrate Laveau," Offrey said.

She cut off the person on the phone, and there was a heavy silence before the conversation continued.

"Why are you calling?" Offrey asked.

"Yes, of course, Magistrate. I'm sorry, I'm just a little overwhelmed because-," she said.

"Clearly," Offrey muttered, cutting her off again.

"Yes. I'll just say it because I don't know any other way. I saw some crazy BS in a dream last night," she said.

"You will not sit here and claim my birthright in such a silly lie. Don't you ever waste my time again, or there will be a formal response," Offrey said.

"Sorry, ma'am, but you just don't know anything about my abilities," The girl on the phone continued.

"What did you just say to me?" Offrey asked.

Her voice was thick with the heat of anger. The young woman did not answer.

"I know all about what you are. You are an unclassifiable imitation of power. A nothing. How could some mere simulacrum walk a dream?" Offrey asked.

"I don't know. I didn't choose to do it; it was more like something called me there, like a voice. Like a song. I heard it as close as a whisper in my ear, and when I turned around to see it, I was standing in another place. I knew it was a dream," she said.

"It was you," Offrey whispered to herself.

"What?" the girl asked.

"Tell me what you saw," Offrey corrected.

"There was an Other with magic that could harm you, and it hurt! It almost made me pass out, but I escaped, and when I came to, I thought my face would be mutilated," she said.

"Heaven forbid. Some mid-tier magic spell is hardly worth my time. Call me when something that requires my attention happens," The Magistrate snapped.

"There was one other thing. I'm pretty sure I saw the end of the world," she said.

There was a long pause where neither of them breathed. The quiet seeped in like cold water on a sinking ship. The woman on the line started to become distressed audibly.

"Hello?" she asked, her voice unsure.

"Who did you see?" Offrey asked.

"I saw the person who is supposed to end the world with my own eyes," The girl said.

There was another long pause before the witch spoke again.

"Did you recognize him?" Offrey asked.

"No, but he had horns and some of things that he was doing felt very prophecy like. I would know more, but some ugly witch tried to…" she started.

"How do you know she was ugly?" Offrey asked quickly.

"What do you mean?" she asked.

"Focus, silly girl. Get to the point of why you called me," Offrey said.

"Well…that was it. I saw someone who might fulfil **the** prophecy. The one… where someone brings about the end of the world. Is that not enough?" she stammered.

The phone went silent again, and Offrey huffed in frustration.

"Avo is on his way over to see you," the girl said

"Why?" Offrey said.

"Because I thought the end of the world was a big deal," she said.

"There is so much more at stake than you realize. The end of this world is hardly the worst of what that prophecy tells of," Offrey said.

"What's worse than the end of the world?" she asked.

"The end of all worlds. The end of Magic. If you've seen that boy, then we must find him immediately," Offrey said.

"That's… is that what… I… I-" the young woman started to panic.

"Don't let it get in your head. Your name is Dizzy. Try to take a deep breath," Offrey said.

To her credit, the young woman seemed to collect herself in just a moment or two. Offrey made a face and sighed audibly during that time.

"I'm just… is that all true?" she asked.

"Never speak against the words of the Queen. She deserves nothing less than your everything; you do not deserve her prophecy," Offrey hissed.

"I didn't mean to insult anyone," Izzy said.

"What could I expect of you. You are not smart or valuable, so I try not to judge you too harshly. How about we both start looking on the bright side. You've been just a bit useful today. That must be exciting for you," Offrey said.

"I… guess. I … never mind," she said.

"Did it appear to be a threat?" Offrey asked.

"He, not it, and no, not threatening. Just not what I expected; he was kind of cute," she said.

"Dizzy, I need you to focus," Offrey said.

"Right, sorry. It's just… he looked older than I thought. I thought it would be like, a kid; I mean, they call him the child so much in the prophecy. He was older, a teenager for sure," she said.

"Dizzy, do you know where he is? It's ok. The Mesalto isn't going to hurt him; we need to find him," Offrey said.

The girl on the line said nothing for a long moment.

"I don't know where he is, but there was something. At first, I thought it was just my mind filling in the gaps, but now I'm sure that he sort of looks like Sixx," she said.

"The prince? Why do you say that?" Offrey asked.

"They could have been brothers," she said.

Offrey hissed again, and the girl stopped abruptly.

"You should be careful about the things you say. Have you told that to anyone else?" Offrey asked.

Again, the girl said nothing on the other side of the line.

"Dizzy!" Offrey snapped.

"No. I thought maybe I shouldn't," The girl said.

"For once, you have done the right thing. I was hoping you wouldn't talk to anyone else about this until seeing me. I'll be in shortly," Offrey said

"Yes. Ma'am. Just. One small thing before you go, not **super** important, but my name is Izzy, as in Isabel. That's ok, people always-" Izzy said.

Offrey ended the call and threw the phone across her bedroom. Then pulled the covers up and squished them hard against her face. It didn't matter, she could still see the sun, and she started to scream repeatedly. She silenced it as best as she could into the hunk of blankets, and when she was done, she let them slide to the floor. It was silly, but it made her feel better about what she would do, what she had to do.

"Right under my nose," Offrey whispered.

She settled back into her bed for a moment and closed her eyes. There was a spark along with her nervous system before anything happened, and a moment later, a man appeared in the center of her bedroom.

"I see that she has already called," A man said.

The man appeared, and the lights turned on in the bedroom simultaneously. As soon as he spoke, he heard a flurry of blankets and saw an empty bed. The woman had disappeared.

"Oh, I've startled you. My apologies," he said.

"Avogorum, the next time you appear in my bedroom, I will find a way to delete you," Offrey said.

"That sounds exciting, if unfavorable to me in the long run. I will also remind you that I am a real person," Avogorum said.

"So, they say," Offrey said.

She spoke from above his head, and Avogorum looked up to greet her with a smile; she was standing on the ceiling and looking down at him with her arms crossed over her chest.

"It still fascinates me when you do things like this; the blood rushing to your head does not affect you?" he asked.

"Why are you here, old man?" Offrey asked.

She didn't make them, but he could feel the air quotes in her words. He smiled through them anyway.

"Thank you for calling me a man but am I old?" he asked.

He was taller than her by a head or two and smiling with perfect teeth, sharp eyes, and a tidy collection of lustrous hair tied back simply behind his head. His face was young-looking, but there was an agelessness to it that made it clear that he was not so young as he looked, a tickle at the back of the mind.

"Perhaps it's the eyes; you should adjust them," Offrey said.

"Right. I'll consider that," he said.

"Get on with it, please," she said.

"Only if you come down," Avogorum teased.

A rushing sound like a zipper was opened as long strands of magical energy started to unwind from the space between her feet and the ceiling. There were dozens of the magical threads moving in unison, unsewing the young woman from the ceiling and letting her body drop. She righted herself and landed on her feet behind him, the magical thread retracting all around her like measuring tape returning to its case. The lines all rewound to her fingers like fishing until they disappeared into dark thimbles on the tips of each one of her fingers and her thumb. Once the threads were gone, she exhaled a thin cloud of water vapor, and the thimbles started to fade from view, growing more and steadily opaque until they were gone.

"Fascinating," Avogorum said.

"Why are you here, Sorcerer?" she said.

"Ah, yes. My apprentice seems to have beat me to the punch on the good news. There is also some bad news. There were more bizarre sleeping deaths last night," he said.

"Again? How many is that this year," Offrey said.

"Approximately 22. The mayor will come to see us about this," Avo said.

"You are exaggerating by a large margin," Offrey said.

"Perhaps, but if the levee breaks, so to speak, the townsfolk will surely come for and viciously kill us all," Avogorum chirped.

"Do you call it killing when things like you die?" she asked.

"Rude. Colleagues are supposed to respect each other," Avogorum said.

"Avo. You teleported into my apartment. Colleagues don't do that. They let their co-workers come into the office and maybe have coffee or an egg **before** they start preaching about the end of the world. You are the most abnormal colleague there has ever been," Offrey said.

"We do most abnormal work," Avo said.

Then he smiled at her.

"You should get dressed," Avo said.

"They know the plan that She laid out for them, and they will do their part," Offrey said.

"Us," He corrected.

"What?"

"The plan she laid out for us," Avogorum said.

"Right. Whatever, go away until I have eggs," she said.

"There is no time for eggs. There is a potentially dangerous Viridescii out there. It is our job to protect it or protect the world from it," Avo said.

Then he vanished. There was a tiny flicker of light around his general personage; then, he slipped out of existence like a ghost—his form faded feet first until he was gone.

"I hate that thing," She whispered.

She combed through her thick curly hair and swiftly braided it in twin tails that started behind her ears and hung down to the floor. Offrey always dressed meticulously and took her appearance seriously. Her style was old-fashioned, her position demanded refinement, and she took to it well. Once she was fully prepared to her liking, she gathered up her purse and slipped a wide-brimmed hat on her head. She adjusted the hat until it sat low and over her eyes. The rest of her clothing changed itself on her body as she ran her fingers along the brim of her hat. Once she was dressed, she took her sweet time making and eating the most decadent breakfast she could make. She used almost everything in her fridge. Once she ate her fill, she threw the plate on the floor, shattering it loudly. Her upstairs neighbor stomped on the floor a few times to tell her to quiet down. Offrey broke about three more plates, giggling with delight at each one before she wandered out of the kitchen. When she passed the stove, she turned every knob to open fully, and with a word, the blue fire snubbed itself out. The sound of hissing followed her out of the room.

She did not have much to take from this place, so she did not take anything. She just walked to the front door and took a key from her dress pocket; the key had a wide round bow at its base and intricate carving up its stem. There were several teeth at the key's pin, dozens circling the pin like a spiral staircase. The spiraling bits did not seem to fit into any door lock, but that was the thing about magic; it was never what it seemed. She pressed the fantastical key into the very normal-looking lock on her door, and it quickly slipped inside; when she turned it, there was a creaking sound. Her doorframe groaned and shifted as it changed shape, and in mere moments, there was a completely different door in its place. She opened it, and on the other side was the interior of another site. She stepped through the door. Then she turned to look at her apartment, the air already murky with gas. With just a twitch of her finger, a thread hurdled forward, landing on the ground before her.

"**Bright,**" she spoke.

The thread began to illuminate immediately until it was as orange as a filament. It was already starting to burn the carpet when she closed the door. As soon as the door was closed, the key ejected slowly from the hole, and she slipped it back into her dress. The lobby was once a grand statement, bustling with the activity of hundreds of volunteers, standing watch over the great secret with pride and diligence. At least that is what her Master had told her of the old days, long before Offrey was born anyway. This place was a great seat of power, and now it was an outdated space with a single attendant. To call her a volunteer would be much more than a stretch. The girl looked up as soon as she arrived and smiled, her cheeks lifting the corners of the dark glasses on her face. There was nothing immediately wrong with her to speak of, but her level of friendliness was unsettling to Offrey.

"Good morning, Miss Offrey… again!" Izzy said.

"You forgot my title… again, simulacrum, " Offrey said casually.

"Oh! I didn't mean to," Izzy started.

Offrey lifted a finger, and Izzy stopped talking mid-word, the witch knew her face was stern, and she laid it on thick for the girl.

"Stop. Don't bother going back to correct it now, Dizzy," Offrey said

"Ma'am, I apologize concerning your title; I'm not used to calling people by their titles. However, I have to say that my name is Izzy, not Dizzy. Now, if I-" Izzy started.

"Is that right? I'd heard that you had taken to calling yourself the sorcerer's apprentice," Offrey said.

Izzy idly adjusted the hems of her suit jacket with one free hand, holding the other behind her back instead of answering.

"You are under a lot of stress; I'm sorry," Izzy said.

Offrey made a mock pity face at her, moving closer to the

young woman and taking the lapel of her pants suit between two fingers.

"You are even starting to dress like him… how… delightful. Not the same quality I see," She whispered.

"Please. I just wanted to look professional if I have to sit here," Izzy said.

She was trying to sound brave, but she instinctively leaned away from Offrey when the woman raised her hand, and the witch started to laugh.

"You pathetic little child. You don't know the cost of pressure yet. There are serious consequences in the real world. Yet here you are," Offrey whispered.

She was looming over the girl now, seeming to grow larger with every word, or perhaps it was just Izzy's fear.

"Playing dress-up, no less," The witch hissed.

"Y…yes, ma'am," Izzy said.

"Look at me, Dizzy… look at my face," Offrey said.

The witch reached out a hand again, and Izzy froze, snapping her eyes shut before she could get a glimpse of those thimbles. The witch only brushed a hand through Izzy's hair. The young woman would have given anything to tell her body not to, but she shuttered anyway. This caused Offrey to laugh, a bright and colorful cackle as she teased the girl until she all but trembled under the gentleness of her touch. A hunter at play.

"Are you still afraid I'll sew you all up?" Offrey said.

Izzy said nothing, but still, the witch teased. Her smile was bright and sinister.

"Why would I bother? I heard you don't even have eyes under there. Just *nasty* little holes," The witch whispered.

She reached toward her face, and Izzy flinched back again.

Instead of grabbing her, however, Offrey shoved her instead. She pushed Izzy down to the ground by her face with much more force than was required. Izzy was forced to sit on her butt, and she grunted as she landed. Offrey laughed at her again. She was cackling ever more menacingly.

"Such fragile things. I pity those not born with the cleverness of a witch," Offrey teased.

"Clever enough to see you through a pinboard," Izzy whispered.

Izzy was humiliated, and her cheeks stung with the angry tears that she hadn't even had time to let out yet. She said something she shouldn't have. It felt so good to say it, but she knew she had made a mistake that could cost her dearly as soon as she did. Offrey reached for the young woman's face again; the witches' fingers were suddenly in a flurry of motion. They didn't move as an average person might; the tips of her fingers seemed to vibrate as they made an uncountable number of actions in a flash. When the movements ended, inky black threads began to unspool slowly from each of her fingers.

"So, that was you," Offrey whispered.

"I knew it," Izzy said.

Her voice was muffled because Offrey had taken a firm grip around Izzy's mouth and nose, covering them with a practiced hand and effectively blocking her airways. Izzy started to panic, but she couldn't move her head away; inky threads slid down her cheeks and crawled over her eyes like tiny black snakes. Offrey had several layers over her own eyes, but the intense glow still seeped from the edges of the blindfold. It illuminated the underside of her hat, transforming the smile on her face into a violet knife's edge.

"I had hoped to have more time to set things in motion before you found me out, but no matter, you've done nothing but move my timetable by a few hours," Offrey said.

Izzy just huffed and puffed into the palm of the witch's hand. Her voice was muffled, and as if that wasn't bad enough, it was getting harder to breathe.

"You see, I hate you, Dizzy. I hate all of you unclassifiable whatever's, but I hate you most. You sold your body for magic. A small portion of the power I was born to. Classless. Disgusting. You are worse than a fool. Do you know why?" the witch asked.

Izzy did not respond, and Offrey shook her head like a snow globe until she did. She tried to say why, but it devolved into a long sob against Offreys palm.

"Because you almost have talent. *If only you were good enough.* Then maybe you would be interesting. Instead, you will die right here. Pretending to be someone else because you aren't really anything. Are you?" Offrey said.

Izzy tried, but she could no longer mask her discomfort, and she started to cry against the witch's hand, the threads slowly starting to creep into her mouth so she couldn't even scream. She was going to die. Izzy could feel it in the pit of her stomach, a thin cold thread inside of her belly, the feel of icy air tickling at her skin. She thought she could even see the desperate puffs of her breath hanging in the air in opaque clouds as she struggled through her last breaths. The room temperature began to drop from pleasant warmth to the chilly cool of a refrigerated truck. Death was coming. The realization made Izzy's heart leap and her stomach drop. She couldn't have been more excited. The door opened, and Death entered the room, or more precisely, one of his children. Just by his presence, the room darkened enough that it was hard to see, even now, in the middle of the morning. The witch relented her grip. Offrey turned to face the door and changed the position of her arms a few times before she chose a pose she liked. Izzy could only stay there looking between the door and the witch still nearly postulated. Somehow, Offrey had gone from cold and murderous to demure just moments before Death started speaking.

"Cut that out," he said.

He spoke to the shadows that dimmed the room, and they scaled back dramatically at his word. In the light, the young man was handsome and tall. He was wearing the sort of smile that said he was minutes from mischief and his enthusiastic gait was playful to match. He seemed to dance into the room instead of walking, moving gracefully to a song only he could hear. His hands were wide and open as he moved, spinning his body around, dipping and gyrating to his private music. The way he moved, you could *almost* hear it when you watched. His skin was exposed to his navel, smooth and glowing like dark copper. There was a mess of twisted dreadlocks on his head and a carefully manicured taper on the sides. There were golden cuffs interspersed in the intentionally unintentional tangle of his hair, and they danced along with him while he strolled toward the two women. For the moment, he was seemingly oblivious of their conflict and re-heating the room with his smile. Death had come, and he his way in.

"Damn, Zora, I ain't know you was into girls too. Y'all need a minute?" he asked.

"Not at all, my prince," Offrey said.

She softened considerably in the presence of the young man.

"Easy with the titles, sweetheart. Just call me Sixx," Sixx said.

He adjusted the lapels of his jacket then attempted to fix the tie where there was no tie to fix. There wasn't even a shirt, just a heavy gold chain with intricate links that hung low on his chest. It had a few charms hanging from it, made of gold and carved bone. There was a golden ring in each ear and one in his nose like a bull; they seemed to reflect the energetic glitter in his eyes. A small section of his locks was silvery white, just over his left eye, pale green as a spirit. His right eye was steady and earthy brown. Both were on the witch who seemed far less dangerous suddenly; this gave Izzy a moment to collect herself. She hadn't meant to say anything out loud, but it came out of her mouth before he could stop it, just a whisper. The young man heard and turned to focus on her simultaneously like a fox.

"Did you say something, sweet Isabella?" Sixx asked.

Sixx smiled, and she softened a little too. There was something about him that was disarming.

"I said, it's not a big deal, but it's Isabel. I also said that her assessment of me was unfair," Izzy said.

"My bad. What assessment?" Sixx asked.

"Forget about her, Saturday; I don't know why you are always so nice to these… people," Offrey said.

"Damn Zora, she is still a person, standing right there. That was rude as hell," Sixx said.

"Saturday," Offrey said demurely.

"Pause. Only my momma gets to call me that," Sixx said.

"Now you're being sensitive?" Offrey asked.

"What did you say to her?" he asked.

"I just told her the truth," Offrey said.

"Go on. Tell him what you told me," Izzy said.

Offrey turned to the girl with a happy face, and Izzy stepped back. She was not the monster about to take her life just a moment ago. Izzy had never seen the young woman she was seeing now, not in her life.

"You think I'm afraid?" Offrey asked.

If Offrey was supposed to be tense, she did not seem to know that. Her body language was as calm and focused as her eyes. Izzy felt a slight tremble start in the space behind her knees.

"You can say that? To him?" Izzy asked.

"You and your whole family are nothing more than criminals, top to bottom. You don't deserve to be in the prince's presence," Offrey said.

"Well, damn, tell her how you really feel," Sixx said.

"Enough of this. Give me the…" Offrey trailed off.

Before completing her sentence, the young woman handed Offrey a tan folder. There was a small stack of papers inside and a paper towel wrapped around something. Offrey took the bundle from the young woman and turned her head toward the bulge on top of the file. It gave off mild steam energy on closer inspection and at least smelled nice.

"What is this?" The witch asked.

"A breakfast sandwich from that place you like across the bridge and the full report on the dream attacks," Izzy said.

Offrey only looked in the young woman's direction, but she said nothing, not even when the young man took the sandwich out from under her.

"Well. It's clear you don't deserve this; I'mma just go 'head and avail myself. Y'all carry on," Sixx said.

He took his prize and moved to sit on the desk near them

and started to gobble it down.

"Thank you for the report… Apprentice," Offrey teased.

Offrey gave Sixx one last look as though she would say something, but she didn't. She seemed like she might cry for a moment, but when he made a strange face at her for starting, she retorted in kind. When she noticed Izzy looking at her, the witch narrowed her eyes and scowled. Then she left the room without giving Izzy a second look; once she was gone, the young man rose from the table and put the sandwich down. He looked down the hall after Offrey, but she was long gone; when she turned back, Izzy had already run into his arms and gave him a tight hug.

"Damn, she really hate yo ass, I mean, I believed you, but when you see it up close like that, **Damn**," Sixx said.

"Thank O'do you showed up, Prince Death," Izzy said.

"You gone start with that shit too? And stop that; it wasn't any God that told me to come here. At least, not the one you are thinking of anyway," Sixx said.

"The O'do isn't a God. It's the infinite source of all magic," Izzy said.

The prince was distracted. He was still looking where Offrey had gone long after she had gone; the emotions on his face were mercurial, but it was clear things were complicated.

"What should I call you instead? Saturday?" Izzy asked.

Sixx made a face.

"Call me Sixx. Think of it as a stage name," he said.

"Where is the stage?" she asked.

"All the world, like Billy, say," he said.

"Billy? Do you mean Shakespeare? I knew I shouldn't have asked," she teased.

Sixx winked and then looked off where Offrey had gone

again. He didn't sigh, but she wouldn't have blamed him if he did.

"You want to talk about it? You look like you have something to talk about. Or you saw a ghost," she said.

"She was gonna kill you, Isabel. I could feel it. If I was a few seconds later, I might have seen a ghost. What the hell happened anyway?" Sixx asked.

"Wait, are you sure?" Izzy asked.

Sixx only stared at her, his head canted to the side so sharply that one of his dreads bounced; his face was devoid of emotion except for his eyebrow. It slowly raised, and he looked back and forth between her eyes, silently asking the same question. *Really?*

"Right. That's fair. Can you do something about the cold?" Izzy said.

Her words were manifested in small clouds of mist as she spoke. The young man smiled sheepishly.

"That's my bad," Sixx said.

He reached up and touched his necklace for a moment, closing his eyes. In seconds the atmosphere began to return to normal.

"You godlings are so incredible," Izzy said.

"Oof. Can you please say, Demigods? Godling makes it sound like we 'bout to hatch," Sixx said.

"I'll work on my vocabulary, prince…" She started.

Sixx raised an eyebrow and pursed his lips in a curl of frustration.

"…Sixx," Izzy said.

"Close enough. Try to loosen up and be spontaneous. You might make more friends," Sixx teased.

"Next time I meet someone I want to be friends with, I'll be sure to remember that!" she teased.

She winked at him.

"I get that she isn't the sweetest pie on the windowsill, but she don't usually kill people as far as I know. So why was Offrey trying to kill you?" Sixx asked.

"I saw something I shouldn't have," Izzy said.

"Did you see her real eyes?" Sixx asked.

"What? What do you mean?" she asked.

"Offrey has… I mean, it's not for me to say. What did you see?" he asked.

"I saw the end of the world. I know what it looks like… what he looks like," Izzy trailed off.

"Imagine being the end of the world, must be heavy," Sixx said.

Sixx laughed before returning to the breakfast sandwich and took careful but massive bites until it was gone.

"I didn't tell her how much I saw," Izzy said.

"That's a big ass omission, isn't it?" he said

"Yes, but… I thought she might be working against us," Izzy said.

"Whoa. Full stop. Offrey is a lot of things. A whole ass party mix of… things, maybe. That still don't mean she a bad guy," Sixx said.

"I wouldn't just say this without proof. I wasn't sure before, but after seeing what I saw. I am pretty damned sure that she is a bad guy," Izzy said.

"Are you sure?" Sixx asked.

"Does that thing also tell you when *you* will die or just the people around you?" she asked.

Sixx unconsciously fingered the chain that hung from his

neck, and he tried, unsuccessfully, to hide it in his sports coat.

"It doesn't do either of those things," he said.

Izzy pursed her lips at him in frustration.

"Why?" Sixx asked.

"How did you know she was going to kill me?" she asked

"Instinct. What did the end of the world look like?" Sixx asked.

"I can't tell you that," Izzy said

"What do you mean? Why can't you tell me?" Sixx said.

"I told her not to tell anyone," Avo said.

He appeared in the room just behind them. If his sudden appearance startled either of them, they didn't show it anywhere. They were so used to his comings and goings that neither looked up. Izzy did seem to perk up with his arrival, however.

"I get it. I don't like it, but I get it," Sixx said.

"Offrey has left the grounds," Avo said.

"Where did she go?" Sixx asked.

"Not sure, but she took the car," Avo said.

"The car? Why would she bother taking something like a car?" Izzy asked.

"That's a question we may never know the answer to," Avo said.

"Should we follow her?" Sixx asked.

"That question at least has an answer," Avo said.

Sixx perked up.

"It's no. Are you serious?" Avo asked.

Sixx shrugged.

"Nothing ventured, and so on," Sixx said.

"Yes. Well, now that that is over with. There is something more important to talk about," Avo said.

"I need to know… We… we need to know where she stands," Sixx said.

"Sixx, there are rules to this thing; we can't just…" Avo slowly went quiet.

Both were now looking at Izzy, dancing back and forth from one foot to the other. She looked between Avo and Sixx, her dark glasses reflecting their faces.

"Was that the secret you were gonna tell me? That Izzy has to pee?" Sixx asked.

"I think she is bursting with information, rather than… You may tell him," Avo said.

"The guy looked so much like you, Sixx," Izzy shouted.

"Stop. We know I ain't the end of the world; I'm a gift to the world," Sixx said.

"That is true, at least the first part. However, there is no denying that she had a vision. Izzy saw the end, and it was someone who looked like you," Avo said.

"Well, thank O'do that there's only one real me," Sixx said.

"There was something weird, though. He seems to have horns on his head," Avo said.

Sixx went stiff, but only for a moment.

"Like a cow or like a devil?" Sixx asked.

"I'm not sure I know the difference," she said.

"Cow has horns on the side of his head like this," Sixx said.

He put his hands on the side of his temples like a cow's horns.

"Hmm. I don't love the pantomime. Three out of five," Avo said.

"That's robbery. Also, that's not the point," Sixx said.

"That's not it. Why are we doing this?" Izzy asked.

"Curiosity," Sixx responded.

"Humor him," Avo said.

The young woman nodded, and Sixx continued.

"A devil, though, got horns above each eye… like this," Sixx said.

He held up his fingers and stuck them around his head in a pantomime of horns. As soon as he touched them to his head, Izzy's eyes went wide.

"Oh, holy crap! That's it, that's him. Devil for sure," Izzy answered.

"Damn, I was hoping you were gonna say cow," Sixx said.

"Also, the guy could be your evil twin," Izzy teased.

"I'm the evil twin," he joked.

Sixx started to laugh. His chest shook a few times before a stillness came over him and his face went incredibly calm. The kind of calm that only comes when you hit a wall in your mind. He was making such a face that Izzy felt the tingle of embarrassment climb to her cheeks.

"Did I say something wrong?" she asked.

"No. You just made me remember something," Sixx said.

"A good something?" Avo asked

Sixx did not answer, so Izzy cleared her throat and spoke instead.

"T-there is something else. I think that Offrey might already know who it is," Izzy said.

"Why do you say that?" Sixx asked.

"She was in the dream with me," Izzy said.

"Are you sure?" Avo asked.

"I wasn't before, but now that she tried to sew up my eyes in the same fashion, I think I'm pretty positive," she said.

"Nobody can argue that logic," Avo said.

"Thank you. She is trying to keep us away from that information. I think that's why she came to kill me today," Izzy said.

"She what? She wouldn't jeopardize her position unless…" Avo started.

"Unless what?" Izzy asked.

"Unless this is real. The end of the world," Avo said.

"Well, damn," Sixx said.

"Indeed," said the Sorcerer.

"I'm sorry," Izzy said.

Sixx stepped over to the young woman and gave her a big bright smile.

"Ain't none of this on you, Izzy girl. We have to find this dude before she does," Sixx said

"We also might have to stop something bad," Izzy said.

"Right. The whole ass-end of the world. But, who knows, that part might be easy," Sixx said.

Izzy nodded and smiled a little, which seemed enough for the young man because he returned to the desktop, crossing his legs under his body. He looked thoughtful for a moment, and then he snapped his fingers and pointed at Avo; that mischievous smile crept back onto his face making his pale eye glow like a flame.

"Get me the keys to the old maintenance truck. I'll follow her and ram her into a wall if she tries anything fishy," he said.

Avo was staring at him, and Sixx gave him a wink and twisted his fingers into the shape of a gun, which he also gave him. Neither of those things seemed to change the look on the sorcerer's face.

"That plan is terrible. Can you even drive a truck?" Avo said.

Izzy smiled again and hid a tiny laugh behind her hands, and Sixx looked at the sorcerer as though he had been gut-punched, but if that affected him, Avo did not show it.

"Right. Let's make a real plan. What are our options?" Avo asked.

"Wow. I thought that was gonna be a home run. I may need a second," Sixx said.

"The other two have been out all morning," Izzy said.

"Doing what?" Avo asked.

"Nic said she had a feeling about the high school, whatever that means," Izzy said.

Avo just nodded.

"That's it? No more questions? You trust them like that?" Sixx asked

Izzy smiled and nodded without any hesitation.

"My sister is strong, and Nic is the closest thing we have to an actual Warden. She will find him if the world's end is out there. She found me," Izzy said.

"That she did," Avo said.

"Aiight. I get it; it still doesn't make no sense to be out there with no plan," Sixx said.

"If only I could show them," Avo said

"Show them what?" Sixx asked.

The sorcerer held out his hand, and a faint glow of a yellow and orange light rose from the surface of his palm, as thick and pale as smoke. It began to move, fold, contort and change colors until a precise three-dimensional image of a young man floating just above his palm. He was frozen in motion, driving a strange weapon through a massive tree. Everything was hard to see because it was not clearly in focus. Only the face was perfectly captured in the three-dimensional projection. Everything else was obscured by green fire. Sixx had to admit; it did look like him except for the two small horns on his head. Sixx looked carefully at it, squinting his eyes, and then he turned to Izzy with a single eyebrow raised.

"This is how I look to you? You lyin!" Sixx said.

"There is absolutely a resemblance," Avo said.

"Well, there was bound to be more than one beautiful black man in the world," Sixx said

There was no denying that he looked very similar to Sixx; they were about the same approximate height and age. The similarities were enormous. Sixx was glaring at the mugshot suddenly, leaning closer and closer until he snapped his head back and laughed loudly.

"It's not funny; this guy could be your brother," Izzy said.

"He could be my cousin," Sixx said.

"Alright, I would believe that too," Izzy said.

"Except my cousin died when I was a kid," Sixx said.

"The dead cannot dream," Avo said.

"I can dream," Sixx said.

"You aren't dead; you classify as undead, I think," Izzy said.

Sixx shot her a look again, but she only smiled back this time.

"Unless your cousin is also undead, he can't dream from the grave," Izzy said.

"Is he undead?" Avo asked.

The room fell silent, and the other two looked at him with blank faces while Sixx was still wearing a slight smirk that never seemed to leave his face. His eyes reflected the confusion they were throwing his way.

"That's a good question," Sixx said.

"I would be satisfied if we knew his name," Avo said.

"His name is Taxxis," Sixx said.

"His name is Taxes?" Izzy asked.

"Not Taxes, it's like axis with a T at the beginning. Not for nothing, he is named after our grandfather," Sixx said.

"This would be a blood cousin? A first cousin?" Avo asked.

"The first and bloodiest," Sixx said.

"Well, this changes everything," Avo said.

"Does it? That's still a weird name," Izzy asked.

"It ain't nice to call someone's name weird, especially when they dead and or your grandfather," Sixx said.

"Oh. I'm so sorry," she said.

Izzy tried to reach out to take Sixx's hand, but the young man pulled away and slipped his hand into his pocket, giving her a wink.

"We good sweetness," he said.

"If he is related to the prince of death, then there is an excellent chance that he is undead. What was your cousin's full name?" Avo asked.

"Calderhys Taxxis Moss," he said.

Avo closed his eyes for a moment.

"Your family has such cool names. I'm named after my grandma," Izzy said.

"I'm named after the day of the week when I was born," Sixx said.

"Oh," Izzy said.

Then they both laughed.

"Well. There were no exact matches in any police databases,

but there was a hit for something close on some transcripts. High school student by the name of Taxxis Kingswood," Avo said.

"When is his birthday?" Sixx asked.

"Birthday is… today. How funny," Avo said.

"It's not just funny. It's uncanny. Today would have been Taxx's birthday too," Sixx said.

"I can do you one better," Avo said.

He pulled up another image in his other hand. Magic energy crackling to life in his palm, moving and changing colors again until it showed a clearer picture of a young man. He looked precisely like Sixx, except he was slightly softer around the edges. He was sitting in front of a massive tree.

"This is an image from the yearbook; maybe I can make a composite," Avo said

He held the two images together, and some of the details from the much clearer yearbook image started to fill in the gaps of the blurry mess. It only took a moment for the composite to complete, the two of them combined, leaving only the unmatchable portions remaining in one hand. Avo shook that away and held up the now much clearer image of the young man. There had been horns in the dream version; there was now a bandana in their place. Even with that, there was no mistake. This was the young man Izzy had seen in the dream. Sixx was staring at it with wide eyes.

"Damn. The family resemblance is strong. That's my cousin," he said.

"I don't think anyone could question that," Izzy said

"Get a message to the others; they have to know what we know. Then we just hope they find our man before Offrey does," Avogorum said.

"I'm on it," Izzy said.

She ran off behind the desk and started to rifle through her drawers furiously until she came up with a very plain-looking pencil, and she began to write on her bare desk. The lead flowed easily and trailed her movements like a regular pencil, creating silvery gray forms of the words in her head, but unlike a regular pencil, the words vanished shortly after they were made.

"What about me?" Sixx asked.

Avo shifted the image in his palm, and it zoomed out to show where the boy was located; where it had once been out of focus, it was clear now. There was a visible school emblem on the wall near him.

"Arkane High. The end of the world has been here, in this city, the whole time?" Sixx asked.

"So, it seems," Avo said.

"Then why hasn't Offrey just taken him before this?" Sixx asked.

"She didn't know," Izzy said.

"Huh?" Sixx asked.

The two men turned toward her while she wrote; she never even looked up.

"She didn't know until the dream. She was there with me," Izzy said.

"That explains these two," Avo said.

The image shifted and zoomed in on what appeared to be two other figures, but they were not cleared up with the composite. It was hard to make them out.

"How could she know about the high school?" Sixx asked.

"She was there in the dream. She may likely know even more than we do," Avo said.

"No, not her. Nic. She and Lyra might already be there. That can't be a coincidence," Sixx said.

"Why does it have to be something so simple as coincidence? You are surrounded by incredible magic all day. You are the son of death, and Nic is…" Avo started.

Sixx raised an eyebrow.

"What, exactly?" Sixx asked.

"In a class of her own. Just like you," Avo said.

"Focus! The end of the world is happening today," Izzy said.

"Good point, back to this awful picture," Sixx said.

"I liked it better when you were impressed. Let's go back to that," Avo said

The details were so fuzzy that it was hard to make out. It could have been in the middle of the ocean to go by the chaotic, out-of-focus, and discolored details.

"It's not much, but if you can find him before they do, we may be able to save him," Avo said.

Sixx looked the image up and down repeatedly, tapping at his chin for a minute.

"Who are they?" Sixx asked.

"That's Offrey," she said, pointing to the masked figure.

"And this guy?" Avo asked.

"No clue, some sword-swinging himbo she was with," Izzy said.

"Himbo. Nice," Sixx said.

"Thanks!" Izzy said.

Sixx shot her a smile and a wink. Avo did not seem to share their enthusiasm.

"Offrey must also know where he is," Avo said.

"If this is my cousin, she will at least have an idea. Offrey has been my grandmothers' assistant since we were kids," Sixx said.

Izzy started to do calculations in her head for a moment. Then she looked at Sixx with wide eyes.

"Sixx… The Magistrate is the second to the head of the Mesalto. THE Mesalto. Is your grandma supposed to be the first chair of the guild of all magicks?" Izzy asked, chuckling a little

"She is," Sixx said flatly.

"I call full BS on that one," Izzy teased.

She was full-on laughing now, but Sixx was just looking at her with level eyes. His expression was so straight she was starting to rethink her position. There was such honesty in his eyes that hers began to grow larger.

"Sixx… hold on," Izzy said

"There is no time for this; Offrey has a head start. Do you think you can get to him before she does?" Avo asked.

"Hell yeah," Sixx said.

The confidence in his response seemed to surprise even him.

"As a hypothetical, what happens if he doesn't?" Izzy asked?

"Somehow, your cousin could end the world before we can do anything to stop it or save his life… or any of our lives," Avo said.

"Well, damn," Sixx said.

"Indeed," said the Sorcerer.

"Ok. I sent the message, but it will take some time. What should we do now?" Izzy asked.

"For now, you and I should wait here," Avo said.

"What about me?" Sixx asked.

Avogorum closed his eyes for a moment and held up a

finger. In about a minute, another version of him came out of a door behind them with a set of keys dangling under his palm. The new Avo gave the keys to the old Avo and promptly flickered from existence in a flash of orange and yellow light.

"Take the truck. Don't ram anyone," Avo said

Sixx opened his mouth to protest, and Avo stopped him with a finger.

"I'll only ram someone if I'm sure it will kill them; I won't make anyone suffer," Sixx said

Avo threw him the keys, and he caught them easily, slipping them into the inner pocket of his jacket and smiling at them with his worst, most ne'er-do-well smile yet. Sixx was already halfway down the hallway when Avo called after him.

"That doesn't instill the confidence that I think you meant it to," Avo said.

"Yes, it one hundred percent does," Sixx said.

His laughter was still echoing in the main hall after he disappeared into another room. Avogorum and Izzy looked down the hall after him before they looked at each other again, Avo smiling hopefully and the girl looking worried.

"This is gonna work out, right?" Izzy asked,

"We have the best people in it. *Our* best people," Avo said.

"That's the kind of thing you say when you can't just say, *yes, of course*," Izzy said.

"That is true. However, it is also true that we have our best people on it. Do you have doubts?" he asked.

"Misgivings, I think. I trust them, but I..," Izzy trailed off.

"Please, the world may well end at any moment. This is no time to hold back," he said.

"Would it be ok to swear?" Izzy asked.

"I think this is the moment that cursing was made for," Avo said.

"I think we all might be fucked," Izzy said.

There was a long pause.

"Indeed," said the Sorcerer.

Chapter | Three

Taxx Moss was dreaming. He was fully aware that he was in a dream, though he had no control over their content. Tonight, he was dreaming about a high school dance. When he wandered out into the courtyard, he stopped walking, and the corners of his mouth dipped. He was staring at the massive tree in the center of the space; it was severely damaged. The damage came from the accidental fire he caused when magic escaped his body. It took down the tree in a single strike. Taxx held up his right hand and looked at the mark on its top; there was a glossy scar from healing and time. The imprint of the fire was evident. The shadows whispered ever so softly sometimes in the dark, he could hear them when they called, but the tree shouted the loudest. Its voice was a warm deep sound, coming from beneath the ground to warn all clever things that could feel its klaxon. Danger was here.

Taxx started to move before he thought it would be a good idea, not in a straight line but moving left to right, making impossibly fast cuts at full speed. His body moved randomly, so **it** could not track him. The flame was not the only thing that had escaped his body; there was also the great beast. He could hear it now and feel it, like the pluck on a spider's web long before sensing it with his body. Once he could feel the ground shaking under its weight and the speed of its feet, the sensation was all the way different. There was a primal reaction to such a massive predator, and when the beast skittered out of the darkness, he felt it tingling through his skin. The sound of its roar was like a diesel truck. The beast had as many as six eyes. All of them were searching for him. It took only a breath to track him and even less to run him down, even with his head start. It was on him almost as fast as he could turn, striking at his legs and neck just a breath too late. He could feel the heat of its breath on the nape of his neck, making his hoodie whip around like a flag as he dashed. He could smell the remains of those who had lost this race before him on that breath. Breath that was just behind him. That fear tingled through his muscles and hung onto his thoughts like thistles. He leaned into it and used its weight to push forward like the sail of a ship. The cat howled in frustration.

Something else began to bubble up from inside of him, but it did not leap out. Instead, it started to draw in magic like a vacuum. Each shadow he passed turned toward him like the stems of a sunflower, bending toward him slightly and reaching out with thin strands like dandelion fluff. The shadows that made contact clung to him, hanging from his body like thorns on a rose stem. Something else was escaping his body and calling to them. There were tiny quills all over him in moments, some as long as a porcupine and others as fine as human hair. The cat was getting closer and closer and closer to him with every moment, but now he had a new problem. The shadows had grown too many, and the thorns had grown so severe that he could no longer run. Black thorns now erupted from every part of his body until he could no longer move, and the very moment he stopped, it leaped on him. Its cavernous mouth closed around his entire body in one motion, and Taxx felt its teeth crush and pierce him all at once. He tried to scream but found no voice after such a blow. In the end, it was the lion that won inevitably. He wound up here between its rows of teeth and under its hooked tongue. In this place, in the dark where there was only death, Taxx could hear her voice.

There was his mother's voice at the moment between breaths, in the space between life and death. He heard it calling to him desperately and straining and struggling to reach him through the thorns. It was through them that he listened to the sound. It spoke in a soft tongue, the way a shadow might communicate. Like whispers within whispers against a black backdrop. He strained to hear it, but there was no need; the voice simply came this time, over the growling of the lion and the involuntary sounds of his body. As though it were whispered in his ear. The sound lashed across him like a whip, and the thorns that grew out of his body became more rigid, complex, and sharper. The lion cried out as they began to pierce its mouth, and Taxx pushed himself, growing more thorns. Its power was enormous, and even with more pointed thorns all over his body like a pufferfish, the beast was still managing to close its mouth. Taxx strained against it, but there was no winning; this was always how it would end.

The young man was still alive, somehow, between its jaws. The sound of that voice was affecting something deep down inside of him, it felt as thin and tight as a wire, a piano string, and it was vibrating. The shaking became so violent that Taxx was sure he was about to split in half, but there was nothing when the tension finally broke with a sudden snap. Then he exploded. Energy came welling up from inside him and burst out in every direction. The feeling was dizzying, and the world around him, lion and all, was gone in a flash. Light, bright, green as grass, volatile, and hot as fire. Everything burned away in the blink of an eye until only he was standing in the courtyard. Alone with the voice for only a moment, he heard it as clear as day.

"You will bring a black summer," it said.

Everything came back with a screaming sound, and Taxx was still in one piece. His body was whole, and there was no Slide. There was the small matter of his hand being on fire. A flame was furiously burning all around his digits like they were logs.

"That's… new," Taxx said.

His hand's torch burned dark like emeralds and bright like tropical birds; the fire showed every green in between. It did not burn him. Instead, the scar on his hand drank it up. He could feel it coursing through him, warm and calm like the first sip of soup. It started to spread through him, and the fire slowly grew. He reached out to stop it with his other hand, and it caught on fire as well, quickly growing up his wrist in seconds. When it threatened to take his neck, the fire was suddenly doused, and the sound of it sizzling out of existence was like the hiss of a thousand snakes.

The flame, the shadows, and the thorns had all gone, and

whatever he had been dreaming had settled. The flame was no more, and whatever put it out was gone; the young man had returned to his original form. A shadow passed over his hand, and Taxx snapped upright and found himself face to face with a woman in a jewel tone dress. She was barefoot and covered from her chin to her nose with a long-knitted scarf, golden and spotted like a leopard. Her skin was dark and beautiful, the same tone as his, and so were her eyes. The color of dark honey and full of the sort of recognition that could only come from family. Her bronze box braids were as long as she was tall and snaked around her head woven through a collection of wooden hairpins. They were long and decorative, each braid carefully laid in a way that made it sit high and proud upon her head like a crown.

"Taxxis," She called to him.

The young man wrinkled up his nose.

"Do you not wish to see me?" she asked.

"This is what you do every year," Taxx said.

"Maybe I've spoiled you," she said.

Taxx stood to his feet and looked around for an exit, but there was a surprising lack of scenery in his dream.

"Where are we?" he asked.

"Somewhere between a dream and the waking world, the place where your mind is closest to the Aether. The humans call it REM sleep. Isn't it fascinating how close to our ways they sometimes get, your mother would...," She mused.

"You are wandering," Taxx said.

The woman moved closer to the young man, smiling as she craned her neck to look up at his face.

"You have grown so tall, so strong," Grandma said.

"You would know that for yourself if you weren't gone for

a month now!" Taxx said.

His Grandmother smiled and disappeared like a wandering firefly. She reappeared to his right a few moments later. Standing next to her was a table that had not been there a moment ago. His grandmother was casually setting the place for a teacup.

"May, what is this?" Taxx asked.

"A special kind of tea that I can only brew for you," May said.

"I meant why am I having these dreams about angry lions, fire, and shadows?" Taxx asked.

"It has to do with what you are," May said.

"What do I need to know about what I am? I know what I am," Taxx said.

"You are you, and that has always been special. You have your mothers' gifts, and there is no doubt that you are your father's son, surely. You are more than that even, and someday you will know it," May said.

"There it is. More riddles than answers," Taxx said.

"Only just. Now come and see to this tea," she said.

She was looking into the small hole at the top of her teapot and becoming him to join her at the table. Taxx walked up next to her, and she welcomed him with open arms as grandma does, and he leaned into her.

"Take a look, tell me what you can see as you are now," May said.

Taxx investigated the teapot. He stared into the amber depths for a long time, but all he saw were leaves and water. His sepia-tone reflection staring back at him, handsome face, dark eyes, and the other things. He had horns growing out of his head.

"It just looks like normal tea with the devil in it," The boy said.

"It is normal tea. It is only through our will that things become magical. Self-control is magic, and magic is the tool of our kind," May pressed.

"I'm not any kind of thing. I'm barely passing for human," Taxx said.

"Neither of us is human," May said.

"Why are you always pretending that we aren't human?" Taxx asked

"I am not a human. I am a witch. I'm here in your dreams, ain't I?" May asked.

He pinched himself but did not wake up, not even when he did again and harder. It only hurt him. May just stood there next to the teacup smiling at him behind her scarf.

"Yes, ma'am," Taxx answered.

"Now, listen carefully. You can't tell anyone about this tea; it is for you alone. The truth in this brew is as bitter as they come,"

"What? Why can't we just have it now?" he asked.

"You're as impatient as your mother!" May snapped.

Taxx opened his mouth to rebut with as much vigor as he could muster, but nothing came out of his mouth; he just stood there staring at her.

"You think I'm like **her**?" He asked.

"In some ways. Yes indeed," she said brightly.

"Yes, ma'am," Taxx said, he balked visibly, but that was all he said about it.

"I have to tell you something that you will not like but cannot change," she said.

The teapot she was now using to fill the cup came from

origins unknown, Taxx had been watching her the whole time, and it simply came to her when she wanted it.

"This is a dream, boy; you can do more than impossible things here," May said.

She didn't even look up from her careful pouring. The tea that came out was heavy and some of the darkest tea he had ever seen, so dark that he could no longer see the bottom of the cup. When the last drop spilled, the teapot slipped away from sight like a mirage, and only the cup and the witch remained. Taxx moved to drink the tea, and she slapped his hand away.

"When you are ready for this tea. When and only when you are. It will come once you drink it. You will come to hate me," May said.

"I could never, May May. You raised me when no one else wanted to," Taxx said.

"Always remember the way you love me now. Remember who you are, and you will survive what is coming," May said.

"Grandma… that was pretty cryptic," Taxx said.

"I know, baby, you right," May said.

Taxx rolled his eyes, and she moved to his side and placed a hand on his shoulder, handing him the teacup. He took it and was surprised by the weight of it. It took two of his hands to hold it, and he looked at his grandmother with a raised eyebrow.

"What the hell kind of tea is this?" He asked.

"The worst kind," she said.

"That was pretty cryptic, too," Taxx said.

She smiled so sweetly with her mouth that the pain in her eyes left the young man more confused than the desperate shadows.

"Don't tell anyone what we talk about until you have this

tea. That's important," She whispered.

"Yes, Ma'am," He whispered back.

She started to fade, and the world around them began to soften with a coming light. May took a moment to look around at the breaking dawn, and she smiled again, so sweet and so painful.

"You are good, Taxx. More hero than any devil they will name you, and they will name you many. Don't ever forget how sweet you are," May said.

Before he could respond, he woke up.

It was like a light switch was flipped into the on position, lying awake in his bed. Her words in his heart and the fading memories of dark dreams of thorns and shadows on his mind. He got up quietly and prepared for his day like he always did. After he washed his face, Taxx was staring at himself in the mirror, specifically at the horns growing out of his forehead. His face was otherwise regular; his fro was thick and much too long, standing straight up on his head, but that was normal too. He quickly finger-combed through it and pulled it into a squat orb on the back of his head about the size of a grapefruit, and he tied it back with an elastic. He was starting to grow a little facial hair, just a dusting, but he thought it looked thick. His eyes were visibly heavy with the weight of his nightmares.

Taxx stepped away from the mirror and dressed for the day. He stepped out of the bathroom, dressed plainly in jeans and a dark hoodie. He was now wearing a bandana on his forehead that covered up and over his hair. It was dark with a strange symbol on it, he didn't know much about it, but he knew it mostly hid his shame. The horns didn't make so much as a dent in the fabric, as long as he didn't get excited, but it had been a while. Taxx adjusted it, and when he did, the conical shape of the horn appeared and then faded away like they were sinking under the sheet. He made his way to the kitchen and, on the way, glanced down the hallway at his grandmother's bedroom door. It was still as closed as it was last night. Taxx grabbed his bag and left the apartment. He descended the stairs in a single jump that cleared the flight of stairs to the ground floor.

"Oy! Stop jumping down the stairs, you little bell end!" Someone yelled.

Taxx looked up to the third floor, but he couldn't see the older man to whom that voice belonged. He knew he was there, though—old man Craw from number Three.

"Whatever, man," Taxx said.

"Tell your Grandma I'm looking for 'er! I need my medicine," Craw shouted.

"Tell her yourself!" Taxx shouted back.

The old man said more, but his accent was thick, and he must have been a pack-a-day smoker with all that rasp. The guy never came out of his place, but he always yelled up there. He was quiet for the most part, though, so Taxx had no issue with him. The young man rounded the house and made his way to the street. He pulled his hood up and started to walk toward his school. There was never much by way of traffic here, foot or otherwise, so he enjoyed a nice quiet walk. The apartment was only a few blocks away from the school, but he had to pass through the city center. He had known that today was going to be a bad day. It was his birthday, and he still had to go to school. He didn't want to get out of bed any morning but today was always the hardest. He never understood why he was expected to learn on his birthday.

He had just about made it to the school when he felt

something strange in the pit of his stomach. At first, he thought he might be hungry, but the feeling went away just as suddenly. There were dozens of other kids, parents, and even a cop milling around, so he tried not to make a scene, but whatever had just happened made him feel ill. The sound of a car horn caught his attention, and he looked up to see a black car pulling up next to the sidewalk. It stopped right next to him, and the window rolled down. A young woman was waiting on the other side. A round hat mostly covered her face with its wide brim. He thought she wore it way too low to be driving, but she greeted him with a smile as soon as he was in eyeshot despite that.

"Can I help you?" Taxx asked.

"Good morning, Calderhys," she said.

"How the hell do you know that name? Calderhys is grandad's name," Taxx said.

"Rest his soul," she said

"Who the hell are you?" Taxx asked.

"Calm down, Calderhys. Your grandmother sent me. Don't you recognize me? It's Offrey," she said.

He nodded, but he did not respond. His toe twisted idly on the ground, and he adjusted his bag on his shoulder.

"No offense, but why are you here, Offrey?" Taxx asked.

"I am afraid you aren't going to school today," Offrey said.

"What's going on? Where is May?" Taxx asked.

"May has been away. It wasn't supposed to be long term, but that's what it has become," Offrey said.

"So, what does that have to do with me going to school?" He asked.

He was becoming visibly upset, and Offrey smiled. She exited the car and moved toward him. She was shorter than he was by more than a few inches, but there was something so imposing about the young woman that Taxx took a step back. He couldn't help himself.

"What the hell just happened to me?" He asked.

His frustrations had turned into fear, and the look on his face changed drastically. Offrey smiled again.

"You are ignorant of all of this. It's not your fault. There are things you don't know, and I don't have time to explain," she said.

Taxx was looking at her carefully. She could almost feel his mind searching her all over for something. He was always such a methodical thinker, even when he was young. Offrey never once believed that he had the eyes of a child, they were brown and straightforward, but there was no end to them. She didn't like to look at his face. He seemed to calm down when she calmed down, which was good enough.

"You have to be moved somewhere if the worst happens," Offrey said.

"What do you mean?" he said.

"Calderhys. You know what I mean," she said.

"Humor me," he said.

"You are sick, and I know you haven't been getting your treatments with May away," Offrey said.

"I'm not sick. I've been feeling better than ever," Taxx said.

"Is that why you are wearing that? Just a fashion statement?" Offrey asked.

Taxx unconsciously reached up to the scarf almost always around his forehead these days. He couldn't remember the last time he hadn't worn it.

"Don't come at me like that! What kind of BS is this

supposed to be? You pop up after years of absence saying all this crap about May? What do you want, Offrey?" Taxx asked.

"I am here to help. I know that your medication helps you keep your… problems in check," Offrey said.

"They aren't problems. They are…" Taxx started, but he slowly trailed off.

"Mutations?" Offrey offered.

Taxx looked at her with contempt, wrinkling his forehead.

"I would say unique constellations, but go off," Taxx said.

"Whatever you call it, it requires treatment," Offrey said.

"No!" Taxx said.

He hadn't meant to shout, but his temper got the best of him; a deep and powerful voice boomed from his chest. The area around them seemed to quiet for a moment. Some of the people stopped talking but did not lookup. In the aftermath, Taxx could only stare at Offrey; neither of them moved. He thought that he might have frightened her, but the look on her face was anything but fear. She even looked amused. Then Taxx saw a flutter of something out of the corner of his eye. It was only for a moment, but he swore he saw *something*. Like a spider's silk that danced on the unseen wind, the wind so soft your skin couldn't feel it. The dancing suddenly stopped, and everything became taut like a fishing line, and then it started to vibrate like a guitar string. He felt something touch him at the center of his chest, pulling at his mind, making it hard to think. It was also hard to stand; his knees began to shake, and he stumbled. It all happened so quickly he almost had no time to react, but Offrey was there. She caught him in surprisingly strong arms.

"Careful," Offrey said.

"Get off of me!" He shouted.

He pushed at her until she let him go, which she did—taking a step back and away from him. The boy was looking at her with those eyes. She wanted to sew them shut right here and now, but that was not how this story was to play out. She took a deep breath.

"Where the hell are you trying to take me?" Taxx asked angrily.

"A special facility to help you get better. This is what May would have wanted. It's dangerous for you to be by yourself," Offrey said.

"I've been just fine," Taxx said smugly.

"BECAUSE I HAVE ALLOWED IT…" Offrey shouted.

Then she fell silent for a long breath.

"I'm sorry, it's just that things are worse than I can say," she said.

"What is this big secret?" Taxx asked.

"I can't tell you," Offrey said.

"Then why even acknowledge it? Isn't that worse?" Taxx shouted.

Offrey did not respond. She simply stood there and watched him with a stoic face. It took him a moment to collect himself, but he managed to do so to his credit while still on the ground.

"It's called the House of Wolf and Raven; it's a special facility that can help you get better," Offrey said.

"Isn't that the boarding school where Sixx lives?" Taxx asked.

She smiled, caught off guard by his knowledge.

"You know about that. Impressive. Yes, it's something like that," she said.

Taxx was still on the ground and making a sour face about

the entire situation. He tried to get up almost half a dozen times without any success. Taxx sighed heavily; it felt like his legs were tied up or something; he could not stand up independently. After taking a moment to collect himself, he turned toward Offrey.

"Help me to the car. Please," Taxx said curtly.

Offrey didn't say anything; she only nodded and led him to a car. She opened the rear door to allow him to enter and closed it behind him, then she got into the driver's seat and started the car. They were moving in no time, and aside from the music in the background, it was primarily quiet until Taxx spoke up.

"Where is Grandma?" Taxx asked.

"She's still away on business," Offrey said.

"Mm. You are just as cryptic as she is. She seemed so distracted last night," Taxx said.

Offrey looked up to the rear-view mirror so sharply that the car swerved slightly. Taxx lifted an eyebrow at her, smiling in response, correcting the vehicle, and continuing.

"You good?" he said.

"Yeah, sorry. You said you talked to her last night?" she said.

"Yeah, she came into my dreams, just like every year," Taxx said.

"What did she say?" she said.

Offrey was smiling, but everything felt off about it. Something in her eyes matched the feeling that had been creeping up in him all morning. Something was wrong today.

"She told me to tell you to mind your business," Taxx teased.

"Next time you talk to her, tell her to visit my dreams," Offrey said.

"You got it," Taxx said.

"Have you heard from anyone else in your dreams?" she

asked.

"What are you, the dream police?" Taxx asked.

"Yes. Have you talked to Saturday?" Offrey asked.

"Still got a thing for him, huh?" Taxx teased.

She turned her face toward him in the rearview, and he returned a smirk that was all too familiar for her taste.

"I haven't seen him in a long time. I wonder if she told him what she told me?" Taxx asked.

Offrey turned to look his way in the rearview again, no emotion on her face, and Taxx just started to laugh.

"Don't look at me like that; if you don't know, I will not tell you," Taxx said.

"You sound like May," she said.

"Is that a compliment?" he said.

"It's just the truth. Just remember that it's not good for a young man to be so much like his grandmother," Offrey said.

"I'll try to keep that in mind," he said.

The car fell silent, and Taxx preferred it that way, Offrey was very courteous to him, but he had this sinking feeling that she didn't like him. He couldn't prove it, but something inside of him had always told him to be wary of the weight between them, and he had never been one to turn against his instincts. They were all he had. The car approached the main street and passed a hand-painted billboard standing in the center of the road that read: Arkane, CT, a magical place. Taxx didn't get out much, admittedly, but there was hardly any magic here from what he had seen of it. No one ever heard of it. Down route 34 in the Naugatuck Valley, the state's smallest city, next to Derby.

The car stopped at the intersection, but Offrey didn't turn down the bustling and colorful main street. She continued down the road, and Taxx quietly watched the sign until it disappeared into the distance. Then he turned back to look at Offrey. They had known each other almost all their lives; she was mercurial and spoke around him very curtly. Admittedly Taxx knew very little about her, but there was always something in the air between them that made him feel uncomfortable. A small weight. She never mentioned it, and he would probably never think to ask. He sometimes imagined that she could feel it. He also believed that if she *could* feel it and ignored it anyway, that would be much worse. He hoped never to find out.

"Sixx used to tell me that I was like her too," Taxx said.

Offrey visibly brightened at the mention of his name, and Taxx rolled his eyes, where she treated him with a careful distance; she had a crush on his cousin. There was no other explanation for why she acted the way she did around him. She was like a different person around his cousin.

"Do you think he still uses that unsightly nickname?" she asked.

Taxx nodded. He looked down at the car's floor between his feet and let out a long sigh that he didn't even know he had been holding.

"You ok, champ?" she asked.

"Offrey, I'm not a child," he said.

She glanced back in the mirror and smirked at him.

"May told me you were making a lot of progress with your condition. That means you'll be able to start doing things like a normal teenager soon enough," she said.

"Great," he said.

"I know what will cheer you up," she said.

Taxx looked up at her in the mirror, confused.

"I didn't forget that today is your birthday. I was teasing you," Offrey said.

"Why would that cheer me up?" Taxx asked.

"Because I have something for you," Offrey said

For a long time, Taxx didn't say anything. He just watched her. He only spoke when she cleared her throat several times. It took him about three to realize that she wouldn't stop until he responded.

"What is it?" Taxx asked.

"A message," she said.

"Ok. What message?" Taxx asked.

"A message from your mother," Offrey said.

Taxx felt his mouth go dry and his stomach drop to the floor. He closed his eyes and did everything he could not to scream or cry or, worse of all, tremble. Not in front of her. It took him a moment to recover, but eventually, he spoke.

"I know I don't want it," He whispered.

"What do you mean?" she asked,

"Why would I want anything from a woman who wanted nothing to do with me? No offense, but it's none of your damned business," Taxx said.

He punctuated his words by sitting hard in the back seat and crossing his arms over his chest—the international symbol for talk-time is over.

"Sheesh. After all, you two aren't so different; you're just a little sweeter about the jabs," Offrey teased.

Taxx made a face at her but maintained his silence strike. It was not a long-lived strike, but Taxx was sure there was some *tense* silence. If Offrey noticed, however, she played it very cool.

"I don't know how Sixx is. I haven't seen him in years. No

one visits us," Taxx said.

"You know why no one can visit," Offrey said.

"Because Grandma is a witch?" Taxx asked.

"No. Because you are sick," Offrey said.

"Sick. Nice," Taxx snapped.

"I meant that you are special," she said.

"Can this ride be over, please?" he asked sarcastically.

"Almost there, smart guy, you can see the gates from here," she said.

The facility's gates were glowing white steel structures with a fancy letter R twisted gracefully from the same metal. It hung just beneath the iron sign: The House of Wolf and Raven. The gates started to swing open before the car even stopped, and Taxx lifted an eyebrow.

"Guess they are expecting us?" he asked.

"Some people here have been waiting a long time to meet you," Offrey said.

"Then why have I never heard of it before?" he said.

"You ask a lot of questions, Calderhys," Offrey said.

"Questions are how we surv-" Taxx started.

"Regurgitating grandma again?" she said, successfully cutting him off with the question.

Taxx said nothing. He only looked at her in the mirror from the back seat, holding back his words and feelings like she taught him. She pulled the car through the gates, and they started across a wide bridge, taking them to an island on land. Sheer walls rose high above a quarry floor and came to a sudden flat top, covered with greenery, a large mesa accessible only by the single bridge.

"What… is this place?" Taxx asked.

As they crossed the bridge, Taxx could see a house in the

distance that was so large that it could have been a palace. It was standing between two smaller buildings in the center of the wild greenery that erupted from every surface of the table-topped hill. The forest was sprawled across a surprisingly wide space, and the house rose above it like a crown at the center. It had many arches and glass that made it glitter like a jewel in the light, the late 50s aesthetic that people paid good money for. All the doors were broader and heavier than they needed to be, and gardens were thick enough to lose a full-sized bus. The building that stood off to the left appeared to be a small medical facility, and he was unsure about the squat building to the right. The building was round at its base with pale stucco walls and a tapered roof that made it look like a plump little mushroom. The driveway of the main house was lined with wild vegetation, flowering trees, and alive with the sounds of nature on all sides.

"You ready for that message from your-," Offrey started.

"Nope," Taxx said.

"Calderhys, you'll have to forgive her some time," she said.

"Ok. No, though," Taxx said.

Offrey sucked at her teeth in frustration and again looked back at him in the mirror.

"Calderhys-" She started.

Taxx let out a long sigh, and then he opened the car door while the vehicle was still in motion, causing Offrey to slam on the brakes and the car to veer sideways in the road. Taxx had already slipped out of the car before she opened her door to chase him.

"Hey, what are you doing!?" Offrey screamed.

Taxx started to run off, but somehow, Offrey was able to grab his arm. Even when he was sure she was nowhere near close enough to do that. He looked down at her hand on his forearm and back up to her face.

"What the hell did you just stab me with?" he said.

"You could see my needle? That's impressive. Still, it's far too late. It's time that you received that message," Offrey said.

"Needle? What the hell are you?" Taxx asked.

"Behold the child born through a curse," Offrey said.

Taxx froze.

He couldn't move his arms or his legs. He couldn't turn his head or even breath. It was as though he had been pushed out of the driver's seat of his mind. He was tossed into the back seat. He could see out of the windows, but someone else controlled him and made him stand perfectly still. Offrey walked up to him with a long think needle between her fingers. It was as white as a bone and covered in delicate carvings. She only pressed it to his chest, but it felt like she was scalding him with a red-hot brand. He screamed so hard that his voice gave out. Taxx was unsure how long it took, but eventually, all of the stinging objects left his body. As they did, there was a tingle in all his nerves that caused him to lose his footing and fall to his knees. The action seemed to force him back into the driver's seat, and Taxx looked at Offrey with confusion.

"What did you just do to me?" Taxx asked.

"A few things, honestly, but I'll try to summarize for you in layperson's terms," Offrey said.

"I feel... strange," Taxx whispered.

"Already? Your body is already starving for magic. How she has been holding you back all this time is beyond a compliment to Maybelline's power," she said.

"You're crazy," Taxx said.

It was getting harder to talk.

"I used an unsealing phrase to release magic that has been locked inside of you. Magic that *was* keeping you safe. Think of it as a birthday gift. Happy Birthday, Taxx. I am sorry," Offrey said.

She looked a little sad for a moment. Even the corner of her mouth turned down.

"What does that mean?" Taxx asked.

The sound of twisted metal exploded around them, and Taxx turned just in time to see the car they were driving start to lurch sideways before it rolled completely onto its side. The sound of broken glass was everywhere, and it started to crumble under its weight, the roof caving on itself in moments.

"What the hell? Offrey?" Taxx said.

When he looked back to see why she was so quiet, he found that she was not there at all, he was standing on the side of the road alone now, and he didn't know what to do. It wasn't just because of the incredible damage to the car, or because his heart was racing so hard that he thought he might collapse, there was something else. He didn't have time to think. A low growling sound came from behind the car, and he froze, staring at the spot as hard as possible. A golden hood ornament preceded the car that slowly crept around the wreckage. The decoration was a golden hand, all five fingers, and a detailed palm, easily the size of an adult man's hand. It was held out as if to say, 'give me that' and served as the gilded cherry on a limousine as white as ivory and trimmed with glittering gold. There were crowns over the headlights, and the spiny golden grill gave it a menacing face and was the source of the low guttural growl he had been hearing. He didn't know the make and model because he had never seen a car like this before. It looked like a car from a movie set in the

1920s. A monster movie set.

"Pass," Taxx said.

He turned and started to run as fast as possible, but before he got more than a few steps, he slammed into something so hard that it took his breath away. Before he could catch it, his body started to move. He was suddenly flying backward and unable to catch his feet. He went end over end off the side of the road until he hit a tree. Hard. The next time that Taxx was conscious, he could hardly move or think and barely see, but he was sure that something was dragging him by his foot, and he couldn't do anything to fight back.

"You weren't supposed to kill him, Fuckwit," A voice said.

Taxx tried to speak and squeezed out something like a scream, but it probably didn't sound as brave as he thought. He felt someone gently tap at his ribs with a foot, not a kick, just a poking, and he tried to curl away.

"Well. You are one lucky son of a bitch; I was going to gut you if he was dead. What did you do to him?" The voice said

"There is a knot in his heart. Her magic won't be able to protect him anymore," a different voice said.

It was scratched up like a record and sounded strange.

"What happens after the procedure?" the voice asked.

"Kingmaker, you are proving to be a very useful person," The voice said.

"Once this is over, he will be as weak as a human. That's the best time to strike. I'll send my best two," Kingmaker said.

"I'll hang on to Kiddo. I've taken a liking to him," The voice said

There was a terrible sound, like the sound of blood being spilled, from the one that dragged him.

The other man laughed, a dry, mirthless cackle.

"What is it?" Kingmaker asked.

"Your boy is made of iron; he is awake," The voice said.

"That could become problematic," Kingmaker said.

"Not at all. Fuckwit Johnny put his ass out. Then go and wake Kiddo," The voice said.

Taxx tried, but he couldn't get a good look at any of them, his head hurt, but there was something else like he couldn't focus his eyes on their faces. Even listening to them speak was a strain, and breathing became problematic. Taxx was beginning to think that he would die on his birthday. Before he could worry about it too much, he was lifted by his leg as easily as a child might lift a doll, and the last thing he heard was that dry cackle before he was slammed into the ground. Headfirst. He went out like a light switch.

Click.

Chapter | Four

Click

Like a light switch, he felt himself starting to come out of the darkness of his unconsciousness. Taxx forced his eyes open as soon as possible, only to be blinded by the sudden light. He lifted his hand to protect himself and gritted his teeth against the pain behind his eyes, but it wasn't just the light. A message started hammering away like a clock ticking in his mind so intensely that it was adding to his headache. When he tried to think of the message, there was nothing there. It existed in a faded place like a dream you couldn't recall, no more than a gentle whisper in the back of his head.

One thing was sure; something was very wrong. His bones were shivering, and the vibration continued throughout his body.

Every shake seemed to bring back another sense. His vision was the first sense to return. He couldn't see clearly but could hear and smell something sweet and heavy with iron. Someone was talking, and he could make out what was being said if he concentrated, he focused not just his eyes but his whole self on the voice, and he could hear him.

"That has honestly never happened before. Normally they die when we do it this much," Spoke the thing sitting on the left.

They were all in the back of a vehicle, himself and two men who made it apparent that neither of these beings was of the human variety.

"What the hell are you?" said the being on the left.

The young man was still baffled by what was happening and why he was in this car with these strange people. Taxx simply could not stop staring at the man on the right. At first glance, he could have been any regular guy, but if you looked for even a moment longer, everything went very wrong. An infant's face sat where an average man's face should have been. An infant's face wearing a pair of designer shades, held up by an adorable button nose. Under that nose sat the lips and mouth of a much larger being. It took up an upsetting amount of real estate on the tiny face. The skull beneath was full-grown, and the way the child's face stretched around the bones was a jarring combination that made the man hard to look at. Baby Face leaned forward and snapped his fingers right next to his ear to get his attention. The sound exploded through him like a gunshot.

"Why?" He shouted.

It was all he could muster now; he couldn't seem to collect his thoughts for anything beyond responses. Everything he could see had a rainbow haze around it like he was on drugs.

Not just his eyes but his mind as well. Try as he might, he could not remember who he was or how he got into this car in the first place. Before he could think about it too hard, Baby Face snapped again, and whatever thought he was chasing slipped out of his grip, and he found it even harder to look at the man on the right. He pressed his hands to his face to try and center himself, but it wasn't helping. As soon as he covered his eyes, there was a rainbow fuzz over everything. Pressing his fingers into his eyelids seemed to help. After a moment, he looked up at the man on the right one last time, straining to see him through the haze.

"Impressive. She is a woman of her word. Get him out of my car, right now," said the voice from earlier.

He could see the car's interior even better now, and everything looked new and expensive like what you see in a movie limousine. There were decanters and bottled water even. He could see the baby-faced man even more clearly and the world outside of the car now like he was coming out of a deep fog, but he couldn't make out the man on the right. No matter how he tried, something seemed to shroud him, bathing in shadows or dark smoky clouds. Baby Face opened the door on his side of the car, and then he clapped his hands until the young man's attention was centered on his strange face.

"Yup, just like that!" Baby Face said.

Then he punched the young man unexpectedly hard in the jaw and sent his head rocking. Before he could recover, he was grabbed by the shirt and ejected from the car, end over end. Maybe it was the punch or being upside down, but the haze around the man on the right lifted, and he saw him clearly for a moment. He couldn't remember his face because his mouth was a gilded horror filled with hundreds of pointy teeth, each one gleamed with gold and diamonds like a glam rapper from hell. They aligned like the teeth of a comb in his smile. He couldn't get that smile out of his head, and it had him so frozen that he slammed into the sidewalk without lifting his arms to defend himself. The doors on the car opened like French doors from the center. Baby Face leaned out and grabbed the hanging handles on both, smiled at him with sinister intent, and slammed the doors closed in his face. The car took off with its horrible growling engine and was gone as mysteriously as it came.

Taxx watched the headlight fade off into the distance directly in front of him but still having some trouble orienting himself, and he made his way to his feet carefully. He didn't recognize this place, but it was quickly apparent that he was nowhere near his grandmother's house anymore. He didn't even know how much time had passed. Wherever they threw him out was at least a little familiar to him, he could barely see the sign for the high school in the distance. A retaining wall with an iron fence running along its top was just across the road from him, and a wide asphalt sidewalk flanked the street. A few cars were parked along the curb and some houses here and there, but mostly there were trees. Just down the road stood what looked to be a library. There was a church on the other side of the street, and just next to it, a large funeral home with wood siding. There was a thick old tree on the corner of the lot where the funeral home sat as wide as it was tall, and someone was standing just in front of it, staring at him. Taxx cried out.

"Holy crap! What are you doing, man? You scared me," Taxx said.

A man was standing against that tree with calm gray eyes, and although he was staring at Taxx, he did not say a word to him. Taxx stopped walking, but the gray-eyed man was already making his way toward him, slowly working on a strange duffel bag hanging across his back.

"Do you need something, bruh?" Taxx asked.

The gray-eyed man said nothing. Then he started to run toward Taxx, never even blinking those terrible gray eyes. Taxx couldn't think of anything else, so he began to run away. As soon as he turned, he found another strange man standing just behind him so close that they collided, and Taxx crumpled against his chest. It felt like running into a brick wall, but there was no response from the man. Even more surprising was the lack of attempt to grab or hold Taxx. Instead, the new stranger helped him to his feet and even dusted off his shirt, he hadn't even noticed this man, but he was enormous and intense, just like gray eyes.

"What the… What?" Taxx said.

"Behind you," The new stranger said.

Gray eyes had reached him. Taxx felt his body heat on his back before turning to face him. He couldn't see it, but he knew that guy was standing just behind his right thigh, there was something in his hands, but he couldn't make it out. Taxx did not see it, but somehow, he could perceive it, like a shadow through a haze of clouds during a thunderstorm, just for a moment. As soon as he did, Taxx felt something like a shiver that started at the center of his being and radiated out of him from his guts to the tips of his fingers. He could even feel it in his hair, tingling from the roots to the ends of his afro; it was like electricity flowing into every cell of his body. The attack came, and before he could think at all, his body reacted all on its own, and he pivoted on the ball of his foot as fast as he had ever moved.

If Taxx had taken a breath, he would be dead, but instead, the two men were now standing back-to-back. It was a somewhat poetic, if partially homicidal, ballet. Taxx opened his mouth to speak, but the words never got the chance to come out. The growl of a vehicle cut him off, and a yellow pickup truck popped a curb behind him. It accelerated on the sidewalk as fast as it could and hammered into the man with gray eyes. There was a loud sound, and the truck carried him off with the terrifying speed of a predator from the dark. Taxx thought for a moment that it was like watching a shark attack. It sped across the road and came to a violent and sudden stop when it crashed into a retaining wall.

"Holy shit, did you see that?" Taxx asked.

There was no answer, and when he turned to look for the other guy standing there, there was no one. Taxx didn't even have the stomach to look at the mangled pile of metal yet, so he took a moment to collect himself before examining it. Miraculously the engine was still running, and it didn't look too bad for the horrific accident that had just gone down. He didn't know what to do about this. He had hoped that someone else would be here to take responsibility for it, and his head was still all over the place. He closed his eyes to collect himself, and when he opened them again, he gasped loudly. There was movement in the car wreck.

"No way," Taxx whispered.

He scrambled behind the squat little tree and watched as the driver-side window was suddenly kicked out. He expected weirdness, some next-level strange horror to come out of that window, but that's not what he got. Once the driver was free, it became clear that this looked like a regular dude. Except he did not seem concerned by the murder he had just committed. He may have even looked happy about it. The killer kid looked over the wreckage with a small smile. Then he searched for something, sniffing the air like a bloodhound. He was wearing dark gray slacks with no shirt under his suit jacket and no socks under his slippers. Taxx thought that he might be looking for him, the thought suddenly crossing his mind for a moment, just a single moment like the brush of a feather. As soon as it did, at that exact instant, the other guy turned suddenly and locked eyes with him as if he could hear the thought, and just like that, the murderer started running toward him. As soon as the killer kid started to run, it became apparent that this person was also not a human; he was so inordinately fast that the distance between them was halved in a second.

"Why is every weirdo looking for me today?" Taxx shouted.

He tried to run, but the killer kid was so fast that Taxx could hardly keep up with his eyes. When he realized how close they were now standing, Taxx thought he had already been stabbed. Taxx didn't get stabbed. However, instead, the killer kid tightly hugged him close around the chest with such warm familiarity that he was caught off guard. For reasons he could not explain, instead of pulling away, he let himself be hugged by this new murderous stranger who was laughing into his shoulder and patting him on the back vigorously.

"I knew I would find you, Taxx!" The guy said.

When the hug was over, the killer kid even looked a bit embarrassed by it but was still all smiles, he didn't look so dangerous like this, and honestly, that was making it worse. Taxx tried to think of what he had been doing before this moment, but his mind was suddenly full of rainbows and smoke. No matter what he did, he couldn't seem to wrap his head around anything, and it was starting to agitate him. Taxx pressed his hands into his face again and tried to force the rainbows away, and when he couldn't do that, he whipped around to the guy and pointed the finger at him accusingly.

"How the hell do you know my name?" Taxx asked.

"You don't recognize me? You are my one and only cousin," Sixx said.

"Huh? You're **not** my cousin. I don't have any cousins that look like Jamaican cartel," Taxx said.

"Serious? You need it delivered Tarzan style, bruh? Me Sixx, you Taxx, man. Look at me!" Sixx said.

Taxx took a good look at him, and he started to see it. Somewhere inside of this handsome, dread-headed, pierced, and tattooed young man was his cousin, Saturday. The last time they had seen each other, Sixx didn't look anything like this. Taxx couldn't stop staring.

"Sixx!? You look so… different," Taxx said.

"I know, it's been a while but listen, brotha, you got into some shit, and we need to get the hell out of here," Sixx said.

"Some weirdos in a limousine beat me up and brought me here. Then you… holy shit. You killed a guy. Sixx. You killed a guy. What the hell are you smiling at?!" Taxx erupted suddenly.

Sixx was watching him with a smile on his face that was so wide that it upset Taxx instantly, and he curled up his face about it.

"Oh him? He probably ain't dead. But look at you, cuh. You are lookin' a little different too. I like. Where your horns?" Sixx asked.

"Pipe down, man. The bandana hides them," Taxx said.

"Taxx, what are you talking about? I killed a guy, and you didn't even care," Sixx said.

"I do!" Taxx shouted.

"Then why you ain't run from me? Why you still here right now?" Sixx asked.

Taxx could only stare at him. He didn't have a good answer for any of that. Nor for the relief he had felt since his cousin appeared. He felt like he let a breath out he didn't know he was holding.

"Exactly. You worried about some horns? It would help if you loosened up," Sixx said.

Taxx hated to admit that he had a point. Though he was sure that he did not run because he was too afraid, he didn't feel scared. He was feeling better than he had in a long time.

"Sixx. I…" Taxx started.

When he tried to tell him about the babyface and the gold mouth man, he could not. The words would not come out of his mouth.

"Sixx. What is happening to me today?" Taxx asked.

Sixx smiled even harder and patted his cousin on the shoulder gingerly.

"Don't worry bout it. I'mma take care of you, but first, we gotta… hold on. Something ain't right," Sixx said

Sixx lifted his nose to the air and took a sniff balking at the smell and pinching his nose.

"Those damned things reek of death, making my chain go crazy. I'm gonna get you out of here," Sixx said.

Sixx closed his eyes. Taxx felt something like the pit in your stomach when you take off in an airplane. His stomach lurched. Not painful but jarring.

"What the hell was that?" Taxx asked.

"Just a little magic, cuh. Chill," Sixx said.

"Don't tell me to chill," Taxx huffed.

"I did miss you, Taxx, you so serious," Sixx said.

Sixx gave him a little push, and Taxx lost his balance and fell. Not just down to the sidewalk but through it, as though a massive hole had opened beneath him. He screamed as he dropped a few feet and landed with a hard thud on his back. Taxx was now looking up his cousin through a hole rimmed in dark energy that swirled at its edges like black smoke. Sixx was sweating, but he was still wearing a big smile. The hole was only open for a moment before it started to close.

"Oh damn. That's my fault," Sixx said.

Sixx looked off into the distance and gave his cousin an even bigger smile.

"Sixx! Come on!" Taxx said.

"Can't do that right now," Sixx said.

"What are you saying to me??" Taxx asked.

"Ran out of juice," Sixx said.

"Then why did you push me?" Taxx asked.

"There's more of them coming," Sixx said.

"Why did you save me?" Taxx asked.

"We family," Sixx said.

Sixx looked exhausted, and he was sweating even more as the hole started to fade between them. Somehow though, he still looked pleased.

"Sixx, you haven't seen me in years!" Taxx shouted.

"That don't matter, cuh," Sixx said.

The hole was rapidly fading, and Taxx was starting to panic. It was so small now that all Taxx could see was the huge smile on Sixx's face.

"Why are you smiling like that!?" Taxx asked.

"I'm happy you still you," Sixx said.

"What does that mean?!" Taxx shouted.

Sixx probably didn't hear that one. The portal was gone, and Taxx was looking up at the slatted ceiling of a front porch. His front porch. Sixx had pushed him through a hole in the sidewalk, and he came out on his porch, safe and sound. Saturday swooped in and saved him just when he thought it was over.

"You are still the same too," Taxx whispered.

Taxx smiled and then ran to the railing to look out at the yard and then back to the space where the hole had been. It was still daytime, which means that almost no time had passed. His cousin created a practical hole in space and time. The same cousin who taught him how to do the butterfly dance made a hole in space and time. The thought hammered through his head and touched at something deeper inside. There was no pain, but a sensation rolled through him that made his toes curl, and his eyes roll for a moment. Something was drawn inside of him, and the haze on his mind went along with it. It cleared like the sky above the clouds, and he shivered again, so hard that he had to steady himself against the wall.

"What the hell?" Taxx whispered.

A powerful wave of panic washed over him. The same kind of panic flashed through him when he was near the man with the glittering horror mouth, the feeling in the pit of his stomach of butterflies and fear that told him that danger was coming. Taxx quickly and quietly slipped behind the door just a moment before it opened. There was no sound, no nothing. A small voice inside of him told him not to move. He didn't know where it came from. He was having a strange day, and the voice at least seemed to be friendly. Trusting a peculiar and helpful voice inside him was the most normal thing he had done in recent memory.

The sound of something approaching the door gave way to the steady hum of insect wings, and a single black house fly buzzed out of the door around eye height. It seemed to hover for a long time, longer than he had ever seen an average fly stay in one place. This was probably some weird mating thing he knew nothing about because he didn't know a damn thing about flies, except that he didn't care for them very much. He looked around to see if there was anything he might swat it with but as soon as he thought it, the tiny little set of eyes turned to look at him, the way a human might react. Taxx and the fly were both startled. He gasped and involuntarily tried to backpedal, which set his back against the wall, and he did the only thing he could think to do. He slapped the fly.

Except it didn't sail away into a wall like a toy dart, it didn't float away. When he slapped the fly, full force, his hand only stopped in midair as if he hit an invisible wall. It felt like he had just punched a brick. Pain suddenly stinging all through his palm, and he was sure if he had swung his hand any harder, it would have punctured right through him. The fly didn't even seem to be angry, it just started to hover slowly toward him, and he quickly ducked under the fly and rolled into the apartment, slamming the door in the fly.

"Ha! Oh, wait…" Taxx said.

He suddenly remembered that the fly had already opened the door, and as he stood to his feet, the door swung open with force until it banged on the wall as if the fly had kicked it in. Taxx stood his ground and held his hands toward the fly in the shape of a cross, he couldn't even remember if he was religious, but this felt like the right thing to do right now. As he was thinking about it, he concluded that the cross was a vampire thing and had nothing to do with aggressive door-opening flies. The fly suddenly rushed him, and he shut his eyes and braced for what he was sure to be a pain, but nothing happened, and when he opened a single eye, the fly appeared to have gone. After a quick look around, he was sure that there didn't seem to be any other flies that he could see. He should have been elated by the sudden departure, but there was something so wrong with it that he couldn't get past it. He had never been much of an animal person. He thought, even less of an insect person. He didn't know much about that kind of thing, but even he knew something was wrong with that fly.

"Are flies supposed to… do that?" he said.

"Do what?" Someone asked.

He wasn't proud of the scream that slipped out of his mouth before the woman had even finished speaking, but it happened, and to her credit, she didn't mention it. She was also kind enough to not give his outthrust hands, in the rudimentary shape of a cross, anything more than a single glance. However, the woman standing with her appeared to have far less poise. Her chest was heaving rapidly, and her eyes were wet. Even though she tried to hide her noticeable laughter with her hand, she did very poorly. Sudden heat rose to his face, and he quickly lowered his hands, moving toward the front of the apartment where the two women waited just outside the screen door.

"You scared the hell out of me! Excuse my language and sorry for the… hand thing. How can I help you?" he asked.

"Good afternoon, sir; my apologies for startling you. My name is Lyra, and this is my partner, Nicole," Lyra said.

Her partner grunted and rolled her eyes but ultimately smiled.

"Nicole is definitely my name," Nicole said.

"We are with the police department," Lyra said.

She held out her hand, and when he accepted it, she gave him a single firm shake that was efficient but somehow succeeded in conveying that she was friendly. She and her partner showed him their badges, and he took a good look as if he knew what he was looking for, but he didn't know a badge number from his elbow. The badges said Detective right in the center, so at least he now knew that much, though he wasn't sure if that was what they were supposed to look like.

"Thank you, I'm Taxxis Kingswood," Taxx said.

"Your name is Taxes?" Nicole asked.

"Taxxis," he corrected.

She still raised an eyebrow slowly, and he shrugged back.

"How can I help you?" Taxx asked.

"Mr. Kingswood, have you had any strange visions today?" Lyra asked.

The question slammed into his chest like a bean bag. He tried his best to keep his composure.

"Um, what? What does that even mean?" he asked.

"Have you experienced any events that you might consider to be abnormal? Specifically, today?" Nicole asked.

Taxx cleared his throat and leaned against the doorframe to look nonchalant.

"Nope. No visions here. What kind of cops did you say you were again?" Taxx asked.

"The good kind," Lyra said.

"The kind that are looking for visions?" Taxx asked.

"Truancy officers," Lyra said.

"Oh," Taxx said.

"Yeah," Nic rebutted.

"Want to tell me why you aren't in school today?" Lyra asked.

Taxx nodded slowly, giving himself time to think, and his mind cooked up a lie faster than any hamburger joint could slap together a burger.

"I was taking care of my upstairs neighbor. He isn't feeling well," Taxx said.

"Tomas Craw? We tried his door, and he didn't answer," Lyra asked.

"Tomas? Huh…that's pretty exotic," Taxx said.

"Yeah, not like Taxxis," Nicole said.

Lyra stopped her partner with just a look.

"I didn't know his first name. I don't talk to the guy. He is just some angry old dude who lives upstairs. Sometimes my grandma asks me to look in on him," Taxx said.

"You are taking care of him, but you didn't know his name?" Lyra asked.

"He isn't much of a talker, super old," he said.

"Thank you, Mr. Kingswood. We will be reached out to your parent or guardian about this absence," Lyra said.

"Go off," Taxx said.

Nicole looked past him and into his apartment with an intensity that got his attention. When she noticed him, the detective smiled.

"You said you have flies?" she asked.

"Uh, no, I had one… that sounds so sad, but it seems to be clearing up, though," he said.

"That's good to hear. Please give us a call if you see anything strange. Remember. If you see something, say something," Nicole said.

She earned an elbow from her partner for that last bit, which was well deserved. He was starting to have a hard time with their status as police officers. Nicole then handed him a business card, but it didn't say police; instead, it read:

The House of Wolf and Raven

Guild Warding

1 (203) 911-4666

1134 Fair E Circle

Arkane, CT 06418

He could only stare at it for a bit before he looked up at the women, they weren't in uniform, which would have been fine, but now that he was looking at them, there were some inconsistencies. He hadn't noticed at first, but Lyra was wearing bright orange flip flop sandals, the kind you get from the dollar store, and black yoga pants. She was also crazy tall and muscular, a loose tee-shirt hung to her knees and an oversized hoodie over the top was fully zipped, and the hood was up though it did not hide her face. It just hung precariously off the back of her head. The outfit didn't hide her frame or height at all, and he was looking up at her face when he was a few inches over six feet tall. The other woman wore a trench coat and ankle boots, red as candy apples, and a pink shirt that read 'Bird Gang' on the chest.

There was no way these two were cops, he thought, but now that he was thinking about it again, he couldn't remember if they had been dressed like this a moment ago. Thinking about it brought the rainbow clouds back to his head, but they were so intense this time; his head started to swim so much that he almost fell over. Lyra caught him easily, as though she were holding a doll and not an admittedly chubby grown man, turned him until he was right side up, and checked his eyes. She did it all so smoothly he thought she might have been an EMT or giant medicine woman because of the round necklace she was wearing. It was all he could look at for a moment, and he could see some words starting to rise from the surface. Taxx was not sure how but he knew they were names. The weird part was that he knew how to say them.

"What kind of police department is called Wolf and Raven?" he said.

"What did you just say, Mr. Kingswood?" Lyra asked.

They were both looking at him with fierce eyes, making him cringe involuntarily. As soon as he did, he felt a sensation like he suddenly breathed ocean water into his nose, and he couldn't quite work his eyes or draw in breath for a moment. When it was over, the two women stared at him even harder.

"Ha, I knew it!" Nic said.

"Please," Lyra rebutted.

"I said the next one would be the guy, didn't I?" Nic asked.

"You said that three times in a row," Lyra said.

"Doesn't matter, still counts when I'm right," Nic said.

"What the hell did you do to me?" he asked.

Taxx was still a bit dizzy, and a headache was starting to stitch its way through the fabric of his thoughts. He pinched the bridge of his nose, but it wasn't helping. There was something stuck in his mind, it was like getting a splinter, but instead of being made of wood, it was a single thought that Taxx couldn't get out of his head. The tingle of it felt familiar, the opening segments of curiosity setting into his mind, but this was different, it was taking over his every thought, and soon, it was the only thing he could think. Taxx's eyes rolled into his head, and he started to speak. Lyra reached out and stifled the word in his mouth before he could say it, and he blinked out of the trance, looking at each of them wildly. He remembered everything he did but not even a single thing about why.

"What just happened?" Taxx asked.

"You first, what were you just about to say?" Nicole asked.

"A name, I think," Taxx said.

"What name were you about to speak?" Lyra asked.

Taxx froze.

He couldn't remember.

"Answer the tall lady-" Nic started.

Lyra stopped her with just a look again.

"You're like my age. Why are you pretending to be a cop and not just a strange girl in red boots?" Taxx asked.

"Who are you calling strange? I saw that fly about to kick your ass. Don't act tough now. I'll punch you right in the di-" Nic stopped suddenly.

Lyra gave her the look a third time.

"Thank you," Lyra said.

Her voice was much heavier now, and she took a step toward him, and Taxx stepped back, he was having a hard time focusing his eyes, but he was sure her hair color changed from blond to brunette just then.

"Was your hair black a second ago? What the hell is going on?" he said.

The rainbow clouds were back with a vengeance, and he was starting to have a hard time remembering even fundamental things. His headache got so bad that he collapsed to his hands and knees. He was chewing at the air to get a breath, but none of it was coming into his lungs. All he could do was make a rasping sound. The two women exchanged a look.

"Did this guy see through my glamor? I mean, that makes sense. He did see through the charm on the card. **This** is why I hate dealing with Guild brokers," Nicole said.

"I do not believe that a poor charm is the issue. I'm not sure of what I am looking at here. This boy is wrapped up in so many curses I can't tell what he is. He is certainly no human," Lyra said.

She hovered her hand over him a moment and closed her eyes.

"There… Do you feel it? This one has some power, it feels so slight through all of this mess, but there is something here," Lyra said.

"What Mess?" Nicole asked.

"Who has done this to you, boy? Come here and hold out your hand, Nic. Can you feel that? He has been the victim of very dark work," Lyra said.

"You say this guy could be an Other? Good kind or the bad kind?" Nic said.

"What's an Other?" Taxx tried to ask.

It came out as more of a moan than the words he intended.

'Nic' had taken a knee next to him, and her hand was hovering over the center of his back. He could feel a beautiful warmth coming from her. It made his head hurt less. He leaned into it and touched his back to her hand and the comfortable heat involuntarily, and as soon as he did, something strange started to happen.

"DON'T!" Nic shouted.

She sounded panicked, but Taxx couldn't stop himself. He couldn't help but lean further into the rushing warmth. He wasn't just leaning; he was pulling that heat into himself at an alarming rate. It was like drinking warm liquid. It spread through every part of him, from the center of his back to the tips of his toes, a comfortable warmth that he couldn't get enough of. Nic tried to pull away, but she didn't seem to be able to. Taxx felt the tingle rise to his eyes, and just for a moment, it filled up his mind, and all of the terrible haze inside of his mind went away in an instant. Like flicking a light switch, the warm feeling went away, and the pain came crashing back so hard that his hands gave out, and he fell flat on his chest. Tears were coming now, but he couldn't even feel them. All he could feel was pressure pulling from the center of him. All he could hear were the women's voices silenced by the rapid, steady rush of his heartbeat in his ears and somewhere inside of him a tiny voice. He couldn't understand any of them now, though, just the fleeting feeling of the rush as it receded into his depths. He assumed his conscience was trying to tell him he was about to die.

"What the hell is this boy?" Nic asked.

Nic was still kneeling next to him, staring at her left hand with a bewildered look on her face. She flexed her fingers and looked from the young man on the ground to Lyra.

"I do not know, but we were both there to see it. There was no doubt that he drew magic from you. Did you see the color in his eyes for a moment? This is… I do not honestly know if this is just a coincidence or what he sent us to find," Lyra said.

"How was he able to touch me? This has prophecy bullshit

written all over it," Nic said.

"Definitely. After dark, we will have to come back for the other one, then I will-" Lyra stopped.

She looked distant for a moment.

"That was Izzy again," Lyra said.

"What is it this time?" Nic asked.

"There is a fire. People are hurt. We need to go," Lyra said

Nic stood up quickly, and a playing card appeared between her first and second fingers from the sleeve of her jacket like a magic trick, threw the card at Taxx's apartment door, and stepped over his body without a second's hesitation. Lyra lingered for a moment and knelt next to the young man again, he strained to look at her, and she gave him a small smile.

"It seems that you have been handed a fate you didn't want due to misfortune or divine intelligence," Lyra said.

"Also. The guy upstairs is a monster. Tell him that part, too," Nic said.

"Right. He is a particularly nasty one, and your situation makes you the rare truffle he could not resist eating. I am confident you will be killed or devoured, but I sincerely hope not," Lyra said.

She reached out and tentatively stroked his tightly coiled hair for a moment, a wave of emotions pouring off of her body so purely that even he could feel them, anger, pain, even joy. Then he felt the pain in his body starting to feel better. Little by little, he could feel himself regaining control.

"That little fly can eat me?" he asked.

It was more of a raspy breath than a voice, but she seemed to understand him anyway, helping him sit up and looking him square in the face.

"The monster it belongs to will eat you. That is simply and cruelly what monsters do. Surviving an encounter with one is not up to fate or luck; it is about your choices. Whatever you choose to do, do it with everything you have and beg the gods for the rest. If you live like this, you cannot die," Lyra said.

"Don't give him that old world, BS. Let's go," Nic said.

"Pray the gods are merciful, Mr. Kingwood, but no matter how terrible your peril, know that it is nothing compared to the regret of inaction," she said.

She smiled at him, her mouth curling into an arch.

"You are cursed with a terrible fate. If you are clever, choose to hide. If you are smart, choose to run. If you are stupid, choose nothing," Lyra said.

"What..." he said.

"I don't have time," Lyra started.

"What if I'm not any of those things?" Taxx asked.

The warden regarded him for a long moment, and something passed between them. He didn't know how but he understood something about her when they stared into each other's eyes. She was not his enemy, and she did not wish for him to die, he could not understand how he knew it, but he understood it as clearly as if she spoke it into his mind.

"What are you?" Lyra asked.

"I don't know... what should I be?" he said.

"Be fearful if you must but be brave if you can," she said.

"What if I can't do either of those things?" he said.

"Then you are probably just going to die," Lyra said.

"You speak very plainly," Taxx said.

"You ask far too many questions when you should be feeling. The truth is that you don't have a choice in what will become of you in the grand scheme. It is the belief that you do that separates the stupid from the brave. The line is thin, and it cuts down many. Good luck," Lyra said.

Then she was gone, stepped over his head just like Nic had, and as soon as she did, the headache went away as though it were anchored to her. It was startlingly fast, and it took him a moment to get his bearings and slowly work his way to his feet. He turned toward his screen door, and another door was hovering just before it. It was more of a hole, the shape of a door where his screen door should have been. It didn't lead into his house. Instead, he looked into a space that appeared to be a hotel lobby or a hospital. Taxx couldn't tell. Nicole looked up briefly and saw Taxxis watching them, so he involuntarily stepped back when she caught his eye, but she didn't move toward him. She sharply turned to Lyra and opened her mouth to speak, without a doubt about him, but the door was gone before he could hear anything.

Chapter | Five

Taxx was not a fool. He had just seen a hole in space, and time took two shape-shifting women to another place. That was magic, without a doubt. The sudden appearance of the supernatural was not something he was having an easy time digesting; he was digesting it but not as quickly as he thought he might. Something about the implicit danger of it all stopped him from being excited. He had seen what he could classify as magic about half a dozen times in the past hour, and the thing that was so strange about all of it was how underwhelmed he was. There was no pop or fizzle or bang. It was all as fast as a heart attack. All of it simply happened with no auspice, and despite his best efforts, somehow, it made him feel small. Even with all of that going on in his head, he couldn't help thinking about what Lyra had said to him instead. He would be stupid to stay here. There was a minor issue, however.

Taxx knew that something was up there and no possibility that he could simply walk back into his home and continue with his life without knowing if what she said was true. He also knew that what she said to him was true as soon as she said it. She didn't seem the type to speak in hypotheticals. Ever since they threw him out of that car, there had been something off inside of him, and that something was urging him forward. His mind was so busy it felt like there were bees in his ears, and he still couldn't stop thinking about what a monster might look like. He was starting to panic and trying his best to stay calm, his body beginning to shiver from the effort of it all coming down on him at once. The day caught up to him all at once, and it took him a minute of deep breathing and focusing his mind on clearing it of the cloudy turmoil before he started to calm down.

There was too much information to go over all at once, so he focused on what he knew. He was cursed. He was in immediate danger. Taxx didn't know that woman from Jane Doe. She entered his life under a pretense and left just as oddly, but she had been candid with him. More than most, and she meant every word that she said, he had no cause to doubt her over anyone else. That fly meant to kill him. If that was before or after it was also supposed to eat him, he did not know, but he knew that he wasn't about to sit here and find out. He ran into the apartment, closed the door behind him, and even though he knew it wouldn't do much, closing the door made him feel safe. He ran back to his bedroom and rummaged through his things. It only took him about ten minutes to go through everything he had in the room, pack a bag, and step out into the hallway. He paused in front of his grandmother's bedroom door. They had been in this apartment alone for as long as he could remember, and, at that time, he had never entered her room. Not even once. May was a kind woman, probably the best grandmother a kid could ask for. She taught him how to speak his mind and throw a punch. She baked him cookies and served him many fine and exotic teas. May was an open book, she spoke to him plainly and openly, but she was deadly serious about her privacy. With everything going on, he hesitated for a moment at the knob before he tried it. To his surprise, it was unlocked, and the door opened. She locked her door even when she was inside the room.

He tried the light switch, and the overhead light popped on, and he saw why his grandmother was so careful to keep him out of here. There was nothing. The walls were bare, and the floor was covered in a fine sheen of dust. Not only did his grandmother not live in this room, but she also may have never even stepped foot in here. Taxx was sure he had seen her go into that bedroom night after night. Wherever she had been going, it was not this place. No one had been in this space for a long time. He felt his heart sink in his chest as he stared at the thick layer of dust in disbelief.

"What is this?" he asked himself.

Taxx was starting to run out of curse words to describe this situation. That's when he saw them. Flies were sitting on the doorknob to the closet. The tiny insects, or whatever they were, clearly saw him too, and as soon as they did, they both slipped between the gap of the closet door. He wanted to follow them, but he was too afraid to move for a moment, there were two now, and he couldn't even handle one before.

"I need to run," He tried to tell himself.

Something was happening inside of him. Something that was preventing him from leaving in the first place, and that feeling began to bubble up inside of him. He thought he felt something leave his body like a fishing line that started from his heart and traveled up to the apartment above. The line brought up an image, something terrible. He could see inside the apartment now, or he felt like he could anyway. It was just a flash, but he was sure he could see something in his mind, a pile of white maggots heaped up knee high on a Persian rug, even more, piled on the coffee table. It wasn't a coffee table. There was what remained of Craw, covered toe to tip in flies in various life cycle stages. The image was so real he felt himself trembling violently from even the idea of what could be up there waiting for him, what could be in there watching him even now.

He returned to his body and took a step back and away from the closet door, just in case any of those flies came back. He was thinking a mile a minute again. He should have been thinking about how he could get his ass out of here and to safety. Instead, every one of his thoughts was centered on opening that closet door. He took a breath. There was no changing it. He simply had to know if the dark vision he had just seen was real. The only way to do that was to open the door and see what was inside, and so he stepped up to the closet and turned the knob. There were no flies here. There was nothing in the closet except a small light with a long pull string. He reached out to pull the string, and the light popped on a mustard yellow, and moments later, it fell to the ground and shattered right in front of him with a loud pop.

"Nice," Taxx said.

A large hole went through the floor into the apartment above, and several maggots were wriggling around the edges of the uneven cavity. What remained of the ceiling in the closet appeared to have been rotting away and was the color of tobacco leaves, and the light had barely been hanging on. The apartment ceiling above was visible, and there appeared to be lights on in the room. The built-ins were arranged so that he could probably climb up, and for reasons he could not understand, he did precisely that. Taxx was not so passive that it could be called a trait, he was curious to a fault, but he was prone to moments of impulse. Moments like this.

Lyra had been pretty clear about his options; smart people ran, clever ones hid, and everyone else was probably going to die. He started hoping that he was smart, but he knew immediately that he wouldn't run. Then he thought he might be clever, but he couldn't even begin to think of a single place to hide, even after he tossed the whole apartment looking for a good idea. He was much too stubborn to sit and let himself be killed; he did not want to die. That was enough for him. So that just left him being stupid.

No matter what lies he tried to believe when he thought he might run and hide, Taxx had decided that he would go up there before the Wardens even left. He was way too curious not to have a harmless look, at least. He could not help himself. He had a plan, at least. It wasn't a good plan, but he had one. Taxx was not the kind to have a death wish. He was worse than that. Taxx was a real-life bleeding-heart romantic. He thought of himself as a good person. Good people were unable to walk away from bad things. It was something he knew at the core of him, something he never had to be told, and something he trusted. Once he saw something wrong, he just couldn't let it go. He knew that if he didn't at least try that he wouldn't be able to sleep no matter where he ran or hid. Even if it was just a trick of his fear, something in his little delusion made him feel obligated, which meant he could not walk away. If there was any chance that anyone was still alive up there, then Taxx wanted to help. He was also terrified.

Filled to the brim with fear, it was a natural reaction, but he knew something worse than fear. The truth of life was that if idiots like him didn't do the stupid things other people wouldn't do to help people, no one else would do it. The magic police were gone and told him that there was no further help coming, he was the only person who could do it, and there was no one backing him up. He didn't direct his feet to move, but he was quietly up and through the hole in the floor and standing in the apartment before he knew it. The room was off-white, not very well lit, and had a solid scary movie vibe. He was standing in a shadowy unknown where an actual monster was possibly lying-in wait, but he continued forward anyway. There was nothing in this room except a few errant flies and maggots, so he moved to the door at the end of the room, and after listening for a moment, he opened the door just enough.

He stepped into the hall, and after a quick look around to be sure he didn't see any flies, he stood up and closed the door behind him. The house didn't smell bad like he expected it to. There were indeed some fascinating smells in the air but not so much of a rotting corpse as he assumed there would be. He walked as softly as he could toward the living room, every step was slow, and he looked around carefully as he moved. Like he had seen in his imagination, the body was on the ground in front of his couch. He appeared to have crashed through the coffee table and lay on his back among the broken glass and splintered wood. The strange thing was that there didn't appear to be any blood, not a single drop anywhere that Taxx could see. Taxx crept over toward the older man as far as he dared, inching up until he was standing just a few feet away.

"Psst. Hey. Old Man, wake up," He called in a hoarse whisper.

There was no response. Not even a toe twitch. Taxx rolled his eyes and decided to throw caution to the wind and say the name the magic feds called him.

"Craw!" He shouted.

As soon as he shouted, the old man lurched violently, and Taxx took a step back into the hallway. There was no other noise, so Taxx leaned around the corner to peer into the living room after a few seconds. The old man stood up, barefoot on the glass and looking at his hands like he was doped up. His mouth was hanging open, and drool leaked down his chin.

"Old man, are you alright?" Taxx asked.

There was no response.

The old man also appeared to have flies crawling all over his face and neck and didn't respond to that either. Taxx was starting to get worried.

"Hey! Listen to me. Some cops were looking for you earlier and said you might be in trouble. They told me some crazy shit about some Mon…ster..,"

Taxx's voice slowly tapered off at the end when Craw suddenly turned to face. There wasn't any need to say what he was going to say; the old man was already long dead. Whatever was standing in front of Taxx now was not any sort of thing he could have imagined. Even while looking right at it, he wasn't quite sure exactly what he was looking at. The body had taken on a grey pallor, and every inch of it that wasn't covered in filthy clothing was now crawling and undulating through his skin. It moved like it was boiling. Craw had taken on an unnatural stance; one of the feet was angled 90 degrees in the wrong direction with all the weight on an angry red ankle. His arms were jutted out in angles that meant broken bones and broken everything else for that matter, but that wasn't the scariest part. His face was the worst of it. It was twisted into a horrifically gleeful smile, and from every orifice, he was leaking white, slimy maggots. His eyes were encrusted with them all the way around, and there was no eyeball to be seen, only a dripping pool of white slime with a single fly in the center of each. Those wandering flies began to act as the pupils, and in perfect unison, both turned to look directly at him.

Craw widened his smile, spilling a thick glob of larvae to the floor. Taxx was frozen where he stood. He wondered how he could look away from those eyes of living maggots slithering and sliding all over a dead man's face? Grown flies marched across his skin, in and out of his ears and mouth, perforating the flesh with thousands of pockmarks as they forced their way out of him. In short order, the tiny black flies began to fill up the room, as thick and shiftless as a storm cloud. Taxx started to step backward involuntarily. It didn't make sense that there could be so many flies inside him. There were so many shiny black insects in the air that they covered everything in shadows, except the body of his neighbor standing amidst that black ocean, eerily glowing and splattering maggots onto the floor in fat piles.

"You woke me up; you skritchy little bastard. I had such a good dream. I dreamed about killing you again," Craw said.

His voice was slow at first, incomprehensible, like a thousand flies buzzing at once, but each subsequent word was more precise than the last. The voice was dark and husky, but it sounded eerily human, and to his shock, there seemed to have been an accent there, but he couldn't immediately place it. He was pretty much shocked to the limit just hearing a corpse full of insects speaking in the first place, he thought, there wasn't much else that could surprise him. He was wrong.

"D'you know what I find funny about all this?" Craw asked.

Taxx only exhaled loudly.

Craw laughed.

He had meant to say something, but his voice didn't come when he reached for it, and his fingers and arms, torso, and legs started to quake slowly. She called him a real-life monster, and Taxx was beginning to understand. Each moment he stood here looking at this walking nightmare, he felt a tidal wave of the fear crash against him again. This man, this monster, didn't make any sense to him. It couldn't have been real or alive. It couldn't be talking or laughing. It shouldn't exist.

"Damn it all. She told me this would happen! That you would pop up here just like this. That old Witch. Prophecy is a quite shit way to have a fuckin' face time, ain't it, squire?" Craw shouted.

Taxx went to speak, and Craw advanced a step, causing Taxx to shut his mouth.

"This damned family is so cryptic. You're as bad as your nan, for the god's sake!" Craw shouted.

"Did you… did you hurt my grandmother?" Taxx asked.

His voice was small at first, but he made it more prominent as he spoke, even taking a step toward the abomination. An action he regretted immediately; Craw was worse up close.

"May? Fuck no. I wish I could kill something like your grandmother. That would make me famous," Craw said.

"Why is there a hole in the floor?" Taxx asked.

Craw only smiled at him, carefully looking over Taxx with those fly eyes. There was a moment where Taxx was sure he could feel something pleasant coming from this being. It was at the very least not as hostile toward him as he assumed. Craw moved to the window so fast that Taxx felt his body turn cold. Craw was even faster than his cousin. The thought smacked into his mind so hard that Taxx might have fallen over.

"Where is my cousin? Do you know who is trying to hurt us?" Taxx asked.

"Someone told me that you were in the hands of the Demon, but that can't be true because you would be dead, so that must be who is after you. That means that I'm either being set up, and I fuckin hate being set up, **or** something worse is going on," Craw said.

He spoke so plainly that all Taxx could do was stare at the glowing corpse animated by flies.

"What do you want?" Taxx asked

"Neither one of those things is what I want. I want to know why you are up here, little Moss?" Craw asked.

The voice was becoming ever more human, which was starting to make him nauseous. He could even hear its emotion now, and he was only more unsettled by it. All of his instincts were thinking about running. Maybe he was the type of person who followed his instincts. All he needed to do was distract it.

"A...are you telling me that you, a gross fly demon monster human eating… thing, are you telling me that you know me?" Taxx asked.

"Come on. For one, I am very clean, don't be that guy, ok? Secondly, don't call me a Demon. They are bad news, and honestly, between us. It's you who is the fuck stick what went and got himself mixed up in their bullshit. I know that you were raised better than that," Craw said.

Craw held up his hands and shook his head with emotion. He even looked a little hurt. Seeing him move in such a human way only upset Taxx further.

"Third. Fuck you. Second again! Where do you people get off calling me a demon? That's the worst one! I'm from London, not hell," Craw said.

"I'm sorry, I just… I don't know what you are," Taxx said.

"I am definitely a monster. I call myself one of a kind, so, stick that up your pipe and-" Craw was interrupted.

"STICK THIS!" Taxx screamed.

"Ew, was that a one-liner?" Craw asked,

"No!" Taxx shouted.

"Yes, it was. That was terrible," Craw said.

"Shut up, it was supposed to be a distraction, but I didn't plan for what came next," Taxx said.

"That's a little sad, innit?" Craw asked.

"Yeah. Thanks. What happens now?" Taxx asked.

"Maybe I kill you," Craw said.

"What? Why?" Taxx asked.

"Cause you were rude," Craw said.

"That's not a reason to kill someone!" Taxx screamed.

"Calm down, you little bell end. One. You don't need a reason to kill a thing; you just do. Or you don't. Two. You are as harmless as a kitten right now. I could accidentally kill you if you try any stupid shit like that one-liner again. Now quiet, let me think," Craw said.

"Don't tell me to calm down," Taxx shouted.

Taxx hurled the bag on his shoulder and started to run. He hadn't meant to do it really, he just came to grips with the reality that he was probably not going to survive, and he wanted to try something, anything! This was all he could do. He would ask the gods for the rest, as that woman Lyra suggested to him, and maybe they would see his stupidity as bravery and give him a blessing. He didn't know how you approached the Gods to kill a swarm of evil flies, but he was doing it now if he had a way to do that. He screamed with everything he had; that was all he could think to do, call for the gods to notice him, and spare his life. Scream for the last time in his life. Scream louder and longer than he could ever have imagined that he could. The bag never even came close to hitting Craw. It exploded like it was hit with a shotgun blast, and it burst like a firework in the air between them. Everything within had been pulverized in just a moment. There was almost no sound except a rapid succession of whipping noises and soft thuds behind him. His shirt ruffled on his chest like a gentle breeze danced through his clothes.

"That was a shitty thing to do, it didn't hurt, but it was seriously fucking rude all over again! I swear if your Ma could see you now. Do you think she would be proud of how you treat people? Honestly?" Craw chided.

Taxx only felt a chill.

"Hello? Can you hear me talking to you?" Craw asked.

Taxx attempted to answer, but instead of speaking, he only coughed up an alarming amount of blood, and it splattered down his shirt.

"Uh oh… that's a fucking yikes, innit?" Craw said.

The chill was starting to get stronger. It started at the back of his skull and slowly traveled down his spine, and he shivered uncontrollably. He didn't even feel cold.

"Oh hell, I didn't mean to kill you," Craw said.

Kill me? Taxx tried to ask.

He could no longer speak.

He looked down and saw more than a dozen holes in him. He lost count when he started to collapse to the floor. He landed in a sticky pool that began to saturate his shirt immediately. It was blood; there was so much, **his** blood. He feebly attempted to stand up, but all he could do was writhe on the ground.

"You know what May told me before she left? She asked me to stick around here for you. I told her that was a shit idea, that I'm more likely to kill you, y'know? Then you know what the witch said to me. She tells me that it's my destiny to do it, even if I didn't want it," Craw said.

The monster knelt next to him and leaned in close with his maggot eyes, and spoke directly into his face. Taxx couldn't even feel the breath on his face, but he could hear Craw when he spoke.

"Want to hear the real funny bit? She told me this would be the sin that…" Craw said.

The hearing went away before the end of the sentence. Suddenly, like someone unplugged a speaker, he hadn't felt any sensations since the slick horror of his blood between his fingers. Vision was the last sense to go, but not before everything took on a blurry haze. Then it was just shadows that only got darker until they became nothing. Thoughts were all he had left, no; he couldn't arrange them. He was worried about everything he never got to do, sad about everything he never could. Mostly though, he was furious about having to die at the hands of whatever this thing was. He thought if he had more time, he could do something. He thought about God. He felt that there probably wasn't one, and if there **was,** he didn't seem to give a single damn about the singular life of a regular person. He realized that this was the precipice between life and death when he ran out of things to regret. His last thoughts were sizzling through a dying brain like water droplets on a hot pan. He had better make them good. He was having a hard time thinking of anything good, so he latched onto the only thing he could, a gibberish word that he didn't know why, but he knew that it was a name. With his last living thought, a boy called Taxx invoked the name of a God he did not know. He pleaded for his life with everything he had left.

Then...

He died.

Chapter | Sixx

There was no way to tell how much time had passed.

There was no time here.

There was nothing here.

Nothing happened here.

Until where once there was nothing, there was now a Voice.

"Broken," it said.

'said' was an overstatement. The Voice appeared suddenly from the quiet nothing of a dreamless sleep with such bright and powerful energy that it felt more like an explosion than sound. Like a sudden scream. Impossibly loud just behind him, the sound set his ears to ringing like a shotgun went off inside of his head. Then came the pain. He reached up to touch his ears and was surprised to find that he could feel them. He was something again; he was unsure if that meant he was alive because he was confident that he had died. He didn't know how long ago that was. It was hard to tell when you were dead. Time seemed so much less critical when you weren't anything anymore, and even now, he was having difficulty tracking time. He was distracted by the sudden awareness of space around him, he couldn't see anything, but he could *feel* the wideness of whatever this place was. It was a peculiar place, an inky black dark void that stretched into infinity. An entire world of darkness. He felt like he was standing on solid ground, a small and tentative leap proved that much, and he landed steadily, with only one issue. Everything suddenly started to move.

He couldn't tell if he was off balance because of his little jump or if the world was moving, but either way, it was happening. Everything started to slide to his front suddenly, the ground jerked hard enough to take his footing, and he toppled head over foot, kicking up a cloud of glittering black dust. The dust looked like there was glitter, and seeing even that slight sparkle was startling starlight in the darkness. He wasn't knocked out of breath or anything, but he couldn't immediately move his body or hear himself breathing now that he thought of it. He couldn't hear… anything. He hadn't even noticed how silent everything had been, even when the whole area was in motion, and he could feel it gliding along even faster now under his back. Everything around him quickly slid into some tremendous unknown and pulled him along for the ride. Only it was all flowing upward. He couldn't fight against the current. He took a breath of what he assumed was air into his lungs, but he never got the chance to let out even a peep.

He emerged from that forever darkness into blinding white

light. He couldn't see anything and scrambled to cover his eyes, but his arms were so heavy that he couldn't move them. His eyes eventually adjusted to the light, and he was greeted with a sky so sapphire blue it was enough to make him cry. Though honestly, his tears may have had something to do with the fact that he was falling and rapidly headed for another violent death. He didn't even bother to scream. He just closed his eyes. The wind pressed against him with such force that he could barely do much more than that. Through it all, not a sound.

"What the hell is this?" he said.

He hadn't expected to hear his voice, let alone echo like his head was in a fishbowl. It startled him, and he started to flail in turning his body until he entered a large bank of clouds and passed through them as quickly as spider webs. The lack of sound made his impending death uninteresting for some reason. He found himself thinking. He found himself missing the sound of the wind, which was such a strange thought. He smirked, which became a smile and evolved into an echoing laugh. This was the worst possible time to laugh, but he couldn't stop, each arc of his laughter bouncing off the invisible fishbowl and laughing along with him with increasing delays. It sounded like a small group of people laughing, making him laugh even more. After a minute, he stopped laughing, and then one by one, the other laughs stopped, and he was alone again in the silent free fall of his second death. After what felt like an hour, he wished he was dead. The thought of falling forever in silence was a thought he found less than appealing. After what felt like 5 hours, he had the craziest idea he probably ever had in his not-so-long life, death, and whatever this was. He missed the voice.

"Not one or the other… curious," it said.

As though on command, the words exploded to life again so loud that he couldn't possibly have heard them, but he understood them again. This time, it was quieter, more like someone was shouting in his ears with a loudspeaker from a point-blank range and less of an explosion.

"Open your eyes," it said.

He found that he was no longer falling when he opened his eyes. Instead, he was standing in the middle of a forest, thick with trees of every color, some with white ash bark and others with bright yellow. Strange plum-colored squat round trees with long-stemmed leaves that faded light to dark. The color of tiny flames. In a rainbow of colors, Ethereal vines traveled through the trees and hung from branches like a kaleidoscope of spider webs. The sun that passed through them was cast on the ground in a color splash that gently swayed with the wind along with the trees, and it was so serene that he forgot about his pain and just stared for a moment. He tried to take a step forward, and he couldn't move his legs, and when he looked down, he found that he had been buried in the ground past the knee. There was upturned earth around his legs, and slowly he felt it turning still, pushing him out of the ground like an elevator.

"What Thing can be both and neither?" The Voice said.

It was much more pleasant at this level, but a few hundred echoes rattled around his mind. It was also much closer this time, and there was a distinction there, some unique infections that made it sound much more like a human voice. However, the echoing continued to bounce around, getting increasingly louder until he had to cover his ears.

"I will go deaf or die if you keep that up!" He screamed.

He mustered enough strength to cover his ears, but the echo

did not fade. It seemed to have increased in power to the point that he was grunting against it now. He could feel it inside his bones like he was standing in a paint mixer.

"You are already quite dead, as I tell you every time you come here," The voice said.

The volume level this time was perfect. Thankfully, the amount of echoing that accompanied it seemed to be under control, which made it easier to tolerate the macabre words. The voice was not a voice, just a noise, a shapeless mass of sound piled on top of each other to make a bizarre tone, like boiling water might sound if it could talk.

"And not so. Such a strange curiosity. Once again...You are here," The Voice said.

There was still no one else in his immediate vision, and he looked all around the area. He didn't want to wander into the forest because the voice could be coming from there. He thought he would have liked to have seen it before he let it eat him or drink his blood or whatever monstrous way monsters went about their work. He didn't like thinking about there being another monster out there plotting against him. Still, his mind wouldn't let go of the image of some large feline hunter imitating a human voice or some other impossible horror. On top of that, he couldn't think of anything worthwhile to say to it in return, but what the hell was he supposed to say to impress a voice, he thought. He was just some kid from a small town in Connecticut, a city he never left, a town his body was probably not so peacefully resting in right now. His mind was racing with ideas about where he might be, he even thought about it being THAT place, but there was no way he was the guy who made the list.

"Were... you were expecting me?" He asked.

"I never expect you, but you are often here," The Voice said.

"Where is here? Where are you? Honestly, can you tell me what is going on?" He asked.

There was nothing. He searched all over the clearing and walked on a thick carpet of fallen leaves that were soft under his feet. It was as soft as a shag carpet and bouncing back under his toes like walking on a mattress. It was strange, but he couldn't help but smile as he jumped, with his footsteps carrying him forward like a trampoline. He had gotten the hang of it in just a few steps. He didn't have time to think about if he was dead because he bounded all around the clearing, jumping as high as possible and landing on the natural springs. He was having so much fun he had nearly forgotten about the voice altogether.

"What is this?" The Voice asked

The voice was back this time, but it was suddenly at a perfectly normal speaking level and directly in front of him. He tried to bounce to a halt, but he couldn't stop himself. He sprung forward but smashed into something directly in front of him that stopped him cold and sent him head over feet. At first, he saw nothing, but when he got to his feet, it became evident that a disembodied hand was floating in the air. It looked like a human hand, but he saw that it was a gemstone carved to look like one on closer inspection. The hand moved and began to sprout a wrist. In moments it extruded an arm and shoulder, then even faster, a torso appeared. The rest of the limbs grew, and finally, a vaguely female head and a spray of white sand that flowed like murky water acted as hair. More stone appeared and covered her body in a simple robe, and on its surface, moss began to grow in large green patches of many tones. Her eyes were holes where only soft light smoldered orange and dangerous, constantly swirling, blackening, and hardening, only to crack again like flowing magma. The only constant in her eyes was a ring of gold at the center, circles that turned slightly to look directly at him. He couldn't look away.

"Are you God?" he asked.

"Te'Amath," she said.

"Oh wow, they *really* got your name wrong back on earth," he said.

"Te'Amath," she said.

One of her hands moved to her chest, indicating that she was Te'Amath.

"Oh no, I get it. Not that God. That makes way more sense. There's no way I would be in that Heaven," Taxx said.

"What is this?" She asked.

"Taxx," he said.

She stared.

"What is this?" She asked.

"Tarzan," he said.

No response.

"Moss?" He whispered

Still, she only stared at him unblinking.

He concluded that she did not ask him what his name was but the question of what 'he was' seemed too difficult even to attempt to think about. There was a strange truth laying there, just under his thoughts, something that popped into his head as soon as she asked him. He decided to see where that would take him.

"I want to know, but I don't know," Taxx said.

"You still don't know what you are?" She asked again.

"I don't know what I am," he said.

Te'Amath smiled so easily that it was unfathomable to think she was stone. Her body moved and looked warm and alive. He had never seen anything like her in his life, and it was difficult not to stare at the marvel in front of him, a woman made of earth as soft as flesh. Her. It. They. Whatever it described itself as was staring at him intently, or at least the golden rings of magma were pointed at him, and she was still smiling.

"Of course, you don't remember. You never do. It is only the magic you take with you, " she said.

It was his turn to stare at her unblinking, and the stone woman nodded as if reading his thoughts.

"You have come here so often. Sometimes it is I who forgets, forgive me," she said.

"For what?" he asked.

Before he could react, she took his head in her hands. He didn't even try to resist as the grip of just her fingertips was incredible. Her hands were soft, and he tried to avoid the much too warm and smooth skin, but he had been unable to. She tilted his head down, and he didn't know if he leaned or she had been the same height, but she had been standing a foot shorter than him until now. She was face to face with him, and he thought that she might kiss him, then he felt that she might chew off his tongue and eat it out of his head.

"That is exactly what I meant to do," She teased.

Taxx was no longer in the mood to kiss. She did something so strange and straightforward that he froze instantly. She pressed their foreheads together and just held there for a few moments. The act was so intimate and sudden that he didn't know what to do but stand there. He could feel warmth passing between them from the skin contact, and he subconsciously leaned into it, so when she pulled away, he had to catch himself on his feet to stop stumbling.

"There, that's better," Te'Amath said.

"What are you?" He asked.

"I am Te'Amath. That is my name. It means 'The Wandering Earth' in your language, but you may call me Am," she said.

"That's a very cool name," he said.

"I've always enjoyed how much you enjoy it," Am said.

Taxx could only stare at the goddess.

"Taxxis is a good strong name. Someone who is blessed with good deep roots. There is much power in your roots," she said.

He meant to speak, but pain blossomed inside of his head severely enough that made him groan against gritted teeth. He couldn't quite see for a moment, and a sharp pain traveled down his spine like an electric shock. Te'Amath squeezed his hand, and the pain passed instantly. He gasped against its sudden absence and pressed back until he was himself again. She let go of his hand, and the pain did not return. Then she pointed at his chest, and he looked down and saw something he would never believe if he was not looking at it. A tree branch had grown from his abdomen, and there was a snake nearly as thick as the branch itself coiled around it. The snake's scales were pitch black and pointed like an arrowhead, just like its head, black eyes looking between the man and the forest woman.

"It looks very much like the serpent has been starving and now is trying to kill you at the core. Perhaps it is no longer able to feed on you. That is a bad thing. A hungry thing that has eaten so well will never leave you," she said.

The snake constricted the branch, and almost all of it was

ashen, and the stumps of new growth choked to death, covering every inch of it. Every bit but the end. On its very tip was the only thing left that was alive, just a single leaf. It was as green as an emerald with a segmented circle in its center as gold as an autumn sunset. The gold continued to the leaf's veins and down the stem sparkling like real gold.

"What is this branch? Why is there a branch sticking out of my body?" Taxx asked.

He was oddly calm, considering.

"I know you cannot help yourself, but you always ask me this, and I tire of answering. You've been here hundreds of times. If you pretend that you don't know, I will do the same," she said.

"It's hard to understand you," Taxx said.

"It is simple. You are my only visitor. I will never forget," she said.

Her face was right up against the leaf. Her eyes scrutinized the snake, taking it in from a few angles. Then she smiled and shook her head as though she remembered something silly. She laughed.

"Very clever on the part of whatever did this to your root, this snake was meant to destroy you. Someone had a plan for this, but that plan did not include me. You were meant to be here exactly now, just like me, probably called here just the same. I could not see why until now," she said.

One of her hands fluidly transformed from five soft digits into a rigid stone blade, black as obsidian and glowing with a faint light. The sword felt heavy in the air, like a coming storm. He couldn't only stare at it. He needed to do something, say something, the ominous feeling in his chest the blade gave off made him want to scream.

"Are you going to kill me?" He asked.

"I had thought of it, yes, but I truly do not know if I could," she said.

She didn't even look angry, just thoughtful. Taxx looked terrified, and Am examined his face a moment before she spoke again.

"Perhaps I should try something a bit less severe. If we can be honest, I'm shit at making people. There are so many parts and things to remember it gets tangled up so easily in all the goop. So boring. Bah," she said.

She waved it off, but she did not change her blade hand back into a normal hand.

"Why do you still need that then?" Taxx asked.

"Oh, this? Well... Instead of being remade, what if I free you of this snake? Before you answer, though, there is a catch," Am said.

"There is always a catch! So, what is it? If you remove the snake, will I die? Turn into a rabbit?" he asked.

"This snake has followed you into death. Should I remove it? I am not sure what will happen to you. I will not tell you that it will be survivable," she said.

"What's the point then?" he asked.

"I will tell you that If I do not remove it, the snake will devour your last bits you will cease to be at some point, how long that will be I cannot say," Am continued.

"So, if I don't keep the snake, I'll probably die again, but if I DO keep the snake, I'll die again?" he asked.

"You have already died. I don't know what happens beyond that, for there has only ever been you and I in this place," Amath said.

Taxx looked confused again.

"I mean to say that whatever plan this universe has made for you is still in motion. At least for now. If you want to see what that plan is, I will remove it. If you would like to stay with me until it gets hungry again so we may both see what becomes of you, I am equally interested," she said.

Taxx said nothing. He just thought for a moment.

"It seems you have made your choice," she said.

She winked at him before he even spoke and gently reached out that dangerous stone blade, and with a quick flick of the edge, she severed the snake as though she was cutting a flower stem. The snake hissed and cursed and screamed. Tiny pain points were born all over his body, even under his toes, until the snake crackled one last stiff burst of energy and went still. The color of its eyes faded dull, and then the rest of its body seemed to gain a deathlike pallor. It took him a moment to realize it had turned to ash. Her blade arm turned back into a hand, and she gently lifted the ashen snake from his root, holding it in her upturned palms so he could see it.

"Fascinating," she said.

Her words broke the perfect ash replica, and every bit of it blew away on an unseen breeze until it was gone.

"I feel… strange, am I supposed to feel strange?" He asked.

"Yes, of course! You are very different from what you were a moment ago. You have 100 percent less snake in you," Amath said.

She leaned down again, looking intently at the leaf growing at the end of his torso branch. It was brighter than it had been, more vibrantly green now. The circle of gold had tripled in thickness and looked more like a heavy ring on the center of the leaf. It almost seemed to be standing prouder.

"I release you from your curse, but I have to apologize for the implications that have been left on you. Should you survive this process, I will apologize to you properly, though I am sure it will kill you," she said.

"Am I in danger?" He asked.

"You are always in danger. If you ask if you will be in situations worse than dangerous, then yes… probably many of them. Is that bad?" She asked

"What the hell are you talking about, you crazy rock lady? That isn't good. I don't want to die!" he said.

"Then it is fortunate that you are already dead," she said.

He was about to lay into her when she pointed at his chest again, and he noticed that there were now many more leaves on the branch. There had only been one before, just a single leaf clinging for life, but here there were dozens, more than he could count immediately anyway. They grew before his eyes, budding and reaching out like hands toward the sky. One after the other, they came. She lifted one of her hands and touched the end leaf on his root, and it began to recede into his body, and in just a moment, it was gone, leaves and all. He touched his chest a few times to confirm and smiled, looking up at her, his eyes were wide, and his breathing was getting heavier.

"You are exactly as he said you would be. I did not believe it until now," Amath said.

"Amath, I can still feel them… growing," he said.

His voice was dreamy, distant. He was starting to feel like he had been drugged, everything was taking on a slight blur, and the rainbow spiderwebs were bleeding together into a halo of every color around her. She smiled at him, and for a moment, he swore he saw actual skin on her face, but only for a moment.

"I choose you. It would be best if you didn't tell me the truth. I need you to be what you are. You are the one. The one I have been waiting for," Amath said.

"What are you?" Taxx asked.

"I am the end of the world, and so are you," she said.

Her right hand was changing shape, growing thinner and longer, more fluid.

"What do-"

She punched the question right out of him. She hit his chest so hard he was sure that he could feel her fist inside his ribcage. Something was there, gripping at the things inside him and filling up the space behind his lungs. He couldn't breathe. It spread all through him under and around his bones. It was too tight, and it just kept coming. It was all too much. First, he thought he might explode, but he didn't. In time he felt his chest return to normal, and he sucked in a breath through his mouth with such vigor that it might have been a meal. His eyes rolled into the back of his head, and he landed hard on his chest, and it knocked the wind out of him. He groaned and tried to open his eyes when he came to, but they didn't open. He reached up to investigate and found a strange crust over his eyes. It was thick and hard, but it came off easily when he started to pick at it. In moments he freed his eyelids and opened his eyes, balking against the light, lifting his hands to cover his face.

Chapter | Seven

"Wait. I heard something," Nic said.

She jerked around toward the living room so hard that the fly she held between two fingers flung across the room and under the couch. Nic winced. Ultimately, she shrugged it off and did not go and retrieve it. Instead, she approached the young man's body, still curled up on the floor in a pool of dried blood and surrounded by salt. The salt was arranged in intricate shapes and spells that slowly spread around the young man. Inch by inch. As the salt spread, it left gaps behind in the form of footprints, revealing more of them as it widened its net.

"I think this guy is still alive, seriously this time. I know I heard him move," Nic said.

She spoke to Lyra, who was just across the way, a pair of

tweezers between her fingers as she carefully removed a black fly from the drywall. The fly was still buzzing and skittering with life when she carefully packed it into a specimen jar and closed the lid. Then she took a copper bullet with no casing and shoved the round into the hole as easily as if the drywall were playdough.

"If he were alive, the salt wouldn't work. You would have heard the salt falling," Lyra said.

"Right, but I don't like what you're implying," Nic answered.

"Did you hear the salt?" Lyra asked.

"No," Nic said.

Under protest.

"Then relax. It is probably just the flies getting to you. They are noisy," Lyra said.

"I know what I know. I heard this guy move," Nic insisted.

"He is dead. I had hopes for him, but... I have completed the task of replacing all the flies with bullets," Lyra said.

"Do you think it's just the world's biggest coincidence that Offrey goes off res the same morning her apartment building catches fire?" Nic asked.

"Another hunch?" Lyra asked.

Nic nodded. She was carefully going about her work.

"As good as they are, your hunches alone will not get you into the Wardens," Lyra said.

"I think this is more than that," Nic said.

"Can we stay on topic? Have you planted the evidence for the human cops?" Lyra asked.

"Yes! I know what I'm doing. I'm just saying...," Nic said.

"Shut up. Do you hear that?" Lyra asked.

As she said the words, a sound like gently falling rain started to fill the room.

"**That** was salt," Lyra said.

They turned to look at the young man just in time to watch his corpse start to move.

"Fu-!" Nic said.

Lyra placed a hand over her mouth.

"Careful with your language. We are Wardens dear, we protect curses," Lyra said

They were distracted when the corpse moved again. At first, it was just a tiny twitch of his arms, but the corpse in front of them was reanimating very rapidly. In less than a minute, the chest began to rise and fall with breath, and then the holes in his body began to close. They were filling in like time was traveling backward. Wrinkled flesh became engorged with life, and the corpse lost its pallor. It coughed out a gasping breath and writhed all over the floor.

"Oh, Shit!" Nic said.

"Better," Lyra said

The young man rolled over, and his eyes focused on them. He tried to speak, but a chunk of congealed blood dribbled out instead.

"Well, I had hoped for smart, but this is equally impressive. It is not every day I get to witness something come back to life," Lyra said.

She held out her hand, and he took it. His grip wasn't just restored, it was sure, and he stood up easily for a man who was previously very dead. He had no pulse. Lyra had examined him herself, the exit wounds were the size of golf balls, and there were dozens of them in his torso and neck. Here he was. He was standing in front of her looking as dumbfounded as she felt. It was all something of a miracle.

"Where am I?" Taxx asked.

When he spoke, Lyra and Nic looked at each other bewildered

"My sister was right," Lyra said.

"Do you know what the hell it is saying?" Nic asked.

"It? What the hell?" Taxx said.

Nic lifted an eyebrow again and started to poke him here and there, finding every hole she saw in his shirt with a swift finger. He tried to swat her away, but she was too fast. Every time he would swat at her, her hand would be somewhere else, and he would hit nothing but air. If he was speaking differently, he could not hear it. He couldn't hear a lot of anything. Taxx pinched his nose, held his mouth closed, and pushed out a breath as hard as possible, forcing his ears to pop. Something came flying out of his ears to his delight and horror, and he felt a surge of immediate relief. It was clotted blood keeping him from hearing, and it was now oozing down his cheeks. He did his best to clean himself, and he could hear again in no time.

"Please stop ignoring me," Taxx said.

When he spoke, it was not words that came out of his mouth. There was a sound like a hundred voices in a chorus all at once, human, animal, and even stranger things. It sounded like wind and fire and violins. He covered his mouth quickly.

"He also does not seem to know what he is saying. I have never heard this language before.

"Same. Sounds like… music," Nic said.

"I've also never known an Other who was so weak come back from the dead," Lyra said.

"I came back from the dead. Wait, weak? Seriously?" Taxx sang.

He understood what he was saying perfectly, he heard the crazy song coming out of his mouth, but the intent was still there in his mind. Neither of them was looking at his face or reacting to his words. They were both examining him like a piece of crime scene evidence. Lyra even used her tweezers to lift some of his bloodied shirt, cut a part of it off, and slipped into a bag. It all happened so fast that it was over when Taxx flinched back from her.

"What the hell are you doing?!" He sang

"Definitely reacting to us and moving around though it doesn't appear to have changed physically yet," Nic said.

"HEY! I'm standing right here, and I hear everything you're saying. Please don't call me an It," Taxx sang.

Still, they did not acknowledge him even though he couldn't hear what they were saying anymore. They moved to the nook between the living room and the hallway. Only that was where he had been standing a moment ago and was now against the far wall, had he been the one that moved, he thought. He looked at his whole body, starting with his hands. Everything appeared in order, but some things were obviously wrong here. He closed his eyes and took a deep breath.

"How did I get here?" Taxx sang.

"I have never known a zombie to have any regenerative ability. This case is getting to be more mysterious than I prefer," Lyra said.

"You're right, of course. I love to play the guessing game when we find them new in the cellophane," Nic said.

Taxx was starting to reach the limit of his patience with being ignored like that, and he was about to say something snarky when he noticed something glowing. It was just out of the corner of his eye, but he saw something. It came from his headband when he tried to look for the glow source. He pulled it off of his head and looked at it. There was a series of glowing symbols where it was usually a solid color. It was a diamond shape with three circles in the center. The center circle was radiating a strange light. He put it back on his forehead and turned to ask the wardens about it. Before he could ask, there was another one sliding across the floor. He followed it as it passed under his feet and then began to slide up the wall. It stopped between the front windows, and in a flash, the glowing rectangle became a blank playing card that looked almost normal except for the image. There was something written on it, but he couldn't read it. Whatever it said, the symbol on the card certainly wasn't a spade.

"Whoa, did you see that? How are you doing that?" He sang.

"Perception is off the charts too. See! I knew something was up when that glam broke. I should have guessed he was an Other," Nic said.

"What is an Other?" He sang.

"I don't think this guy is a zombie, he is talking to us, but I have no idea what the hell he is singing about," Nic said

"Was I singing?" Taxx said.

When ordinary words came out of his mouth, Taxx looked just as astonished as Nic, excitedly pointing at him.

"Oh shit! Oh shit! That was English!" Nic said.

"Yes. This is exciting. Watch your language," Lyra said.

"Not my boss," Nic teased.

They were both standing just before him, but he hadn't heard them move. They were just there, Lyra looking at him intently while Nic seemed to be smiling at him.

"What is your name?" Lyra asked.

"Is this a freaking joke? Taxx. We met like half an hour ago! You pretended to be a cop with Red Boots, but you are not cops," Taxx said.

The two women looked at each other and smiled.

"I'm glad that singing is over. I was starting to get worried," Lyra said.

"Bro, who are you calling red boots? Why do I feel like that's an insult?" Nic asked.

Then she pinched the bridge of her nose and held up her hand.

"Stop. Wait. Do you think that recently happened? Did you say half an hour?" Nic asked.

"Yeah, it **just** happened," Taxx said.

Lyra and Nic exchanged a look. Taxx wasn't clever enough to read their faces, but it was easy to guess that sharing a look like that was probably not anything positive.

"What? What is it?" Taxx asked.

"It's been hours since we were here," Nic said

"I've been dead for...?" He trailed off.

"Yes. Typically, humans do not come back from the dead unless they are a certain type. So as a test, I offered you my hand, but since you took it instead of trying to eat, you aren't a zombie," Lyra said.

"Do you a fuc-" Taxx started.

Nic put her hand over his mouth.

"Excessive swearing makes each use less meaningful for all of us. We protect curses," Nic said

Lyra nodded sagely.

Taxx also nodded, and Nic removed her hand.

"A **flippin'** zombie. But I don't think I'm craving the flesh of the living. I'm not even hungry. Shouldn't I be hungry?" He asked.

"It's hard to say. Magic sometimes lacks the repeatable nature of science, so there isn't an explanation for most of it. That's why it's called magic in the first place. Our job is attempting to document and explain magic. We represent The Mesalto. We are Wardens from the House of Wolf and Raven," Nic said.

"...Nic," Lyra said.

"As far as he knows," Nic said.

"What?" He asked.

"The point is that nothing we know of has ever come back from the dead after a long time, with basically everything intact. Many things come back from the dead, but the cost is usually high. You died in here conceivably half a day ago and just came back to life minutes ago. Does that sound normal to you?" Nic asked.

He didn't have to think about it hard at all. He wondered why the outside looked so much like night when it was mid-day when he was last here. It wasn't just the light. There was a light blanket of dust on everything, even some dust on his clothes, which were ripped to shreds for the most part. His shirt was hanging on by a thread and covered in long dried blood. The rust color was all over his hands and arms. He could feel it on his face. The evidence was piling up. Taxx didn't know what to do right then, and he tried to come up with something to say, but all he could do was stare at all the crusted blood all over him. His blood.

"Oh, God. What am I?" He asked.

Nic placed her hand on his shoulder.

"In the most basic sense, there are certain categories to the creatures that inhabit the world, some you know like Humans and insects and shit like that. Those are things that humans can understand. At the same time, there are things you know nothing about. That's us. Other things. The sort of things that humans absolutely cannot understand," Nic said.

"You mean like Cryptids?" Taxx asked.

"That's not a bad headspace. Some Others are a lot like humans, but some are not like them at all. The proper name of our species is Homoceterus because, as far as we can guess, we are at least based on humans somewhere in the past. Most folks call it being Other,'" Nic said.

"What do you mean?" Taxx asked.

"Imagine you had to take a standardized test that asked what kind of a thing you were, and there were only three choices, Human, monster, and Other," Nic said.

"Oh, that is a good one," Lyra said.

"Thank you," Nic answered.

"Is this getting to a place?" Taxx asked.

"Yes. You are no longer able to choose the option for humans. You also don't appear afflicted with wild magic or otherwise driven to eat people, so probably not a monster. That means you fall under the term we use for the **MANY** types of nonhuman entities that exist. Are you still with me?" She asked.

Taxx only stared at her.

"Perfect. Most of these Others can do things you cannot imagine, and all of them are out there, doing Other shit. Some of them, for whatever reason, are overcome with wild magic, which drives them mad and makes them eat or engage in the general destruction of Humans. We call them monsters or Wildlings. You don't seem to want to eat people. So, that's out. Easy, right?"

Nic said.

"Literally not at all," Taxx said.

"Anyway. Humans generally exhibit all the usual functions that a typical human does, bleeding, crying, eating, shitting, and oh yeah, they stay dead," she said.

"I feel like you are generalizing a lot of things," Taxx said.

"You got murdered today. You did not stay dead. **That** is some Other shit. So… you don't fit the classification of Human," she said.

"Obviously," Taxx said.

"It's wonderful that you can be so receptive," Lyra said.

"That was sarcasm," Taxx said.

"You are official Homoceterus. A nonhuman entity," Nic said.

"None of this should make **any** sense, so I refuse to agree with your reasonable explanation. People don't come back from the dead," Taxx said.

"No, they don't. Not if they are normal, but you did. That means you aren't normal," Nic said.

"I know that this is confusing, and you are right to feel fear. Nicole and I are not real cops, Mr. Kingswood. However, we are cops of a sort. Apparently, we are Wardens," Lyra said.

"There's that word again! And it's Mr. Moss. Kingswood is just a made-up name I use for school… never mind," Taxx said.

The fake cops stared at him. He stared back with a smug look.

"Look, we all got secrets. Am I supposed to know what a Warden is?" Taxx asked.

"Think more along the lines of Magic Federal Agents," Nic said.

Lyra paused but ultimately nodded when Nic glanced her way and winked.

"What the hell do you mean, Magic Federal Agents?" Taxx asked.

"Nicole and I are members of a powerful group of Others who work together to defend the many worlds, maintain order and understand the nature of magic. We are called the Mesalto, though some refer to us as the Guild," Lyra said.

"You were right. That is hard to believe," Taxx said.

"Let her finish, and it will be much easier," Nic said.

"Thank you. Every member of The Mesalto is a being, much like you, who is not classified as human. Each of us is decided to use our unique abilities for the good of everyone. There are many in our number and many faces and roles within the Guild, and we represent one of those faces, the Order of Warding, what you might think of as law enforcement," Lyra said.

"Oh… I see now, Magic Federal Agents. That makes way more sense now," Taxx said.

"Why do you keep interrupting her?" Nic asked.

Taxx opened his mouth to speak and received a look from both at the same time that told him not to. Even though he couldn't remember his mother, he knew she raised no fool.

"If you would continue to educate this unworthy neophyte," Nic said.

"The Order of Warding is the shield and spear that keeps the peace and protects the nexus from potential threats," Lyra said.

"The Nexus?" Taxx asked.

"You were so smart a second ago. I am flabbergasted. The

Nexus of Worlds is where every world bisects in the Infinite Aether, aka the planet Earth in space. Wardens protect the earth. Keep up," Nic said.

"How?" Taxx asked.

"We do so by investigating reported incidents, stopping bad guys. Things of that nature," Lyra said.

"No, I meant how am I supposed to keep up, everything was normal just a little while ago, and now...," Taxx said.

"You still look pretty normal for a guy who was dead for half a day," Nic said.

"Fair," Taxx conceded.

"You have been through something that no one has ever been through. Whatever is happening to you, we can try to help you understand it. If, and only if, you want to come with us," Lyra said.

"Where?" Taxx asked.

"To the House. That seems to be the best place to start, " Nic said.

"The House?" Taxx asked.

"The House of Wolf and Raven. An entity of the Mesalto that studies and catalogs magic. The Curator is very wise, so he at the very least may be able to shed some light on what exactly you are," Lyra said.

"That is the same place Offrey was trying to take me earlier," Taxx said.

"You know Offrey?" Nic asked.

She looked much more concerned than surprised, but Taxx continued anyway, choosing to ignore that.

"She works with my grandmother. She isn't someone I would call a friend," Taxx said.

That was the first time he had seen the mask on Lyra's face crack, and she looked genuinely surprised. Nic was staring at him with new eyes. Eyes searching his face for the answer to something on the tip of her mind.

"Did you say your name was Moss?" Nic asked.

Nic elbowed Lyra, and the taller warden was staring at him.

"Mr. Moss. Who is your grandmother?" Lyra asked.

"Who cares about that! I need to know what happens after you come back from the dead. Are you here to arrest me? What brought me back?" Taxx asked.

"Hmm. You usually vomit, but you did not seem to do that," Lyra said.

"That's a win!" Nic chimed in.

"We are also not here to arrest you," Lyra said.

"Right. We just came to collect… the… body. Damn, it feels **way** worse to say that when they are looking right at your face," Nic said.

Then she laughed and likely would have continued without Lyra getting her attention. The young man looked like he might begin to unravel, so she stopped.

"Oh, right," Nic said.

"What happens to me?" Taxx asked.

"Huh?" Nic said.

She looked so uncomfortable and confused that Taxx turned his attention to Lyra instead.

"What happens to… my life?" He asked.

"That is for you to decide," A woman said.

Her voice came from behind him, and he turned quickly to see another of those holes in space and time. On the other side of it, there was a completely different room. The ceilings were much higher, and the room itself made the space they were in look like a closet. There were bookshelves stacked to the ceiling on every wall and some strange glass boxes on pedestals here and there. In the center of the room, in front of a large red leather door, sat a young woman in a bright blue suit and glasses tinted so darkly they could have been in a welder's mask. He saw that they were entirely enclosed around her eyes with leather-like goggles upon closer inspection. He had never seen anything like that. Her skin was olive, and she wore a dark plum lipstick that matched the well-manicured nails on her fingers. He realized he was staring when she cleared her throat to get his attention.

"Oh, I'm sorry. Wait, no. No, what the hell is going on here?" He asked.

"May I help you?" The woman asked.

"Honestly, I don't know if I'm qualified to answer that question. I just found out I am not a human about a minute ago, and I'm having a hard time with that," he said.

"You appear to be in distress, your clothing is covered in what looks like blood, and you seem like you could use some assistance. So, may I help **you**?" The woman said.

"I don't know if anyone can help me. I might be a living dead," he said.

"Well, lucky for you, that is nothing I haven't seen before," she said.

"I am sorry, but who are you?" Taxx asked.

"Ah yes, I forgot to introduce myself. My name is Isabel. What is your name?" Isabel asked.

"Taxx," he said.

"It's a pleasure to meet you, Taxx. You can call me Izzy. I know this has to be a lot to take in. If you can trust us enough to have a seat, I will try to answer as many of them as possible," Izzy said.

He looked back at the two Wardens and then into the space-time hole where Izzy waited, still smiling, and back to Lyra and Nic again.

"This is a portal, a real portal, that goes to another place," Taxx said

"That is correct," Lyra said.

"Sorry to hold you all up, but do you expect me to walk through this without asking any questions like it's **not** a hole in space-time? The last time he got me because he pushed me, this time I need answers," Taxx said.

"Who pushed you? What happened to you, Mr. Kingswood?"

"You first!" Taxx said.

Izzy started to laugh this time. Her laugh was nothing like the belly laugh of the warden. It was soft and almost kind. It completely derailed his anger. When she noticed that everyone was looking at her, she covered her face in embarrassment.

"I am **so** sorry. It's just that you are so much like him," Izzy said.

"Like who?" Taxx asked.

"The son of Death," Izzy said.

"Lady, what the **HELL** are you talking about? Am I honestly supposed to accept all of this? Disregard that I'm no longer a human being, nor have I ever been?" Taxx said.

He was getting more upset by the moment, and his breathing was starting to get heavy. A tingle in his forehead started as an itch and slowly turned into a burning sensation.

"I am not finished!" Taxx shouted.

The rooms darkened significantly on both sides of the

portal for a moment when he shouted. Taxx did not notice, but everyone was staring at him openly.

"Now I have to pretend that a hole in space-time is something other than honest to goodness witchcraft meant to be feared and respected?" Taxx asked.

"You are right. There's a lot to take in," Nic conceded.

"That's all I wanted. Just... I've had a crazy day," Taxx said.

Nic nodded and guided him through the portal slowly. Taxx expected to feel pressure or hear the sound, but there was nothing. Taxx stepped across into the other room, and a slight floral scent took the place of the smelly corpse odor in the apartment. The three of them had crossed over, and with just a flick of her wrist, the hole that had been as tall and wide as a garage door was gone, and a card took its place. Nothing indicated that anything else had ever been there except the book stack and a small pedestal with a man's bust. He thought it was someone famous from history, but the name didn't ring any bells for him. He looked up to ask and noticed that all three were looking at him. He decided against it and took the open seat between the Wardens.

"The Curator should be along shortly, and then we can begin, but you must have loads of questions. I'll do what I can," Izzy said.

"Thank you. I don't even know where to begin." Taxx said.

"Lots of us probably feel like that," Izzy said.

"So, I've never been a human?" He asked.

"The research seems to suggest so, but it's not as black and white as all that because of magic. It has a way of circumventing our understanding in ways we still cannot imagine," Izzy said.

"You guys keep talking about magic. Like witches and

demons and Merlin magic? Magic is real?" He asked.

"Obviously yes, except Merlin. He is based on a few Others, but there is no actual Merlin that we have heard of. However, absolutely powerful others are very similar to the common understanding of Witches, Wizards, and Demons," Izzy said.

"Am I magic?" Taxx said.

"Resurrection is caused by magic, as to who performed it, you, or someone else, that is still a mystery. You've certainly been touched by magic. I can feel its presence in you at enormous amounts," Lyra said.

He rubbed his hands on his face.

"What happens to me now? Do I go back to my apartment?" He asked.

Izzy looked to Lyra, who quietly shook her head before she started to speak.

"That may not be possible at this point," Lyra said.

"What? Why not?" He asked.

"Craw," Nic said.

"Gross," Izzy said.

"My neighbor? He is dead, remember? Also, the thing in his body doesn't like it when you call him gross," Taxx said.

His hands went to his chest subconsciously.

"He was never your neighbor; Crawford is a powerful Other whose body is composed of a seemingly endless nest of black flies that appear to be under the control of a single mind. His. He is not only a confirmed eater of humans but has been known to participate in targeted killings for money and trade," Izzy said.

"Wait… wait. Craw was always a monster and an assassin?" He asked.

"Yes. His age and most of his abilities are undocumented.

He is a fascinating specimen. We aren't even sure if he is truly male as he changes his outer appearance often," She continued.

"I don't want to deal with that sack of maggots again. What do I do? how do I get away from him?" He asked.

"That's not the issue here. Craw is affiliated with a group of killers that rarely fail to fulfill a contract," Nic said

"So, what does that mean? Do I get to cash in the bounty because I survived?" Taxx asked

"That's not how bounties work… how do you think bounties work?" Izzy asked.

"If the person with the bounty on their head challenges the bounty hunter to a duel and wins, then the bounty is erased, right? Are we not working on Shonen rules?" Taxx asked.

Lyra just stared at him.

"Seriously? Tell me that was a joke? You are joking?" Nic asked.

Taxx winked.

"I can see your nipples," Nic teased.

His hands covered his chest, and when he finally really looked down, there were a few places on his chest where he had been injured. It was surreal to see the size and the sheer number of holes in him.

"I'm sorry, I hadn't even realized," Taxx said.

"Oh, how did I forget to do that? Excuse me, Mr. Kingwood," Izzy said

The woman whispered something in a language that he did not understand, not just because he didn't understand her words, the way she spoke was something else. Whatever she said didn't sound like language or even the sounds that a human could make. She sounded like an electric keyboard. It was a noise he would never expect to hear, and as soon as she said it, he felt warmth on his whole body, and it was moving, like wind, if only for a single moment. It only got about as hot as bathwater, and then it was gone, but in a flash, his clothing was free of holes, and not just that, he was clean. His skin was clean even under his nails, and the tiny echo of a headache in the back of his head that had been there since he came back from the dead was dulled. It was incredible.

"What the hell was that?" Taxx asked.

"My words can heal, it works best in living things, but it is effective elsewhere," Izzy said.

"That's incredible," Taxx said

"Oh well, thank you," Izzy replied.

She smiled, and Taxx smiled back reflexively. Then the smile fell from his face, and he shook his head in disbelief.

"Hold on… let's go back a step. Did you say that there was a whole group of killers possibly coming after me?" Taxx asked.

"It's a maybe at best," Nic said.

"What the hell is it with you people and saying such serious and terrifying things like it's no big deal?" Taxx asked.

"Magic is dangerous and unfortunately everywhere," Izzy said.

"This sort of thing happens to many people if I am honest with you, Mr. Moss. If we are lucky, we can intervene, but generally, if magic is involved, they are dead before we arrive," Lyra said.

"But he said he wasn't supposed to kill me," Taxx said.

He was desperate now. He was grasping at the honesty of a maggot monster.

"Then he promptly shot you through the chest, many times.

So, Craw is very clearly not the most reliable source for honesty," Nic said

"Right. Fine. Then tell me, not counting myself, how many times have you successfully stopped something like this BEFORE the killing started? In the past year?" Taxx asked.

"Counting you? That would make a total of… two," Nic said.

Taxx's mouth went dry.

"But why keep count?" Nic asked.

"How many times have you failed?" He asked.

The tension in the room was so thick he felt it descend like cellophane over the entire space. Nic looked uncomfortable, while Lyra was simply looking at him with her calm features. Izzy cleared her throat and took the reins.

"Well, I don't think-" Izzy began.

"Unexpectedly, I appear!" A man shouted.

A man had appeared in the room in a pose that you might see at the end of a large Broadway number. He was still as if he were performing a stage freeze, even holding a white top hat. He was posed in a mid-kick like a dancer. Head to toe, he wore white, from his tux with tails to his shiny shoes. Taxx had not even realized there was anyone else in the room until the white tuxedo was so close to him that they could touch. Taxx screamed a little, but no one else seemed surprised. There was a surge of relief in the room as soon as he entered. Taxx didn't feel any of that.

He was terrified.

Chapter | Eight

"What the hell!? Who is this guy?" Taxx asked.

"I will take it from here, Izzy," The man said.

He was still frozen in his silly pose.

"As you say. Good luck," Izzy said.

Isabel was pleasant enough, even smiling at the odd haberdasher who came out of nowhere. Taxx was starting to calm down. Everyone in the room seemed to know the guy.

"Avogorum Zorrum Illunorum, but you may call me Avo for short as my full name is long on the tongue. I am also very proud to be the acting Curator of the House of Wolf and Raven and an all-around snappy dresser. A pleasure to finally meet you," Avo said.

The Curator was tall, even taller than Lyra and his hair was long and straight, jet black like ink spilling over his shoulder. His eyes were sharp and violet like amethyst. His skin was perfectly tan, and a short beard framed his face. He looked like a stage magician, Taxx thought.

"Tell me, which stage magician do I remind you of?" Avogorum asked.

Taxx was speechless and staring at this strange man, and the strange man was staring back. For a time, there was no sound, then surely everyone heard the ding of Taxx's mind when he figured it out. Copperfield was reading his mind, he thought.

"I'm sorry?" Taxx said.

"Copperfield!" Avogorum said.

He started to laugh, and Taxx gasped loudly, not because his laugh was odd but because his outfit would change drastically every time Avo's body shook. Not just color, shape, fabric, and pattern too. It was unlike anything he had ever seen before, and he subconsciously began to climb his chair backward and away from this… this? Taxx couldn't think of anything to describe what he saw; it was like scrolling through a website at full speed but only his clothing.

"Holy F-" Taxx stopped himself.

"Oh my, that was unintentional," Avogorum said.

He settled into a single set of clothing that was much more casual than the white tux. He even had moccasins and his hair in a ponytail.

"Well, that's at least period appropriate," Avogorum said.

"That was incredible. Can you read my mind?" Taxx said.

He didn't know what to do or say. There hadn't been many experiences in his life to preparing him for a sorcerer or whatever the hell this guy was, he thought.

"Moss then and, No. I can't read your mind, but I can hear your thoughts. They are very different ideologies; I will have to avail you of the intricacies later. We have much to do and not much time to do it. Follow me to my office," Avogorum said.

He turned toward the wall, and a large, quilted set of doors stood there. Taxx was sure they had not been there before, but the heavy doors started to swing open. The room they revealed had vaulted ceilings like some cathedral. Deep red tapestries depicted magic tricks of all types throughout history. Sawing people in half, escapes, straitjackets, and levitation. The floors were dark wood but shined to a mirror polish to reflect everything in the room so clearly that it was unnerving to stand on them. There were hundreds of books all over the space, overcrowding bookshelves and stacked on the floor, and carpets by the dozens rolled up and splayed about randomly. Some of them still and others gently hovering above the ground and floating above tables. It looked like a library crashed into a caravan. The magician waved a hand, and a round table appeared in the center of the room right in front of him, along with a giant crystal ball that materialized at the center. The ball was a dark black orb that swam with a murky depth that crawled beneath the surface. He didn't want to look at it at all and only wanted to investigate its depths forever, all at once. At its center was a perfect circle of color that was somehow darker than black and looked like an iris. He didn't know how the odd eyeball was looking directly at him, but he knew it was true. He could feel it.

"What is that?" he asked.

He was already walking towards the table before the man answered, and he took a seat in front of the orb, still staring into its murky nothingness. He swore he could almost hear it whispering to him.

"This is a looking glass, a type of oracle that allows us to look inside of ourselves and reveal something true. Its name is Blackest Eye," Avo said.

As if it had heard its name spoken, the eye began to shimmer with reflective sparkles like a billion stars. A low violet light bloomed at its center like a candle flame.

"Only look into its eye, Mr. Moss, to see what truths await within. Stare into the abyss and let it stare back into you," he said.

His voice was smokey and dark, and it filled the room with a heavy and powerful mood that crackled in the air around them like static electricity. He couldn't look away from the dazzling orb, and he slowly reached out his hand to touch it, pausing to look at Avo before he did. He was suddenly unsure of himself.

"There is nothing to fear of the truth, Mr. Moss," Avo said.

Avo was probably trying to be reassuring, but there was some fear inside him. Taxx wanted answers, and the whispering orb was offering them. He reached out and pressed his hand to the surface. It was so smooth that there was almost no friction. It felt like he was still holding solid air in his hand. He could also feel a warm heartbeat steadily drumming inside of it. His heart was beating in time, and the sound became the only thing he could hear. Only the thumping of his own heart and this dark magic heart rippling through him was so loud he couldn't hear anything. The violet light was everywhere, and Avo was shouting something, but he couldn't hear him anymore, the violet light got so bright he couldn't see, and a constant noise was sawing through him with a shrill gurgling whistle.

Then everything was still.

Taxx was now standing in a field of grass surrounded by

little snow-capped mountains on all sides and grey-blue sky as far as he could see. The sun was warm and prominent in the air, and the smells of honeysuckle and violet were everywhere. He took a deep breath and closed his eyes, drinking in the scene before he started to pick it apart. Of course, he said the ball looked inside you, which meant it investigated your mind. That meant this was some projection of his from the sound of music or some other such family film as his vision of a happy place. He knelt, ripped up a fistful of grass from the root, and rolled it between his fingers. It felt so real he could even feel the crunch of the earth under his nails.

"This is some impressive Virtual Reality," he said.

His voice carried in an echo, and he turned to follow it around the valley, and when he did, he found that he was not alone. Standing just behind him was someone or something that looked just like him, only he was made of what looked to be oil. He was shiny and slick, but his body was perfectly recreated like some eerie gelatin mold, even down to the barely tied laces of his shoes. After standing still for so long and letting Taxx study it, the figure lunged for him with both hands out, Taxx ducked out of its path, and the copy tumbled through the grass. It righted itself immediately and came at him again. Taxx was not a small person by any means. He was built sturdy, solid, and he sometimes acted a touch reckless where most might run. This was one of those times. Instead of running away, he decided to run toward the thing, and he took hold of one of its arms, ducked underneath it, and pressed his back to its chest. The creature tried to wrap its arms around him, which he wanted. Taxx planted his foot and threw all of his weight into the creature's hip. The Clone came off the ground quickly, and Taxx snapped its arm forward to slam it on the ground, crushing its chest against the earth.

"Stay down, Shadow Taxx," Taxx said.

His grandmother thought it was good to teach him how to fight. A few new schools and bruised egos later, he figured his way around a scrap or two. The creature rose much more slowly this time but was back on its feet and growling at him now like an animal, it gnashed its teeth and circled, but it seemed to have learned not to attack straight on.

"There are many roads on the magic mountains, more than we could ever name. That has not stopped us from trying some broader categorization," Avo said.

He was not here, but his voice was everywhere, or maybe it was inside his head. He couldn't tell. He was too busy watching Shadow as it circled him and sized him up. He knew that he would be attacked if he slipped even a little.

"Shifters are gifted with balance. Walking the knife-edge between self and the infinite allows them to call on power beyond imagination without losing their original nature," Avo's voice said.

Shadow growled again, but it was much deeper and started to change shape this time. It leaped around, lunging at him and snarling, moving much faster, with long and controlled movements. His shadow-self began to grow with a roar until it was twice as large and bristling with muscles and then feathers and fur. It was a comprehensive set of beasts, as it changed in front of his eyes to reflect hundreds of different types of creatures. Werewolves to a feathery dinosaur, a great bear man with huge, clawed hands. It all happened so quickly that he didn't know what to make of it. Before the thing could attack, it returned to its standard form.

"Hunters have the gift of rebirth. They are granted power beyond the limitations of the human form and are born again within it," The voice said.

Shadow version of him sprouted fangs and glowing red eyes like a vampire and then turned into a tiger with a human body. It melted into a tiny house cat then grew into a massive ferocious dragon that whipped the flowers with its wing thrust. The dragon's chest filled with light, and golden fire came to life between its fangs, and when it opened its mouth, fire leaped toward him. It was thick and flowing all around him, but it did not burn, it burned the grass and flowers, but it may have been bathwater to him. The fire was gone in that next moment along with the dragon, and only the shadow version of himself remained, looking at him with eyes like the looking glass. He could even see the slightly different shade of black that made up its iris here in this double, just like the orb in the office, and just like then, he was sure it was looking at him.

"Speakers are gifted with secrets. A speaker can use the secrets of power and harness its energies to do impossible things," Avo's voice said.

There was a sentiment in his voice as he was a speaker, and the emotion was not lost on the environment or his dark copy. Black electricity sprang to life around its body, clawing and dancing all around him. Then it became fire, so intense that it scorched the earth, then water so pure and clean that the grass drank it up and started to grow again. The water purified the ground, spreading warmth through his body as it lapped upon his shins. The water was cool, but its energy lightly sizzled on his skin like fizzing bubbles. The water melted away, and weight in the air pressed down on his chest with such force that he fell to the ground. It pressed down on him like a great hand, crushing him and forcing all the air from his lungs. Then once again, everything was still. He got to his feet, and Shadow was back to normal, or whatever you might consider being normal in a place like this, he thought. There was no longer any such thing as normal.

"Demigods are gifted by blood. Their power is sharpened with each generation and grants them abilities that once saw them worshipped as gods," The voice said.

"If we could maybe take a break? This is all starting to feel strange," Taxx said.

There was no response. Not even Shadow did much of anything until the wind picked up, and his shadow self was suddenly illuminated in white light. Shadow came for him again, only this time he was so fast that Taxx couldn't keep up and slammed into Taxx's chest. He was easily tackled to the ground, and both his arms were held down with just one glowing white hand. The glow went away, but the strength did not. In place of the light was a hammer with a head the size of a cinder block. The hammer was crackling with electricity, and it rose in the air for a moment before it drove down toward his face. This incredible display was something he would not dare look away from, so he forced his eyes to stay open. Even if this was the end, he wanted to see it through. As the hammer came down on his face, it fell away in a shower of sparks, and in its place was the hand of the dark copy alive with a corona of light encircling it. Only two fingers gently touched his forehead, and instantly he knew that the intense violet light he was seeing now was pouring into his body. It was warm and heavy like bathwater, and it flowed all through him like the heat from the sun. It soothed all of his pain at that moment. He had never felt more alive or whole than when the light was filling him. The color shifted through many things until it became green. Not just any green, deep and rich green with hints of gold, and for some reason, it made him think of leaves, leaves with rings on them… was it a dream he had? He hadn't remembered much of that strange dream for most of the day, but he could see the leaves now with their proud golden rings. No, they weren't rings at all, he thought, they were crowns, and that made sense because...

"Kingswood," Taxx said.

The green light became so intense that he thought it might swallow him up, but it didn't. Instead, it poured into him at a rate he could not even hope to perceive. He didn't know how he could hold it all, it was all through his body now, from his nose to his toes, and then, when he thought he couldn't take any more of it, it was gone. His shadow-self was no longer standing over him, and Taxx got to his feet slowly. This was taking a lot out of him. Shadow was just a few feet away, holding a sword in his hand, a long shining blade that had runes all over it.

"Mediums are gifted with duality. They live in perfect harmony between the worlds of man and worlds far beyond. This allows them to channel incredible power in both," Avo's voice said.

The sword came alive with light, and its furious power made the air howl and hiss as it passed. He could hear and feel the air screaming around the edge of that wicked blade and its unearthly glow with every swipe. The sword fell away to ash in Shadow's hands, and so did the grass around his feet, and slowly he began to bulge, like an overfilled balloon. He continued for a few moments until he was comically large. Before Taxx could laugh, the clone exploded violently. A vapor came from his body, a thick dark cloud the color of sage that sucked the life out of everything it touched, it rolled past his ankles, and he could feel its poison trying to gnaw through his skin. The poison was suddenly gone, and Shadow held up some small tube in his hand. It appeared to have a small white stone in it. When he kissed the small pendant, his body changed instantly. Now he had a set of large black feathery wings and a halo over his head. The halo bubbled away in black boiling liquid, and Shadow was floating off the ground with black oil dripping from its fingertips. It grumbled and growled and snarled, but it didn't move, just hovered in place over some strange marking on the ground.

Then it all stopped. It didn't shift or anything like that. It simply was not there anymore. He was standing in the plain meadow again, and Shadow was standing just in front of him. Its hand was held out toward real Taxx, and it was asking him to take its hand, not with words, but he knew what it wanted. He didn't hesitate. He reached out and took its hand, it was like trying to grasp at slime, and the black goop was all over him and crawling up his body. He panicked and tried to scrape it off, but more of it crawled on him every time he touched it. It had his arms up to the forearm and wrapped around his middle. In no time at all, he was covered entirely by the black fluid, even over his eyeballs, but he could still see and breathe just like usual. He lifted his arms to look at them, and he was just as shiny and reflective as the clone had been. It was strange, but he wasn't suffocating or on fire.

"So, what happens now?" Taxx asked.

His voice was slightly muffled, and there was a strange, distorted sound that he assumed was because he was speaking through this… stuff. He didn't want to think about what it was.

"It is time for us to see what you will become. Allow the blackest eye to search your power, and your nature will be shown," Avo said.

It tingled all over him like icy little raindrops, it was unsettling at first, but he was starting not to notice it so much. Minutes passed, and nothing happened.

"Is it supposed to take this-" He was cut off.

The goo began to screech a high-pitched sound that he wasn't sure if he was actually hearing it or his eardrums were vibrating so hard it made him think he could. It started to squeeze tight to his body, and he couldn't breathe.

"Avo, help!" Taxx screamed.

"Relax, young Kingswood, everything is under control," Avo said.

There was something very unsettling about hearing the concern in a sorcerer's voice. He saw that man change clothing hundreds of times in a single moment. When someone like Avo is nervous, someone like Taxx should be **more** so, and right on cue, everything around him began to flash violently. Now Taxx could see the meadow and Avo's office flashing in and out of reality quickly. It was disorienting. Blackest Eye was boiling under his palm like a pot on the stovetop, and black fluid that spilled out of the orb had overtaken his body in Avo's office. Taxx could hear a voice whispering something repeatedly, so quickly that he couldn't understand it.

"What? What are you saying to me, Avo?" Taxx asked.

"Nothing, what do you hear?" Avo said.

The sorcerer was standing on the other side of the table with both hands on the ball. There was a sheen of sweat on his forehead. It was apparent now that he had not said anything with his mouth. The voice was coming from inside his head.

"I see you, Taxxis, you are finally here," said a voice.

This was not the voice of Am in his head. It wasn't in his head. The sound came from the ball, still boiling around his hand.

"The Black Summer is coming," it said again.

The words slithered and oozed from some unknown place in the orb that he could half see spliced with the illusion projected into his mind, one vision in each eye. It felt like his head would tear in two, and just like that, everything snapped away like an elastic band, and the illusion was gone, and he was back in the room again. He was also nearly completely covered in a viscous black fluid creeping, crawling, and pouring out the looking glass. It was tingling all over him, and he could feel something strange happening inside of him.

"What is it doing to me? And what is a Black Summer?" Taxx asked.

Taxx's voice was still modulating up and down and back as he spoke, like half of the air that came out of his lungs had become helium.

"I haven't the faintest idea. However, there is a more pressing matter. I feel it is no longer prudent to lie to you about it as you know something is wrong. Blackest Eye seems to be making a play toward eating you," Avo said.

"What? Tell it I'm not for eating!" Taxx screamed.

"I don't know why it's doing this, but I'm sure it wouldn't get you mixed up just because of a name. This is just a tool to unlock potential and my favorite one to boot. It's a demon that eats a bit of your power and uses its amorphous nature to show us what form your power might take," Avo said.

"That's great. That sounds fun, but this isn't so fun," Taxx

said.

"It seems to have had a taste of something in you that it does not want to let go of. Just a moment," he said.

He was nodding his head furiously, and with each nod, a perfect copy of him appeared and stepped to the side until the room had about 6 Avo's standing around.

"You go and fetch Izzy. You go and cover the boy's eyes. You cover my eyes. You two go and fetch a containment vessel, Sumerian if we have it. And lastly, can you get us a spot of tea? I am going to miss this ball while it recovers. English Breakfast, please," he said.

He spoke at a hard pace to keep up with, but all Avo clones moved to their jobs immediately, and the last thing Taxx saw was the real Avo get his own eyes covered and Izzy being hustled into the room, gently complaining all the while.

Then his own eyes were covered.

"-sort of half-assed thick-headed... Oh, I see. Blackest eye. That's a shame. This one is a very useful tool. You're two for two this year-old man," Izzy said.

"Later, we have someone in danger, if you please," Avo said.

"Settle down. Look at me, blackest eye," she said.

Then she spoke a single word in that language of power. It was like a light switch was flipped. Everything stopped, and the Avo covering his eyes fell to the ground asleep, as did the Avo covering the real one's eyes and the other 2 in the room. All of them were crumpled on the floor, asleep. The looking glass was solid polished black stone again and nothing more. Izzy was putting her goggled glasses back on, but for a moment, Taxx was sure that she did not have any eyes inside her head. He saw a healed but a puckered hole where her eyes should be, black as pitch with a dying ember of green light in its depths. As soon as he noticed it, the light turned on him like an iris, and there was a pop like a camera flash before everything in the world went black. He could still hear, but couldn't move, see, smell, or feel anything. It was as though his senses were turned off except for his ears.

"Oh whoops, didn't holster the girls fast enough," Izzy said.

"So, it would seem. Wake him up, would you," Avo said.

"It doesn't work like that, even if I call him back, he will have to pay for it at some point and the longer we put it off the longer he will sleep," Izzy said.

"I understand. Its only sleep," Avo said.

"I'm not sure you do. He could sleep for a week," she cautioned.

"Isabel. Please," Avo said.

"Fine, but you know I hate using it on people," Izzy said.

There was another word from her power language. Another pop of light, and Taxx was himself again. He took a moment to collect his bearings and watched as the sorcerer's clones faded away like dimmed light until they were completely gone. Blackest Eye was gone too, but where he didn't know, thinking about it made him uneasy. He could still hear the voice in the back of his head... *I see you, Taxxis.*

"Why did it try to eat me?" he asked.

"Who can say, demons are a funny sort, they just sort of do what they do," Izzy said.

Her eyes were fully goggled, and she gently placed a hand on his shoulder.

"Demons? I thought demons were from hell, and I was **sure** they would look more intimidating than a perfect sphere,"

Taxx said.

"Taxxis. The Blackest eye is a looking glass. Inside of it, there is a lesser Demon. It's the best one we have, but it took a liking to you, which means you have powerful magic. However, we could not see what you are," Avo said.

"Don't fret. This is not an uncommon occurrence. You are an unclassifiable Other. That means it will take more time to figure out what sort of thing you are. That's exciting if you ask me," Izzy said.

She sounded like she believed what she was saying to him even though that was not what he wanted to hear. He had already spent so much of his life being the odd one, and now there was magical evidence. It didn't exactly make him feel positive.

"There are other methods, Young Kingswood. I will reach out to an associate of mine who may be able to shed some light. I am sure one of them will be able to tell us something," Avogorum said.

"The Tailor?" Lyra asked.

Her voice startled Taxx as everything that happened made him temporarily forget that the other women were also standing in the office.

"More precisely, his wife. I think she is going to be the one we need this time. Can you go and see to that, Lyra?" Avo asked.

Lyra only nodded and looked at Nic, and in mere moments Nic had created a portal on the wall with just the flick of her wrist, a card sliding out and stretching until it was large enough. The rectangular portal opened on a busy street in the middle of a city, which was strange but not as odd as the people who passed on the other side. They could easily see through the hole, as easily as he could see out of it, but most of them didn't even lookup. He stepped forward suddenly.

"Hey!" He shouted.

He didn't know why; an impulse came to him at that moment, and he acted on it. In the back of his mind, he held on to the notion that all of this was a dream, something he would wake up from and be back in his stagnant but quietly peaceful life. No one looked up when he spoke, and he could hear them. The light from the room he was standing in was glowing on the sidewalk, and a few people even walked through it. Not one of them looked up or acknowledged anything happening, not Nic or Izzy, or him. They moved aside when Lyra stepped out of it but still none of them seemed to see her. He felt like he was standing in an elevator, and it suddenly started to fall. His stomach felt like it was going to leap out of his body. Lyra gave him a small nod and then closed the door.

"They don't want to see us, so they don't. It's the only ability all humans share. They are completely ignorant of magic, so they are mostly unable to see it. There are exceptions, as there are in all things and more than a few, but on the whole, normal folk don't want anything to do with Other shit," Nic said.

The fact that he had been living in a world like that his whole life and never knew that there was another world outside his periphery was an astounding revelation. monsters were real, they ate people, and there were Magic Feds that tried to stop them. He was learning too many things all at once. The most recent is that he was no longer a human because as much as those people ignored the magic, they also ignored him. He was no longer they.

"You look like you could use some air," Izzy said.

"Huh? I mean, yeah, I… it's just been a long day," Taxx said.

"I can show you to your room for the night?" Izzy offered.

"Yes, please," Taxx answered.

Isabel smiled and stood up from her chair. She was much younger than Taxx had assumed. Having her come around the desk like that took away some of her administrative mystique. She appeared to be somewhere around his age, like Nic. Then there was Lyra, whose age he couldn't guess on his life and who could even know how old Avo was. Izzy pulled a key from her suit jacket and walked toward the door of Avo's office. The key had so many more teeth than a standard key. It looks like the frills down the back of a metal lizard. Taxx was puzzled because she said they were going to his room, and now she seemed to be locking the door. The other, and admittedly stranger, thing about all of this is that she appeared as though she were going to put a key into a door that lacked a keyhole.

Taxx opened his mouth to ask about that.

Izzy shot him a look to cut him off.

Not only did the key simply slide into a place with no keyhole, but it also made a satisfying click when she turned it and opened the door. What was on the other side could not have been possible. He was looking at a bedroom where there had not been a bedroom before. There was a large bed, a desk, and even a balcony at the rear of the space. It was large and luxurious.

"Is this more Magic?" Taxx asked.

"You will have a tough time about the rest of this if you can't get used to Magic, my dude," Nic said.

She popped up from her chair just after him and clapped him on the back like an old college bud, harder than he assumed. After she nudged him on the shoulder, he even smiled a little. Something was reassuring about her all too human attitude. The fact that she was card-wielding, whatever she was, helped sober him. There was never going to be normal as he knew it. Not ever again.

"Whoa, this guy is headed down a real sad hallway. Who died? Oh… right, it was you. Damn, sorry. I'm out," Nic said.

Then she fell onto the floor, just disappeared as though a trap door opened under her feet, and she was gone. When Taxx looked down, he could see a card, but its face was replaced by a vision of somewhere else, a kitchen in what looked like an upscale home. He was looking down at the top of Nic's head, and she was poking through the fridge. He could hear the sound in stereo, softly from the other room down the hall and loudly through the card.

"Do all of you pop in and out of everywhere like that?" Taxx asked.

"Not everyone. Just the lucky ones. Nic is a special case for a lot of reasons. There are not many like her," Izzy said.

"That I believe," Taxx said.

Nic had taken half a dozen clementines from the fridge and was sitting just in front of it on the floor and meticulously peeling them one by one before stuffing them into her mouth, whole. She looked up at him with an orange mouth and gave him a wink. He had to admit it was adorable, but the speed she was swallowing citrus fruits was slightly alarming. The card face changed from a portal to a regular card face in a single motion. Then, it turned on its side and threw itself out of the room, spinning like a frisbee and gliding around the corner.

"Huh," Taxx said.

"What is it?" Izzy asked.

"That. That wasn't that weird to me. That should have been **super** weird, right? This is all pretty damned weird. I think I should be more shocked, but instead, I feel so… so…" he said.

"Normal?" Izzy offered.

"YES! Exactly that. I've always kind of been… What I mean is that I didn't fit in with people… humans. At least I didn't feel like I did, but I am in a sorcerer's office with a woman with flames for eyes and a seemingly feral card flinging magic cop, and I'm right as rain," Taxx said.

"You're one of us. Even if you didn't know it this morning, you always have been. We all feel that we aren't humans at some point, as much as we want to be, as badly as we may have wanted it to be true. It never was. I'm sorry to drop all this on you at once," Izzy said.

"No, please, you have all been so helpful. What if I just woke up alone in that apartment? I couldn't even imagine…" he said.

Then he started to imagine it.

Izzy had clearly said something in her magic language, and immediately, the thought left his mind. There was something different this time. He understood it.

"Is it possible to hear magic?" He asked.

"Nic is right. You ask a lot of questions," She laughed.

He couldn't help but smile when she started to laugh, and he even laughed a little too. It did seem like a ridiculous thing to say, considering all that happened. She turned to the door and kicked off her shoes.

"Come on," Izzy said.

The two of them stepped into the bedroom space. The air was cooler here, and there was a gentle humming from the air conditioning. It was all so typical.

"What were you expecting?" Izzy asked.

"Great, you can read minds too?" Taxx asked.

"Nah. Just faces," she answered.

Taxx looked down at the ground sheepishly.

"I know this is a lot to take in. Try to get some sleep, and you'll feel better in the morning," she said.

"What if I can't?" he asked.

"Well, there's bound to be some therapy that can help," she said.

"No. That's not what I meant. What if I can't sleep?" Taxx asked.

"Then you come down the stairs and take a left. That's the TV room. I'll be in there," she said.

"Maybe I'll run into you in the night," Taxx said.

"You will," she said.

"Did you have a vision?" he asked.

She laughed.

"No. I don't sleep well," Izzy said.

Taxx thought about whether he should ask if she was serious, but he decided it was probably better not to ask. Izzy gave him one last smile before she stepped back through the door. Once the door was closed, the frame mutated and changed shape back into the average door. Taxx opened it and found a hall that led to a stairwell and several other doors, presumably bedrooms. He wondered how many charity cases like him this place catered to. He thought maybe he didn't want to know. He moved to the bed and took a seat. It was soft, and the blankets were heavy and smelled like fresh laundry. Taxx lay face down on top of the covered and took two deep breaths of that fresh scent, and by the time he tried to inhale for the third, he was already asleep.

Chapter | Nine

Taxx awoke with a start and his breath caught in his throat. He did not recognize his surroundings, and he felt the weight of panic tugging at his heart. It wasn't until he sat up in bed that he realized where he was and why. He had somehow gotten himself very tangled in the top covers of the bedding, but it only took a bit of rolling to free himself. Once he was up, he reached for his phone to check the time and saw that it was still very broken, and he threw the device in frustration. It landed on the nearby nightstand and stopped when it hit a clock radio that told him it was just past midnight now and that he had at least gotten a few hours of sleep. He tried to lay back down, but now that his mind was awake, he was awake, so that was a no-go. He paced the room for about 5 minutes before he crept to the door and gently tried the handle.

It was unlocked. For some reason, he was surprised, and he didn't know why. These people had been nothing but pleasant to him. There was no reason to suspect that they would lock him in an honestly lovely room. He opened the door and stepped out into the hall. Her directions had been clear enough, and he was thankful for them. There were many doors than he had imagined. Luckily there was only a single massive staircase that he could find. He had to descend three floors to get to the main floor, and once he was there, he looked to his right. That appeared to be where he had arrived earlier, and now, he was standing in front of a central staircase. There was a kitchen just behind the stairs, and to his right was a large door that stood half-closed. The sound of television and flashing lights made it clear that this was his destination. He made his way across the hall and peeked inside; at first, he didn't see anyone, just things. A massive sectional couch was in front of a large TV, and a coffee table was covered in snack wrappers and notebooks with doodles. The TV was much louder inside the space than outside the door, and all the lights were on. Izzy was lying across the couch and furiously drawing in a notebook, heedless of the sci-fi action happening on the TV.

"Even when I knew you would be there, it was still creepy. Isn't that funny?" She said.

"You knew I was coming here?" Taxx said.

The girl adjusted her glasses and turned to look at him, holding the notebook she had been working on so he could see. A very accurate image of him peeking around a door with half a dozen or so pictures of clocks around him was on the page. Some were digital, and others had hands, but each showed the same time. 12:21. The precise time it was right now.

"That's…," Taxx said.

He couldn't think of a way to end that sentence that would not be rude, so he just trailed off into silence. After staring at him for a bit, Izzy laughed to break the tension.

"It is a little weird, right? I don't always get them, but they come at random," she said.

"Heavy," Taxx said.

"I am just so glad you are awake," she said.

"I had such a long day. Guess I needed a nap," Taxx said.

"I'm sure everyone will be glad that you are awake," she said.

"What do you mean?" Taxx asked.

"We didn't think you were ever going to wake up. How does it feel to sleep like that?" Izzy asked.

"It was rejuvenating. Best nap ever," Taxx said.

"Nap? Oh no, dude. It's Thursday night," she said.

Taxx could only blink at her.

"Its… Tuesday. Well, ok, it's after midnight, but still," he said.

"Oh, you're right! Technically I think it might be Friday now," she said.

Izzy pulled up the channel guide on the TV, and the date and time were there in cobalt. They were floating beneath the image of a TV news person. Friday. 12:30 am.

"I'm sorry, friend. You've been asleep for a while," Izzy said.

He was staring at her again, and she smiled.

"Avo examined you. It seems like you just needed the sleep, I guess. You did come back from the dead," Izzy said.

"I guess so…" Taxx said.

He felt more rested than he had in a long time.

"I'm still tripping over being dead," Taxx said.

Izzy gave him a small lopsided smile that turned into a giggle, and then suddenly, she looked sad. It happened so fast that Taxx almost couldn't keep up.

"You ok, Izzy?" he asked.

"Yeah. It's just. You remind me of this other guy that lives here. He hasn't come back yet, and I'm starting to worry about him," she said.

"Oh yeah? That can't be easy," Taxx said.

"It's been days now. I guess he can be a wildcard, but this is a long time even by his standards," Izzy said.

"I can't even imagine. That does remind me that there are things I need to do too," Taxx said.

Izzy sat up on the couch and patted the spot next to her. Taxx hesitated for a moment, and then he joined her there. She pulled her knees up to her chest.

"So, tell me about him," Taxx said.

" Who?" she asked.

"The guy you are pining over. It's kind of obvious. What's he like?" Taxx asked.

Isabel blushed softly, and after a moment, she shook her head.

"No. Well, I mean… No, it's not like that," she said.

"It sounds like that," Taxx teased.

"Hey, you. I'm supposed to be the wise mentor here. Don't tease me. Mr. Moss," she said.

"Not at all," he said.

The two of them laughed, and Taxx started to notice things about her that he hadn't before. She looked to be around the same age that he was. She was dressed down quite a bit and wearing ballet slippers and leggings under an oversized sweater. Her laugh was infectious, and he felt himself relax in a way he hadn't all day. When she noticed he was starting, he looked someplace else.

"You remind me of him. A lot. Except he is a little different," Izzy said.

"Like he doesn't sleep for 30 hours?" Taxx asked.

"Not that I've seen, but who knows with him. He is so secretive about himself for a guy with such a big personality," Izzy said.

"Sounds like the kind of guy you would go for," he said.

"Meaning what, exactly?" she said.

"He sounds like one of those cute boys with the wrong attitude that girls love so much. Honey to the bees," Taxx said.

She looked affronted, and then she started to laugh uncontrollably. Taxx was far less amused.

"I promise I'm not laughing at you," she said between breaths.

"Sure…," Taxx said.

"No, it's just… You said he was a cute boy, and I thought you were fishing for a compliment," Izzy said.

"Why would I be fishing for a compliment?" he asked.

"I already told you that he looks like you," Izzy said.

Taxx didn't know what to say, so he looked at her silently for a second. It was no harder to gauge her emotions through her face with the glasses on, and he knew she was looking right at him. He was looking right back. He cleared his throat. Izzy seemed to come out of her trance, and her cheeks went red again. She hastily changed the subject.

"You want to watch Star Trail? I know it's old-school, but it's the best old-school," she offered.

"No thanks. I think I just need some time to work all of this out," he said.

"How about some air?" Izzy offered.

"That could be nice," Taxx said.

Izzy flipped off the TV. Then she took off her shoes and tossed them aside.

"What are you… doing?" Taxx asked.

"Being spontaneous! A friend told me to try it. Stay right there," Izzy said.

She left the room and returned quickly. Her bare feet echoed in the hall even when she was out of sight. When she returned, she was holding something up. She smiled and waved the strange key around in the air.

"What's that?" Taxx asked.

"A skeleton key. This one will take us to cotton candy," she said.

"A place made of cotton candy?" Taxx said.

Izzy only shrugged. Then she closed the door to the TV room and held up the key to the spot on the door where a keyhole should be. There was no actual keyhole.

"What happens when there is no keyhole?" Taxx asked.

"The door is not the thing that makes it magic. It's the key. A skeleton key will open any door if the basic shape is right. The magic does the rest," Izzy said.

The door began to change shape under the key, and even where there was no keyhole, it accepted the strange key. The staircase of teeth slipped into the invisible keyhole, and he could even hear tumblers working. Once the key was in, she gave it a hearty turn, and the door began to change shape. The orange tan wood transmogrified and changed color, even material, until it looked like the inside of a portable toilet. Izzy opened the door, and on the other side were white sands, humidity pouring out of the rounded door shape and filling the TV room.

"Whoa," Taxx said.

"I know! I can smell it too!" Izzy said.

Taxx could smell the cotton candy then. There was a sweetness in the breeze and quite a bit of sand. It made a small pile on the carpet at the door's threshold. Izzy stepped through, and Taxx was through the door moments later. She closed it behind them, pulling the key out of the door and causing the small view window to change from Occupied to Available.

"Did we just come through a portable toilet?" Taxx asked

"Seems like," Izzy said.

"What the hell kind of key is that?" He asked.

"I already said. A Skeleton Key. Normally they can only open one door, but this one is the Any Key. It can open any door you can think of from any other door. If the door is closed and unlocked," Izzy said

"You also say impossible things quite plainly," Taxx said.

"Why, thank you. You can choose next time, right after we walk down there. I smell cotton candy," she said.

"Sounds good. Really good, actually," Taxx said.

They walked for a long time in silence. It was nice just to be, Taxx thought, and the scenery was incredible. A beach with a long boardwalk lit up the night and wafted scents and sounds into the breeze. There was a pier a little way down the coast, and there were many people on it; he expected that **some** of them would notice the pair. No one appeared to, even when Izzy took a cotton candy right off the display and started to eat it.

"Where are we?" Taxx asked.

"Muumuu," Izzy replied.

She had a mouthful of cotton candy that turned her mouth blue immediately. Once she swallowed the much too large chunk, she answered him again.

"I don't know. It's not a freakin' GPS. It's a magic key. You think of where you want to go, and it brings you. I thought, beach and cotton candy, and so here we are. It sounds like Greece. I can understand some of it," she said.

"Interesting. I didn't know you could speak Greek," he said.

"Well. You don't know me," she said.

"Tell me about you, Isabel. Where are you from? How did you get mixed up with the house of What and Ever?" Taxx asked.

Isabel looked at him for a moment before she answered.

"Izzy. When I hear someone call me Isabel, I think of my nana. So, Izzy," Izzy said.

"Izzy then," Taxx said.

"It's The House of Wolf and Raven," she said.

"Got it," Taxx said.

He did not get it.

"Anyways, let's see, what is there to know about me? My name is Isabell Serena Carvalho. I am half Greek. I am from… everywhere. Well, not **actually**, but the place where I grew up had windows that could see the whole world," Izzy said.

"That sounds amazing. Is that some kind of magic thing?" Taxx asked.

"Location, really," she said.

"That's… cryptic," Taxx said.

Izzy only shrugged.

"Let's see. Oh! Lyra is my younger sister.," she said.

"Actual blood sister? **Wait**. *Younger?*" Taxx asked.

"Yes, I know. She seems older than she is," Izzy said.

"She has to be in her twenties," Taxx said.

"Lyra is 16. I'm almost 18," Izzy answered.

"Me too. I still can't believe she is your blood sister," Taxx said.

"The bloodiest?" Izzy responded.

He didn't have an answer for that, and she was kind enough not to ask for one.

"You guys pulled me out of the fire today," Taxx said.

"We try to protect people. I know he seems out there, but Avo is a prodigy turned genius. He can do things with his power that no one else can imagine. He wouldn't let anything happen to you," she said.

It got quiet after that. He was thinking about Magic and what all this would mean for him. It never even occurred to him that he could have become a werewolf or something. There was so much he didn't know. She wasn't offering up any conversation either, so they walked on in silence. It was not an uncomfortable silence for Taxx in any way. He thought Izzy was a good person to have around, and she seemed to know a lot. He was happy to walk quietly with her for a while, so they did. Before he knew it, they had walked in a massive circle out from the midway and back to the portable toilets.

"Ok. Your turn," Izzy said.

They reached the door they had used previously and found it to be in use. Or at least the flag on the door said so.

"Should we still?" Taxx asked.

"Feels rude, right?" Izzy said.

They moved to the next portable toilet, and though it was

unoccupied, it lacked a physical door of any kind. Only the empty frame remained and the bathroom beyond.

"This will work. It's time for a scenery change. Think of where you want to go and then put the key in," Izzy said.

"There is no door here, so where do I put it?" Taxx asked.

"It's. Magic," she said.

Izzy handed him the key, and Taxx was surprised to see how normal it was. He expected it to be hewn of gold with jewels and magical things, but it was made like a regular key. He had the same kind for his apartment, except this one had a few more sets of teeth on it. It was even the same off silver color, and there was a brand name across the broadest part. He would ask about it, but he didn't want to seem blown away by magic again. Instead, he took the key out and pretended to put it into a door. There was a slight resistance at first, and he gasped. When he heard Izzy quietly giggling behind him, he rolled his eyes and pressed the key harder. The key went in easily, into thin air, he could feel each tumbler as it pushed further in and stopped against something solid, but there was nothing there. He turned the key, and the space between the toilet and the door became a completely different place. It was green and alive. There was some thick forest there, the air was much cooler, and the moon hung low in the sky.

"You just did magic, new boy. The people rejoiced," Izzy said.

"Hooray!" Taxx said.

The two of them laughed as they walked through together. Izzy stopped and looked around, then punched Taxx right in the shoulder.

"Huh?" he said.

"Do you know where you brought us?" Izzy said.

He wasn't sure. When he put the key into the door, he thought he wanted to go to Myrtle Beach. He and May used to go there a few times in the summer, and it was one of the only places he felt normal. Sixx would often come when they were kids. Then he couldn't stop thinking about his cousin.

"What does it mean if I've never been here before?" Taxx asked.

She laughed and shook her head, pointing at him with the paper cone that once held cotton candy.

"This is the quarry around High Table," she said.

He still looked lost.

"That's the name of the mountain under the House. Haven't you ever seen the high table from town?" Izzy asked.

"Offrey tried to bring me there this morning, but we never made it," Taxx said.

"Cause she tried to murder you?" Izzy asked.

Taxx could only stare at her. She held up both hands and the key, then she flailed them wildly. Taxx took a step back but he was smiling again.

"I'm sorry. Wait, no, I didn't mean that," Izzy said.

"She did. I see you know her too," Taxx said.

They both laughed. Taxx reached out and took the key, and the gateway closed, leaving a door-shaped arrangement of branches.

"That's impressive, door-to-tree teleportation. I have never seen that one before. Well done," Izzy said.

"Thanks, I guess," Taxx said.

He turned to hand her the key, and she was not there. Instead, she seemed to have run off into the trees, and he took off after her, stopping short again. It was not a tree this time. On the other side of the pines was a clear view of a deep quarry. You could see out for miles in almost every direction and down hundreds of feet into the quarry. Izzy walked to the edge and took a deep breath before she let out a scream that was so loud it echoed throughout the quarry dozens of times.

"Whoa!" he said.

In a grand motion, she stood aside and indicated that he should step up himself. He even bowed as he stepped up, looking out over the quarry, and then he took a very deep breath. Shortly after, a loud shout came, only it wasn't from his mouth, and Taxx and Izzy looked at each other abruptly.

"Did you?" he said

"Hear that? Yes, I did," She answered.

They both moved and searched the quarry for the sound source, and it didn't take them long to find it. A man was running in the quarry and screaming his head off. The thing he was screaming about seemed to be related to the two trucks behind him overflowing with people. The trucks circled the man on foot, cutting in front of him and revving up behind him. When one of the trucks finally hit him, it sent him sailing to the ground. His body landed so hard that Taxx wasn't sure he would get up. The trucks stopped, and just short of twelve men were now standing around the single body in the dirt.

"We have to help him," They both said in unison.

"I don't have my phone, you?" Taxx said.

"You're what? Oh yeah, no, that's ok. We can take the key," Izzy said

"We need to go now!" Taxx said.

"Ahh, you're right, come on!" She shouted

They nodded at each other, and Taxx started in one direction and she in the other. She stopped and looked at him like he had suddenly grown a second head.

"What the hell are you doing? There are a bunch of those guys. Other or not, you could get killed. We need to go back and get help," she said.

"Why don't you just use your magic?" Taxx asked.

"Humans don't respond well to it. Sometimes they really hurt themselves... to death," Izzy said.

"What the heck…" he started.

"WE DON'T HAVE TIME FOR THIS!" Izzy shouted.

It made sense what she was saying, and he knew that in his logical mind, but Taxx was not much for logic at times. Once he got on a thread, he just couldn't let it go, and that man needed his help, so he was going to give it to him.

"You go get help. I will make sure he is still alive when help gets here. Just trust me, I'll be ok. Get help, and I'll-" he said.

"Good idea!" she said.

Then Izzy took off.

"Oh shit, oh shit, I'm having one of my things," Izzy shouted.

She came running back suddenly, waving her hands frantically and dancing around like she had to pee.

"Uh?" Taxx asked.

Izzy looked at him, and instead of speaking, she just started to chant, a low and fast language that he could not understand at first. It sounded like she was chattering her teeth, but each sound was a separate word. The goggled shades she wore around her eyes started to leak green fire from every seam. Taxx couldn't be more confused, he opened his mouth to speak, but she put her hand on his mouth before he could.

"You must follow the dawn," Izzy said.

"What?" Taxx mumbled.

"Follow the dawn or hang in the night," Izzy said.

The fire went away from her eyes, and the two stood quietly between the trees with her hand on his mouth still.

"I'm sorry, that was probably weird," she said.

"Mhmm," Taxx said.

"I'm a seer. I don't have control over what I see or when. They come like migraines when I'm awake," Izzy said.

"Mmhm," said Taxx.

"Oh poops," Izzy said.

She took her hand off Taxx's mouth.

"Maybe you should-" Taxx started.

"OH!" she shouted, interrupting him.

Then without another word, Izzy took off running again.

Taxx was so surprised about it that when she ran off in the middle of his sentence, he just stood there for a moment before he started running himself. He was running a full sprint halfway down the steep grade of the quarry wall, and somehow, he was able to keep his footing. Maybe it was because he wasn't thinking about his feet, the ground, or the air on his face. The only thing he could think about was the metal object. He saw it when he started to run, catching the moonlight just so in the hands of one of those men, and he didn't have to think twice to know what it was. A gun. He ran as fast as he could push himself, focused only on that glittering thing, and before he knew it, he was on top of the man holding it. Even when Taxx was right on top of him, the man did not flinch. His eyes were on Taxx the whole time, and he didn't shrink back even a bit. He even spoke as calmly as a greeting.

"Where did you-" the man said.

Taxx's body couldn't have stopped if he wanted it to, so it slammed into the man and his rifle, sending him and the gun tumbling away from the person on the ground. Taxx wheeled on the other men and put up his fist, he didn't know how intimidating he thought he was going to look, but he didn't expect them to start laughing at him. A few of them shook their heads in disbelief.

"What the hell is this supposed to be?" One of them asked.

One of them sniffed the air, and there was meaning there. Many of the others were looking at him as if waiting for a verdict. The Sniffer.

"I don't know what I smell, my brothers... but it smells... strange," Sniffer whispered.

"Is that a... human?" Another one said.

"No... not quite. He smells like a human, but something else too," Sniffer said.

"Just what the hell is it?" One of them said.

"Don't matter none if it's strange that means unique, and that means valuable. We will take him too. Master'll take 'em both," Sniffer said.

They did not run as he hoped they would, but there were many of them, and they were much larger up close than they were from up on the ridge where this seemed like a good idea. They kept their distance but mainly formed a circle around Taxx and the body on the ground. The one he shoved had stood up when Taxx wasn't looking but now made his way through the ring, and they stood aside from him. He was imposingly tall and thick with muscles; this one was the leader.

"Yes, this appears to be a blessing, brothers. Whatever this little morsel may be, Serrano is right. We must collect him for the Master," he said.

He picked up the shiny rifle-like object Taxx saw from the ridge, but it was not a rifle. It was an actual sword glowing in the night like a nightmare, a massive hunk of metal longer than his arm. It had a fat belly like a pelican's beak, but it was not a scimitar. It was more like a massive meat cleaver as thick as a butcher block and etched with age. The edge was wickedly sharp, and the man somehow easily held it in one hand. He was a massive human, standing well over 7 feet tall, but there was no way, even at that size. Something was very wrong. He couldn't help but think that he had made a mistake with this one. He couldn't help the slight tremble that went down his spine when they all went silent, and he felt their eyes on him. He knew that wispy feeling in the middle of his stomach. He felt it right before Craw nailed him to the wall. It meant he was about to die.

"Take them," The Leader said.

Taxx was circling the person on the ground and trying to watch them all as best as possible, but he couldn't tell who it was. There was so much blood on the face and clothing. Taxx was starting to feel dizzy from the circling, scared and thinking that Izzy had a better idea than his. His heart was beating so loud in his ears he couldn't even hear the guy on the ground talking to him until he reached up and grabbed Taxx's shirt to get his attention. Taxx looked down at the young man smiling up at him with blood caked on his face. When the man on the ground started to stir, the men circling them seemed less eager to get close to him. Some even took a step back once he began to stand again. He shouldn't have been able to do that, but then again,

Taxx had seen a lot of weird shit tonight. That didn't explain why so many people should be worried about them.

"You have a light?" he said.

"No, I don't. Wait, Sixx!?" Taxx shouted.

He was circling him still, but he got a good look this time. He could see the gold cuffs in his dreads sparkling like the smile on his bloody face. Sixx was still down and holding Taxx's shirt like a safety strap.

"That's too bad. I was 'bout to do something wild, boy! Hold up, let me see what I got," Sixx said.

He held up a stick with a long string hanging out of it. If Taxx didn't know any better, he would have thought it was a stick of dynamite, but there was no way, right?

"What is that?" Taxx asked.

"Oh, this here is a stick of, watcha call it? Trinitrotoluene," Sixx said.

"Trini?…" Taxx asked.

"Trinit-," Sixx started.

"Trinitrotoluene?" Taxx said.

"Good job, Taxxy!" Sixx said.

"Taxxy?" Taxx asked.

"Trying it on. Can't you see we are in danger right now? I'm trying to save us, Cuh. Relax and help me find a light," he said.

"Save us? What do you mean, save us?" Taxx asked.

"I kept these stank ass monsters off you, Taxx, and now you second guessin-" Sixx started.

He was interrupted by the leader, who Taxx could see clearly now that he caught his breath, and sure enough, he was the Gray-eyed stranger from earlier, and sniffer was the second guy; it was like a weirdo reunion.

"Hate to interrupt you, but we are on the clock. Do you think we might carry on here?" Gray eyes asked.

"Hey! I am conversing with my cousin right now. Take a 5, baby," Sixx said.

"Wait… Trinitrotoluene is TNT!" Taxx said.

"Good job again! Oh wait, this is only a blasting cap. This isn't TNT at all," he said.

He sounded disappointed.

"No offense, but I'm a little busy now," Taxx said.

Sixx struggled to his feet and sighed when he was up, he was a little taller than Taxx but not much, and he seemed a bit older. He kept patting his jacket and coughing even as the men started to close in on them. Some of them had bare hands, and others held knives, he saw a bat too, but only the Grey eyes had anything as ridiculous as that pelican beak sword. He did not move. He only watched them with a smile on his face. Taxx suddenly had a very urgent thought concerning the person he was trying to protect… He was sure he heard him say the words blasting cap, he thought. He was sure of it. Blasting caps were also explosives. He didn't take his eyes off the men, but he spoke over his shoulder.

"Hey, wait, what was that about a-?" Taxx said.

"Hoo! There we go. *This one* is **definitely** TNT," Sixx said.

A green spark bloomed on the end of a wick like a dandelion, and it started to burn down at the same speed that Taxx felt his heart sinking into his feet.

"Listen here, if y'all want to kill **my** black ass, you gonna need to COME. GET. IT! You heard me!?" Sixx said.

He waved the dynamite over his head and smiled with such a feverish madness that Taxx felt his bottom lip quiver, and then

Sixx screamed in a high-pitched voice.

"Who is dying' with daddy tonight?!"

The crackling hiss of a burning wick held the attention of all ten men standing in the quarry. No one paid more attention than Taxx. He could only stare with his mouth agape as the person he had come down to rescue twirled the lit stick of dynamite around like a menacing ribbon dance.

"Come on, move, you rotten bastards!" Sixx said.

Every time he waved the stick, someone would skitter away and back from him accordingly, except for the leader. He was the one that Sixx was yelling at the most now, swiping the stick of dynamite at him like a bullwhip. The wick was long but not long enough for Taxx. There was less than half left. The leader didn't seem to notice. He was staring at Sixx with calm, level eyes, grey as a somber morning and striking against the dark black sclera behind them. These were not the eyes of a man, perhaps, but in Taxx's assessment, this one seemed to be the thinker of the group, so maybe they could appeal to him to think logically. They at least had backup coming. He thought, as long as they could keep them from frenzying because they were outnumbered. Taxx did not understand why he was so calm right now, but he was acutely aware that his heart was pretty damned quiet for someone in the blast radius for a lit stick of dynamite. He didn't have time to think about it because he knew somewhere inside of him that he had to mitigate the danger they were facing right now. He knew he had to reason with the leader, use the explosive as leverage and keep them from getting too upset and making any emotional moves. If he could get them to stall for just a few minutes, they might get to walk away from here AND hopefully not get blown up. Taxx sidled up to Sixx and started speaking in a low voice.

"I love where your head is with this whole bluff, but I don't think the tall one is buying it, so let's stay calm and try to reason with..." Taxx said.

"ANY muh'fucka even looks our way with some side-eye type shit and KA-BOOM bitches. This is **not** a bluff!" Sixx interrupted.

"Seriously?" Taxx said.

"That's right; I'm **serious**! I will straight up KILL every damn one of us! I can NOT be reasoned with!" Sixx shouted.

Sixx looked over at Taxx and gave such a wink that he was sure he could hear the sound of his lids snapping closed like a guillotine over the burning wick. Sixx then mouthed something along the lines of 'I got this' and turned back to the group of men, still waving the explosive.

"You, the bold but stupid one, tell me your name. I must know," The leader said.

"What the hell you wanna know my name for?" Sixx asked.

The Leader did not look amused or agitated, his face was collected, but there was an emptiness to it that hung lifeless against the sharpness of those gray eyes.

"It is of no importance. You have amused me, and I would honor your death by remembering your name, but you may remember mine. I am sometimes called Jackdaw by my Master; when you are dead, take my name to the underworld," Jackdaw said.

Jackdaw bowed at the hip.

The other men visibly cooled when he spoke, his voice was calm but commanding, and it seemed to clear the haze. There was only the sound of the wick then. Even Sixx had stopped and was now watching the man much more seriously. Sixx mimicked Jackdaw's body language mockingly, but where the man held a sword, Sixx had a stick of lit dynamite that he held between his teeth like a cigar.

"Well ...since you want to do this like the first day of school and shit, let us do it. My name is Saturday Romaine St. Martin, and I'm the son of Death," Sixx said.

He pulled the explosive from his mouth and spat a little at Jackdaw, pointing the dynamite at him like a baton.

"I will remember you, Mr. St. Martin," Jackdaw said.

"Did you say somethin' bitc- Oh shit!" Sixx said.

Jackdaw only seemed to flinch, but he threw his sword out of nowhere with such force and accuracy that it sailed through the air like a flying disk. The blade slammed into Sixx's chest and took him off his feet before it passed through him ultimately and dropped him hard to the ground in two pieces. The insides of his body fell to the quarry floor in wet heaps. A soft haze of steam came from them as they started to cool in the night air. Taxx did not want to look, he did not want to see this, but he could not look away for a moment. He wasn't even sure when he began to scream.

One of them dove on the dynamite and held a knife to the wick at the base, and just like that, it was tossed uselessly aside and left to burn out.

"Hell of a shot, Brother," Serrano said.

Serrano clapped him on the shoulder, but Jackdaw seemed to be the only one decent enough not to look proud of himself, Taxx could only stare at him, and at that exact moment, the group turned to look his way. They seemed to have forgotten he was there.

"Tell me I get to take this one?" Serrano said.

"Alive?" Jackdaw asked.

"Fine. How about intact?" Serrano asked.

Jackdaw smiled and slowly shook his head, and the rest of the group descended on Taxx like a pack of wolves, attacking from all sides. They were on him, grabbing him from all angles, slashing with impossibly sharp fingers, and kicking him hard to the ground. They battered him with fists and boots, and Taxx was sure he saw a weapon like a pipe or a bat and even more positive when it struck him in the head and neck a few times. He closed his eyes against the impact, but it felt like a soft slap instead of what he expected when it came. Oh, it hurt, but the effect didn't feel right. Where pain should have been, there was only pressure. Even the bat which crushed across his cheekbone felt more like a punch than a bat to the face. There was a strange sort of understanding coming over him as he lay on the ground of the quarry, his body curled up defensively now as he was kicked and punched repeatedly. The blows seemed to come slower and much more predictably. Some were even slow enough that he thought he could avoid them, and after some quick adjustments, he did exactly that.

He couldn't dodge them all, but it seemed to rob his attackers of their confidence and boost his own each time he did. He could see them before they came. No, that wasn't true. It was not like seeing with his eyes. It was like knowing where your limbs are even when you aren't looking at them. He was aware of the attack in his periphery even when he wasn't looking. He could see it in his mind, like a shadow crossing behind clouds. Not enough to tell him what it was, but just enough to make him aware of it, he couldn't explain it, but every second he spent focusing on that feeling seemed to make him feel faster. Serrano took a misstep and slightly lost his footing, and the bat lolled ineffectively to the ground for just a moment. Taxx broke free of the pack at that same moment and rushed him, toppling him with a wild shoulder.

Taxx stumbled over Serrano and lashed out at Jackdaw, clamping down on his wrist with as much force as he could gather. To his surprise, the wrist under his hand crumpled easily until it hung limp. Taxx even felt some small bones pop like dry pasta under his palm. He didn't care. He wanted revenge. He didn't know why he was so angry, but seeing his cousin murdered seemed to drive him to action. Taxx's other hand struck Jackdaw across the face and sent his head whipping to the right; he reared back to punch him again. Before he could, his arm was taken by another man who struck Taxx in the face at the same time. Serrano held his arm and attempted to punch him again, but Taxx was ready and batted him away with a well-placed punch of his own. Serrano crumbled.

Whoever these people were, his counterattack seemed to have broken their resolve, and they were huddled around Jackdaw, a few running back toward their trucks. Taxx ran over to what was left of Sixx's body, and he silently swore, glancing over at the group. They were staring at him with a mix of fear and confusion like he was some monster. He found himself enjoying the looks on their faces. The removal of their strength in numbers seemed to have cooled their boldness. They at least seemed to be as intelligent as any other animals, though they did not approach him or Sixx's body. They only stared wide-eyed, and that suited him just fine.

"I'm so sorry. I shouldn't have come down here... this is all my fault," Taxx whispered.

He couldn't let go of the body yet. He didn't know why, but he could never leave him here like this. There was no way he would let them have their way with the body. A little voice inside his mind was telling him not to, not his conscious. No, this was not a thought that belonged to him. It was something else. *Stay right where you are. We are coming.* Though it wasn't words he heard, the voice was just an idea he knew came from somewhere else. It was Izzy. He didn't know how he knew it, but he knew it, and somehow it made him feel better.

"Just a little while longer, Saturday, they are coming. I'm so sorry I let you die. I am so sorry I didn't try and save you," he said again.

He felt compelled to say something every time he looked down at Sixx's face, but these tiny round sunglasses on Sixx's nose hid his eyes, so Taxx didn't know if they were closed or open. He reached out and lifted the glasses to find that his eyes were open, and Sixx was looking right at him. His right eye was so pale green that it almost disappeared into the white, and his other eye was brown like Taxx's.

"That was some pretty shit you said. For real, I couldn't say nothin' cause I was having some feelings about all that. While you are a sweetheart, don't nobody call me Saturday but my momma. Now hand me my legs, please," Sixx said.

Sixx was smirking at him. Taxx gasped and backed away a few steps. He saw him get perforated, and there was blood all over the ground and everything. But… there wasn't any blood. He looked all around the body, but he didn't see very much blood at all. There were some splatters, but nowhere near the amount, there should have been.

"...How?" Taxx asked.

"Whatchu mean? You pick them up and bring 'em here," Sixx said.

"You know what I mean! Your intestines are on the ground, man, literally on the ground. How are you alive?" Taxx asked.

"Taxxy... can we finish this later? This is wildly uncomfortable," Sixx said.

"Oh wow, yes, I'm so sorry," Taxx said.

Then Taxx helped him to his feet, literally. He picked up the disembodied legs and carried them over to the torso half. Before Taxx even reached it, the lower half leaped out of his hands like a hot potato. The pair of legs flipped, flopped, and slopped until they were in place all their own, and just like a building block, Sixx put himself back together. He was standing moments later, adjusting his blazer and poking at the tattered edges with disdain. Taxx was on the verge of shock.

"W...why can you do that?" Taxx asked.

Sixx smiled at him. Grinned more like. Then he started to laugh and cackle, and his green eye danced with glee and electricity that made Taxx want to run away. Sixx had always been a handful, but right this second, he looked dangerous. Sixx flipped his dreads out his face and winked at his cousin with a wild flourish, then said something completely outrageous as casually as he could.

"That's easy. I'm the son of Death," Sixx said.

Chapter | Ten

"Don't look so shocked. For damn sure ain't no hopped-up machete gonna put my pretty black ass in the ground," Sixx said.

"The son of Death? Like the Grim Reaper? The Grim Reaper has a kid?" Taxx asked.

Taxx's voice was becoming higher and higher as he spoke, and each time he did, he went up an octave. Sixx raised an eyebrow until they were both looking at each other foolishly.

"Yes. Yes. And to answer your last question, yes. A lot of them last I heard," Sixx said.

"Wait… wait. I have so many questions," Taxx said.

"That's gonna have to wait. This is prolly gonna be an issue for us in the immediate," Sixx said.

"You have injured this vessel. That is uncommon. I will

grant you a quick death for that excitement," Jackdaw said.

Sixx and Taxx turned to face Jackdaw and the other men, some of whom were still reacting to what they had just seen and screaming curses and prayers. Jackdaw did not seem to be distracted by his damaged hand. He simply tore his hand off his own body like a heel of bread. He tossed the twisted mass aside, never moving his eyes from Sixx. Jackdaw held up the gory end of his arm to the young men, dripping viscera to the ground in alarming amounts. Then, the bleeding stopped in moments, and long oil black shapes began to force themselves out of the end of the stump where his hand had once been.

"This will take some time to heal as my regenerative abilities are not as impressive as the boisterous one," Jackdaw said.

"Oh, you 'bout to see so many more impressive things," Sixx said.

"Smart one," Jackdaw said.

"You think he means me?" Taxx said.

"I get it. I don't like that shit, but I get it," Sixx said.

"Indeed. May I impart to you a clairvoyance?" Jackdaw asked.

"I don't give a damn what you do," Taxx said.

He tried to sound as angry and desperate as he could. The longer he kept this monster talking, the closer the backup was. All he had to do was keep him distracted.

"I will tell you who is responsible for your death. You see, it is the fault of your loudmouth friend who was too busy listening to me and not watching your back," Jackdaw said

"Oh, Shit!" Sixx said

Taxx became aware of the danger too late, and he gasped. It seemed that he was not the only one who was stalling for time and the cool logic in Jackdaw's eyes only made it worse. He had been outsmarted. Without a sound, Serrano had slipped up behind him. Taxx could feel him like a shadow on the edge of his vision and the long-curved knife coming toward his neck. It would all be over faster than he could imagine, just like the last time he died. Except the pain never came.

There was a sound like a roar, screaming or gushing blood, he couldn't tell, but it was loud and sudden and over as quickly as he came. He could still hear it echoing off the quarry walls, and because of that, he could be sure that he was not dead. Hearing was the first sense that failed when you were about to die. Also, there was no knife ripping through his neck. Taxx turned around slowly toward Serrano but only found Sixx in his place, wearing the biggest grin that Taxx had ever seen. Sixx's right hand was missing its flesh. It had been exposed to the bone from tip to wrist and was sizzling like a cartoon gun barrel. There was pale green smoke still billowing from his fingertips. When he noticed Taxx staring at his bony appendage, he gave him a wink and started to put the skin back on like a winter glove.

"What am I looking at?" Taxx asked.

"Hooo! Watch out for that hand, Bo! Taxx, did you see that? I slapped his ass into next week. Tell me you did. I bet he didn't think that was gonna happen to him today," Sixx said.

"Sixx. What did you just do?" Taxx asked.

Even now that the hand was repaired, he couldn't unsee the moving bones and the incredible magical energy they radiated.

"Whooped his ass," Sixx said.

Sixx indicated with his head, and Taxx followed until he finally found what he was looking for. Serrano had been struck and moved almost twenty feet away to be planted headfirst into the quarry wall like a dart. Sixx laughed so heartily that even Taxx had to smile. There was something infectious about the boisterous laughter of this man even when he did something impossible.

"What did you just do?" Taxx asked.

"Come on, Taxxy, I'm giving you solid gold over here, and what are you lookin' at? That dude?" Sixx said.

He thrust a hand toward Jackdaw, still watching them with calm eyes.

"That dude sucks. I don't even remember his name, Jago? Sounds French," Sixx said.

"I'm pretty sure he said, Jackdaw, which sounds English. Like England English… wait... why the hell am I talking about this? Tell me how you did that? What the hell are you?" Taxx asked.

Sixx had been standing so close to Taxx that what happened next seemed impossible. It all happened in the blink of an eye, faster than Taxx's brain could follow. Before he became aware of the shadow falling over his face, the monster had closed the gap between them silently and faster than anything Taxx had ever seen in his life. On the other hand, Sixx had both eyes firmly on the monster. Unfortunately, his mouth had been opened to speak, but the sound never got out. Jackdaw smashed his fist into Sixx's lower jaw, and it clamped his teeth closed on his tongue like a scissor. A gush of blood forced its way between Sixx's lips before his head snapped back and his body left the ground, and the force of the uppercut lifted him into the air.

Sixx's body gained altitude and speed and was flung more than a dozen feet, flipping end over end, eventually settling to the ground with explosive upheaval. Sand exploded in a cloud, and in that same instant, there was a loud burst of sound, like a roar or a scream. It rumbled in Taxx's chest like a bomb had gone off, and the air pressure changed so dramatically that it ripped his legs out from under him, and he lost his balance. Taxx's ears were ringing so hard that he could barely keep his thoughts together, and he had to shield his eyes from a massive cloud of steam that boiled up all around Jackdaw's hulking mass. Sixx was grounded, and Taxx was barely standing, holding both hands to his ears to keep himself from going deaf. He was sure he would never hear again. Tee steam started to clear up, and Jackdaw flexed his arms and shook the long cleaver-like blade toward Taxx.

"Enough. Tell me your name, or you shall die without honor," Jackdaw said.

Taxx couldn't find his voice just then. He just stood there staring at the man in front of him who could move faster than the speed of sound. None of this was making sense to him. This was a real monster who could destroy him with the blink of an eye, and Jackdaw's eyes promised to do just that.

"Oh, a souvenir," Jackdaw said.

The monster knelt and gingerly lifted the severed tip of Sixx's tongue between his fingers. He peered at the little pink hunk of flesh for a moment before something terrible happened. Somehow Taxx knew that he would eat it before he took the bite. He could not have imagined that he would take that bite with a beak. A large beak, oil black and shiny, came tearing through the bridge of Jackdaw's nose and chin, devouring the tongue tip in a single bite. The breakthrough left a ragged edge and caused his face to sag like an old awning clinging to the bones of his skull.

"This you will not understand, but I must tell you that I take no pleasure in the eating of flesh. I do it purely for the sense of horror it paints on your human-like faces. So when I look into your face and see nothing, you take from me one of the few joys I have in this wretched life," Jackdaw Cawed.

Jackdaw had spoken but not in any way that could be considered a human language. Where words should have been, there was a guttural birdsong. It sounded like a crow and the low growl of a large animal all at once. As he sang, Jackdaw's jagged black beak whipped and danced, and he flicked his neck quickly, giving a loud caw that ended in staccato. All that sound entered Taxx's head and passed through the wall that separated him from his memories. When it came back, it was instantly translated so efficiently that the bird monster might as well have been speaking English. Again, he thought, something extraordinary and terrifying was happening to him, and he wasn't as surprised as he should have been. Worse than that, no matter how much he wanted to be afraid of all the unimaginable things he was seeing, he couldn't feel even a single drop of fear. He felt some fear, or perhaps it was just a hyper-awareness of the area around him that became clearer with each passing moment. He thought maybe the electricity that was humming along every nerve ending within him, and somehow, somewhere deep down, there was something even more. It was calling to him like a song.

"You will show me fear," Jackdaw Cawed.

Nothing was an accident. Taxx didn't know why he thought that phrase, but it lingered in his mind. He could hear the music again, but it was not just in his mind this time. He swore he could hear it in his ears, and although it wasn't what most would call music in the traditional sense, it was beautiful to Taxx. It sounded like the uneven drumbeats of rain falling through a canopy and dripping down to the dense leaves on the floor or the slow rush of a wild burning fire as it gobbled up anything in its path. It felt like falling ice shattering as it crashed to the earth. Animals baying for the moon's attention, to greet the morning, and simply to feel the joy of screaming all at once. Somehow all of that came together inside of him in that secret place and became painfully beautiful music. Music that somehow Taxx knew that he could sing, he could feel it thumping along in his chest and then behind his tongue as though the song were crawling its way out of his body, and when he opened his mouth, the song leaped out of him.

"STOP!" Taxx sang.

Jackdaw froze in place.

Taxx could feel that single word burning inside his chest, hear it echoing in his ears in every language he had ever known, and hundreds he could barely make out. The song was heavy with magic, and it dipped and iced and rolled over him like cool summer air on wet skin, making him shiver and shake as it washed over and through him like a wave.

"Speak again. Let me hear it once more," Jackdaw cawed.

He did not know how to start or stop speaking, but everything Jackdaw said was still coming through clearly and easily. It was as natural as hearing the wind. Jackdaw cooed happily from his jagged black beak and even hopped backward in joy. His once cold empty eyes were suddenly full of life and energy. When Taxx did not speak immediately, however, the man with the beak shook his head angrily for a moment but cooled, and after looking pensive for a moment, he began to sing again.

"You have blessed me with the old tongue. For this, I will give you a gift," Jackdaw cawed.

He began to open and close his beak, but he made no sound

but a terrible gasping of air, and in moments a wad of unknown wet matter came rolling up and out of that beak. Jackdaw sifted through the pile of damp flesh and whatever else could have been until he found what he was after. He produced a small pink mound that he tossed to Taxx. It was a reflex to extend his palm to catch it even if he did not want to, especially when he realized that the little blob was the tip of Sixx's tongue. He caught it and quietly slipped it into his pocket.

"What happens now?" Taxx asked.

"Now. You die," Jackdaw cawed.

Taxx once again became aware of him a moment too late and a surprisingly powerful set of arms enclosed around Taxx's torso, and though he tried to fight back, he could do nothing. Serrano had a grip like a stone statue around his waist and neck. The hold was so tight that if Taxx was not perfectly still, he could not breathe properly. Once Taxx went still, Serrano peeked over the young man's shoulder, and they were face to face. Serrano's face was slightly concave in a pit where his nose had once been, like a cartoon character, but the joke ended in the many places where the face was bloody and torn. There was no gore to be seen. There were no bones and muscles to be found, only light-colored scales and a pair of slitted eyes through that false human face. A massive snake's head with a long scaly hood draped around it like a cloak in its place. Serrano pulled his captured arms behind his body so that Taxx had no choice but to get up on his toes. There was no way he could move or dodge. Serrano's grip felt like being encased in iron. Taxx struggled against it just the same, but there was simply no escape, he had been caught, and Jackdaw was coming at him again. He did not use his supernatural speed. He stalked toward Taxx at an average rate holding the cleaver used to split Sixx in half, still bloody along its edge.

"You do not look afraid, but I will not allow you to take my joy from this," Jackdaw cawed.

"I've had a long day," Taxx said.

"Sarcasm is my least favorite human trait. I will cut it out of you," Jackdaw cawed.

"Somehow, I don't think you can," Taxx began.

His words were stopped when the cleaver caught him where the shoulder met the neck and easily entered his body, he couldn't hear his bones breaking, but he felt the pressure of the separation. The violence unfolding on his shoulder made him think of how different it was to be cut than it was to be shot for some reason, and Taxx could not help but think that he would rather be shot. Unsurprisingly they were both terrible, he thought, but being shot was over much sooner, and there was far less blood. The warmth spilled down his back and the side of his torso like shower water. He went slack, and there was a strange sense of relief when the pressure under the blade finally gave way, and he felt it pass through him completely. He was suddenly missing the weight of his left arm. The edge was so sharp that he didn't feel the limb as it was removed, just a distant and gentle release like plucking a grape from the vine. Taxx stared at his disembodied limb and where he was sure he would feel shocked or awe but what he felt was very strange. It hurt incredibly, so the pain made the muscles in his chest spasm and caused more blood to spill from the wound where his shoulder should have been but was very much not. Every time he looked at the arm, he had to close his eyes, but his captor's iron grip was surprisingly helpful for shouldering the pain. He leaned into Serrano and his grip. He gritted his teeth and breathed heavily, but Taxx did not make a sound; he would not because there was something more important than the white-hot fire of pain. He simply could not give Jackdaw the satisfaction, and watching him start to lose his cool was seemingly worth it for him. He had to question the kind of person that he was again.

But not deeply.

"YOU ARE SUPPOSED TO SCREAM!" Jackdaw cawed.

His birdsong was harsh and ragged this time, full of blood and echoing off the quarry walls. It washed over Taxx so hard he blinked. Jackdaw lost his composure and was basically stomping his feet and swinging his cleaver around like a mad man in his rage. He even splattered Taxx with some of his own gore. The weight of his blood hitting him made him want to slip away, but something was amusing about terrorizing this monster. Perhaps Lyra was more correct than he had previously allowed when she said that he was the sort to fight and that that sort was foolish. This wasn't very smart, but he simply could not stop.

"I'm sorry. I don't want to die again, but for some reason. Making this as shitty as possible for you feels like a better use of my time," he said.

He laughed.

"How F'ed up is that?" Taxx said.

Taxx was speaking in plain English, but there was some of that song behind it, in its periphery, maybe so that he could be sure this bastard could understand. Perhaps he lost too much blood to speak like that anymore, the contrarian that lived inside us all whispered to his mind. Maybe he was already dead again. Jackdaw cackled as only a bird could, a musical horror that shook out of his beak with a steady and patronizing mimicry of the all too human tone of mockery. The tip cleaver touched Taxx's chin and smeared blood on his chin when he forced Taxx's faceup to look right at Jackdaws. Taxx didn't have the energy to fight back, so he was nose to beak with the monster.

"You are not brave nor bold, and no one will come and save you. You will accomplish nothing. You are simple, and you will soon be dead," Jackdaw cawed.

"But you forgot the one thing," Taxx forced out.

His voice was hoarse, and he couldn't control the volume because he was in such pain, but he forced himself to look Jackdaw squarely in the eyes.

"Which is?" The monster cawed.

"At least I'm not… as… ugly as you are," Taxx said.

Jackdaw cackled. Then he nodded, and on command, someone punched Taxx in the chin so hard he was sure it would be dislocated. In truth, his silence had very little to do with robbing the beaked monster of his amusement anymore. He had become distracted by a little voice inside of him that was so insistent and strong that he could feel it in his bones. It was just a mild diversion at first, but now it was all he could think about, like an idea he could only remember but not wrap his mind around. For reasons he could not explain at that moment, he understood that this little voice was necessary, that he needed to find it more than he needed to stand.

More than he needed his arm. More than he needed to breathe, he didn't even notice any of the other men approaching. Taxx had all but forgotten that there were more of them. The punch was meant to serve as a timely reminder, but he didn't even bother to respond to it. None of it mattered if he was going to die anyway. He just had to keep chasing that voice, if he could only hear it, it was on the edge of his consciousness, and he could almost make it out.

"Go and bring the truck," Jackdaw said.

Serrano let go of him immediately and took off, and although Taxx was on his feet, he slipped down to his knees and ultimately down on his face with no resistance. He was still alive, as far as he could tell anyway, he could still hear, and his body was still wracked with pain so intense that it was easier to stay away. His body felt light on the earth of that quarry. Even as he was slowly starting to fade from consciousness, he felt better than he could remember ever feeling in his life. Mainly because the voice in his head finally said the thing he had wanted to hear, and it was such a relief that he chuckled a little. Jackdaw lifted his head and looked into his eyes, canting his head like a real bird. If Taxx could have mustered another laugh, he would have.

"Perhaps not so human after all? He still lives. The rest of you go and bring the other boy, and do NOT let him escape again," Jackdaw said.

There was no answer.

"What in hellfire are you doing now, you idiots?" Jackdaw cawed.

Jackdaw dropped Taxx to the ground and turned to find the rest of his men missing and in their place a young woman in a red peacoat and boots. She was holding what looked like a single playing card in her hand.

"Who-" Jackdaw started.

"My name is Nic White. I'm a Warden, and I'm here for those two," Nic said.

"Warden… where are my people?" Jackdaw cawed.

"According to the Rules of Order, they will be taken into

custody," Nic said.

She was looking past him at the boy, and Jackdaw stood up straight to obstruct her view of him. The monster visibly adjusted the cleaver in his hands as if he were checking its weight. Nic only smiled at him, her hands still in the pockets of her coat.

"What are these objects?" Jackdaw cawed.

More of the cards had been scattered on the ground between Jackdaw and the Warden, but the monster did not look away long enough to count them.

"Tell me what magic these objects possess, and I will favor you with a painless death," Jackdaw said.

"Honestly, the list goes on, but they are tiny jail cells right now. Tell me what you would do with these guys, and I'll pretend you didn't just threaten my life. How about that?" Nic asked

Jackdaw cackled.

"Come on, Big Bird, it was worth a shot, right? Any chance you want to turn yourself in?" Nic asked.

Jackdaw moved suddenly and with tremendous speed, simply appearing in front of the young warden who still had her hands in her pockets, he was not only several times her size, but she couldn't even seem to keep up with him with her eyes. The cleaver came down on her head with such force that the blade warped because he used too much of his power, and the once rectangular blade took on a nasty curl, but it never got the chance to touch the warden. Jackdaw's blade only met with the backside of a playing card which did not budge when hit. It shattered the blade on impact, leaving only a tiny rectangle behind. A shadow covered his face instantly, and Jackdaw looked up to see a playing card sailing in the air over his head. The Warden materialized where the card had been in the space between a breath, and she left a card on his forehead as gently as if she were placing it on a tabletop. Her body was gone as soon as the card touched his face, and Jackdaw finally completed the motion of his attack, and what remained of his cleaver slammed into the ground. All of that transpired in a single swing of his blade. Her speed was so impressive that instead of raging, Jackdaw let out a huff of noise that might have been a whistle on the lips of a bird.

"Could have turned yourself in," Nic said.

"You will soon understand why I am feared in worlds beyond this lowly place," Jackdaw said.

The monster moved, but as soon as Jackdaw twitched a single muscle, he was sucked into the playing card placed on his forehead as though this body was made of liquid. The card absorbed him like a towel drinking milk. He was gone, and the playing card landed heavily on the ground, joining the others that contained his men.

"They all say some cool shit 'til they are in the trap card. And scene," Nic said.

She even curtsied to the playing cards.

"If you are about done, I could use some assistance," Lyra said.

"Oh yeah, sorry. I was just… never mind," Nic said.

Lyra was just behind her now, standing over Taxx, who seemed to be missing an arm that Sixx seemed to have been collecting. He was looking at the severed arm with concern. Once Sixx reached Lyra, he gave over the limb, and she placed it next to its owner, who was still awake though his eyes were a million miles away.

"Mr. Kingswood, are you still with us?" Lyra asked.

Sixx groaned in frustration in place of words. His mouth was distended and forcibly held shut, a steady line of blood leaking out of either side. Sixx looked at Nic, and she looked from his mouth to his eyes and then back to his mouth. She laughed, figuring out that he could not talk because he was injured. It quickly became a cackle.

"Actually, that's not a bad idea," Nic started.

The twin looks Nic got from them both seemed to be enough to make her stop for the moment. Though she did wink at Sixx, who said something foul in response, it was forcibly demoted to a simple grunt. Taxx seemed to be trying to say something, and he slowly held out his hand, holding it up to Sixx. Taxx placed the end of Sixx's tongue, still very pink and alive, into his hand and carefully tried to smile. Sixx smiled back, and blood poured out of his mouth through his teeth.

"Hot," Nic said.

Sixx shoved the tongue into his mouth, and after a moment of swishing around, he opened his mouth with a satisfied 'ahh' sound and subsequent nonsense sounds and rolled his tongue. When he was done, he laughed and whooped a little.

"Aww yeah, can't nobody shut me up," Sixx said.

"That guy is bleeding out… so…" Nic said.

"You can relax. Taxxis is made of tougher stuff than that," Sixx said.

"Sixx, this much blood loss is well past fatal…," Nic said.

"Not for us," Sixx whispered.

Nic opened her mouth to speak again, but Lyra put a hand on her shoulder. The older Warden stepped forward.

"Saturday. Are you saying that this young man is the cousin?" Lyra asked

"Wait, the zombie guy is **the** guy? " Nic asked.

"What the hell do you mean, zombie guy? Yes, this is my cousin, Taxxis Moss," Sixx said.

"THIS guy is the guy we've been looking for? Damn, I'm good," Nic said.

She even smirked before making her way toward the small group, looking down at Taxx's face and Sixx's face a few more times before she wrinkled her nose.

"You do look alike. I guess I didn't see it before, but you guys could be brothers," Nic said.

"Cousins, in point of fact, but we are so much more than that," Sixx said.

"What did you say?" Lyra asked.

Nic turned to her but ultimately looked at the young man kneeling over his cousin and flexing his hands.

"My ol' granny used to call us twin cousins, her little joke because our birthdays are the same day," he said.

"When is your birthday?" Nic asked.

"That's a family secret," Sixx said.

"What the hell kind of shit is that?" Nic asked.

Lyra only made a noncommittal noise, and Nic made a sour face.

"Sorry. I meant to say, do go on," Nic said.

Sixx continued, eventually holding out his hand in front of him with a tiny bit of light glowing at the center of his palm, the size of a marble at first, but it quickly grew to the size of a coconut. The light bloomed into the shape of a flame, which was folding in on itself instead of billowing outward and colored a soft pastel green. It flowed like liquid smoke and burned from within with a bright light of a similar color. This light began to spread until it reached the edges of the fire. Sixx lifted the strange little orb and blew on it, instantly creating a glass-like coating on the outside and framing the energy within it neatly like a bottle of soda. Sixx took it in his hands and started to work it between his palms with a well-practiced motion, and the magical energy reacted by taking shape between his hands. He produced what looked like a glass bottle, opaque with no label but filled to the brim with a slightly iridescent dark fluid. There was even a stopper sitting atop the neck of the bottle made of the same glass-like material.

"There we go. Can you sit him up?" Sixx asked.

"First, we are gonna talk about what the hell that is," Nic said.

"More importantly, I have to know why this boy has rings?" Lyra asked.

"What are you saying?" Nic asked.

"There, look at his arm," she said.

True to her word, there were dozens of rings around the exposed central bone where his arm had been. Black as ink and echoing throughout the crimson flesh of his muscles, there had to be hundreds of them. They made the inside of his arm look like the interior of a felled tree. Nic could not believe her eyes.

"Ok. What the hell is that?" She asked.

"Taxx is a little different," Sixx said.

"That is an understatement, Mr. St. Martin," Lyra said.

"Trust me. He just needs a little jump start to work it out himself. This will do it, I promise," Sixx said.

"You really want to hedge all your bets on some juiced-up moonshine you literally just pulled out of your ass?" Nic asked.

"This isn't moonshine. It's… well, hell, I don't really know how to explain that, but you're gonna have to trust me," Sixx

said.

Sixx pulled the stopper from the bottle, and the smell of spices took over the area. Lyra exchanged a look with her partner but ultimately helped Taxx up so he could more easily drink. Taxx was barely conscious. His mouth was moving in silent whispers, but he was alive, which was all that mattered. Sixx poured, and the fluid spattered on his lips like liquid, but whatever splashed from his body and into the air immediately changed form and floated away like vapor instead. Taxx started to drink, and in just a moment, the bottle's contents were gone, and Sixx tossed it over his shoulders. Nic caught it with a quick hand and examined the bottle.

"That's a new one," Nic said.

"May I?" Lyra asked.

Nic tossed the glass toward her partner, but before it could reach her, it seemed to lose the ability to hold its shape, and it too changed form into a vapor that wafted away on the breeze like smoke.

"They don't last long when they empty like that, but we have other things to worry about," Sixx said.

"He always takes a second for the drama. It's about time, lazy ass. We got work to do, now stand up!" Sixx said.

"If that works ill-" Lyra paused.

Taxx stirred a bit, and Sixx nodded triumphantly.

"I retract my bet. Well done, Mr. St. Martin," Lyra said.

She had only looked away for a moment, but Taxx was already awake in her arms when she looked back. He was almost sitting up on his own even, bracing himself with both hands on the ground. His arm was fully mended, but he also no longer seemed to be on the verge of death. He was looking very lively.

The places where his blood had spilled left strange remnants, lush green plant life. Grasses, weeds, and even some flowers grew wildly from the quarry floor all around him. He did not seem to notice. Taxx held out his left arm, and he flexed his fingers a few times as if he didn't believe it was real either, and then he touched his face. Then Taxx felt Sixx's face, and Sixx swatted him away like a gnat sniffing the air wildly around the other young man. Sixx narrowed his eyes and grabbed Taxx on either side of his face with a solid grip.

"Get out of my cousin, " Sixx said.

Chapter | Eleven

"What exactly are you doing?" Lyra asked.

"He is probably drunk from your healing potion," Nic said. Complete with air quotes.

"That wasn't no healing potion. That was just some of my magic to help him shake off what's got him so twisted up. Taxx can usually take care of things just fine all on his own," Sixx said.

"So, it would seem," Lyra said

She was investigating Taxx's arm with interest, especially in the space where the shoulder met the torso. It seemed to have reattached cleanly at the joint. She had never seen anything like it. She examined his pulse and pupils and snapped next to one of his ears, but he did not respond. She let him support himself and stood to her feet, looking down at Sixx as he continued to watch

Taxx as though he was waiting for something. Taxx had done little more than wave his head back and forth like a newborn and examine his limbs up to this point.

"What is the matter with him?" Lyra asked.

"Nothing I can't fix. Now, let me say one more 'gain. I am the son of shadow. Heed my words. Get up outta my cousin, son," Sixx said.

Taxx turned his face to Sixx, and they locked eyes, Sixx's starting to glow with a soft green, and then Taxx's eyes began to glow with a similar inner light. Then Sixx slammed his palm into Taxx's forehead with such force that Taxx's head snapped back and stayed that way, his mouth pointed up at the sky. Sixx stood up and took a few steps back, and as soon as he did, Taxx began to tremble, his body shaking violently and randomly as though he were being electrocuted. After a minute or so, he began to settle and finally came to a stop face down on the ground, and a black ooze seeped out of his mouth and pooled on the quarry floor. It seemed to be leaking out, but as more and more of it was exposed to the air, it became clear that the fluid was crawling out. It was wriggling like thousands of inky black worms dangling from his open mouth. Eventually, the march ended and what was left appeared to be a squat little knot of worms no bigger than a golf ball. It was slowly crawling around as a single organism using worms as makeshift legs. Though it was covered in black slime, the worms beneath it appeared to be a much lighter color. Some of them even seemed to sparkle.

"That's not normal. What the hell are these?" Sixx asked.

"That is a complex shadow curse; several are hinged together at their core, like A knot. I have never seen one inside a living being," Lyra said.

"That is a nasty bit of magic," Nic said.

"I thought that was illegal. Living curses..." Sixx said.

"How did you remove a curse like that?" Nic asked.

Sixx looked a little startled that someone would ask, and for a moment, he only smiled.

"You know what I am," he said.

"Nobody knows what we are; that's why they call us that terrible word. That I understand, but you told a curse to jump, and then... it jumped. That's not normal, is it?" Nic asked.

Lyra looked between them slowly and stepped in, turning their attention back to the wriggling ball of curses positioned so that it seemed to be listening to them. When it noticed they were looking at it, the worms flopped on the ground and pretended to play dead.

"They are very illegal," Nic said.

"And smart. That's kind of dope," Sixx said.

"What isn't dope is what this all means. Before I get into that, Nic, would you?" Lyra asked.

"Whoever did this broke many laws just to kill a teenager," Lyra said.

Nic flung a card at the Knot. It skimmed the ground twice before it landed right on top of the small collection of worms, gobbling it up entirely in a single go leaving nothing behind.

"Damn, that must come in handy, huh?" Sixx asked.

Nic flexed a finger and the card returned to her like it was on a wire. It stopped and she caught it between her fingers, then the card was gone into the sleeves of her red peacoat.

"It's faster than walking, but... wait..." Nic said.

There was a sudden weight in the air, and all of them seemed to become aware of it simultaneously, but only Lyra and Nic were turned toward its source. It seemed to come from one of the cards Nic used to trap the monsters. It seemed like one of them was starting to stir. At first, it was just a little wiggle here and there, but soon one of the cards was up and spinning on its corner like a top. Lyra glanced at Nic, who had an eyebrow raised in confusion.

"No way one of these jokers is powerful enough to split my trap card. I'll bet you lunch," Nic said.

"Normally, I would leap at the opportunity for a free lunch, but I think it is time for us to take the boys and go," Lyra said.

"If I try to use a gate card right now, all those trap cards **will** fail, and whatever comes out of that card will need all my attention," Nic said.

"I will leave you to your work," Lyra said.

"Should I help?" Sixx asked.

"See to your cousin. Don't worry," Nic said.

"Here we-" Lyra started.

"Jackdaw!" Taxx said.

The young man sat up suddenly, his eyes illuminated with a light from within, green and dark like a forest canopy and rimmed in something that could have been black. The dark rim was gone before Lyra could get a good look, and the boy was staring past all of them at the spinning card. At that exact moment, the card fractured with explosive results and left the figure of Jackdaw in its wake. Jackdaw seemed to have a much bigger body now, standing well over seven feet tall, and his shoulders and chest were hulking like a bodybuilder. The remnant of his cleaver was still in one hand though his larger size made it look more like a hatchet now, and he was emanating a very dangerous aura. Even Taxx could feel it tingle against his skin like a thousand insects.

The rage in this creature burned so hotly that Taxx was sure it was making him sweat. There was still a beak pushed through the middle of his human face, and somehow, though there was no evidence of it on the monster, Taxx knew Jackdaw was smiling at him.

"Ah, you have been healed. I see now why he wants you," Jackdaw cawed.

"Who wants me?" Sixx said.

"If this works, I will eat a shoe," Lyra said.

Jackdaw regarded her for a long time. It was hard to tell when he was thinking, but there were undoubtedly some gears turning, and her presence did seem to change his actions. Sixx looked from the birdman to the Warden again.

"So interesting. All of you have such stimulating parlor tricks. You may tease all you like, Guild dog, but your tricks will not work on me," Jackdaw cawed.

No sooner had the sound escaped his beak did the large mass of Jackdaw explode forward. Somehow, he did not seem to be as fast as before, but he rushed Nic all the same. Nic had put her hands into her pockets again and only smiled at him as he approached, and just like she had the last time, she quickly averted the wild haymaker he threw. Her body was simply gone before the punch could connect, replaced by a card. Jackdaw slammed his fist into the card with all of his weight but could only move it a few inches like hitting an iron wall. Once the force was gone, the card gently floated to the ground like an ordinary playing card. It didn't seem any worse for wear either. The Warden was behind him now. Jackdaw didn't even have to look up to feel it; he knew she was there. Jackdaw huffed and slowly turned toward the warden, but he kept his eyes on the ground all around them for a long moment before he looked up at Nic again.

"Wow… who the hell are you? Most people don't figure it out at all, and even the good ones don't get it until it's too late but look at you! Ready to turn yourself in?" Nic asked.

She had her hands in her pockets, tapping the toe of her red boots into the ground one after the other. Jackdaw did not make any moves, he just watched her with a growing contempt, cawing low and deep in his throat, not precisely a growl, but the effect was the same.

"A gimmick is always a pale copy of true power," Jackdaw cawed.

Jackdaw launched himself into the air with such force that the ground gave way beneath his feet, and in just a few seconds, he rose to an unimaginable height. He was carried up and up in the sky on a massive pair of wings that sprouted from his back. Even as he rose, more mass was added to the wings until, with one last heave, he spread them wide enough to support his weight. He was well over one hundred feet in the air now, coasting on the updrafts and searching for the Warden with his sharp eyes. She had not moved, and she wasn't even looking up. He started a divebomb on her without hesitation, holding his body in a tight knot for maximum speed. His more considerable bodyweight made him fall like a cannonball and did the impossible again. Jackdaw broke the sound barrier, appearing on the ground in a three-point stance. The ground gave way under his body before the explosion came, and a massive burst of wind unsettled the loose earth of the quarry floor. It sent stones, Sixx, Taxx, and dozens of playing cards flying off in every direction, effectively clearing the cards from the area in a single move.

"Now then," Jackdaw cawed.

"WHAT?!" Nic shouted.

She squinted her eyes and leaned her ear toward him, teasing that Jackdaw did not find amusing. He took off toward her and closed the space between them quickly. Jackdaw increased the size of his body again, but only his fist this time, and it happened so fast there would have been no warning. He suddenly brought his fist down toward the center of the warden's mass, connecting with his fist and driving it into what he thought was her chest. The blow was mighty, and though it moved her back a few feet, it didn't have the kind of impact that he was looking for, and Jackdaw realized his mistake a second too late. The palm of her hand intercepted the strike, but the skin of his fist had started to fry well before he made complete contact, sizzling gently. There was a visible field where the air temperature around her increased dramatically. Instantly. The visible arcs looked more like amber lightning than fire. When Jackdaw connected with her palm, his arm was blackened and mostly smoldering up to the elbow, and the heat continued to rise. He had to leave his arm behind or risk his entire body going with it, so he ripped it off at the shoulder and made his escape from the super-heated zone.

There was another flash like a lightning strike in that space, and when it was over, the warden was holding the remains of that still smoldering limb. It had been blackened to ash and burned away like a forgotten cigar. Nic tossed it to the side and smiled at Jackdaw. She never even took her other hand from her pocket. Jackdaw was a few feet away, holding the remains of his arm and staring at this woman with something that looked like caution. Nic exhaled a thick white line of steam from the corner of her mouth, and flecks in her eyes were glowing a dangerous red-orange like embers in the night sky. The warden took a step forward, and the quarry floor boiled and sizzled, steaming a bit around her legs, and with every step of her red-hot boots, the stone curled away from her toes like receding sand.

"I hate those skin suits. Could you show me what you look like, Big Bird? I promise I won't use a single card," 'Nic said.

"I must apologize for my flippant remark earlier, Warden. You are more dangerous than you look," Jackdaw said.

"Not usually. That was revenge for the kid's arm," Nic said.

Jackdaw glanced at Taxx and then back to the little Warden in the flaming red boots.

"Now that I have your attention let me ask again. Are you ready to turn yourself in? Or perhaps I should show you my offensive magic?" Nic asked.

"Nic, I must remind you that we need him as alive as possible," Lyra said.

Jackdaw turned his eye toward Lyra, who was standing between the monster and the two boys he was after, then he looked back to Nic. He was effectively surrounded. He peered at her face and then back to the younger warden. She was just a girl but did not look concerned. Jackdaw huffed again.

"It seems that I have underestimated you to my detriment. Please excuse the crude path to victory I must take now. We will argue about it in the next life," Jackdaw said.

The air around him started to become heavy for a moment. Then his remaining shoulder began to bulge to nearly twice its size, and large black feathers, dripping with black slime, were starting to leak out of his skin like spores on a mushroom. Lyra and Nic moved to defensive positions around Sixx and Taxx when a part of his head joined the shoulder, ballooning in size like a cartoon and leaking black feathers at an alarming rate. The ground was littered with feathers now, and the air was swirling with them. The massive wings on his back started to break down too. Each feather that fell to the ground landed like a lead weight, the ones that collided in the air did so with explosive results.

"Are you gonna suicide bomb us? What a flippin' cop-out!" Nic shouted.

"I think it would be more of a suicide claymore mine," Lyra said.

"You right. This is very claymore-like," Sixx agreed.

"Can we **please** remain focused on the crazy dangerous shit happening in front of us?" Taxx asked.

"Should we be running?" Sixx asked.

"No time. He is going to explode in seconds. Nic?" Lyra asked.

"I'm tapped. I might send us into space," Nic said.

Sixx laughed while Taxx looked on in horror at the monster bomb that was about to explode and probably kill them all. He couldn't help but think about the day he'd had. Ever since he had come back from the dead, it felt like everyone was trying to kill him, maybe everything had always been trying to kill him, and he was only just noticing it for himself. Even now, when things were looking bleak, he was more upset about how easy-going Sixx was than the imminent doom they were facing. Taxx had survived death and dismemberment with astonishing luck thus far. He had no idea if he could come back from the dead again. He wasn't looking to find out, but he couldn't bring himself to be afraid. He could only watch.

"How can you all be so calm?" Taxx asked.

"Shit like this is always happening. The trick is knowing

when to be afraid and when to ask for help. Carvalho?" Nic said.

"I am happy to assist..." Lyra said.

She reached into her coat and pulled out what looked like a regular spoon, crisscrossed with tiny scratch marks from use.

"Whoa, Lyra, calm down," Nic said.

"Wait," Sixx said.

Sixx started to smile. Then he reached out into thin air to grab something. To say that Sixx reached out was making a simple matter of something that did not make sense. Even in the world of magic. He reached into thin air, and his hand disappeared and entered the darkness of a shadow. A shadow that rose from the ground. It grew out of his shadow and attached to his hand, moving like a ferrofluid attracted to a magnet. It swallowed up his arm to the elbow until he drew it back and produced a cane. The wardens gasped in unison, but Sixx didn't seem to notice. Sixx continued to pull the long cane out of the shadows, and when it was gone, the shadow sank back into the ground. The young man visibly cooled. The air cooled too, and their breath became visible at that moment. There was a sudden weight around Sixx that made him look taller. Powerful. Taxx took a step away from him, and Sixx smirked.

"Don't be afraid, cousin. Be amazed," Sixx said.

"What are you?" Taxx asked.

"The Prince of Death," Sixx whispered.

Sixx's pale eye started to glow violently, throwing off a pale green light. Flame licked out of his eyes like the dancing heart of a candle.

"I've never seen this before," Taxx said.

"I have. That green flame," Lyra said.

"Bingo," Sixx said.

"How did we not know you were a Reaper?" Nic asked.

"I wanted to tell you-" Sixx started.

"Enough, I pray that hell is silent," Jackdaw said.

Jackdaw exploded. Iron-hard feathers screamed out in every direction, and a steady drumbeat echoed across the quarry as they slammed into the walls around them as fast as machine gunfire. As quickly as heavy rain. Sixx didn't hold up his hand. He didn't posture or speak. He didn't show any emotion on his face. His eyes were laser-focused, the air didn't shake, and there was no flash of light. There was a slight buzz like static electricity that danced over the skin. The feathers that should have torn them the shreds seemed suspended in midair. It was unclear due to the strange darkness all around them. It had not become darker. The shadows around them were in odd positions, making the whole area seem strange. Taxx's shadow was long and thin like a cable underneath him, and it stretched so it could reach his cousin. Lyra and Nic had the same thing happening to the shadows that should have been under their feet. They lost their human shape and leaned toward the cane. Even a lot of the shadows that had once been on the ground were now flowing toward Sixx like a river. They all leaned toward him by the dozens like they were magnetically drawn, pulled by thin strands. He changed the shape of every shadow around them for a great distance. Those shadows were not gone, but they had been repurposed instantly from noncorporeal silhouettes into something else.

Now they were deep and dark objects with weight and shape. At his direction, they took the form of hands. Then erupted from the ground before him, reaching up to the sky and grasping feathers out of the air. One by one, until there was an uncountable amount of hands growing out of the ground and out of each other. The number of hands grew, budding from the others like sinister trees and creating a macabre forest. Only Sixx's burning green eyes could be seen through the black forest of hands.

"...how unlikely..." Jackdaw sang.

His song was weak and more of a croak than a caw. This was likely since most of his body seemed to have been destroyed in the explosion. He looked like a bundle of feathers held together by bloody slime and piled to about the size of a trash can with a human face draped over the top. The remnants of a beak stood out of that face like an ingrown nail, and only one eye remained in that head, desperately trying to focus on the small group. The hands continued to multiply from each other, and the patch of black continued to propagate forward, the fingers grasping at the quarry floor to reach the birdman. The uncountable number of feathers floating in the air before them were being drawn down into the shadows and were gone without a trace. Not even a fragment had been left behind. Jackdaw cawed in disgust, but there were no words to hear, just low lamenting singing from a broken animal as the hands closed in on him.

"First of all. Don't interrupt me. Second. You got all poetic about meeting us in the afterlife, and then you ain't even die. So full of shit!" Sixx said.

"I underestimated you too. This is the cost of my mistakes," Jackdaw sang.

"Tell it to my daddy," Sixx said.

The hands were still flowing toward Jackdaw like a tidal wave made of a slowly increasing number of black hands. Each of them reached out and grasped with every ounce of strength, obeying the command they had been given. They would tear what remained of the bird to pieces.

"Alright, bro! Stop!" Nic said.

The hands stopped suddenly. Some of them had taken hold of Jackdaw already. The tips of inky hands were only just a moment away from taking his remaining eye. The tips drew back from his face and regressed away. The hands pulled away into the shadows. They took the feathers with them, hundreds of them dragged down into the darkness and gone. Sixx adjusted his jacket and tried to button it, but when he was chopped in half, the button appeared to have fallen off.

"Damn. I liked this jacket," Sixx said.

"Mr. St. Martin, there are more important things to discuss. What exactly are you?" Lyra asked.

"Ok. That feels rude," Sixx said.

"Wait. He lives here, and you guys don't know what he is either?" Taxx asked.

"He has only lived here for a few months, and I've never seen him do this," Nic said.

"Look, there is an excellent explanation for this," Sixx said.

He had been shrouded by the heavy shadows that his magic created until that point. The shadows returned to their rightful objects, and the light returned to normal. That's when they got their first good look at his face.

"Sixx… what the… hell?" Taxx asked.

He was openly staring at his cousin with a look of confusion.

"What's wrong with y'all? Don't you have to take care of the monsters I just SAVED us from?" Sixx asked.

"He does have a point," Nic said.

She was still watching Jackdaw for the moment.

"We will be coming back to this. I've never seen anyone able to do what you can do without so much as hinting at the higher states of ma...," Lyra said.

Then she slowly faded out and joined Taxx, silently staring at Sixx and looking horrified. Sixx turned toward them fully, and Lyra took a step back.

"Everything good witcha?" Sixx asked.

"Listen, if it helps any, all monsters are full of shit. Try to remember that one if you remember nothing else," Nic said.

She was the last horse to cross the finish line, staring at him, eyes wide.

"Aiight. Now I'm starting to get a bruised ego," Sixx said.

"Bruised or not, we need to talk about why your face is gone," Nic said.

"Oh. That," Sixx said.

He smiled. Somehow. Where his face had been, all that remained were skeletal bones. Bones that glittered in the dark, colored copper where they should be white and covered in strange markings. The area around the cheekbones and orbit of his left eye was particularly crawling with magical power. That magic channeled through the lines engraved directly into the bone. They might have been words, but there was no time to read them. Even as Taxx started to see the pattern of the tattoo-like markings on those bones, Sixx started to heal. Whatever magic fueled this impossible sight began to replace the tissues of his face at an alarming rate. In moments it started to fill in like expanding foam.

"That is... kind of mesmerizing," Nic said.

"Don't look until it's healed," Sixx whimpered.

"Rapid regeneration after using such a high level of shadow magic. I've never seen puppetry like that," Lyra said.

"Thank you sounds weird in your language," Sixx said.

The corner of Lyra's mouth turned up at the ends in what could almost be considered a smile.

"Let's go and collect this Jackdaw creature and see what he knows. Then we will talk about why you've been lying to us," Lyra said.

Serrano seemed to have a way to shroud his presence so potently that none of them could even hear the truck until it was so close that Taxx was sure they were going to be hit. Lyra reached out and pulled Taxx close to her body, and somehow the vehicle passed through the group without incident, narrowly missing Sixx and Nic as its tires screeched by. Jackdaw was gathered up, and soon the noise and taillights of it all were speeding away and quickly disappeared into the darkness.

"What the hell was that?" Sixx asked.

Taxx let go of Lyra, who he was holding tight around the middle. It was something to gauge how tall she was from so close. She was also much more solid than she looked. He was stumbling over himself a little. Her body wasn't just fit; it was so hard that he felt like holding a statue. He had underestimated this woman in a way that made something inside of him suddenly fearful. Sixx smirked at him when he noticed the other young man staring. His wounds were fully healed now, so that smirk was on his whole face.

"Looks like you seen a ghost," Sixx said.

Taxx stepped toward his cousin and took him in a hard hug, a hug that Sixx returned in earnest. For a moment, the two of them just held each other, patting each other on the back. Lyra turned away to give them a moment, and Nic stepped away from them to examine the tire tracks. Then Nic held up her hand, and about a dozen playing cards began to make their way toward her as though they were on a rope. Some of them flew and tumbled and struggled out from under objects, but they all gathered neatly into a pile in her palm.

"Everyone is alive. So, I would call this a win," Nic said.

"Things as they are," Lyra said.

"Can you take us back to the house?" Lyra asked.

"Nah. I'm beat," Nic said.

"Allow me," Sixx offered.

He tapped the cane on the ground, and a long shadow grew out before him. It changed shape until it was rectangular and large like a tarp laid out end to end. It wasn't until it rose from the ground like a ramp that it became clear that this shadow was a door. The endless black faded away until it revealed the outside front porch of the House of Wolf and Raven. A large wooden door with a square window said as much beyond the shadow gate.

"We have much to talk about," Lyra said.

She was first through the gate. Nic followed, holding a few cards in her hand that seemed to be wiggling a little.

"Honestly, I am more impressed than mad, but I agree," Nic said.

She winked on her way through, and Sixx smiled, holding out his hand for his cousin to proceed.

"Sixx. If you are Death, what am I?" Taxx asked.

There was a tone in his voice that made Sixx pause. He stepped away from the gate and took on a severe look that made Taxx focus on him.

"Taxes?" Sixx teased.

He started laughing, and he passed through the portal. He

held out his hand to his cousin, and though Taxx took it, he was making a sour face.

"Not funny," Taxx said.

Chapter | Twelve

There was a knock on his door early the following day. He had fallen asleep in his clothes, and when he woke up, he was again disoriented by his surroundings. It only took him a moment to figure it out this time. Taxx answered the door while one of his eyes was still closed. He was still able to recognize Izzy.

"Oh no, what day is it now?" Taxx asked.

Izzy started to laugh, and Taxx couldn't help but be infected by it, even though he was more than half asleep.

"It's only been a normal amount of hours. It's early. Avo thought you might want to see what they found," she said.

"What could be worth getting up this early?" Taxx asked.

Izzy tugged at his arm and pulled him out of the room. He went along with her, and they made their way down the stairs.

Two flights. Izzy stamped three times rhythmically like a tap dancer when they reached the bottom step. Once she did, the ground collapsed into itself like dominoes, the floor falling away to reveal a deeper set of stairs.

"Ok. That was cool. What is this?" Taxx asked.

"This is the entrance to the Mountain," Izzy said.

"Sounds ominous," Taxx said.

"It kind of is," she said.

She started down the stairs, and he followed her down. He didn't know how far they descended, but it was colder wherever they were now. There was also a sort of silence that had weight. He could feel it in his ears and deeper. Something strange. His head was tingling, just under his bandana, where his secrets grew. He gasped when he felt them react and stopped cold on the stairs. Izzy looked back at him with concern, making him even more uncomfortable. She was looking right at him. He thought he might vomit, which brought up even more uncomfortable thoughts.

"Oh right! It's your first time," she said.

"HUH?" Taxx asked.

He hadn't meant to shout. There was a sound happening that was ramping up slowly as she spoke. She only blinked at him. He smiled sheepishly, and mercifully she continued down the stairs. They were hard under his shoes, like stepping on marble, but there was something else. Not just the terrible sound that grew louder and louder as they descended. It was like standing next to a jet engine, and Taxx found it hard to focus. Once they were halfway down, the room opened to cavernous proportions. They were standing on a staircase built into the wall of a much larger room. Beneath the floors of the mansion, there was a room more extensive than an aircraft hangar, possibly even larger than that. If the strange space had an end, he couldn't see it. The space was full of strange things, towering shelves filled will books and stranger things. There was a large water tank that could have easily housed the entire cast for a dolphin show, but there were no dolphins here. Dark and massive creatures darted around in the murky space, there was no light in the water, but those nightmare shapes were clear enough. Izzy did not seem to notice. She continued down the steps, carrying the conversation forward. She spoke at average volume, but Taxx strained to hear her against the onslaught of the horrible sound.

"Being so near the machine can sometimes make you feel strange things. It has this dampening field," Izzy said.

"I'm sorry. What is damp!? Taxx shouted.

The shouting seemed to have caught the attention of the people below. He was sure that one of them was looking directly at him, but they were still far away. He couldn't be sure. He lowered his voice as much as possible, but he spoke very loudly over the incredible churning sound. He was astounded that she could not hear such a tremendous noise. He thought it might split his skull open, and his body was starting to feel its effects. He felt stiff, and his teeth were clenched together. When Izzy looked back at him again, he did his best to make that grimace into a smile. She looked confused, but she smiled back anyway and continued.

"Dampening. It makes all of us feel weird. This staircase and almost everything else is made of Nullun. It is a stone that eats magic. The whole mountain is made of it. That's why it's the perfect place," she said.

"Perfect for what!?" Taxx said.

"A prison," A strange woman said.

Taxx screamed. He turned toward the woman who spoke. They were so far away he should not have heard her. Her voice was shockingly clear. It cut through the sound of the machine with ease and a heavy Scottish accent. The woman was becoming clearer the longer he stared at her. She was wearing a lot of denim. A jacket with rhinestones and embroidered flowers matched her skirt, pink leggings, and checkered sneakers. She looked like she could have been a runway model from the eighties. At this point, he realized that his vision was not getting more precise. She was getting closer. This woman was walking in the air as easily as he walked down the stairs. She was moving toward him, but the way she moved was anything but normal.

The way she walked looked out of place in the world. She was simply closer than she had been without flexing a toe. Every time she slithered or teleported or whatever the rapid and sudden egress she was doing was called, Taxx couldn't help but step back up a step. There was something about the feeling of her magic that made him wary. He couldn't get the feeling out of him. She had the longest reddest hair he had ever seen in his life, and her skin was so pale and perfect it made her look almost alien. He had to admit that he had also never seen a more beautiful woman. He was sure that such a flawless face could not belong to a human. She was tall and long in places not achievable by human forms.

Her eyes were too large, and her cheekbones were impossibly high. There were tiny points of light around her body and swimming in her hair like diamonds. Like morning dew on a rose petal, it made the space around her shimmer and seemed to gather just around her edges. It looked like glitter in a snow globe, but something behind that glitter felt more like danger than wonder as she approached. The woman stopped walking in midair and turned toward the group.

"The prince is removing himself from the machine," she said.

Just after she spoke, an alarm started to sound. There was a crashing sound, and Sixx began to scream from somewhere else.

"Taxx, you stay away from that red-haired **demon**. That glitter ain't nothing friendly," Sixx said.

"What is going on?!" Taxx shouted.

He was trying to look around, but the sound kept him from opening his eyes.

"Don't listen to him. He is upset because she had to use her powers on him. Simply for appraisal," Avo said.

The sorcerer was waiting at the bottom of the stairs to greet them. Taxx did not move. He was still looking at the woman floating in midair and the secret basement cave. He also couldn't get that noise out of his head or bones. He swore he could feel them vibrating down to his toes. It was Izzy who came to his aid. He gasped when she took his hand, but he did not pull away from her. Her hands were so soft and delightfully warm. He had not even realized his body was so cold until just then. She squeezed his fingers and held his oversized fist in hers for a moment. After a while, he nodded and followed her down the stairs. She took her time and held his hand firmly until they reached the bottom. The sound was so loud now that it was making his teeth chatter. It felt like his bones were going to rattle out of his body.

"Good to see you again, Mr. Moss. I heard you comported yourself quite bravely last night," Avo said.

"Sometimes stupidity looks like bravery," Taxx said.

He was starting to get the hang of speaking, but every word was huffed out. Avo looked concerned and led him to a computer system that looked normal enough. Whatever it was made of, however, seemed very odd. It was like clay, but also metal. The whole room was made of it. The entire room was the source of the constant hum.

"If it hurts you, you should probably take it off," the red-haired woman said.

"Take what off?" He asked.

"That sound you are hearing is resonance," she said.

"From what?" he asked.

The red-haired woman tapped at her forehead and glanced up at his headband. He reached up and touched his headband, and sure enough, it was vibrating like a running engine.

"What's happening to my headband?" he asked.

"Were you unaware that you have a series of potent spells meant to siphon magic right on your head? Its mere proximity to the Nullun is causing a feedback loop. It must be removed," she said.

"I won't!" Taxx shouted.

The red-haired woman looked surprised for a moment, but ultimately, she smiled.

"Very well. Then allow me to help you," she said.

Taxx flinched when she reached out her hand, and she stopped.

"Do not be afraid," she said.

The red-haired woman was suddenly standing so close now that her glitter was falling all around them like sparkling snow. It resembled the kind of snowy tv static from early televisions. All black and white and moving so fast they were impossibly hard to follow with the eyes. Several of them had landed on his clothing and vanished without a trace, like a good dream. The red-haired woman stopped moving in front of him. Her feet finally came to a soft landing on the ground, and objects manifested on her back when she did. A set of four strange extensions, nearly invisible, glittering like the wings on the back of a dragonfly. They were pink and glossy with delicate veining like stained glass and in more shades and colors than he could imagine. They were twinkling so much that they could have glowed, even when still.

"Who are you?" Taxx asked.

"She is a Fairy and more. I think the title of The Pink Fairy makes her practically royalty," Sixx said.

His cousin stepped into the room with the aid of Nic, who was under his arm and helping him forward.

"What happened to you?" Taxx asked.

"Relax, cuh, I just used up too much of the juice. Feeling it now," Sixx said.

Taxx was going to say more, but Rosen spoke instead.

"You know me?" The fairy asked.

Sixx nodded.

"You do not?" she asked.

Taxx was horrified to see that she was looking very much at him. He felt so suddenly embarrassed he couldn't even speak, so he found something else to look at. However, the fairy was unrelenting and moved where his gaze went several times before he learned to look at her.

"My legend here in the Nexus is ancient. Do not hang your head. I remember when the Fae were not such rare things," she said.

The pink fairy reached out and touched his bandana for just

a moment, and the vibration went away. The sound dulled so suddenly that Taxx gasped out loud. It felt like stones had been taken off his chest. It was still there, but down to the humming of a satisfied cat instead of an industrial machine inside of him.

"What did you do?" he asked,

"I disabled the Nullun thread. A tricky task for most anyone except the tailor," she said.

"You… made this?" Taxx asked.

The fairy smiled and looked distant for a moment, thinking of things only she could say. It was only a moment, and she was back, glowing more acutely now with pink energy. It radiated from her like an inner light and formed a visible aura around her. It made her shine like a lantern for a moment. Taxx had never seen so much magic all at once. Her body was now the center of a pink star, and her skin was not visible. There was only the blush-colored heart of this just-born sun. The fairy turned toward Taxx, and her aura twinkled away in a brilliant haze of red rose confetti that sparkled all around. A sense of overwhelming joy settled on him in the wake of her magic, and he felt his skin become hot. The fairy cleared her throat and tried to compose herself.

"Suffice it to say that I am familiar with this tailors work," she said sheepishly.

Taxx could only nod and openly stare at her. He couldn't help it. He had never seen anything like her display. It was not attacking magic or defending magic. It was… he didn't know what that was. He looked down at his hand and then to hers, and he felt a tingle in his palm. He heard distant flutes and felt the wind on his skin. It tickled and sent a tremble through his body, ending in his horns. He felt them vibrate with such a clean sound it could have been a bell. The sound rang through him like a chime. It felt like his bones were… singing.

"What… is this?" he asked.

"I apologize, young man. I had no idea you had such sensitivity to magic," she said.

"What? I don't have…" he faded.

The ringing inside of him was changing pitch and tone, vibrating from the crown of his head to the tip of his toes. It did not hurt. It felt incredible. It felt like joy and love and abundance. He thought he might fly if he picked up his feet. Taxx reached up and touched his face and found it very hot under his fingers. His entire body was uncomfortably hot.

"I think something is *very* wrong with me," Taxx whispered.

The fairy looked at him carefully then. She leaned in close and squinted her eyes. Her eyes were the color and texture of rose petals, sharp velvety red. Probing through him so closely that he was sure that he could feel its fingers skimming through him. They were fluttering through the pages of him like a book. When she found what she had been looking for, the fairy nodded and laughed. She opened her mouth and released a song like he had made in the quarry with Jackdaw. The similarities ended with the sound. Hers was quite jarring at first, like the sound of thousands of voices singing songs of their own devices.

"What the **hell**, lady?" Sixx asked.

"Just testing a theory," she said in English.

"Test that in a room that isn't a cave," Nic said.

"Hmm… that perhaps is wise. I apologize but was I correct?" she asked.

"Correct about what?" Sixx asked.

"He knows what I mean… don't you?" she asked.

Taxx slowly nodded his head.

"Remarkable," she said.

"Mrs. Graves?" Avo asked.

"May I see?" Rosen asked.

Taxx was bathed in her magic. The chamber was heavy with the glow of pink magic. The Nullun itself seemed to reflect its warmth and with it was something soothing, like sunlight and the smell of flowers. It served to calm him down. He was standing much straighter now, but his deep dark eyes were only on that rose-colored woman.

"How did you know?" Taxx asked.

"The headband. I am married to the tailor who made it. How did you come by this?" The pink fairy asked.

"It was a gift from my grandmother," he said.

"A… what?" she asked.

The smile left her face. Taxx was sure he saw her bottom lip quiver, and she had to turn away for a moment before she spoke again.

"This is a tool. A device with many names, but the one most know is a taker's cloth. Called so because it is infused with Nullun thread to absorb the magic of whoever is wearing it continuously until they die," she said.

"No, that's not what this does. This headband keeps my… you know what's hidden," Taxx insisted.

She shook her head slowly.

"Trust your ears," she said.

He listened carefully for something, but all he could hear were the usual sounds of the room. Then he realized what she meant; the buzzing sound was gone. He had not heard it since she touched the headband. He hadn't felt sleepy anymore either.

He assumed it was due to excitement, but now she was offering another path. He reached up the touched the cloth. Even now, he was having a hard time taking it off.

"You may keep it on if it comforts you. Here you are free to be whoever or whatever you are," she said.

He nodded, but he did not take off the bandana. The fairy did not pursue it.

"You are a fairy?" Taxx asked.

"That I am," she said.

"I hope this doesn't seem rude, but… fairies are supposed to be small, aren't they?" he asked.

"The Fae come in many shapes and sizes. They were once so bountiful that they lived among humans. Now they mostly keep to themselves. Most are benevolent," Sixx said.

"Very good," the fairy said.

"A fae with a name whose name is a color is about as ancient, powerful, and rare as they come," Sixx said.

The fairy regarded Sixx for a long moment with a similarly placid but somehow expressive face that reminded him of Lyra.

"I assumed you were just a loudmouth, but you are well informed, Wiccani," The Rosen lady said.

"What is that word?" Sixx asked.

"Just an old name for a witch's son," the fairy said.

"Kinda tight," he said.

There was the sound of a printer suddenly in motion, and after just a few moments, the squat little machine produced a tiny domed object. The fairy slung an arm around his shoulder, and they moved toward the station.

"Come, let us see what your relative is made of and perhaps give us some insight into you," the fairy said.

He had not looked around the room because he was captivated by the fairy. There were several stations around a massive machine at the center of the room. It looked like something out of a science fiction movie. Massive cables were snaking from it, as wide as an elephant's trunk, and climbing the walls in geometric patterns and shapes. The machine was giant with a central pillar that rose to the ceiling, filled with multicolored eyes. One of them was Blackest Eye. Each of them appeared to be a looking glass, and they numbered in the dozens. The massive computer was almost always in motion, visibly. Moving cogs and gears, but mostly it moved through a series of tubes filled with green fluid. They were all over the machine and the cavernous space, sticking out like cathode tubes. Taxx couldn't count them all.

"What the hell is this thing?" Taxx asked.

"The inquisitor," Nic said plainly.

She and Sixx sat on a different computer around the massive machine connected to a particular set of tubes. He thought they were empty but could now see they were full of things. Creatures of many shapes and sizes.

"It is a research facility," Avo said.

"This is also where they lock up all the criminal magic users," Sixx said.

"Right. That too. But it is also the most advanced research facility for Others, probably ever. It helps us understand magic," Izzy said.

"Among other things," Avo said.

The sorcerer handed some cards back to Nic, who stuffed them into her pocket without a glance.

"Empty. What did we find out?" she asked.

"There wasn't much they could tell us. The surprise was in their magical composition. They are comprised of necrotized tissues animated by a strong core of life magic," Avo said.

"Is that bad?" Taxx asked.

"Someone is using dead parts to make monsters. Nah, no worries," Nic said.

"They are specifically looking for you, as well," Lyra added

She had been quiet up to this point, but now she was standing near Avo and looking concerned.

"They captured me for a bit, and before I escaped, I'm sure I saw dozens. There could be more. Hundreds even," Sixx said.

"That is bad news. The worse is probably who is at the top of all of this," Avo said.

"Moreover, what that has to do with Mr. Moss," Avo said.

"Perhaps they will be more pliable after a few weeks in the machine," the fairy said.

"The same prison you want me to step into willingly. That machine?" Taxx asked.

"Well, that's different," the fairy started.

"Different, how? No way! Give me one good reason why I should willingly walk into prison?" Taxx asked.

They all fell silent. He looked around the room, landing on Sixx last. His cousin was the only person who could meet his eye.

"I know what it look like. You can trust these people. They good. If anything look sideways, I'll bust you up out of there," Sixx said.

"Sixx. Come on, man," Taxx said.

"Look. I think you have all these questions, and this thing can give you answers. I'll be honest. Magic is its own set of gambling. I got in, and it answered some questions for me. If that helps at all," Nic said.

"Honestly, it does," Taxx said.

She put her hand on his shoulder, and they smiled at each other.

"You are a strange guy, Taxx, but you've never been in better company," she teased.

He didn't want to, but he laughed a little anyway. Nic had a knack for diffusing a situation, and her energy was always positive. If playful.

"I don't think you will lock me up or anything, but… try to see this from my perspective," Taxx said.

"Trust me, we do. Me more than most. No one will force you to enter the Inquisitor. But I will ask. Will you agree to enter the Inquisitor and allow us to try to reread you?" Avo asked.

Taxx frowned. He couldn't help but remember Blackest Eye trying to eat him, and it was sitting just there above his head. He wanted to know what was going on with him but not if it would kill him.

"I promise its safety," Avo said.

"Me too," Izzy said.

Taxx nodded.

"Ok then. Let's do it," he said.

"Excellent! Begin the experiment. Inquisitor, you may take him," Rosen said.

"Wait, what?" Taxx asked.

"Relax, Mr. Moss. This process is like falling asleep," Avo said.

"Bullshit. It's scary as hell. Clench your cheeks, trust me," Sixx said.

"That's not bad advice," Nic agreed.

That was how he knew immediately that it was **not** true. The two of them were smiling too much and waiting for him to do it.

"He saw through us," Sixx said.

"Must be magic," Nic teased.

"Why are you two being so stupid?" Taxx asked.

There was something wrong with this voice.

"To help you with the scary part. Last one. Don't look down," the fairy said.

Taxx immediately looked down and regretted it. There was a tentacle of that strange stone moving like a living creature. It reached up for his right forearm and touched him so gently he couldn't even feel it. It felt like air. Then it slowly injected a needle-like appendage into his arm that was bigger than his pinky without even a breath of feeling. Taxx watched as it snaked up and into his forearm, inch after inch. He could see it under his skin. He couldn't feel a thing. Once the needle was inside his forearm, the tentacle stopped moving.

"Oof. I wouldn't have looked," Sixx said.

"Is this thing alive?" Taxx asked.

"Yes. It speaks and has its own mind. It eats secrets. That's why we call her the Inquisitor. She has a curious mind," Avo said.

"She used to be called the Tree of Knowledge, which I think is much more appropriate. This is only a branch," The pink fairy said.

"The secret of the mountain and a place of great power. You never had anything to fear from her," Avo said.

Taxx lifted his forearm. A huge tentacle was embedded so deeply that it hardly moved when he did. Its tongue-like needle had wound its way into his bicep by now.

"You call this needle safe?" Taxx asked.

"That's not a needle," Lyra said.

"Screw that. Tell him 'bout the one in his neck," Sixx teased.

Taxx reached up to his neck and felt the tentacle firmly implanted at the base of his skull. He hadn't even thought about it because they were distracting him. This thing was a tree unlike any he had ever heard of. The tentacles he was seeing were root systems, and they were absorbing their nutrients. Something he thought was magic, but the more it reached into him, the more he understood. The thing he was looking at was much clearer to him now. He understood why the chamber was so tall, to accommodate its endless branches. The tubes, himself, and even the looking glass orbs were not a part of the tree. Its hunger trapped them. It gave that knowledge to him freely because that is not what it wanted. Absorbing magic was only a side effect of its origins. What this tree ate was even stranger than secrets.

"It doesn't eat secrets," he said.

"What? What did you say?" Nic asked.

"He said it don't eat secrets," Sixx parroted.

"Then what does it eat?" Avo asked.

"Give him time to answer!" Izzy huffed.

The fairy gently touched her shoulder, and everyone fell quiet. Just enough to hear his breathy murmur.

"It eats questions," Taxx whispered.

"I knew it! I was right. He spoke to it!" The fairy exclaimed.

The tentacles lifted him high into the air. Whatever anesthesia the tree used was so good that he couldn't feel anything. Not when it started to place him within a tube or when he was planted into its trunk. He was vaguely aware of it, but he couldn't move his body. His head felt like it weighed a thousand pounds. Green fluid began to fill the tube, and Taxx started to panic, only he couldn't speak or move. Something was crawling over his face and into his mouth. He tried to fight back, but he could hardly flex his jaw and close his mouth. The Inquisitor had him, and the dreams came like the blue-black darkness when the sun disappeared beyond the horizon.

Taxx watched the shadow of night crawl over the forest as the sun disappeared with his consciousness, and he was standing alone in the woods. He blinked against the sudden change. He could see his breath here, and the air carried the sort of chill that made it heavy when it blew past. This place was dark but somehow familiar. It was like the world that the blackest eye projected into his mind but infinitely more real. He could feel the weight of gravity here, and he was so aware of his body that it was hard to believe this wasn't real.

"Hello? Avo?" Taxx called.

There was no answer. A part of him knew it wouldn't be that easy, but he still wanted to try. After getting his bearings, Taxx started walking off in one direction, and he did not stop. He stepped over stumps and roots, shrubs, and rocks. He stopped suddenly when he noticed something on the ground. He kneeled to check it out. There were footprints here just under some leaves, and he moved them to investigate. He was no tracker, but he was sure these were his tracks. He had walked in a complete circle.

"Ok. This is good VR," Taxx said.

Still, there was no answer. The night here was lit up by a full moon so vast that he could not see the stars around it. The silvery disk gave him great light, at least. There was not much to see here, and a part of him was thankful for that. There was no shadow version of himself here either, and he had been afraid of that. So far, it was just him and the dark. He didn't know how much time had passed, he had gone from wandering to climbing, and now Taxx was sitting on a fallen tree and looking up at the moon. It was complicated to tell time here, much harder than the black glass. There was something here that kept him from thinking about it too hard. Right around then, he heard the noise for the first time. The sound of a gently snapping twig. Taxx felt his entire body respond to the tiny sound. The hairs on his skin shifted, and his senses converged on that area. There was something there. He could not see it with his eyes. He could perceive it with his gifts, and it was like seeing the outline of a human shape behind a veil of light mist. He could not see the details, but he was sure it was there, as sure as he was about the creatures in the quarry.

"I know you are there," Taxx said.

The figure moved just slightly. At first, he didn't think it would show itself, but it did just that in a few moments. A figure stepped out of the woods; hands held up on both sides of his head and a smile on his face. The man looked familiar, but Taxx was sure he had never seen him before. He was wearing an olive fedora over kind eyes and a T-shirt with suspenders. Slacks and leather shoes. His eyes were dark and deep, more than brown but less than black. He was a black man and handsome, his smile was gentle, and he looked happy. There was something about his face that was all too familiar. It all felt too convenient. He thought he was looking at his cousin, older, with different eyes, but the facial similarities were stunning.

"Who are you? What are you doing here?" Taxx asked.

"Whatcha say now, son. When two men meet on equally unknown terms, it's customary to come in peace. As I am," he

said.

"Don't call me son, old man," Taxx snapped back.

In truth, he was not so old of a man. However, an air about him spoke of older days, not ancient, just before his time. Somewhere in the 70s, by the way he wore his fro and that hat at a sharp angle. There was a bounce in the way he stepped, and a ne'er do well smile on his face.

"What should I call you then, young blood?" he asked.

"Call me what you want, but don't call me late for dinner," Taxx said.

That was something his grandmother would say. It flowed out of him so easily. The strange man made an even stranger face at him. Taxx didn't like it. It wasn't malicious per se, but he knew there was more to it than just a smile.

"What's your problem?" Taxx asked.

"You always been this hostile, my man?" the man asked.

"Ain't never had a choice. Now start answering or start **stepping**," Taxx said.

He affected the most dangerous voice he could muster and inflated his chest slightly. He did not know this man, and he was only getting closer. His bolstering seemed to work as the man stopped approaching him.

"I won't come closer. I only want to speak with you," he said.

"Speak from there. Who are you, bruh?" Taxx asked.

He was still posturing with an aggressive tone. The stranger did not seem to mind. He might have been smiling more now.

"You can call me Rhys," he said.

"What are you doing here, Rhys?" Taxx asked.

"Nah. Bruh," Rhys said.

Taxx wrinkled his eyebrows. Rhys laughed. At least until he noticed how much it upset the boy. Then he quickly and smoothly composed himself.

"I told you mine. Now you tell me your name," Rhys said.

"Taxx," he answered.

"That's a good name," Rhys said.

"A strange woman told me that once," Taxx said

"She sounds pretty wise to me," Rhys said.

The two of them looked at each other for a moment. Rhys was all smiles, his hands still up at the sides of his head.

"Can I lower my hands now?" he asked.

Taxx nodded. The older man lowered his hands slowly, and before Taxx knew it, Rhys was standing in front of him. He moved so quickly that Taxx couldn't keep up.

"What the hell?" Taxx said.

Rhys plunged the tip of one of his fingers into Taxx's neck. There was a sting like a needle, and the man was gone. Taxx tried to swing at him, but there was nothing to hit. By the time his body reacted, Rhys had taken what he wanted and put distance between them. Taxx was furious and holding the bleeding cut on his neck. It was small, but it burned like acid on his skin.

"What did you do to me?" Taxx demanded.

"You are so easily riled up, my man. I just took a little drop of blood. Try and chill, baby," Rhys said.

"I cannot chill when someone takes my blood against my will. I am no one's baby. What the hell are you, Rhys. No more bullshit," Taxx said.

His voice took on a darker tone. He called up his magic as best he could. He still wasn't sure how he had been doing any of that, to be honest. The air around him did change, enough for the strange man to notice. Rhys held up one hand, the other hand with the blood he held to his mouth, and popped his crimson fingertip in. Once he removed the blood with his tongue, he removed the finger and raised his hands again.

"I am Rhys like I said. I'm an Other. Like you, I taste. I am what you might call a Hemoturge. I use blood magic. I only took a little bitty drop of blood to examine you. I can tell your fortune with just a taste," Rhys said.

Taxx looked off for a moment and then back to Rhys. He thought of how much better the illusion in this space was than the blackest eye. Perhaps this man was the equivalent of shadow Taxx. The tree seemed to enter him in strange ways, which may have been a part of that process.

"Are you part of the Inquisitor?" Taxx asked.

"I am a part of you," Rhys said.

Taxx visibly relaxed, and Rhys slowly lowered his hands. There was no way that wasn't some magical BS. He put his face in his hands for a moment to calm down.

"I'm sorry. I didn't mean to threaten you. That's not what I do, really. I'm not used to all of this," Taxx said.

"No prob, young blood. May I continue?" Rhys asked.

Taxx nodded, and the Hemoturge returned the seemingly clean finger to his mouth and closed his eyes. Taxx observed him. There was something about the way he savored the tasting that was unsettling. The man did not give off any dangerous vibes, though. He was just strange. After a minute or two passed, Rhys opened his eyes and nodded slowly.

"You are different than I expected," Rhys said.

"Is that bad?" Taxx asked.

"Being different? Shit, no. That's the best thing you could

ever be. Listen here. If you were the same as everyone else, you would be boring. I meant to say that you are more powerful than I assumed," Rhys said.

Taxx brightened. The two were now sitting on the ground near each other in the bright moonlight.

"How is that fine ass grand momma of yours?" Rhys asked suddenly.

"Bro, **who**?" Taxx answered, his voice full of anger.

"Your blood told me. You are the grandson of Maybe Meadows. If that's true, you and I have much to talk about," Rhys said.

Taxx stood up and moved away from him a few steps. He was still feeling angry and generally upset by all of this. They told him the Inquisitor was alive, but this was too much.

"What the hell kind of machine is this?" Taxx asked.

"Oh. Is that what you meant? No. I ain't no silly question machine," he said.

"You said you were a part of it," Taxx said.

Rhys stood up and smiled again.

"You look just like her when you're mad," Rhys said.

Taxx screamed.

"What do you mean?" he shouted.

"I mean, I am your grandfather," Rhys said.

He may as well have hit him in the chest with a gut punch. There was something so familiar about this man that those words carried weight. He could see it in his eyes, in his reflection in them. There was something else too, something strange. A tingle in this most secret place, the horns on his head. He felt it now more vital than ever, a vibration from this man.

"Do you feel it?" Rhys said.

He looked amazed for a moment, the older man looking directly at the bandana on his head. He looked hopeful.

"Feel… what?" Taxx asked.

"That reverb in your horns," Rhys said.

"You know about me… my," Taxx started.

Rhys not only nodded, but he also started to laugh. Then he lifted the hat on his head just a little, and there they were. A set of horns very much like his but thick and layered with plates and deep ridges. Rhys had such long horns that they appeared like a magic trick from his fedora. They were different than Taxx's, recurved at the center, and many feet long. It was mesmerizing to see such a thing on a face like his.

"What are you? What am I?" Taxx asked.

"I am an unclassifiable what such. I prefer the term Nature Boy. My horns tell me you are too. Whatever else you are is more than I can say, and, young blood, you are something else," Rhys said.

Taxx reached up to his bandana, and he could feel them pulsing behind it. Reacting excitedly to the proximity of his horns, they gave off such power that Taxx could feel it in his toes.

"You can show me, see. I'm like you. I remember from when you were born," Rhys said.

Taxx touched his bandana, but he didn't take it off. Rhys nodded slowly after a while and walked over to his grandson. He hugged him around the shoulders.

"You must have so many questions," Rhys said.

"How can any of this be happening?" Taxx asked.

Rhys lowered his fedora and tucked away his horns. The tingle reduced in intensity as soon as he did, and Taxx sighed in relief.

"Magic is powerful but unpredictable. You are made of it down to your bones, just like me. Those things are your head are just the buds of the pride of a long line," Rhys said.

Taxx looked at him blankly.

"You don't know about your family? What you are? These aren't even horns. They are so much more important. You don't need to fear them. They are a part of you as sure as your hand. Many times more capable. But only if you free them. I could show you so much if we had more time," Rhys said.

He was so passionate that Taxx felt terrible for not wanting to show him. The older man seemed to key in on that, and he smiled.

"We don't have time anyway. It doesn't matter. What matters is that you are here, and we got to meet," Rhys said.

"Why don't we have time?" Taxx asked.

"This machine is helping me speak to you. I'm surprised it lasted this long. All these years and all I could do was watch," Rhys said.

Taxx stared at him blankly for a long moment. Rhys looked confused at first, but then he seemed to understand.

"She didn't... You have no idea where I have been, do you?" Rhys asked.

"What do you mean? You were supposed to be dead. Where have you been?" Taxx asked.

"Dead? Close, but I've been here with you all along. Inside of you, Taxx," Rhys said.

He may as well have been speaking Greek. Taxx was still stuck on the fact that he was talking to a man that was supposed to be dead.

"But. You died before I was born," Taxx said.

"I died because you were born," Rhys said.

Taxx felt the air leave his lungs.

"You don't know anything about what you've done?" Rhys asked.

"What I've done?" Taxx whispered.

He couldn't think of anything he had ever done to this man. He was dead before Taxx even had his first memory. The only thing he knew was that they shared a name.

"If you are my grandfather, why are you called Rhys?" Taxx asked.

"Calderhys Taxxis Moss is my name. I go by the name my father used. Rhys," he said.

"That's my name. I'm named after… Shit," Taxx said.

"Language," Rhys said.

Taxx looked him over again. It was uncanny, the resemblance had been there from the start, but now it was almost glowing off his face. He looked like Taxx, like Sixx. He looked like his mother. This was his grandfather.

"Do we hug now?" Taxx asked.

"I mean… if that's what you want," Rhys said.

Taxx firmly took his grandfather in a hug around the chest. They were around the same height; his grandfather was taller and more fit. He smelled like something… something he couldn't quite place. They hugged for a long while before the boy stepped away.

"Sorry," Taxx said.

"No need. I have always dreamed I could speak to you this way," Rhys said.

"Now what?" Taxx asked.

"Now. You will help me get out of here," Rhys said.

Rhys smiled. Taxx thought he saw a flash of crimson in the man's eyes for a moment, but whatever that was had gone. Taxx slowly nodded his head.

"Let's say I believe you. How can I help?" Taxx asked.

"You don't have to do anything," Rhys said.

Taxx made a face.

"No, what I mean is I can do it. If you trust me. Can you trust me?" Rhys asked.

Taxx thought about it for a moment.

"I will if you tell me what happened when I was born," Taxx said.

"You got a deal, Taxxy," Rhys said.

"So, what do I do?" Taxx asked.

"Just watch," Rhys said.

His grandfather took a bite of his own finger, just enough to draw blood. Taxx winced. Rhys only continued to smile as the blood began to pool at the end of his finger. It gathered until there was more blood than there should have been, piled high. The blood started to move on its own, take on a gelatin-like texture, and flop here and there. Then it began to scurry. It launched off his finger in long strands like hair. They moved out in every direction, passing around Taxx and through the air. Taxx had never seen anything like this.

"What is this?" Taxx asked.

"Blood magic," Rhys said.

"What are you doing?" Taxx asked.

Rhys suddenly changed his mood. He seemed stressed and uncomfortable. He started to sweat. More and more blood poured out of him, splashing on the ground, crawling around until it made a shape. All around Taxx, there were geometric shapes and strange symbols, all made of energetic blood. It pulsed with energy.

"Forcing open the door inside of you. Only it's taking too long," Rhys said.

"Why?" Taxx asked.

"No idea. It should have been done by now, I've had plenty of time to think of this spell, and I've run so many contingencies. Only. Something is wrong, something I hadn't considered," Rhys said.

"What does that mean?" Taxx asked.

"I didn't imagine there would be something blocking the door," Rhys said.

"What could it possibly be? What's inside of me?" Taxx asked.

"Not what. Who. Someone already used a spell similar to this on you.

"What does that mean?" Taxx asked.

"There is already someone inside. Something dangerous. Hot damn. Taxx. Listen… grandma… she," Rhys started.

He knew what it meant. He knew exactly what those words meant when arranged in that way. It was not understanding he lacked. He was in disbelief.

"What can I do?" Taxx asked.

"Force it out, and it will make… your grandma… she…" Rhys started.

His voice and the dream world faded away. Like the rays of the coming dawn, beams of light burned every bit of this reality away in a breath, and Taxx was forced awake.

Chapter | Thirteen

The dream of the inquisitor was torn away, and reality came back to him all at once. The sensation was jarring, and he felt something lurch in his stomach. The fluid receded from the tank, and he was standing on the platform again. The mask was removed from his mouth, and he took a long deep breath. Then his body shifted suddenly as though he would vomit, but nothing came up. He took another long breath. He was trying to collect himself.

"What happened? Why did I come out?" Taxx said frantically.

"Calm down, Taxx. Something came up," Sixx said.

"No, you don't understand. I saw him. I saw him," Taxx said.

"That will have to wait. The guild has ended the experiment,"

Avo said.

Taxx was unable to see. The green goo was still draining from the tube, and he could not see. It was so hard to talk. He was still gasping for air.

"No, I have to go back in. I saw my grandfather," Taxx said.

"Now that is interesting," the fairy said.

"You saw him?" Sixx asked.

Taxx nodded and cleared the goop away from his eyes. The machine released him and removed its tentacles painlessly from his body. Once he was free, he checked his forearm, and there was no scar. The green fluid had not even made him or his clothes feel wet. There were so many questions to ask and no time to ask them. The tree placed him back down on the ground once he was clear of the tube. Everyone in the room looked apprehensively at the staircase, and Taxx did the same. Just in time to see Offrey descending them.

"Offrey? What are you-" Taxx began.

She raised her hand to stop him and shook her head, her braids bounced, but the weight of their enormous length held them in place. She was dressed so officially this time. Taxx could only stare at her as she looked past him to the Wardens and Rosen, who greeted her with a low bow. Sixx looked his way for a moment, and what Taxx saw on his face only added to his confusion. Sixx was bowing as well, and he felt like he was missing out on a joke.

"Taxx, it's customary to bow before the-" Nic began.

Offrey smiled and waved her off.

"He knows me. Calderhys, please give me a moment, and I will explain everything," Offrey said.

Then she turned to his cousin, looking him in the eyes.

"Sixx," Offrey said.

She said Sixx's name with a bit of stoicism, to which he responded with an incendiary smirk. He rose from a deep bow, but he did not speak. Taxx couldn't stop looking between them.

"What the heck is going on with the two of you? Sixx, it's Offrey, man. Who is she supposed to be?" Taxx asked

"Taxxis!" Lyra said.

Offrey waved her off again with a hand, and Taxx was staring at that hand like he kept expecting a beam of light to leap out of it and explain why all these people were acting like this. Maybe he had lost more blood than he thought.

"I speak for She," Offrey said.

Her voice was heavy with power. It shook the air enough to make him step back.

"I am the Magistrate and 5th Chair of the Mesalto. I speak for my Master, the 1st Chair," Offrey said.

"Wait, your master?" Taxx asked.

She didn't seem to hear him.

"We welcome you, Magistrate, but I must tell you that I am surprised that Queen Moss would trouble herself with such simple matters," The Rosen Lady said.

She and Offrey greeted each other with a familiar hug before the young woman turned to face Taxx and Sixx again, shaking her head.

"Circumstances required her immediate intervention," Offrey said.

"Queen!?" Taxx shouted.

Sixx moved toward him and tried to calm him down, but Taxx looked like he had been hit by a city bus, and that's when things started to click into place for a certain young Warden.

"No way, no way. Look at me, guy, look at my eyes. Capital F. This is way above our pay grade. Who does he look like?" Nic asked.

She took his face in her hands and looked it over carefully before she stepped away and started to swear, shaking her head at Sixx and Taxx, Lyra was not nearly so dramatic, but even she looked worried.

"Please elaborate on those circumstances, Magistrate," Lyra said.

"Taxx…" Sixx started.

"Did you know about all of this, Sixx? How… Why didn't I know any of this about Grandma?" Taxx asked.

"Who is your grandmother Mr. Kingswood?" Lyra asked.

"His name is Calderhys Taxxis Moss II. He and **that** one there are the only grandchildren of Lady Maybelline Marigold Meadows Moss, 1st Chair of the Mesalto and the living queen to all witches," Offrey said.

"The WHO?!" Taxx asked.

Offrey had been a member of his grandmother's household since Taxx could remember, and he was still unclear on the particulars of their relationship. There were parts of her that had not changed since he had last seen her. She was still wearing a flat brim hat so wide that he did not know how she balanced. Now he could see that she had some light tattooing on one of her cheeks, cascading down her face like the shadow of tears. Her aura was different, and she reeked of power. Not just a mysterious strength like the Warden, but something more tangible. It was the air around her, he realized. It was alive with sizzling energy, just like the fairy. He could see it now and then warping around her like a heat haze, and he could feel it on his skin like warmth from a distance. It was clear that whatever her title was, she was powerful.

"What circumstances?" Avo asked.

"She prophesied the end of the world would be reborn here," Offrey said.

"So, you've come to stop that from happening, then?" the fairy asked.

"Something like that," Offrey said.

Avo nodded. Offrey continued to descend the stairs, and shortly after her, another woman followed. She was shorter, and her skin was pale. She was well dressed like Offrey, but what she wore had been cut much more straightforwardly. This woman's hair was red, and she wore no hat, just a high pony. Her eyes were amber and burning with excitement. Somehow Taxx knew that she was not to be trusted. Once they reached the ground floor, the pair slowly walked toward them. High pony waved at Sixx, and he gave her a look that said things Taxx couldn't read. Did they know each other? He wondered. Avo stepped away from the computer, and Offrey took over the space. She started typing on the keyboard with practiced familiarity. The machine was in motion in moments, and the tubes he could see started to move. They vanished into the ground and were replaced by a different. Each one held an Other, some shaped like nightmares, and some just like them.

"Now I understand what you were doing down here on your own so much," Avo said, shaking his head.

"Yes. I learned everything there was to know about the Nullun. You told me to learn its secrets, and I have… along with yours," Offrey said.

She entered another set of commands, and all of the screens

in the room started to flash. They were all showing the same thing, a name, his name. Avogorum Zorrum Illunorum.

"How long have you known?" Avo said.

If he was tense, he did not show it. The corner of his mouth was curled up in a smirk.

"How could you think you ever fooled me, light show," Offrey said.

The sound of a klaxon was blaring over their heads, and other alarms chimed into the chorus. There were red lights and green lights, all flashing. There were chirps and bells and whistles.

"You still think you can threaten my life? Even knowing what I am, it is clear that you know nothing," Avo said.

"Tell me that in a day or two, if you still can," Offrey said.

The alarms all stopped with a final keypress, and the computer in the strange language calmed down. There was a low sound, deep beneath their feet, and a tremble rolled up to the walls of the Nullun. Avogorum was the only one who did not look unsure and terrified by all of the commotions. Even when it all settled, he was standing there smiling.

"You are braver than I gave you credit for," Offrey said.

"Not at all. I am terrified. How thrilling," Avo said.

"Avo…" Izzy whispered.

The sorcerer held up a hand to stop her.

"Now that you have condemned me. What's next?" Avo asked.

The tubes started to move again and at a much faster pace. There was no sense in trying to count them. There seemed to be an endless number of them cascading off into the depths of the Nullun. Thousands upon thousands of occupied cells.

"How many of those do you have? What is all of this?"

Taxx asked.

"Status tubes. They keep the subject inside under effective sedation, and an illusion injected directly into their minds," Avo said.

Taxx nodded slowly. Blackest Eye was the looking glass that had tried to kill him the other day. Remembering how real it all felt inside of that glass made him shiver.

"There are more of them than grains of sand on the beach," Nic said.

"Technically, this is just a lab outside the Inquisitor. The entire mountain is its body. The Tree of knowledge grows through this world and beyond," Rosen said.

"That's impossible," Taxx said.

"You are talking to a fairy," Lyra reminded him.

"Point," Taxx said.

Everyone turned toward the tube that Offrey brought to the surface. It came to a slow stop, and the green cylinder was completely clear and sat empty.

"Dear Gods," Avo said.

"I knew it," Offrey whispered.

"What does that mean? Who's cell is this?" Sixx asked.

Izzy had been quiet up to this point, but she read the number aloud.

"Looks like… number 00001," Izzy said.

She read each zero. Then she read the number all over again. Every time she said it, the energy in the room got worse.

"That can't be possible," Izzy said.

"What can't be? What's supposed to be in there?" Taxx asked.

"A nasty type of Other with unprecedented elemental

power," Avo said.

"The wandering earth," Offrey said.

Taxx felt his skin go cold. That was a name he had heard before. A name he had started to think was a dream. He instinctually touched his belly. There was nothing there, but he did feel it gurgle strangely.

"Te'Amath," Taxx said.

Offrey was looking at his face when he spoke her name, and the two of them locked eyes. He didn't see fear there. There was something worse. Offrey was happy, and she was smiling.

"Tell us what's happening," Avo said.

"There is no time. I have seen it. This is the place for the rebirth of a God," Offrey said.

"A what?" Taxx started.

Something was wrong with him.

"She always said it was you. That you would bring about the end. I did not know she meant literally. Now I see why she had to kill you. How wonderful that she could not," Offrey said.

She had been staring at him for a long time before she spoke to him. As if she were waiting for something, and when he opened his mouth to respond, the words would not come. At first, it just seemed to be an average bout of shock at hearing something unbelievable. He was standing there staring at his childhood friend and his cousin. He looked from them to the fairy and the stoic magic fed and her young. All of them were looking at him expectantly as if he was supposed to say something or do something, but he couldn't think of anything to do but stand there. The quiet was already heavy, and it did not let up, or maybe that was just the pressure inside his head from trying to cram all the new things he just leaned into his mind all at once. Whatever the cause, the effect was a headache that started very deep in the recesses of his mind, the place where he put all the dark and terrible things that you couldn't even remember, a dark well beyond the wall of his memory. The pain came just after it like a trailing banner, and just like that, the sensation of a sharp thorn digging into his eye spread all over him like fire.

"Taxx!?" Sixx shouted.

Taxx screamed and tried to clutch at his eye, but he couldn't move his hands, so he settled on collapsing to his knees and starting to curl up into himself. Sixx tried to rush to his side, but Lyra grabbed him before he could continue.

"Restrain yourself in the face of the Magistrate, please. Look and do not speak, " Lyra said.

"What are you doing to him!" Sixx shouted.

The sound echoed all around them from the shadows, like a hundred Sixx's were screaming all at once. The sound vibrated off the walls. None of them seemed to notice. Lyra might have looked a bit disappointed in him.

"If you throw a tantrum, I will have to treat you like a petulant child, Mr. St. Martin," Lyra warned.

Nic disappeared, and Lyra locked eyes with the young shadow user.

"Where she go?" Sixx asked.

"To find handcuffs," Lyra said.

Sixx looked her up and down, sizing her up for a moment before turning his attention back to Taxx, who had stopped screaming and was now groaning, and when he looked back to the warden, he seemed to have changed tactics.

"Please help him. I won't fight," Sixx said.

"I believe you," Nic said from behind him.

Sixx jumped, but he could not move his hands from behind his back. Nic was there and already securing them by the time he flinched. She locked him tightly.

"Damn, that was slick. You crafty as hell. Imma have to use this one," Sixx said.

"On the house," Nic said.

Nic punctuated her words with a wink, clapped him on the shoulder, then leaned in close and whispered something in his ear. He froze for a moment before he nodded.

"My apologies, Magistrate," Lyra said.

"Indeed," Offrey nodded.

She never took her eyes from Taxx.

There was a tension in the air that Taxx was hyper-aware of, he couldn't control his voice or his body anymore, but he still moved and spoke, groaned, and screamed without any impulse. When he tried to speak, nothing happened. It was like being a passenger in his own body while something else was at the wheel, or worse, no one. The thought made him want to scream, but he couldn't even do that. He could barely think, and soon he felt he was about to be squeezed out. He would be crushed by whatever was occupying the places he had once been, and soon even these thoughts would be the only remnant of his old self.

"Zora, please don't let him die!" Sixx pleaded.

She did not answer.

Taxx's body started to heave and shiver and quake, and just like when he retched up the Knot, something began to crawl out of him, only this time it was not worms. It was wood. Shreds and ribbons were coming out of his mouth. Then came chips and shims of all shapes, accompanied by a dark and gelatinous slime. The pieces were unmistakably wood. The sound made it harder to watch. No one looked away except for Nic, who was heaving all by herself behind the Amazonian warden. It took a while before it was done, but eventually, there was silence, and Taxx was lying on his back with black slime all over his face. Horrifyingly he was wide awake and seemed to be completely calm.

"What the…" Sixx started.

"Do not speak, only watch," Lyra said.

The pile of goo started to move on its own, not like it was sentient but perhaps like some grand design was driving its purpose, each flake and piece slammed into one another. Pushed by the black slime that was all around and sandwiched between each piece, it seemed to be the thing that made the wood move. The sound was like a steady tapping or grinding as the wood crushed and squeezed and crashed together, and separate piles started to take on uniform shapes. The random mass of misshapen timber came together into a rectangle and, finally, a door in just a few moments. Once it was fully formed, it rose from the ground. The last remnants of slime slithered into the many cracks and imperfections of the door and started the handle on both sides, and when it was done, there was just a perfect door. A strange and heavy door studded with shiny brass rings hammered into its surface, each one punching a small dimple into the thick violet wood. The handle was black and long as though someone had made a long deep ink stroke in the air, and it froze in place, glistening like dark metal in the air.

"Why did I throw up a door?" Taxx asked.

"Taxx! Thank goodness!" Sixx said.

Sixx ran to his cousin's side and slid down on the floor next to him. Looking him over, Sixx looked relieved.

"You smell right at least… somehow," Sixx said.

His eyes went to the slime on his cousin's face and then back to his eyes.

"Taxx. There was a door inside of you," Sixx said.

"Yeah," Taxx said.

"You threw up a door," Sixx said.

"Yeah," Taxx whispered.

He sounded a little sad.

"Nobody looks cool throwing up anything, but that was some of the coolest stuff I ever saw in my life, cousin," Sixx said.

"Yeah?" Taxx asked.

"Hey man, what the hell wrong witcha? You keep saying 'yeah' like you have gone simple or something. You freakin' me out, man," Sixx shouted.

"Sixx. I just threw up a door. I'm just a little… like, can I have a hug?" Taxx said.

"Nah, man… You **really** just did that, but nah," Sixx said.

"I'm having an extraordinary day," Taxx said.

"We both had a strange one. You gonna have to come with something harder than that if you want some of this love, Cuh," Sixx said.

"I'm pretty sure a baby called me a bitch the other day," Taxx said

Sixx had the courtesy to look a little shocked.

"Damn. A real baby or something that only looked like a baby?" Sixx asked.

"Honestly? Maybe it was both," Taxx said.

For a moment, Sixx didn't say anything. He just looked at his cousin's face and scanned his dark eyes for any signs that he might have been lying. When he didn't find anything, he turned and offered his shoulder to Taxx.

"…Aiight den, come on," Sixx said.

Taxx lowered his head to rest on Sixx's shoulder tentatively, and Sixx leaned in. He could not sling his arms around him because of the handcuffs, but the two of them settled their heads together. Neither of them said anything. Taxx closed his eyes, and he took a very deep breath and exhaled the air from his lungs. The breath was long and inelegant, maybe even a bit ragged, but Taxx could not remember the last time he felt anything so good. Once it was over, he lingered for a moment. Sixx pulled free of his cousin and leaped to his feet without his hands.

"You better now?" Sixx asked.

"Almost…," Taxx said.

Maybe Sixx was feeling idealistic, but he even seemed to be standing straighter, like he was raised right, Sixx thought. Overall, he was pleased with what he saw. Taxx caught him staring and smiled awkwardly before he turned to look at the people around them again. It was as if he was seeing it with new eyes and those eyes were damned angry from the look of things if Sixx had anything to say about it.

"Why are you in handcuffs?" Taxx asked.

"Public safety, prolly," Sixx answered.

"Noted. You and I need to talk about Offrey later," Taxx said

"What about?" Offrey asked.

Taxx turned to look at her, and he frowned a little.

"Where have you been?" Taxx asked.

"There will be time for that later. First, we need to secure this vessel. Serafima," Offrey said.

The red-haired woman who accompanied her immediately

went into motion. She had only just approached the door when small objects fell from the sky and clattered on the ground. They rang like bells with every bounce and landed just at her feet. Two small gold coins that were no bigger than a pinky nail. Serafima stopped cold. A figure darkened the stairwell, and a man started to descend. Whoever it was had a hulking form, he was easily the largest man that Taxx had ever seen, taller than Lyra, and his skin was as pale as alabaster stone. His eyes were gold pools in a salt ocean, but there was no glittering horror show of teeth when he smiled. There was only a single twisted gold tooth among a small patch of pale-yellow cousins. The man looked right at Taxx, but these could not be the eyes from before. His memory was hazy, but this was not him.

"The adjudicator of the Midnight Auction is here? That's not good," Nick whispered.

"Who or what in the hell is the adjudicator of the Midnight Auction?" Sixx said.

He did not whisper.

"Well, you heard him call for me. Stand aside, you useless white turd," said the Adjudicator.

A second person appeared behind the pale behemoth; this one was much smaller. Everything about him was smaller and sharper than the larger man, like a machete and a razor blade. This one had similar eyes and white skin, but Taxx felt the blood in his veins go cold when he smiled. He now had a face to attach to the glittering horror he could not get out of his mind since he had first seen it. It was staring him right in the face again beneath crisp rectangular sunglasses as dark as night and attached to an unexpectedly handsome face. The man who tried to murder him was dressed head to toe in clean white with gold accents, he was about average height, and his body looked fit. Entirely too human for the thing that Taxx knew was lurking beneath that skinsuit. Once they descended the stairs, Offrey rushed to meet him, and they shook hands.

"Cornelio. I was not expecting you," Offrey said.

"I told you a thousand times, girl. My name is Mr. Drip. That name you always use is not my real name. Did I ever tell you?" Drip asked.

"No," Offrey said politely.

Drip nodded and smiled again, the room reflected in the endless glittering rows of his encrusted and horrifying teeth.

"You were never wrong. I suppose it does belong to me. Took it as payment for debts owed. It belonged to a human I used to know. One of my very first deals. Long before the time of electricity. He was a wonderful murderous tyrant, a real credit to those monkeys," Cornelio said.

Offrey was smiling nervously, and everyone else in the room was on such an edge that even Taxx could feel it. He tried to keep his temper in check, but it spoke every moment. Taxx could only stare at his mouth. The mouth that he burned into his memory. He felt his fists clench.

"If I have offended you," Offrey started.

Drip stopped her with only a raised finger. His golden eyes were locked on Taxx. He was openly staring at him. The light in his golden eyes was so intense that the dark shades only served to dim the pools of shimmering metal. They were gilded craters, and the molten centers were pinned on him as surely as any eye.

"Shh. I am talking," Drip said.

He turned his eyes to Offrey only for a moment. She quietly nodded. The Adjudicator looked pleased as the tension in the room grey to stifling heights. They reached the bottom of the stairs, and the dapper man adjusted his lapels.

"Now Cornelio was a human with vast wealth and reach. A human to be admired with a collection of delicious antiquities the world would never see again. He had a hundred sons and daughters and connections to every crown on earth," he said.

This being was sharp all over, like a living knife. His magic was dangerous, even from a distance like molten lava. Taxx swore he could feel the heat of it. The smell of flowers and blood preceded him, and Taxx couldn't help but think that its sweet horror suited him well.

"Fuckwit, get your ass over here. I want to sit," he said.

The massive man curled himself down to the ground with all the grace of an enormous bear, settling on one knee. The other was raised up and carefully adjusted. Once that was done, the massive man pulled out a small dustpan and brush and, with impressive ability, cleaned his knee. Cornelio perched himself on that knee and crossed one of his legs over the other.

"That will do, FW," he said.

"Mr. Drip," Offrey said.

"Now, now," Drip said.

He cut her off and waved his finger in front of him with a golden nail that tapered to a point with a beveled edge. He was impeccably manicured from head to toe. Even FW, his associate, was dressed well for a living chair. Something about this was getting Taxx more disgusted by the second, and his anger was seething.

"Let me finish. Cornelio had everything in the world. Power. More money than a human could need, but he needed more than that," Drip said.

Serafima stepped away from the coins. Drip only looked at her, and she froze. Everyone in the room was frozen, even worse than when Offrey showed up. She made them react like danger was near. Drip changed the air into a predatory weight that hung on everyone's shoulders. The only person who seemed unaffected was Taxx.

"In exchange for just one of those coins, I stole the ears of kings and waged wars with his blessing. He poisoned the mouths of his sons and daughters and fed them to me one by one. He watched as I sold and ate every piece of his wealth and drank the blood of his kin. When that wasn't enough, he offered me more. This name. This face. Even his life. Such value does just one of them hold. I, of course, took it all with zeal, but even then, it was not enough to balance the scales for just one of those coins," Drip said.

"What does that have to do with us?" Taxx shouted.

Everyone in the room looked at him. Drip did not. The man was still sitting casually on the knee of his associate as he observed Offrey. The witch was staring at the coins.

"If you understand what I am offering you, you will take them," Drip said.

Offrey went still. Her face lost all emotion, and she stared at the demon, watching the liquid gold in its never-ending torrent from his mouth.

"You lie," she whispered. She sounded bewildered.

"I never lie when it comes to a deal. You can take them both with my blessing and the promise of safety for you and your female. All I want from you is that door. Off the books," Drip said.

Offrey said nothing. The air in the room was so heavy that it would have forced Taxx to lower his head any other time. He was too angry, and it was only getting worse. The more he listened to that smug thing speak. He wanted to punch him in his gold teeth. Taxx couldn't take it anymore, and he stepped forward, screaming with rage.

"What did he trade you to leave me on the side of the road?" Taxx asked.

Drip did not react. Offrey turned to look at him and then to Sixx, who moved to his cousin's side.

"What does he mean, Zora?" Sixx asked.

"I mean, she left me to this… thing. Those monsters that have been after us are definitely related to him," Taxx said.

Offrey was looking more and more distant as time passed. Each accusation he hurled at her seemed to send her farther away.

"And YOU. How dare you show your face after what you did!" Taxx shouted.

He pointed his finger at Mr. Drip, and the man raised an eyebrow above his shades. FW looked confused, but he might have always looked cluttered.

"Mr. Drip, I-" Offrey started.

Mr. Drip only looked at Offrey, and she stopped speaking. The rest of the room filled with tension like a slow leak, but Taxx couldn't hold back anymore. He's had enough.

"What the hell are you doing here?" Taxx asked.

"Yeah! And what the hell kind of name is Mr. Drip?" Sixx added.

"Your name is a number, dude," Nic said.

Lyra touched Nic gently on the shoulder, and the other warden immediately quieted down.

"Mr. Drip. These boys are-," Offrey started.

Drip gave her one last look, and Offrey quieted down completely. The magistrate looked at Serafima and nodded only once, slowly. Then Serafima knelt and retrieved the coins from the ground quietly. Izzy openly gasped, and Avogorum looked as though he had been gutted.

"So, it's true, you are working with the Midnight Auction?" he asked.

"Go on," Offrey said.

Serafima gave her a stern look, and then she looked at Drip, who was still all smiled.

"You are sure about this?" she asked.

"Take them and go. You know the plan," Offrey said.

Serafima gave her a hard look but ultimately, she nodded. Offrey reached out and touched the coins in her hands, running her fingers over them. When she was done, Serafima took off for the stairs and started up them without looking back. Once she was gone, Offrey turned around toward the group. She shook her head. She was holding her hands folded in prayer out in front of her. She looked like a politician, and that was never good.

"Save your lies for someone else," Izzy said.

"You wouldn't believe the stress I am under. There are things that you cannot understand. Just do as I say and take the boys and get," Offrey started.

Taxx cut her off with a guttural sound. Even though he hadn't meant it to be, his voice was full of magic. It was pouring off him in increasing amounts, fueled by his anger and wildness in the air.

"No! I'm done with people showing up and trying to kill me with no consequence. You will apologize to me or...," Taxx trailed off.

"Or. What?" Mr. Drip said.

The golden horror of his mouth released such power in his voice that Taxx could barely understand what he said like he was underwater or speaking in the lowest bass he had ever heard. He felt the words in his bones. There was a moment when he felt a familiar fear starting to grow in his belly, the same sharpness that slowly stabbed through him. Then he felt his cousin at his side, and suddenly there was no cold. There was more. It was more than warmth, and not just heat but Fire too. Burning brighter now with the presence of his childhood best friend and relative, Taxx could not put it out.

"Tell him how the Moss boys handle 'em," Sixx said.

Maybe he felt emboldened by his brash companions' words, but he knew what was happening too well. Sixx was released some of his magic into Taxx's body. Sixx was born with a bottomless well of volatile magic, and Taxx was born unique in his way. Taxx could absorb magic. He didn't even have to try to do it, his body was made to drink magic, and his cousin's magic was spicy, making him likewise. Drawing magic from Sixx felt like taking a shot of rum with jalapenos in it, and it spread through him like hot tea on a cold morning, and before he could stop himself, the words slipped out of his mouth.

"Or **I'm gonna whoop your ass**," Taxx said.

He meant to say it with the same sort of ne'er do well flair that his cousin had, but Taxx didn't have the swagger in his step. However, there was magic in his voice, which made the air tremble with his power to punctuate his words. The area dimmed, and the quarry floor kicked up some dust. There was magic in the air, angry magic that tossed sand and small debris in a straight line toward Mr. Drip, kicking just a bit of dirt onto his white shoes. The adjudicator adjusted his jacket.

"For your sake, I will let you off with words just this once. Listen closely. First, don't you ever come at me like that. I don't play. If you speak out of turn again, I will have my man here pop your head like a grape," Drip said.

Taxx opened his mouth to speak a rebuttal, but the Demon continued talking right over him.

"Second, if I wanted you dead. Then you would die," Drip said.

"And yet, I live," Taxx said.

"Are you certain?" Drip asked.

"No!" Nic shouted.

Drip snapped his fingers. FW was as tall as a basketball player and built like the kind of strongman that wrestled bears. His arms were anacondas in a suit. He was practically armored in thick muscles as pale as the moon. That alarming pallor made his eyes stand out like gold coins on a corpse. This creature looked human, but his proportions exceeded the limits of the form. His hands were so large that Taxx couldn't help but think that one of them might easily fit the entire way around a human head. As soon as he had the thought, Nic screamed, and the alabaster man made his move. Drip stood up, and FW vanished from sight. He was gone. There was no sound or flash, and the hulking mass just vanished. Only for a moment, he reappeared in front of the boys, and with a single twist of his wrist, he swatted Sixx out of the way. Sixx was sent launching so hard that if Lyra had not caught him, there was no telling where he might have traveled. There was a handprint at the center of his chest slowly filling with blood, and Sixx gasped and gargled. Taxx tried to call out his cousin's name, but he couldn't speak. He couldn't breathe. The world went black all around him as he discovered that he had been right earlier. That creature easily fit its hand around Taxx's head, and Taxx felt his neck stretch with a satisfying crack. Then a **far** less satisfying one.

Taxx tried to scream, but he couldn't breathe or hear either. The giant was trying to pull off his head and making excellent progress. Taxx struggled against him, but he could not escape. He tried with everything he had in him, and for a moment, he thought he could feel those stiff iron fingers starting to give way to his prying fingers, slowly beginning to draw them apart. Then he felt something bubble up from inside him, and his body heaved. This would be the perfect time to throw up another door. Maybe a window, he thought. Instead, he heard a voice within him that sounded like blood splattering on concrete. He could see it. Feel every peal of laughter that came from such a sinister voice. Then he heard a voice in his heart before he heard it in his head. The voice only said one word, but he felt changed as soon as he heard it like a lightning bolt. Taxx could no longer feel the squeezing of the monster's hand anymore. There was only pressure. The voice said the same thing the shadows whispered in his dreams all these nights. It told him to devour. Only this time was different. Taxx said yes.

"Finally. That motha' fucka' had some fight in him, didn't he?" Drip teased.

FW did not seem to share his sentiment and made a sound like meh. The monster held the boy longer and longer while the others looked on. Sixx lunged for the monstrous man but was held back by Lyra and Nic, they both looked somber, but the tingle of impending violence hung in the air like humidity and was shared amongst almost all present.

"If my cousin is dead, you and your boy are done," Sixx said.

Sixx was unseasonably calm, but his hands trembled with rage or fear. If Drip noticed or cared, he did not seem to react. He didn't even acknowledge the threat.

"Magistrate. I don't care for whatever this is. I've made my offer for the door. You may take the rest and go, but for my trouble, I now claim this house," Drip said

"You bastard!" Lyra shouted.

"You would never do this if she were here," Avo said.

"Silence the children, or I will," Drip said.

"The house is not available. I will also require the boy be-" Offrey started.

"You will not tell me what I can and cannot heave," Drip said.

Offrey pursed her lips and nodded, saying nothing. Sixx struggled against Lyra and Nic, screaming, roaring, and about to unleash a flurry of expletives. He never got the chance. Offrey only twitched a few fingers, and a black thread wound its way up Sixx's body until it reached his mouth like a living being. In a breath, the thread dug into Sixx's lips and sewed his mouth completely shut. He huffed and hummed what was indeed a vicious collection of choice American swear words. Only mumbles came out.

"Mr. Drip," Offrey said.

"Enough. FW, hurry and finish up. We have things to do," Drip said.

"What exactly are you here to do?" Avo asked.

"Never you mind, child," Drip answered.

FW looked up at his master with his golden eyes and nodded, but he did not move. He seemed to be unable to remove his hand from the boy's head. The gentle tugging turned into a firm yank, but none of that seemed to be able to remove his hand. FW looked back to his master, looking confused and gurgling loudly. Drip let out a slow dry cackle fit for the demon hiding behind that face. And those very angular sunglasses, he shook his head and started to walk toward FW.

"Next time, don't squeeze so hard, you idiot. Now you've become tangled up in that child's brain. I should just tear your arm off," Drip said.

FW gurgled.

"You a wild mother fucka, FW. I love it, but you can free yourself with that mouth," Drip said.

There was something heavy in the air. Severe enough to make Drip stop walking, the smile fell from his face. There was magic radiating from the body in thick waves. Like a wild ocean. Like a wild star. Drip looked closely at the boy in his assistant's grip, and for a moment, he looked upset.

"FW, move away from that thing. NOW," Drip shouted.

He spoke just a moment too late. FW was already caught up in them. Black Thorns. They appeared suddenly out of the young man's body like porcupine quills, as black as the back of midnight's eyelids and by the dozens. Dozens by the Dozens. Taxx felt them coming long before they broke the skin. He called them here when he gave his answer to the shadows. Somehow, he could say it out loud, and they heard him. The shadows that slept inside him were awake and dancing inside his bones. Clamoring to get out and hungry for magic. They tore out of him at every angle, coming out of his hands and elbows, forearms, and feet. Even the back of his neck was bristling with thorns that glistened like claws. Taxx felt no pain. In those dark and terrible dreams, where hungering shadows chased him, not once was he ever afraid. There was something he always knew at the center of himself. Even when the thorns came from his eyes and skin, he knew the truth. The thorns were his protection. He had never called on them before, and still, they had come. They weren't the claws of a rose. They were as thick as pencils and nearly as long, each as sharp as a quill and tapered to pierce. They punctured through FWs palm and forearm like an iron dandelion, disregarding muscles, and bone, tearing and plunging ever deeper into his torso as they grew even longer. After just a few breaths, the thorns already rose to the length of daggers and now threatened to skewer FW, who could not remove himself from the coming points.

"How interesting," Drip said.

Then he moved so quickly that two of him appeared to be standing near the computer and the other standing next to his assistant. The version next to the computer faded, and the remaining Drip laid a hand on FW's forearm. His hand appeared so small by comparison that he might as well have been grabbing at a felled log. That much smaller hand snapped FW's forearm off just before the elbow in the blink of an eye. It made the sounds of a celery stalk. His fingers cleanly cut and pinched flesh and bone like a garden sheer on fresh weeds. Drip pinched the end of FW's arm with a vice-like grip to stem the tide of blood. There was only a flash of golden light for an instant, then the sound of sizzling flesh and a bright metal cap was placed on the end of the nub where his arm had been. The gold was glowing red hot on the end of FW's arm, but he did not scream. He did not make any noise during his impromptu surgery either. The beastly man did not react, not a nod, a gurgle, or a sideways glance. He only stared at Mr. Drip with a simple smile on his face.

"What are you?" Drip asked.

Drip was staring at Taxx, who was still hanging limp in the air in the remaining hand and arm FW left behind, his feet not touching the ground. He was floating as though the disembodied arm were still holding him aloft when that was impossible. Drip could not look away. He could only stare. A single tear of pure gold slowly oozed out of the bottom of his shades. Then the other eye began to drip liquid gold that inched slowly down his cheeks. The thick lines flowed over the apple of his cheeks as his smile widened, and the gold poured down from his eyes directly into his mouth. It danced along the lower ridges of his spiny teeth and down his bottom lip.

"He is…" Offrey began.

Mr. Drip cut her off by waving his hand at her dismissively. That action set Sixx off, mumbling incoherently, but the intent was directed in Drip's general direction.

"I want him," Drip said.

He then reached into his jacket's interior pocket and pulled out a golden handkerchief which he gently held out and slowly let float down to the earth until it landed softly next to his shoe. There were still some remnants of the dust just on the tip there but never once did he remove his eyes from Taxx.

"FW, come and see this, you useless pile," Drip said.

FW dutifully moved to his side and reached out with the gold-capped severed arm first before he changed to the other and carefully hunched to retrieve the square. It looked like a cotton swab in his hands, but those massive hands gently cleared the shoe of all debris, and when he was done, FW stood and smiled at his master. Drip slapped the handkerchief out of his hand and waved him off with disgust, never moving his eyes from Taxx.

"I should have left the other arm; this is a piss poor job. Go and fetch the case for the Magistrate and bring the whistle case for the boy," Drip said.

Sixx huffed.

Nic took a step forward, and Offrey held out a hand to stop her, glancing back at the warden for a moment before she turned back to Drip.

"Queen Moss would become… cross, were I to sell her grandson for any amount. We cannot accept it. You understand," Offrey said.

Drip stopped FW from leaving with a look. Then he turned back to Offrey, searching her face with the gold crucibles he called eyes. Once he was convinced that she was serious, he nodded slowly.

"If I cannot have him, perhaps I will help you end his misery. On the house," Drip said.

"No, don't!" Offrey shouted.

Drip had already completed his action before she completed her protest. He used his magic to create a large coin. Then he flipped it. The seemingly innocuous act sent a gold coin flying at the young man with such speed that it was hard to see with the naked eye. The coin left a trail in its wake as it broke the sound barrier, and the noise crackled like lightning in the small room. A thorn attempted to intercept the projectile and splintered under the force of the gold coin, the thorn shattering to pieces as the going cut through its center like it was halving a stalk of celery. The currency traveled on and intercepted more thorns, crushing them on impact as well at first until the thorns began to change. They stopped growing in single stalks and started to grow in twisted bunches that tapered to a point like the head of an arrow. This time it was successfully contained in midair by the convergence of the shadowy spears. The gold coin stopped just inches from Taxx's face. Offrey gasped, and Drip looked as shocked as a demon could look, his gold smile faltering only slightly.

"How?" Drip asked.

Drip was in the middle of speaking when the boy's body twitched just a bit, and Drip stopped. Taxx's body had not moved since the thorns grew out of him. The gory arm and some parts of FW left behind were still caught up in the thorns that had grown as long as spears. FW's disembodied hand was still clenched around Taxx's head. It started to darken as though it were rotting. The earthy dark that only decomposed things can create, and the arm began to dry out until the remaining skin fell away and crumbled to pieces. The pieces never touched the floor, they were caught up in the thorns, and every touch seemed to take more and more. Soon the remains were minimized to dust and beyond, leaving only Taxx hovering in the center of a corona of black thorns. His eyes were wide open with the light of wild magic furiously pouring out of them. They were glowing with bright green light like tiny suns. They burned so hot that the corners of his eyes began to crack with their force.

Above his eyes, his horns grew thicker and longer, half straight with a small recurve. Horns that were aflame with green light. Taxx's mouth fell open, and the greensong spilled out as soon as it did. The song had many voices harmonizing sweetly though his face was contorted in horror. The light from his horns grew so intense it seemed to surround his whole body, and the thorns grew longer. They even pierced the Nullun beneath his feet and began to take from it, drawing power like straws until the stone crumbled and cracked. The stone in the room started to blacken, and wisp-like threads grew up and out from the cracks, white and slight as hairs. They grew toward the boy, stretching upwards and growing longer every moment, turning and reaching like sunflowers. As soon as they touched his thorns, they were drawn in like a vacuum, and Taxx began to drain the area of all energy, slowly expanding the circle beneath his feet.

"He is drawing magic from the Nullun. There is no telling what that might do," Avo said.

"You don't even know what you are looking at here. This is a rare beauty," Drip said.

Drip gave them all a slight bow.

"Good luck, Magistrate. However, I hope he kills at least one of you, out of spite, you understand," Drip said.

The demon opened his mouth, and a flood of gold fluid erupted out of him, reaching into the air like a fountain. When it was large enough, it started to change shape. The gold changed into a massive mouth with teeth on all sides like a lamprey. The golden maw grew until it was the size of a shark, then it fell on all sides of the door and swallowed it whole. There was nothing left when it pulled away, and the gold returned to its liquid form, collapsed in mid-air, and retreated into Drip's mouth as though he slurped it up. He snapped his fingers, and FW moved toward him, gently dabbing at the corners of his mouth. The larger man scooped up Drip in his remaining arm and carried the demon out of the room with a terrifying speed. Nic started after them, a card appearing between her fingers as she ran.

"Someone stop him," Nic said.

"Don't bother… we have bigger problems," Lyra said.

She stopped, but Nic was not happy about it.

"If we don't get out of here soon, he will overtake and probably kill us all," Avo said.

Taxx was drawing in more energy, magic, and whatever else he could. Each moment filled him with dangerous levels of power for his body. His eyes were cracked on almost every side, and his mouth, still singing the harmony, was starting to break apart.

"Miss Laveau, I believe that young man possesses the ability to absorb energies. Your particular talents could be of great use," Lyra said.

Offrey could only stare.

Sixx was wailing and looking between his cousin and Offrey.

"Magistrate?" Nic asked.

Sixx screamed in his sealed mouth and wept, fighting with everything he had, tossing his head toward Offrey, and throwing his body in her direction, making as much noise as possible.

"Oh, to hell with it!" Nic shouted.

A card appeared between her fingers, and just the edge sparked up like an ember, and she slashed it through some of the treads that sealed Sixx's mouth. A few popped in succession, and the red-hot card cut his mouth a little on the way out, and he winched. He didn't scream. There was no time. Nic freed his hands with the same card, and Sixx reached up, ripped out the final stitches, and took a deep breath to scream as loud as possible.

"ZORA!" Sixx screamed.

As if waking from a trance, Offrey snapped into action and started to close in on Taxx without moving her feet as if she was on a wire. She was pulled along at an incredible speed. The thorns changed the direction of their growth and started to chase after the witch. She had precise control of her movements, making her hard to follow. She could change direction on the head of a pin and did so often, causing the black thorns to miss her entirely. Her movements were not arbitrary. She circled him several times using her untraceable actions, forcing many of the thorns to chase her and move further out and away from his body. Once they were clear, Offrey moved even faster than she had been, disappearing as she launched right for him.

Her body was entirely too fast for the thorns to keep up, and in the blink of an eye, Offrey stopped on a pin right in front of Taxx. She held up her right hand and pointed toward his chest with all her fingers, there was a thimble on every one of them, and each one was covered in tiny designs and words. She manipulated her fingers around swiftly, her fingers moving and locking with precision as though she was typing in slow motion. Once her hands stopped, a single white thread burst from the center of Offrey's chest and speared into Taxx like a harpoon. The thorns stopped chasing her, just a few feet away from her body. The wispy white hairs began to retreat into the earth, and once they were gone, the thorns and the green light disappeared all at once. Taxx's body fell to the ground, and though he seemed to be conscious, he did not move. The glowing thread was still connecting him to Offrey.

"Offrey. What… happened?" Taxx asked.

"You tried to kill everybody. Just because he is your cousin, you don't have to act as stupid as he does, Calderhys," Offrey

said.

"Not funny. You almost choked, Zora. We all saw it," Sixx teased.

"It's Miss Laveau, boy," Offrey said.

She seemed to have loosened up considerably since Drip had left the scene.

"It's Taxx, Offrey," Taxx said.

"HEY! Can one of you idiots fix that other idiot **before** the witty banter… please?" Nic asked.

She seemed to realize that she was yelling at the magistrate at the end, and her tone changed entirely. The rest of her did not seem to get the memo of the tone change. She stamped a foot and huffed, which drew a curious look from Lyra, but she only nodded.

"Of course, excuse me. Taxx, try to remain still," Offrey said.

"Why do people keep doing things to my insides?" Taxx asked.

"There are residual magics inside of you from far too many sources. Something foul was done here. How did you survive?" Offrey asked.

"Well, he did die earlier, so *technically*, he didn't," Nic said.

"You can come back from the dead? How did… what happened?" Offrey asked.

"It's a long story, and I'm uncomfortable right now. I told a demon I was gonna beat his butt. I'm clearly not thinking," Taxx said.

"You said Whoop. Whoop his **ass**, specifically," Sixx said.

"Yes, thank you," Taxx said.

"I got you. Hold up! Did you come back from the dead?

That's my man!" Sixx shouted.

Then he started to scream.

The webbing of his mouth appeared to have been perforated by a slip up from Nic's earlier work, and yelling separated his cheek, leaving it to hang like a filet. Sixx pressed it back to his face, and It started to heal even as he was complaining about it. Mysterious green energy sizzled under the flesh and sealed it closed. Nic couldn't help but watch.

"Alright. What the hell are you, boys? You can regenerate fatal wounds, no big deal, and I watched that one get rehydrated like ramen noodles when he should have stayed dead. I need some explanations, or everyone's ass is getting whooped!" She shouted.

"They are the grandsons of the most powerful witch who ever lived. Is that not enough?" Offrey asked.

"No offense, ma'am, and please don't take this the wrong way, but that is a crap-ass answer. There isn't a witch I have ever met who can do anything like what these boys can do," Nic said.

"What do you know of witches? You who are unclassifiable should practice respect," The Magistrate said.

Nic was smoldering. The embers flew through her grey-blue eyes like a brush fire in a cloudy afternoon sky.

"Before you say such hurtful things about the unclassified, you should probably know that I am not the only one here," Nic said.

The restraint was so apparent in her voice that you could almost hear her true feelings straining against them in her voice, the magistrate looking from Nic to Sixx. Sixx shook his head at her slowly, and Offrey moved her eyes to Taxx, who was looking up at her and working his jaw.

"What's wrong with being unclassifiable? Is that bad?" Taxx asked.

"N-no, not at all," Offrey said.

Lyra and Sixx were standing on either side of Nic, watching the magistrate with cooling anger on her face. Then the younger warden looked at Taxx and smiled.

"It just means that no one can imagine what we are, don't let that mean old witch get you down," Nic said

"Don't mean nothing' to nobody we know, ain't that right, Zora?" Sixx asked.

"You left me earlier, Offrey," Taxx said.

"Never. The Demon used a spell to move me somewhere else, so he could get to you," Offrey said.

"You knew they were looking for Taxx?" Nic asked.

"Not soon enough. I tried to get him to the House, but," Offrey started.

"You let him die?" Sixx asked.

He looked shocked, and Offrey looked at Sixx for a long moment before she slowly nodded.

"It's not that simple. I was under her orders not to tell anyone what he was until now until I was free of our contract," Offrey said.

"We are running out of time," Lyra said.

"Magistrate, please," Nic said.

Offrey looked at Sixx for a long moment, and when the young man did not return her gaze, she turned back to Taxx. Offrey brought up both hands and all ten thimbles. She manipulated invisible threads with her fingers, and Taxx started to feel a pulling inside his chest that made him cry out.

"There are many curses inside of you, I will draw as many

out as possible, but I can't promise it will be pleasant," Offrey said.

Taxx nodded through clenched teeth.

Offrey drew the thread out of his chest, and after about an inch, a bundle of black coagulated evil was stitched around the thread, encased in a spider's lunchbox. Out they came, the thread stretching between them and pulling the bundles of dripping black ooze out of him and into her body. The instant the first black ball touched her chest, it was drawn into her as if she were made of wet sand, and it vanished inside her. Then something came out of the other side. It was just as tall as the woman herself but looked more like a wireframe effigy of her than a complete copy. The threaded doll resembled a pencil line drawing of its creator. It was like a three-dimensional outline of a girl with a bundle of black goo at her center. The threaded doll stepped out of Offreys back fully formed, if simplistic. Moments after it was free of her, the puppet came alight with a blue fire and annihilated itself along with the attached curse. They continued to step out of her back until more than a dozen of them had stepped out of her body and annihilated themselves in blue flame. Offrey was sweating profusely. She took a step back, causing the thread between them to pull so tight that Taxx moaned. Then it snapped.

"I'm sorry, I will need time to rest before continuing," Offrey said.

"How many more of them are inside of me?" Taxx asked.

"Maybe 2, maybe two dozen, it's not as easy as just reading the newspaper, it's like reading the paper through a wall with only your heart, and it's inside another person," Offrey said.

"Fair. Thank you," Taxx said.

"You can thank me at the Guild. May wanted you there as soon as possible," Offrey said.

"Taxx don't ever get involved with the guild. That's her rule," Sixx said.

"Saturday, don't be stupid. Did you not hear me say she **wants** you?" Offrey said.

"I don't give a damn about that," Sixx said.

"Sixx! Offrey, of course, we will come with you," Taxx said.

"Thank you, you've always been the smart one," Offrey said.

"Hey!" Six shouted.

Offrey pulled a key from her pockets, and the flick of a finger made a thread doorway in front of her. She plunged the key into the air, and it slipped into a keyhole that should not have been there. Taxx had seen a key like that before, a skeleton key, where there had been only air a moment ago now stood a door. Offrey opened the door, and it led to a well-appointed chamber with a massive window overlooking a nighttime sky. There was a large ornate desk in front of it, but no one was behind it.

"I would like to enter into a pact with you. Protect my cousin, and I will trade you a family secret that no one else knows," Sixx said.

Rosen perked up and smiled at the young man broadly and brightly. Offrey turned to face him quickly with a surprised look on her face, her eyebrows, which had raised, were starting to slowly lower, and she narrowed her eyes at him.

"What is this?" Offrey asked.

"You heard him; he has made me an offer for protection. A juicy one from a young one like that. I fear I may have to accept," Rosen said.

"Do not be foolish. It would be best if you came back with

me," Offrey said.

"Sixx, what are you doing?" Taxx asked.

"We have made a pact with the fairy, and we are in the custody of the Court of All," Sixx said.

Rosen was practically cackling with laughter. She danced around the young man a bit, her pink glitter-like energy falling all around her again. Her eyes were bright, and her smile was more radiant.

"Such a clever Wiccani. I accept and pledge to protect you and your companions," Rosen said.

The magistrate seemed agitated, but she took a deep breath and smiled at the group in front of her.

"Don't be silly. It would help if you came with us. You can't rely on these children to protect you. That fae is dangerous. She was removed from the guild for not following orders," Offrey said.

"I was removed for doing what's right. You know nothing of that. Is this woman an approved companion?" Rosen asked.

"No, ma'am," Sixx said.

"Well, that was easy enough. Good day Magistrate, or should I say. Signing off," Rosen said.

"D-" Offrey started

Offrey opened her mouth to protest, and Rosen flapped those fairy wings. They moved so quickly that they made an ethereal sound when they tore through the wind around them, like chimes. The chimes rippled in the air, and that strange TV snow-like fuzz appeared all around Offrey instantly, and she winked out of existence. Taxx and Sixx started to scream.

"No! NO!" Taxx shouted.

"GOD DAMN, you ain't had to kill her!" Sixx yelled.

"Relax, I just borrowed a trick from my husband and sent her surfing a bit. She will return to this spot in a little while, unharmed, of course," Rosen said.

"That's... cool as hell! You made way better friends than I did today," Sixx said.

"So, it would seem," Lyra said.

"Then we should probably get out of here before she comes back," Nic said

"But where do we go?" Taxx asked.

Everyone looked a little lost except Rosen, who was only smiling brightly at Sixx.

"You are a quick one, Wiccani," she said.

"Thank you," he said.

"You are under my protection now, so I will take you someplace safe," Rosen said.

Rosen gathered up some of her glittering magic at the tip of her finger and drew a sizeable glittering rectangle the size of a garage door in the air. She lifted her body off the ground by stepping on the air, as though there were platforms there that only she could see. When she was done, she produced a skeleton key. Taxx could tell by the staircase teeth on it. Rosen inserted the key and opened a doorway larger than Taxx had seen. It swung up and away to reveal a bright and colorful space around the silhouette of the fairy. A building shaped like a toadstool was just beyond a giant portal in space-time. A toadstool with impossible height and an uncountable number of lights on throughout, glowing out of windows that went from the base to the tip on an unknowable number of floors. The very top of the structure ended with a massive hood covered in opaque gills like any other mushroom but as tall as a mountain, and Sixx was sure he could see even further lights in the gills. It stood at the base of a tree that itself could not exist on earth because its height went even further beyond the doors than he could see. There was thick grass that looked as high as his knee and wildflowers growing in a patchwork of colors as though someone splattered a rainbow of paint across that landscape. The plants were alive and bioluminescent with magic coursing through them as strong as any Other he had seen before, some sparkling bright and colorful even in the night so that it defied all reality.

"What is that place... ?" Sixx asked.

"The Court of All," Rosen said.

The five of them made their way toward the still standing portal that led to the fairy's domain, the gigantic mushroom looming over them. Taxx hesitated for a moment at the mouth of the doorway, watching the other pass through it. He looked back to the space where Offrey had been for a moment. The air made a popping sound, and Offrey reappeared, winking back into existence in a haze of tv snow like magic.

"…on't you dare! Damn it!" Offrey said.

She looked at Taxx, and their eyes met for a moment before he stepped through the portal to space-time, and the portal began to close behind him. Sixx slid up next to his cousin in the fading portal and sent Offrey a mischievous wink, then he blew her a kiss and waggled his fingers in her direction.

"Tootles," Sixx said.

The magistrate was alone in the quarry. She looked around more than twice before her hand lifted into the open air. She closed it around nothing and slipped her hand back into her pocket.

"Tootles, you idiot," She whispered.

Chapter | Fourteen

The Court of All was in a world apart from the Nexus. A sacred space, but just a small point on a whole planet that existed in the space between spaces. Beyond reach and within the endless Aether, the birthplace of all magic and home to the impossible. All Lost Worlds also call the Aether home. There are whole galaxies and more buried deep in the Aether stream. The stream was where the energy flowed strongest, where the magic is wild, and most do not dare to tread. The most famous and lawless is the Nexus of Worlds, but some call it Earth. They were no longer on earth. They were on one of the many worlds under the order of The Fae. The Fae were many and varied, but all of them were mysterious and powerful. Others who were long-lived and had a deep connection with magic. Some were so far beyond human that they often evolved beyond the methods of communicating with men.

"…if I'm being honest, most of that's just grade school BS. The most real thing to remember about the Fae is that they ain't got no laws against eating people, or anything really," Sixx concluded.

Taxx looked at his cousin with a calm face that was perhaps contemplative or reflective about the plethora of information he had just received. Sixx sucked his teeth.

"You get all that? You ain't even listening to me, are you?" Sixx asked.

"No, I heard you. I just want to know why both of you are staring at me?" Taxx asked.

"Huh, are we staring?" Nic asked.

She and Sixx had not once since they had come through the portal taken their eyes from his forehead. Sixx didn't even look away while spewing his knowledge about the fae. The only person who hadn't been staring at his forehead was Lyra.

"What's up with you guys?" Taxx asked.

Sixx was silent for a moment, but the warden didn't seem as afflicted.

"You have horns, my guy. Big shiny ones," Nic said.

"My horns are out?" Taxx shouted.

He reached up and felt solid structures growing out of his skull. They felt bigger than his fingers and seemed to go up high. Taxx had horns.

"I guess I forgot to mention. I have horns," he said.

"Ever since you was little, you had a couple bits on your head. Them thangs have been growing like an impala," Sixx teased.

"Tell me they aren't **that** long?" Taxx asked.

"They **absolutely** are. Also, what is an Impala?" Nic asked.

"It's like an antelope. You ain't never heard of an Impala?" Sixx asked

"Nah. I guess I've seen one now," Nic teased.

"Screw you!" Taxx shouted.

"Taxx. We are on another planet surrounded by Fairies. Just. Don't fuck around," Sixx said.

"Also, don't eat anything they offer you or give them your name or take any gifts," Nic said.

"Ok. That sounds dangerous. Are we in danger?" Taxx asked,

"No, but even a small looking thing could be powerful and liable to kidnap and kill you by accident," Sixx said.

"Or for fun," Nic added.

"True. They do be like that sometimes," Sixx said.

"...Oh," Taxx said.

"You need not fear any of that here. We are under her protection. Also, the horns are handsome," Lyra said.

"Thank you, Lyra. At least your boss knows how to speak to someone who just grew horns," Taxx said.

"That is not my boss," Nic said.

There were so many fairies bounding through the thick forest, so many eyes on them that it was foolish to count, but there was no malice. Taxx didn't even really feel afraid. He had known that there would be no conflict in this place because of her. The Pink Fairy. The beings all around them didn't even give them a second glance. They were here to see the lady.

"What is this place?" Taxx asked.

"It's a Fae planet called Rozsavad," Sixx said.

"Planet? A planet like not earth?" Taxx asked.

"Yup," Sixx said.

"We left the earth?" Taxx asked.

"Is this your first time leaving the Earth?" Nic asked.

"Isn't it supposed to be?" Taxx said.

She smiled at him.

"Relax. Try to breathe. You'll get used to it," Nic said.

"You don't have to cuddle him. He is more powerful than he looks," Sixx responded.

"I'm not, it's his first planet hop, and he died a few days ago. Cut him some slack," Nic said.

"I'm not a powerful anything. I also don't need to be cuddled. It's just… there is so much to take in all at once," Taxx said.

"You'll get used to that too," Nic said.

"Keep up, please," Lyra said.

"Not my boss!" Nic yelled back.

The young warden did start walking faster despite her attitude. Taxx couldn't bring himself to do it. The scenery was too incredible to speed past. The sky was all colors of the rainbow-like spilled paint and slowly changing. The group moved further into the knee-high grass that seemed to bow aside as they walked, led by the Rosen lady. The grass they were moving through was not some wild field but a garden being tended to by hundreds of much smaller fairies of all colors flitting from one flower. These tiny glowing beings were the light source that seemed to come from the flowers. There was hardly a single flower that did not have at least one of them sitting, dancing, or gossiping in impossibly tiny voices; these Fae were giving the humanoids very little attention. However, the Rosen lady was showered with their affections. They flitted up to her hands which she held outstretched, and they left small kisses and tiny bits of various things from rocks to what was indeed pollen. Some gave, others took, but one by one, the insect-sized fairies flocked to the Lady, offering her their blessings in an indecipherable whispering sound that was so quiet you had to strain to hear. Once you could listen to it, though, it somehow echoed all around. There were more of them than he could count, filling the air and moving at the same strange gait that their impossibly fast wings gave them. They moved so fast they were often blinking out of existence only to appear somewhere else at the exact moment. The sound of their wings was not a chopping hum like he expected, but it had a musical, almost choral quality that came to sweeping rushes of sound when they amassed. It didn't take him long to understand that they were singing a song along to the melody of that brassy and beautiful wing beat. He could hear it all around them. He was mesmerized while the rest of them just stood by and waited, Lyra and Nic were neither interested nor paying attention, and even Sixx didn't look surprised.

"What am I looking at?" Taxx asked.

"This is old magic. Like ancient type shit from before the time of man, or so they say, whatever they are, the Fae are powerful, and she is powerful among them. They offer her blessings and take them as well," Sixx said.

"That's kind of beautiful," Taxx said.

"Not a bad late birthday present," Sixx said.

"I didn't get you anything," Taxx teased.

Nic slipped between them and threw an arm over each of their shoulders.

"It's your birthday too?" she asked.

"It was. The day we met. Sixx and I have the same birthday,"

Taxx said.

"That's funny," she said.

"It's not that weird," Taxx said.

"No, I meant, it's funny that you died on your birthday," Nic said.

All of them gave her a look, and she smiled back fearlessly.

"Not funny, ha-ha, like morbid funny," Nic said.

"Your bedside manner is really awful," Taxx said sourly.

"Well, I'm not a freakin' nurse, and someday you will be grateful for that," Nic said.

"I like you, you wild," Sixx said.

Then he started to laugh, and once Nic gave him a wink, Taxx finally cracked a smile, too, despite himself.

"Hol up, something is cookin' here," Sixx said.

The small colorful creatures began moving like a school of fish in an ocean current, and he was distracted as he watched them as they converged around the much larger fairy. The Rosen lady stood taller than both he and Sixx, who was over six feet tall. Taxx was unfamiliar with Fairies and the Fae in general. He had never been in the company of so many. He knew that the Witches and the Fae did not get along very well. When the rest of the group passed, the fairies spread out and away from them as though they moved on invisible currents to keep them clear. It was not until they had paid her tribute that the pink fairy turned to address them. They were now standing in front of the toadstool tower that climbed so high that he could barely see the gills in the cap from the ground. There was a grand staircase to the Court of All, draped in ivy and flowers of all colors. Vines provided the handrails and posts with illuminated flower bulbs on every landing. The pink fairy in her studded denim and checkered sneakers turned to face them and held up a single hand. Many of the creatures around them quieted down gradually. The wind also began to blow at a slightly gentler gale, and Taxx could not tell if it was a terrifying coincidence or terrifying reality, either way, it had worked on him.

The Rosen Lady began to speak, or more accurately, she began to sing an overwhelming and unearthly song with words that he couldn't follow but somehow, it was still the most beautiful song that Taxx had ever heard. Her body was bathed in a pink light that crawled all over her like clouds, forming a dress and changing colors until they were a gradient, the dark colors starting at her feet and fading to white at the crown of her head. He couldn't even see her denim anymore, just the smoke light dress and her eyes slowly illuminating with more and more intensity. They were looking only at him. The shapes on her body continued to shift and translate all over her and become clearer. They weren't clouds but hundreds of flowers intricately arranged all over her body. They moved and changed color with impossible ease, and the longer that Taxx looked, the more he could see. Each flower was alive with a deep green stem that disappeared into the flowers around it. She was not wearing a dress by any conventional means. What she wore was a living nature that propagated in the air around her body, this level of magic was little seen. He felt something strange starting to happen to him as her singing continued, and before he could stop it, the song invaded him. It was all through his mind, and he couldn't seem to hear anything else, and it was starting to weigh him down.

"Something is… what is this?" Taxx asked.

As soon as he finished speaking, he quietly lost consciousness.

"Did… you do that?" Nic asked.

It was unclear who she was asking because the three of them were looking at each other for an explanation that did not seem to be anywhere between them.

"Do y'all think he'll be ok?" Sixx asked.

Lyra stood over Taxx and stared at him for a long moment as though she were gathering a thought, then she leaned down and leveled a quick slap across his cheek. It was so fast and strong that his head flopped around for a second before it came to rest, and to no one's surprise, Taxx did not wake up. Lyra seemed not only displeased at the outcome but surprised, even if she never showed it on her face.

"Great! Now **you** killed him too!" Nic said.

"He lives. I was careful only to use minimal force," Lyra said.

"Why does he look so troubled then?" Sixx asked.

"That is only for him to know Mr. St. Martin, it may be another curse, or perhaps he was somehow affected by the power of her transformation. Old magic does not settle well with everyone," Lyra said.

"What did she do to him?" Sixx asked.

"Nothing directly," Lyra said.

Lyra picked Taxx up easily and gently hung him over her shoulder like a stole, and started to walk on. She paused after a moment as though she had forgotten something and turned back to Sixx.

"Oh yes, happy birthday Mr. St. Martin," Lyra said.

Sixx pretended to tip a cap and gave an exaggerated but well-practiced bow that he punctuated with a wink.

"Happy birthday," Nic added.

"Thank you, ladies, honestly as far as birthdays go… not so bad," Sixx said.

"Except for all the," Nic started.

"Yeah, yeah. Except for all that stuff," Sixx said.

Nic gave him a cheesing smile, and he pursed his lips to signify his annoyance in her general direction.

"Still, I got him back. That's all that matters," Sixx said.

Nic only nodded, and they moved on, finally coming to the end of the walkway. After a few more minutes of fairy song, there was a reply from the gathered masses, and almost all the fairies that had gathered here were swiftly and suddenly gone. Most faded away from view with a burst of light like a spent firework. Some took to the bare earth, literally crashing into it and disappearing, some flew and walked and wandered, but the field was clear of the fairies in mere moments. The sounds around them changed into the music of nature, running water, and even some animal and insect sounds that were almost soothing against the deafening absence of those beating wings. It took a moment for Sixx to adjust, and by the time he had, the pink fairy had rejoined them, wispy threads of her cloudlike dress still clinging like cotton candy as they continued to fade away. She was back to her studded denim jacket and checkered canvas shoes, and staring right at him, she walked right up to him and poked him in the chest.

"You two are very interesting, aren't you?" Rosen asked.

"Your Scottish accent is lovely," Sixx responded.

"What you are hearing as Scottish is the accent of the fairy song when it tries to conform to the dimensionless void of the English language. It is the human accent that sounds like **our** tongue. They used to worship us and proper-like in more enlightened times," Rosen said.

She did not sound like the great and ancient thing he had been expecting, she looked much younger, and her energy was curious and playful. It was difficult to dislike this woman even though she was his judge and likely executioner if it came to that. He was not going to let it come to that, however. While he pondered her, she looked him over and analyzed him, tapping a long delicate finger to her chin.

"Do you still claim to be a witch after all I have seen?" She asked.

"She woman, my cousin, and I both are the sons of witches. Beyond that… we couldn't say," Sixx said.

"Sidhe woman. Sidhe is the name of my people, not She. Similar, but there is a slight difference. A nuance. Though I again appreciate your knowledge in our ways," She responded.

Sixx was unsure what to say. To his ears, he had said the word the same, but he was not about to argue with a creature who had been alive longer than his grandmother, who up until this point had been the oldest woman he had ever known.

"You will know it when you speak it correctly. Now, tell me your name," she said

"Sixx," He answered.

"The name that was given to you by your mother. In full," she said.

He hesitated, and when she looked at him with exasperation, he only watched her back in silence. There was a growing tension in that silence that he could feel like a slowly inflating balloon. She surely could not mean for him to freely give his name to a fairy. He was no sort of witch by comparison to his grandmother but not a fool.

"I admire that mind! There is no man as handsome as a bright man," The fairy said.

Sixx smiled, but it was small and clipped.

"Thank you kindly," he said.

"You are in no danger here, Sixx. I have given you my word that you will be safe. That includes any magic you have not brought in on your own. My proper name is The Rosen Child of Morning, Mathair Dreallag, and Lady of Graves.

"That's a long name," Sixx said.

"So it is. I also lived life as a mortal and took a shorter name. Then, I was called Rosenda Morningchild-Graves. You may use Rosen for short," Rosen said.

"Thank you, Rosen. My name is Saturday Romaine St. Martin, just like my momma said it," he said.

"You need not fear me just now. I can never promise never, but not the now. I will respect your wishes and call you by your chosen name, but there is something I must ask, something of a… personal nature," Rosen said.

Her eyes lit up like a child's, but the light was not imaginary, Sixx could clearly see the mischief dancing there, but his curiosity would never let him live it down if he didn't at least hear a personal question from a fairy. Reluctantly he answered.

"You may," Sixx said.

"What terrors have you seen to give you such a pale eye and that bit of hair?" She asked.

She reached up and touched at the small collection of white dreaded twists over his pale green eye, and Sixx pretended to bite her, making her pull back, looking pleased and amused.

"You have lovely humor. Tell me… who or what has marked you? What evil?" She asked.

"The unspeakable sort. Family," Sixx answered.

"I know the family with such eyes," Rosen said.

Sixx froze, and Lyra reacted as well, Nic was carefully watching her master and the fairy with interest, but there was only silence until Rosen broke the silence.

"Do not fear, child of Samedi. I find you and your… cousin quite charming for Wiccani," Rosen said.

"What's a Wiccani?" Sixx asked.

Rosen opened her mouth to answer and turned her eyes beyond the young man toward Lyra, and something passed between the two, causing Rosen to change course.

"*Maitheanas cailleach airson seann fhacal beag, an seo agus an sin,*" Rosen said

"What the hell was that?" Nic asked

"She asked us to excuse her for using old words," Sixx said.

"You do have the gift. I thought as much. Bright men are always dangerous to have about," She teased.

"In exchange for telling me what that old word means, I'll do you a favor of your choice, beautiful fairy queen," Sixx said.

A slow mischievous smile slid across the pale and perfect face of the pink fairy, and her wings danced on her back, in concert with the temptation in her eyes. Lyra stepped between them and blocked the young man from the destructive energies of an excited fairy, maybe for both of their sakes.

"It's an old word for unclassifiable," Lyra injected.

Sixx seemed to accept that answer, but the fairy was practically giddy at the moment and flitted between the boy on the large warden's shoulders and then behind Sixx. She giggled and danced, and a pink trail followed her as she moved back and forth half a dozen times until she finally stopped on her toes and clapped her hands.

"They've both got quite a knack for the speaking ways… Viridescii never ceases to amaze me," Rosen said.

"We should move on from here, my friend. These boys are being targeted," Lyra said.

"As you say, sweet daughter. Come and let me kiss you, Milyra," she said.

Rosen looked at the Warden with delight, and in moments her wings went from still and ornamental to invisible and carried her into a hug, then higher so she might kiss the much taller woman in greeting. Once she was done, Rosen flitted around her body with such speed and eased that Sixx felt the tickle of fear in the back of his throat. Rosen stopped to examine Taxx's sleeping face one more time, but this time she got so close that her nose just barely touched him with a gentle poke, and there was a spark of dabbled black and white between them the size of a match head. This little point of contact caused Taxx to scream awake, shifting so suddenly that he fell from Lyra's shoulder and tumbled to the ground.

"Someone has put great effort into keeping you suppressed. There are more curses in your future, Viridescii, and worse coming. Were you anywhere else that would be problematic, but thankfully you've caught my attention," Rosen said.

"T…thank you?" Taxx asked.

"Don't thank me yet. That sleeping curse was meant to last a decade or so. Whatever is coming next might be even more dangerous," Rosen said.

She offered her hand to Taxx and helped him to his feet. The two of them just regarded one another for a moment without speaking but still holding hands.

"I will solve the riddle of you two boys… such interesting boys you are. Lyra, please bring them in to see the old man. He should be in his study. I must go and prepare, and I can only delay the guild for so long," she said.

Lyra nodded, and the group started toward the front door of the impossibly colossal building. The young men followed along with no issue, and Rosen disappeared into the sky in the space of a breath, out of sight before Taxx could look after her.

"What happened to you?" Sixx asked.

"I don't know… I think I might be in trouble," Taxx said.

Lyra turned back and gave them a sharp look to remind them of the speaking curse, and both young men fell silent but not before giving each other knowing eyes. They spoke no more as they entered the house. They were standing in the atrium of what looked like an old-money mansion in southern Connecticut, complete with coffered ceilings. Sixx had been expecting a lobby, but this was curated so much more like a home than he could have imagined, the ceilings were vaulted, and the furniture was mid-century and comfortable. He simply had not been expecting a fairy dressed up like an 80s sitcom older sister to have such a clean tuxedo black style like this, and he found himself looking around at the neutral walls and bold patterns rather than the garden of fairies outside.

"Are… is this the same building?" Sixx asked.

"Surely you have heard of The Transom Authority. They are responsible for almost all high-speed travel in the modern world. If you do not have a Nicole of your own," Lyra said.

"Unlike the keys, I require food, cannot be housebroken, and bite," Nic said.

"You have already used it, in fact, Taxx. The TA is where all skeleton keys come from," Lyra said.

"That's a neat trick," Taxx said.

"These coffered ceilings are a neat trick. That fairy has some nice tastes," Sixx said.

"That she does, but the real jewel is the conservatory for me. The way she captured the light in there is like a jewelry box," An older man said.

"What the hell is a conservatory? Also, who the hell are you?" Sixx asked.

The man he spoke to was standing among the group as if he had always been there, casually working his thumb into a smoking pipe's business end. He was not notably short or tall but handsome, and his skin was much darker than he and Taxx, which made his even gray eyes stand out. His hair was perfectly gray, not white, as were his clothes and the pipe he finally finished packing. The initial sparks on the match head he struck were the typical orange, but the flame that was born of it was as gray as a black and white film. There was something else too, there were tiny bits of light afloat around him, like Rosen, and they too were colored like the snow on an old school TV set, spotted black and white and alive with movement. If not for Taxx and the warden's presence and fully colored personages, Sixx would have thought they had stepped into a black and white film, complete with a well-manicured and handsome man in a suit gently puffing on a pipe.

"Seriously… who the hell is this, Sidney Poitier?" Sixx asked again.

"Say now! I'll take that as a compliment," The man said.

The man smiled and took a puff of his pipe, the ember glowing gray and then white, before letting out a smooth pillar of smoke, and after a moment, he spoke again, holding out his hand to Sixx.

"We haven't been formally introduced; I am The Tailor. My given name is Grayson Montague Morningchild-Graves,"

"Damn, that's a fancy name," Sixx said.

"I aspire to be the man to match," Grayson said.

"What's going on with you?" Sixx asked.

"I am an Other, like you, and like you in a class of my own. I am a master of Arcanology and a few other things. I've also been called a shadow broker. Allow me to welcome you to our home Mr...?" He asked.

"Sixx, the loveable scamp of this ragtag group of misfits," he said.

The two exchanged firm handshakes.

"We shall see. A conservatory is a greenhouse attached to the home, to answer your earlier question. Ours is lovely for a nice conversation and a cup of tea if my wife has any say. But first, gentleman, I can't have you wandering around with so much blood on you. Please follow me," Grayson said.

They all moved past the main stairs of the home and to a wide cased opening that led to a room where each wall was covered in colored glass windows with black piping between the panels. There were many plants here but few flowers, a backdrop of living green and ethereal color from the light that instantly made the space more comfortable. In the center of the room, with black and white checkered floors, were some red velvet upholstered seats, a chaise, a couch, and a few chairs in a semicircle. Sixx could not tell if this setup was for a four-piece band or a psychologist, but he took a seat anyway, and Taxx was just next to him on the Chaise.

"This is all very strange," Sixx said.

"You were brought here to be assisted, " Grayson said.

"How are you going to help us?" Taxx asked.

"Patience," Lyra said.

"Indeed, firstly, you boys need to clean up. Come along. Ladies, I trust you can settle in independently," Grayson said.

The boys followed him away from the conservatory and through a modern, strangely standard-looking family room, Taxx and Sixx exchanging glances. Grayson didn't seem to notice. They continued down a wide hallway flanked with pictures of Rosen and Grayson from all over the world and a few Taxx was sure weren't the world at all. Sixx froze in front of a particular photograph, and after his eyes went wide, he leaned in close and strained to see.

"These… these pictures...how can this be possible?" Sixx asked.

"She says she simply wasn't familiar with photography, but I think she knew quite well what she was doing… you will have to ask her," Grayson said.

"These are from," Sixx started.

"Cottingley. I believe it made a paper or two way back when. You have a knack for memory, Mr. Sixx," Grayson said.

"That I do," Sixx said.

"What am I looking at?" Taxx asked.

Taxx joined his cousin, and there sat an old photograph of a dark-haired girl kneeling in front of a branch. Standing on the branch across from her was a miniature version of Rosen. The picture was black and white, and the fairy was hard to see details on, but there was no mistake. Even without color, her bright red hair was clear. She couldn't have stood any higher than a doll, and she was handing a small bunch of flowers to the girl who looked on in wonder.

"I don't get it," Taxx said

"Just an old hoax from simpler times. Come now, boys, let's get you washed up for the big show," Grayson said.

Chapter | Fifteen

Taxx did not know that he could enjoy something so simple as a shower as much as he did. There was something cathartic about washing away the kind of day he had. He didn't have the guts to keep his eyes open when he scraped away all the gore, but he was sure to be thorough. This was the first time he had been clean since he died and the first time he felt like he was away from the near-constant deadly situation he found himself in. The first time he had a moment to think about everything that happened, and as the water fell rhythmically on his head, he was suddenly aware of the growths on his forehead. He turned off the shower and moved to the mirror, clearing it with his bare hands to examine his forehead in the strip of the mirror he could see. He gingerly touched his horns, and an electric shock passed through his body. He lost his legs and crumbled to the ground. Thankfully, he was already wrapped in a towel because as soon as he fell, Sixx burst into the bathroom.

"Taxx, are you ok?" he asked.

"Were you camping outside? I just fell," Taxx said.

"That's not… that's not what I mean," Sixx said.

Taxx stood to his feet and searched his cousin's face, it had to be something dire for Sixx to be so focused, and Taxx nodded.

"I know, man. I'm ok… I just… it has been a lot,"

"You and I got separated, and then I got kidnapped, and you got murdered **and** came back from the dead! That counts as a lot, Cuh," Sixx said.

"Sixx, what the hell are you wearing?" Taxx asked.

Sixx pretended to wipe himself down again, but now he was wearing a deep burgundy suit with gold pinstripes. He was also wearing a vest but still no shirt or tie. Taxx whistled low.

"You look like a pimp," Taxx said.

Sixx smiled at first and then made a sour face.

"Modern pimp or 70's pimp?" Sixx asked.

"Uh. The 70s, I guess," Taxx said.

Sixx smiled and preened a little bit.

"See, you always sayin pretty shit. That's my man," Sixx said.

"I didn't mean that as a compliment," Taxx said.

"Maybe not, but Grayson left this stuff for us, so don't hate. Come on," Sixx said.

Taxx followed Sixx to a bedroom and into a walk-in closet that looked like a department store. There were so many kinds of men's clothes that Taxx didn't know where to start. He was certainly not as keen to dress up as his cousin, but Sixx wouldn't let him out of the closet without at least a vest.

"You ain't gonna be wearing shit like this again," Sixx said.

"I don't want to look like a bellhop," Taxx returned.

"This is silk, homie," Sixx said.

He wound up in a pair of jeans and a vest with two rows of buttons and a black tie that Sixx put on him by slinging it over his head like a dog catcher. Taxx won the battle on the blazer when it was all said and done but was forced to wear sleeve garters over his biceps to 'complete the look.'

"You black, stop pretending you don't like these preacher clothes," Sixx said.

Taxx pulled his long afro into a much neater version of the puff tail on the back of his head, and the twin mounds on his forehead were even more pronounced.

"Your horns are still growin'," Sixx said.

Taxx reached up to touch them. He never got a chance to answer because Grayson entered the bedroom and slowly smiled as he appraised them, slapping his hands together with joy.

"Well, hot damn, you two young men clean up well. Now you may come and greet my beautiful wife like gentlemen. It's time," he said.

The three of them returned to the conservatory, and Nic wolf-whistled, immediately earning an elbow from Lyra, who was nodding approvingly.

"You were cute this whole time? Who knew," Nic said.

"Girl, I was **born** cute," Sixx answered.

"Bold of you to assume I was talking to you. You look like a pimp," Nic said.

"Smoove like one too," Sixx rebutted

The three of them were laughing so loud that they didn't hear the sound of the knocker. So, when the door appeared in front of them with a burst like a camera flash, it caught everyone off guard. A door changed from dark wood into a white painted door with a shiny brass handle in the shape of a dragonfly. The entire door seemed to have a rainbow shimmer like mother of pearl. When it opened, Izzy and Avo entered the room, and Sixx let out a breath he had been holding, the door closed behind them, but it did not change back.

"Ah, this is good. Now we can begin," Grayson said.

Up close, Grayson was much younger looking than Taxx had assumed he had been because of his unusual coloring. Every thread he wore was various shades of gray, jacket, vest, collared shirt, trousers, shoes, and socks. With his watch and the stud earrings he wore in each ear, the tortoiseshell glasses on his face, all gray, Taxx noticed that even his tongue was similarly colored as he spoke.

"I am sometimes called a Shadow Broker, always second best, but some might say that I'm the best in the game," Grayson said.

"Only you say that," Avo said.

"And you, Avo," Lyra rebutted.

Grayson pulled a small loupe from his pocket and pressed the cone of the small magnifier to his glasses, where it stuck and immediately turned gray. Then much like a jeweler, he began to inspect Taxx, walking around him in a slow circle, crouching, then standing as tall as possible, which was quite tall because this man towered over Taxx. He was long and lithe, and honestly, Taxx couldn't tell if he was in his late forties or his mid-twenties. His hair was bright and gray, but his skin was dark and smooth, his eyes were wise, but his smile was mischievous. There was so much about him that was either or both extremes that it was confusing.

"Tell me your name," Grayson asked.

Taxx hesitated for a moment, and Sixx touched his shoulder reassuringly.

"They cool, man," Sixx said.

Taxx nodded.

"Calderhys Taxxis Moss II, I'm the son of a witch born with no magic," Taxx said.

"Born without perhaps, but the Second Sorcerer has seen magic in you, a vast and spectacular amount... perhaps a concerning amount? I don't think so, but more than I've got. You need an appraisal," he said.

"Am I supposed to know what any of that is?" Taxx asked.

"Mr. Graves is an independent purveyor of magical goods; he also happens to be an excellent friend," Avo said.

"Are you here to buy me?" Taxx asked.

He hadn't meant his voice to be so small, but it was all the same. Izzy smiled and shook her head at him.

"Hardly, you are here to see his wife," Izzy said.

"Who has appeared just in time to stop a self-indulgent speech about shadow broking, methinks," Rosen said.

She had come in through the dragonfly door while they were speaking, and the door had already changed back to the dark wood color.

"Of course, my love, forgive an old man his vices," Grayson said.

"Old man?" Taxx asked.

Grayson only winked.

"It's complicated, but first, Mr. Moss, allow me to introduce you to my unspeakably beautiful wife, The Rosen Lady of

Dreallag and Graves," Grayson said.

"We've met," Taxx said.

"So, we have, but there is so much more to know. It has been a long time since I've had so many men in my home. I must make tea!" Rosen said.

Taxx expected her to leave the room, but instead, she lifted her hands, and the plants around them began to move, all of them doing different things. Some of them snaked into other rooms, and others crept toward the group, undulating all over each other like snakes until they weaved themselves into sturdy legs and twisted and rolled themselves into round tabletops. Taxx could not stop looking at this woman while she worked. Up close, she was even more of an ethereal beauty. Her skin was as white as snow and smattered with freckles, her hair and eyes were as bloody red as roses and glowing mildly with her power, but her smile was just as bright. He had never seen such a perfect face. She looked like a marble statue come to life, even with the dated denim and pink cotton covering her long willowy body. Taxx thought she might have been the most beautiful thing he had ever seen in his life, and so to illustrate that beautiful notion, he opened his mouth to speak poetry.

"God da-," Taxx said.

Sixx covered his mouth to prevent him from swearing.

"Amen, brotha," Sixx said.

"Impressive for an old woman, eh?" Rosen teased.

"Old woman?" Taxx asked.

"It's complicated," Gray said.

"Hardly. As a Faerie, great and powerful, just like the ones you've read about in your little human books, I am fickle and dangerous, and I tend to do what I like. So, I choose to be as beautiful as a flower and as old as a tree because I always do what I damn well please," Rosen said.

Grayson only smiled at her and adjusted the loupe periodically; he was holding a small pad of paper and a pencil worked furiously over the surface. The tables had been fully formed now, and several creeping vines were setting table service with saucers and cups for all of them except him and Rosen, a large pot of tea that was placed into her hands instead. She carefully filled each cup with the surprisingly bright magenta liquid and a single fat berry.

"Simply hibiscus and catnip for a spot of joy. Please, enjoy this while I appraise him," Rosen said.

"Appraise?" Taxx asked.

While the others quietly drank their tea, Rosen stepped in front of Taxx and used her hands to adjust his shoulders, making him stand up straighter while her eyes were calmly searching over his body. Her hands were under his jaw on either side, moving to his shoulders and chest, then up to his eyes, opening his eyelids forcibly.

"What I do for a living, dear heart, is a function known as appraising. Some say I'm the best in the biz," She teased.

She even affected her husband's tone when she spoke with uncanny accuracy and tossed him a wink over her shoulder.

"What I appraise, with great care and renown, is magical potential," Rosen continued.

"I felt you like a stone in the river the moment I saw you, you are throwing it off like a brush fire, and it's only getting hotter. Now I understand your urgency," Rosen said.

Avo was standing with Grayson, and the two of them were exchanging a complicated handshake that Avo appeared to be less sure of than the other man. Grayson looked up at his wife once they had finished their greeting, and he patted Avo on the shoulder, canting his head in Rosen's direction.

"The Lady beckons," Grayson said.

"I would never impose on you so suddenly without great need. I have never seen anything quite like him. He drove the blackest eye to madness," Avo said.

"Truly. Which of your parents is the Other?" Rosen asked.

"My mother. She is a Witch, and my dad was just some fling she had in the peace corps. If my father is, or was, who can say? Sorry," Taxx said.

"There is no need to apologize at all," she said.

"What does your grandma call you?" She asked.

"Cally," he said.

"What do friends call you?" She asked

"Taxx," he said.

"Taxx then," Rosen said.

Rosen reached up and gingerly touched her fingers to the mounds on either side of his forehead, and he winced, sucking air into his mouth.

"Excuse me for the pain, I had heard you were unclassifiable, but this is remarkable," Rosen said.

"What do you mean?" Taxx asked.

"You appear to be growing horns out of your head," Rosen said.

"Why does everyone assume they are **horns!?**" Taxx said.

"Well, you are certainly growing a pair of something on your head. Pray they are only horns," Rosen said.

"Wait, are horns the good option? What's the bad option?" Taxx asked.

"Are you always so inquisitive?" Rosen asked.

"Yes," Came the voices of everyone present all at once.

The only person who didn't say 'Yes' was Grayson, who looked around at the rest of them amused, Taxx did not look so amused, but he didn't protest in good conscience.

"Come. Perhaps this will answer some of our questions," Rosen said.

She held her hand over his eyes until he closed them and then moved it around to the back of his neck and gently pressed. As soon as she did, he felt something like an electric charge tingle all over his skin. It was enough to make him gasp.

"Do not be afraid. What you are feeling is a part of you, your power. I am simply helping to direct it. Magic is similar to electricity in some ways. In its raw state, it is dangerous but not good for much. It is only energy. Your power is still just beneath the surface. I can access a bit of it if you allow me," Rosen said.

Taxx nodded, and Rosen tapped into him. He could feel the electricity slowly intensifying the longer she held her fingers to his neck. He could feel it coursing through and around him and racing to her fingers and rushing toward freedom. He could almost feel it pouring out of him, thick as honey and just as sweet. Each burst that left him sent waves of tingling tickles through his spin. It was like drinking water for the first time in a long time, and he leaned into it. Allowing it to flow freely was incredibly easy. As soon as he thought to do it, it was happening. It felt so good he started to drift off, and as soon as he closed his eyes, an alarmingly bright light greeted him. The light was green and had such an intense glow that it faded to almost pure white. It reminded him of a flame. It was smooth and pulsing from its center like a heartbeat.

"What did you do to me?" Taxx said.

His voice was heavy and garbled by some unseen thing like he was talking into a moving fan.

"You are responsible for this," Rosen said.

She released him, and he had to catch himself, so he didn't fall over. The power was no longer gushing out of him, but he could still feel it moving around inside him. It didn't feel bad or ticklish, and it didn't feel like any physical thing he could think of. It just felt like something gently flowing around the core of him. There was tingling all over his body in random places like tiny needles touching him, even between his toes and behind his knees.

"What's happening to me?" Taxx asked.

"I am releasing your magic and drawing it into myself. It will let me appraise you properly and show you what I can see. Now then," Rosen said.

She was staring down at something in her hand, which she slowly held out toward him, and there in the center of his palm was a small flame floating just above her skin. It was as black as pitch, and each lick of flame sat around the core like an inky rose.

"Energetic shadows, just like mine," Sixx said.

"Indeed, but there is something else here... Deeper," she said.

The squat little flame changed shape, and hundreds of thorns erupted from the blackness, growing from all sides, even into the hand of the fairy. Mauve blood pooled there and spilled down the sides of her fingers as she held on to the flame despite her injuries.

"Magnificent," Rosen said.

"Rosey," Grayson said.

"No, not yet. There is something further still… something," Rosen said.

Taxx felt her probing him now, reaching inside a part of him he was unfamiliar with. It felt like she was digging around inside of his stomach, she wasn't, but it still felt the same.

"What… are you doing?" Taxx asked.

"These thorns are only a part of your power. There is something else here. Many somethings. Oh my…" Rosen said.

The probing stopped at once, and a different flame appeared in her hand. It was not a squat little thing like the shadow had been. This was larger than her head, and it enveloped her hand completely in its green light. The energy danced and flickered like a candle flame. Thorns were all over it, growing and changing as the flame danced like seagrass and moved with the ocean. The grass green faded into a paler color that was nearly white, just like the flames he had seen in the darkness of his mind, he knew that flame, but he asked anyway.

"What is that?" Taxx asked

"That was nature magic," Rosen said.

"If I may elaborate, just a touch," Avogorum began.

Grayson stepped between

"Rosey…" Grayson said.

"Oh, fine, it isn't as simple as all that. This is a great flame," she said.

"I'm sorry, but what does any of that mean?" Taxx asked.

"My wife means that you, son, are an unclassifiable non-human entity," Grayson said.

"We knew that already," Sixx said.

"Let me finish. You are also as powerful as any Demigod I've ever seen, maybe more. You have demonstrated commands of several abilities from all over the Odo. Both sides," Grayson said.

Taxx was staring at Avo so hard that he was sure that his eyes would bulge out of his skull.

"Couple questions. What the hell is an Odo? Is anyone going to talk about Avo melting? Oh, right, small thing, I'm not a human?" Taxx asked.

"The Odo is the sign of all magic. It is a map, a guide, and the grace of the Aether. Every spell makes use of its shape," Rosen said.

"Sure," Taxx said.

"There is much more to say about it. It's the symbol on your headband. All magic uses it," she said.

Taxx had seen it before, a few times now. It was nice to have a name for the thing, but that didn't help him with everything going on. He was starting to feel a sinking in the center of him. The kind of thing he felt when there was bad news coming.

"There's more, isn't there?" he asked.

"As for your being a human being? Strictly in a scientific sense, no, you are not," Grayson said.

"I'm some kind of jacked-up Demigod?" Taxx asked.

"Think of yourself as being in a larval stage, you have more room to grow and into what no one knows," Grayson added.

"Holy shit," Nic said.

"Damn. I always knew this family was dope," Sixx said.

"No one knows?" Taxx asked.

"Yet. Until then, technically, you are labeled Viridescii. Like me," Nic corrected.

"Like us. It means that the Aether has blessed you," Lyra slipped in.

"I am not a God!" Taxx shouted.

He didn't mean to sound alarmed, but it had been a long day. He thought there was something to be said about discovering that you might be a God. It sounded like a lot of work he didn't want.

"Calm down, 'God' doesn't mean what you think it does. It means you have a certain magic advantage," Nic said.

"What kind of advantage?" Taxx asked.

"The dangerous kind," Sixx added.

Sixx was smiling like a sinner while Taxx was in shock, but instead, he was staring off into a memory that he hadn't allowed himself to dream about in a while. It had been so long now that he had nearly convinced himself that this was really who he was, feeling that magic in his body, being around these people. It was crushing him. He needed to get out.

"This is all too much, I… I need," Taxx said.

He tried to walk toward the exit, suddenly desperate, but he didn't make it. As soon as he took two steps, Grayson closed the space between them and stood in the way of the door. He looked pensive but not angry.

"Stop. I had hoped to have more time for this, but you'd probably be dead by now if Rosen hadn't stepped in," Avo said.

"Technically, I already was killed, so…," Taxx said.

"Still, I can't let you walk around with targets on your back, not even knowing what they are," Avo said.

"What do you mean? What the hell does that mean?" Taxx asked.

"A lot of people will be looking for you. Especially when they find out what you are," Grayson said.

"What do you mean?" Sixx asked.

"Viridescii aren't just powerful and valuable. We are rare. You have at least two powers which makes you even more valuable," Lyra said.

"Didn't you wonder why that gold tooth sumbitch was after yo ass?" Sixx said.

"I didn't think he was after me," Taxx said.

"He sure seems like he wants you. My intuition says so anyway," Nic teased.

"The word Viridescii comes from an old tongue. It used to be used to describe a forest that is always green. Bursting with life. The Aether does not merely bless Viridescii with the gift of magic," Rosen said.

"What do you mean?" Taxx asked.

The fairy smiled at him.

"We are gifted with a ferocious lifeforce that can sustain you through injuries that would kill anything else. You are one of us, Taxx. That is why you heal so fast," Rosen said.

"Isn't it pretty damned unlikely that there are two gods in the same family? Is Grandma a God? Did they say the same thing to you?" Taxx asked.

"It's not impossible. Grandma ain't no God, not like us anyway. When I was four years old, she laid this on me, so I believed it hard then," Sixx said.

"What the hell? You knew all this since we were 4?" Taxx asked.

"Yeah. I used to tell you all the time accidentally. Remember, I used to tell you I was a secret agent all those times?" Sixx teased.

Taxx was only staring at his cousin as if he had never seen him before. Taxx could see the magic coursing through Sixx with his naked eyes now. It was moving under his skin like an underground river system. Strong as a hurricane.

"This is all so… unlikely," Taxx said.

"As unlikely as cousins being born at the same time?" Grayson asked.

Taxx didn't have an answer.

"There… is… something else he needs to know," Avo muttered.

"Avogorum, are you running low?" Grayson asked.

"Tell him!" Avo shouted.

"Tell me WHAT!?" Taxx shouted.

"The entire Warden program is just a happy face put on a probationary system for anyone who could be the end of the world," Rosen said.

"I thought you were magic feds?" Taxx asked.

"Their secondary function is to act as an investigatory arm of the Guild, but the main function is… preventative in nature," Grayson said.

"Preventative of what? How do we know any of this is true?" Taxx asked.

"Because. Rosen is the founder of the Wardens," Avo said.

"And I was its first member. Many summers ago," Grayson said.

"See, this is why I have trust issues. You are supposed to be the leader here. Why you never said anything?" Sixx asked of Avo.

"I could not tell you anything because I am not the leader, and I never was. I'm a Viridescii too, just like you all," Avo said.

Except for the Fae woman, who stepped toward Taxx and touched his hand, the room fell silent.

"I know this is a lot to take in," Rosen said.

"It is. I just… I don't understand why being a Veridian is such a big deal. I don't feel dangerous," Taxx said.

"A long time ago, someone foresaw that a Viridescii would bring about the world's end," Lyra said.

"What does that have to do with me?" Taxx asked.

"That was a prophecy with no endpoint, no clues to tell us who or when or why. Until Lady Moss came along. Your grandmother is the one who told us when it would happen and where," Grayson said.

"How can you be sure she was talking about me?" Taxx asked.

"We can't. The general rule has been that all Viridescii are candidates to bring about the end of the world. So, they either work for the House or get incarcerated," Grayson said.

"That doesn't sound fair," Taxx said.

"It ain't. It's like magical Alcatraz, and only the first chair knows how to get people in or out, and she been missing for 'bout a month," Sixx said.

"You mean Grandma?" Taxx asked.

He was still trying to wrap his head around his sweet and kind old grandmother being a witch. She had never really lied about it, not even once. He just didn't want to believe her. He believed now. He had so many questions he wanted to ask her, so many things he wanted to know, but something was nagging him about what they were saying. Taxx sucked in his bottom lip for a moment and fell silent.

"Ha. You both make the same thinking face," Nic teased.

"Like hell, we do," Sixx said.

Taxx continued, ignoring them both.

"For argument's sake, let's pretend I understand the part

where some magical whatever ends the world. Why do you all think it's me?" Taxx asked.

Avogorum smiled weakly, his form still distorted and strange from whatever was going on with him.

"We don't know exactly. It could be any of us," Avo said.

"Any of us?" Taxx said.

"Any Viridescii born until...well, the end of the world," Rosen asked

"That seems irresponsible," Taxx said.

"Well, it is, I suppose. We can do better," Izzy said.

"She created the house to protect those of us who were prime candidates," Grayson started.

"Let me guess. Unclassifiable Others?" Taxx asked.

"Correct," Grayson said.

The boys exchanged looks, and Sixx sucked his teeth in anger.

"This is Maybelline Moss's grandson," Sixx said.

"All of us are candidates, even you," Avo said.

"Are you doing okay?" Taxx asked.

Avogorum was barely standing, and some parts of his face were starting to change, receding into him like he was growing more diminutive in size, piece by piece.

"Lower the field. It's time," Avo said.

"Avo, please," Izzy said.

Avo held out a hand to her and looked up at the boys. Izzy reached up to the side of her goggles and adjusted a small dial. As she did so, Avogorum began to change shape. He fluctuated like a poor signal for a moment, and his image became blurry before he started to break down. However, it became apparent quickly that he was not breaking down or growing smaller. He was growing younger. Avogorum had the look of a middle-aged man before, and now the face he wore was that of a teenager. He could have been 17 himself. His beard was gone, and his face was smooth except for the sweat on his brow and a wry smile.

"You look so confused, young Moss," Avo said.

"I won't lie, this is pretty freaky, and I've seen some shit today," Taxx said.

"That you have, but don't be afraid. You are among some of the only people who could understand how you feel," Avo said.

His voice and his body were younger. He sounded like a different man, but there was something that had not changed at all. His eyes were the same.

"My real name is Zebulon Valentes. I was born a Viridescii with the ability to manipulate matter on the molecular level when that sort of science was still fiction," Avo said.

"Then who is Avogorum?" Taxx asked.

His regression seemed to stop, and before them stood a young man around their age with the same long hair and ridiculous clothing. His face was the same but saturated with youth.

"When I was 17, I was bonded with the Avogorum Zorrum Illunorum. It is a computer system beyond anything you could imagine. It runs on theoretical magic. Even after all this time, I do not know all its untold abilities, the least of which has kept me alive far longer than a normal man," Avo said.

"You're a damned computer?" Sixx asked.

"I am a living computer that is kept at the House. My current form is nothing more than a projection of light and magic. I am a simulated flesh. A paradoxical illusion,"

"You didn't know this?" Taxx asked.

Nic and Lyra also looked stunned by this revelation, but Izzy and the others did not look so amazed.

"Why tell us this now?" Taxx said.

"Because we are running out of time. I need you to trust me, or none of this will matter," Avo said.

"Why am I so goddamn important?" Taxx asked.

"Nobody knew you existed until today, and you are a Viridescii of age to fulfill the prophecy," Nic said.

"Coincidence?" Taxx asked.

"The person who hid you away from the world is also the same person who had the prophecy in the first place," Lyra said.

"Have you stopped to consider that maybe it's just bad luck?" Taxx asked.

"She intentionally hid you from people. None of that throws up red flags for you?" Nic asked.

"I don't want it to throw red flags," he said.

"You don't have a choice. You really might be **the** guy," Sixx said.

"You too?" Taxx asked.

He turned to his cousin, who was only smiling bigger at him.

"I was sure it would be me until I read the part about the horns. How lame is this?" Sixx quipped.

"Can someone tell me the prophecy?" Taxx asked.

"It ain't the sort of thing you can tell. See May May got a strange medium for magic. She a Tea Witch. Her prophecy come from a cup," Sixx said.

Taxx blinked. His cousin shrugged.

"Grandma is the one who gave the prophecy?" Taxx asked.

"Did we not mention that? I thought we mentioned that

part," Nic said.

Rosen, who looked contemplative, then leveled her eyes on Taxx.

"She never told you?" she asked.

The young man looked stunned before he looked down at the floor.

"No. She never told me anything. I drank lots of her tea, but it never made me feel anything but sleepy. If all of you are Virgos, couldn't any of us be the world's end?" Taxx asked.

He stopped talking when he remembered something. The memory hit him like a punch to the face, and it came so sharply that he could almost feel her knuckles against his face. See the fire of her eyes and her skin's warm and soft stone.

"Te'Amath," Taxx said.

As soon as he spoke her name, the energy in the room changed. Taxx touched his chest, which was beginning to tighten. Lyra turned toward him. Her eyes were sharp, and the power around her changed dramatically.

"How can you speak her name?" Lyra asked.

"I saw her. After I died, she came to me and," Taxx started.

He put his hand on his chest subconsciously. He swore sometimes he could still feel the leaves growing inside him.

"You didn't think to tell us that the first Viridescii just stumbled into you after you died?" Nic shouted.

"The first? I was going through a lot at the time. She told me she had never seen anything like me," Taxx said.

"She probably hasn't. She has been sealed in the mountain since before there was even a mountain. Seriously? None of this? Not a single red flag at all?" Nic asked.

"There's more. She referred to herself as the end of the

world," Taxx said.

His voice faded to a whisper at the end, and everyone was looking at him with a different shade of annoyance on their face, except Lyra. She was just openly staring at him.

"Wow," Nic said.

"I know! I guess I should have brought that up," Taxx said.

"Yeah, maybe," Nic retorted.

"Enough! We can discuss all of that later. You are here now, which means there may still be a chance," Avo said.

Taxx touched the center of his chest gently.

"Wait… something is wrong," he said.

"Te'Amath. You are sure it was her?" Rosen asked.

Taxxis slowly widened his eyes as he stared at her, his face changing into something between confused and terrified.

"What did you just say?" a voice whispered.

"I said, are you sure it was," Rosen said.

She trailed off at the end. She was sure she was going to say a name just now, but for her life, she could not think of it now. Rosen froze. She had been looking right at his face while he spoke, and all she did was blink, just once, and he was gone. She only looked away for a movement, but whoever was standing here just a moment ago had melted away from reality. The memory of him was slipping away from her like sand through her fingers, and she could do nothing to stop it. She tried to grasp a detail and say it out loud because it was important.

"Thorns!" Rosen shouted.

Then she forgot too. A second too late, everyone in the room was startled, and Rosen's sudden exclamation was met with a chorus of hisses and boos from the others in the room.

"What does that mean?" Sixx asked.

"It means that the flower fairy finally lost her marbles," Nic said.

"The real question is why we are all here," Lyra said.

"Why are we all here?" Avo asked.

"I do not know," Lyra replied

Sixx looked around with one finger on his lip, but he wasn't saying anything. That in and of itself should have been a red flag, but still, Rosen couldn't wrap her head around it. Why was she coming back to this same spot in the room? An area where moments ago she had been trying to remember something important at the time but lost now, like when you go into a room and forget the purpose you came for. This was not an aggressive loss of memory but something gradual and nuanced, almost natural, and somehow forgettable. It was the *almost* nature of it that gave her pause. There must have been something there.

"I've never seen you leave the house. Have you ever seen Avo leave the house?" Nic asked.

"There was something else I was supposed to do," Grayson said.

"Lyra must have summoned you for the looking glass, isn't that right, Izzy?" Avo offered.

"I remember the blackest eye acting wildly, but what I don't remember is why. Do you?" Izzy asked.

Avo shook his head instead of speaking when Rosen held up a finger sternly and then pointed to the strange area she had been staring at.

"Stop talking. Everyone. Stop moving and thinking, and for the love of the Gods, don't say a single thing for a moment. I believe we have all just witnessed a curse. I can feel it. Just on the edge of my mind. It was…" Rosen said.

"The forgetting curse," Rosen and Grayson said in unison.

"How do you know?" Lyra asked.

"Easy. This person is no longer in the room," Grayson said.

He turned the drawing pad he had in his hands toward the group, and on it was a very detailed pencil drawing of a young man with a long afro standing in front of Rosen in this room. They each had a series of numbers written around their bodies in several concentric circles though none were as clear as the mysterious young man.

"That is definitely Taxxis," Grayson said.

"Taxes? I know someone named Taxes?" Nic asked

"Can we just dismantle the curse?" Sixx asked.

"Normally, yes, but the numbers in his aura tell me that we have a whole new problem to worry about. This person will die soon," Grayson said.

"Are you certain?" Avo asked.

"It's pretty certain, and we don't have much time. He isn't here anymore. If it were simply the forgetting curse, he would still be in the room, but he is no longer in this house," Grayson said.

Grayson pulled what looked like a pocket watch out of lord knows where and opened the face. It was a compass, and he held it flat in his palm until a strange needle appeared and began to float above its face. The needle started to spin, stopping here and there to slowly point for a moment or two. Until it suddenly stopped. The needle was now standing straight up vertically like a sundial.

"That don't look like it's working, man," Sixx said.

"This is a seeker's needle, and inside of it is a small demon that once properly calibrated can find its target no matter where they are, but this… this is," Grayson started.

"The Other side," Rosen continued.

"Of course! What a brilliant and terrible piece of magical engineering," Grayson said.

"He must have triggered it and been drawn into the Aether," Rosen said.

"I don't mean to interrupt whatever that was, but can you share with the rest of the class?" Sixx asked.

"You are young. Can you describe to me the current image of a telephonic device?" Grayson asked.

"I'll do you one better; I have one in my pocket. What's it for?" Sixx asked.

"To prevent my wife from acting on her heart," Grayson said.

"What you mean?" Sixx asked

"Your cousin has stepped on the equivalent of a magical landmine. Only it doesn't explode. It implodes and pulls the body it's affecting into the Aether," Grayson said.

"The Aether?

"Doesn't that mean he is already dead?" Nic asked.

Sixx wheeled on her.

"Chill, you guys are Viridescii. That much power will protect him the absolute longest. At least, it can't get any worse," Nic said.

"It will be worse if Rosen gets it in her head to do something dangerous," Grayson said.

"Stand back, everyone," Rosen shouted.

"You may want to brace yourselves," Grayson said.

"Why?" Sixx asked.

The fairy crossed her arms, and the energy in the room

turned from comfortable to wild; the air was heavy with danger, and nature responded. The plants began to move, and some started to hiss and whispered along with the fairy when she spoke.

"I'm about to do something dangerous," Rosen shouted.

Chapter | Sixteen

Sixx and Grayson shared a look, and the phone was delivered quickly to the older man who stepped forward, holding the sleek device with just two fingers.

"There is no need, my sweetness. Modern problems call for modern solutions," Grayson said.

Lyra gently lowered herself into a seated position with her legs crossed and quietly started to meditate. Sixx looked between her and Grayson with increasingly bewildered eyes.

"What the hell are you two doing right now?" He asked.

"I'm trying to reach your cousin," Grayson said.

He produced a small object no bigger than a pencil lead and stuck it on the back of the phone. The thing disappeared, and in its place was a long thin strand as delicate as a filament, and it gently arched up from the phone and into the ceiling.

"With a cup and string?" Sixx asked.

"Precisely! An excellent summation, now, if you'll excuse me," Grayson asked.

He started to wander around the room, dragging the string along with him through the far end of it did not often move. He looked like he was flying a kite.

"The Tailor is being weird," Sixx said.

"So is she," Nic followed up.

Nic canted her head to Lyra, who was posed with her back straight and her eyes closed. Sixx swore he saw something flowing out of her like smoke, but when he blinked, it was gone.

"What can I do?" Sixx asked

"You can always try praying. You might **feel** better," Nic said.

"I don't pray," Sixx said.

"Me neither. Whatever is out there, though, I think I'll think a few things a person could probably call a prayer for your cousin," Nic said.

Sixx looked at her for a long moment, and then he and Nic closed their eyes. Not much time passed, but the two were silent for it. Saturday broke the moment when he opened an eye to look around.

"Did I do that right?" he asked.

"Exactly right, young man. You have settled a Fairy," Grayson said.

The tailor was standing just behind him, along with the others in the room who had gathered close. Rosen stood in a direct line of sunlight and let it pass through her hair, her eyes were closed, and she was smiling at the sun. Her lips were moving, and Sixx could see that she was saying his cousin's name. Grayson had taken a single knee behind him and placed a hand on his shoulder. Lyra sat alongside Nic with her legs crossed on the floor. Izzy and Avo stood close as well, heads bowed. Each of them reached out in their way to the beyond, and all of them thought of Taxx.

"What is this?" Sixx asked

"The old way," Rosen said dreamily.

"What can I do? I don't think I was doing all that," Sixx said.

He looked around at everyone, feeling suddenly sheepish and smiling.

"You can be silent," Lyra said.

Sixx opened his mouth to say that he was good at being silent, but instead, Grayson squeezed his shoulder with enough intent to get his attention.

"Why don't you help me complete my cup and string while the others do things the old-fashioned way," Grayson said.

***

Till now, Taxx had never seen the visions, his dreams were empty, forgettable, and faded, and he had never once been thankful for that. Today he would have given his left arm to go back to the way a normal thing sleeps because right then, Taxxis Moss was caught up in a very witchy sleep.

When it started, he thought he had died again because, at first, it was just an endless stream of indecipherable madness as though he was falling through a sea of nightmares. Then he was pulled hard in every direction he could feel, and more than a few, he did not know that a thing could travel, a whipping and roaring loud rollercoaster of a trip that he could still see even when he closed his eyes. He was afraid that in moments he would lose the ability to keep himself together and sizzle away in the wild magic of the Aether to be lost forever. At what he was sure was the last moment, he was drawn in another direction, and the madness seemed to ebb, at least enough for him to begin to be aware of himself again. He couldn't precisely feel his body, but he knew he had one, which was a vast improvement over where he had been just a moment ago. He opened his eyes and was met with the same endless darkness behind his lids, but here in this place, he could see his own body. His body was illuminated from within with a light so bright against the nothingness that he could see everything in such incredible clarity. When he held his hand up to his face, he could differentiate the spaces between his fingerprints. When he tried to look down at his chest, the collected light was so bright that he could hardly make out anything. It was like staring into the sun in that he could not do it for very long without having to look away.

He was unsure how much time had passed because he couldn't feel it in the same way here, but it was not much later that everything began to shift like suddenly moving water. It was pooling around his ankles like he was standing in a pond. He hadn't felt the sensation before, and though it was not wet like water, the substance sliding against his ankles unnerved him. He tried to fight against the current and found that, unlike when he had been dead when he tried to work away from the pull, he was easily able to keep himself not only stable but still. This allowed him to look at where he was, and when he focused his eyes against the darkness, he could just barely see the vague outline of what could have the wall on either side of him. He moved against the current with his arm out in front of him until he felt the wall's surface under his palm, and after a test, he pressed both of his hands against it. For the time being, it was solid. He moved closer to the wall and began to explore it with his hand, feeling along the rest of the border with broad but slow sweeps. He was careful not to commit too much pressure so he didn't stumble. There was nothing but the surprisingly smooth texture of the wall until his finger rolled over something very familiar to him. To be sure, he rubbed his hand all over it again. There was a smooth surface with two textured bumps in the center, one at the very top and the other at the bottom, and a knob between them. He flipped the light switch, and to his surprise, a very typical light came on, and he could suddenly see he was in a room and a room he recognized easily.

This was his room.

He was in the bedroom where he grew up. In his grandmother's old house. The door to the hall was just next to the light switch, and he felt a sudden temptation to open it because across the hall was Sixx's room. He might have opened it if not for another door he did not remember. There was a framed and free-standing door in the center of the room, grander than an ordinary door in height and weight and covered in purple quilted leather with brass rivets punching each dimple. The handle was black and long as though someone had made a long deep ink stroke in the air, and it froze in place and pointed down at the moment as the door was slightly ajar. A line of light peeking around it's even from such a small crack, but he could feel the weight of what lay beyond it very lightly drawing him toward the door like an invisible undercurrent.

"Why would I choose this door as my waypoint," he said.

He sometimes spoke out of turn as a reflexive habit from a lifetime of living with Sixx, and every time he caught himself, it made him swear under his breath. Waypoints were the visual representation of a door into the soul. A connection to the Aether rationalized it in his mind. Some were doors. Some were caves and any number of things. A way to ease into the madness of the Aether in a controlled manner, not safe, there was no safe way, but with a waypoint, there was at least the option of shutting it out. He moved toward the door and reached for the handle, which unexpectedly moved toward his grip like a tentacle until it rested in his palm. He pressed the door, and with a burst of multicolored light and smoke along the edges, it closed, and the lock fell heavily into place. As soon as he closed the door, the pulling ended, and there was such a feeling of relief in his whole body that he wasn't expecting. He felt like an elephant had been sitting on his chest, and he had to take a few breaths to clear his head and get himself collected. However, he could not pull his hand away from the knob for the moment.

His hand was not stuck, mind you, but the knob was warm and tingling with the promise of magic under his fingers, the door wanted to be opened, and though he would never admit it, he wanted to open it. He could feel its intent rolling over his hands like creeping insects, the door asking him to open it with those feelings, and for a moment, he felt his hand tightening. There were so many questions that could be answered if he would open the door, his grandmother told him once that the Aether knew everything that ever was or would be, but nothing that has ever lived could understand it in its entirety. This door in the center of him was protection from that storm and a Rosetta stone that could show him the way if he was so gifted. If he were not so talented, the Aether would supposedly enter him and burn him alive from the inside, driving him mad and destroying his body or something to that flavor. That thought ultimately helped him pull his hand away despite wondering what it would be like to swing it open. The feeling of his stomach dropping to his feet was very helpful in moving him away from the door. As soon as he did, something extraordinary happened. A phone started to ring.

Three rings, sharp and clear, and then there was only the sound of his breathing much more deeply and rapidly than before and looking all around the room in the center of his mind. He had been here before, everyone has a neutral space in their mind if they have the sense to see it, but until this point in his life, he had never been able to do much more than look at this thing. He had certainly never seen or heard a phone in here before. He would have remembered that… maybe, he hoped now that he was clear of all mind-altering curses. He stepped back and away from his waypoint and moved to the door that led to the hall as quickly as he could, reaching for the knob, but when he tried to move it, the knob did nothing. It didn't click or make any sound; it was solid in his hand and looked the part, but there was no weight to it, so it felt like plastic fruit. Then the ringing came again, so he did the only thing he could think to do. He yelled.

"Go Away!" Taxx shouted.

The ringing immediately stopped to his surprise, and after he waited for a few minutes before he made his way toward the quilted door and held his ear as close to it as he could, just in case, but there was no sound on the other side of the door. Once he was sure there was nothing, he pulled back and heard something move around under his feet. When he knelt to examine it, he found a thin white cord. It looked so much like a phone cord that he could not get it out of his head, so he followed the line, and it led him to the bed and disappeared beneath. He tugged on the cord, and there was resistance there but not enough to stop him, and in just a few seconds, he dragged out a phone. He had been expecting a rotary phone, but it was a cell phone on the end of a charging cable, he didn't know what it could have been, but he had not been expecting this. As he looked at it dumbfounded, the screen went dark, and an unknown caller appeared. He pressed the green button to answer on instinct more than desire and held the phone up to his ear.

"Hello?" He answered.

"Good man! Everyone picks up on the third ring. That's almost a fact. This is The Tailor. What I have to say is time-sensitive, so you'll have to listen very closely, Mr. Taxx," he said.

"What… happened to me?" Taxx asked.

"We aren't sure. What we thought was a simple forgetting curse seems to be something worse. However, don't be fearful; there are only two things I need you to know," he said.

"Ok. That sounds like good news," Taxx said.

"Firstly, it seems that you are, for lack of a better word, stuck in the Aether, and none of us can get to you, so you are basically on your own. Oh, yes, and this last bit is important. If you can't figure out how to wake up, you will die between worlds," Grayson said.

"Not good news but that tracks," Taxx said.

"Secondly, and I want to apologize for this one sincerely, but we may have spent a lot of your time figuring that first part out. So you don't have much time, but all you have to do is…," Grayson said.

The sound was gone as the call dropped, but that wasn't it. The device was no longer in his hands, the cable that was charging it was gone too, and just like that, Taxx was alone again. Only this time, there was peril.

"That also tracks," Taxx said.

Others could leave the safe confines of their minds to explore the depths of the Aether, perhaps the Witches more than any other, so they knew a thing or two about it. Why take the risk at all? When you can navigate it, the Aether is like a sea of magic, an energy that can lead to self-discovery and platforms for ideas that a regular thing could never conceive of. Searching the depths of magic meant surrendering to a powerful current older than the earth, older than time, something truly wild. That was always overwhelming. Even a single slip-up came with a dangerous consequence. It was never more complicated than the first time. Usually, that was after years of reverence and practiced meditation and a deep understanding of the paths of magic as defined by the witches. This and only this, they say, led to balance, and balance was the only thing that could save you from the madness of the chaotic Aether stream. A pure sense of self.

It was easy to tell yourself that you had a pure sense of who you are, but when you have to fight back against the full force hurricane of madness that is the birthplace of all magic and nightmares, it hits differently. He had to keep reminding himself that there **was** a possibility that he could succeed with his current understanding of magic. Somehow, it didn't make him think of anything except failing to recall some tiny bit, some simple piece, and facing a horrible, possibly eternal death. A fair percentage of those did all the reverence shit and still succumbed to the chaos and went mad. Sometimes it wasn't just mental disfigurement. It was often very physical and deadly, or worse, as some have been said to disappear without a trace.

"That must be how I got here. Damn, I can remember everything in here," Taxx said aloud.

He couldn't help but start to put things together now that most of his memories seemed to have been returned to him, but he was still trying to wrap his head around many things. A fail-safe in case the memory wipe or the assassin didn't work that somehow thrust him into the Aether stream to be stuck between the many worlds and tossed about the undertow of the Aether until the heat death of the universe. If not for the presence of the Door, he would have already been gone, but if he didn't open it soon, he was going to be gone.

"It is so easy to think when trapped inside your mind. Maybe I can figure out who would go through all of this trouble to kill me?" He asked no one.

There was no time to think about all of the horrible things going on **and** save his own life, so he decided he would instead save his own life and worry later. He sat down on the ground and took a deep breath to collect himself, and reached into the center of him where his magic lived. Usually, this was a slow-going process, and eventually, he could gather enough to do some basic magic. When he reached for his magic, it came easily and instantly this time. As soon as he tried to call up a bit of magic, it was there, tingling on the outer edges of his skin. He had always pulled as hard as he could to draw up even a drop and when he tried to draw on it this time, what came was a burst of so much energy that it slammed into his body. There was raw power sizzling all over his body, coursing through him and dancing along his nerve endings. His ears were ringing, and his eyes couldn't focus. None of his senses were working normally. He couldn't even think straight, so the simple idea to release his hold on that power did not immediately come to him, so he let go of it like a hot potato after a moment of suffering.

As soon as he let go of his magic, he felt better, and after a mild wave of nausea, he was back to his old self surprisingly fast. He might have even been feeling a bit better than he had been. He could still feel that touch of magic on his body like the residual heat of a hand on your skin. He was afraid to reach for it again, so he tried to stop thinking. As soon as the idea that he should shut himself off from his magic passed through his mind, he felt a sharp rustle under his palm that made him jerk his hand up and away. Where his hand had been, the floor appeared to be moving, not crawling or anything like that, but it bubbled like it was suddenly boiling and violently.

"Ok, what did I do?" Taxx asked no one.

The boil came to a fever pitch, and then something came out of it, a large malformed object that looked like an arm. It grew into a thick white stemmed mushroom. It was as tall as his waist and thicker than his body with a shiny red cap that speckled, and it only continued to grow wider and taller until it was about to rise over Taxx's body. He stood up and backed away as the stem grew thicker and darker, and the cap bulged as though it would explode. He briefly thought about the dangers of magic mushroom spores and took a diving leap away. The bed squeaked in protest when Taxx landed on it in his retreat from the strange plant, and for the moment, he just lay there and watched it grow and grow. Once the cap couldn't hold back anymore, it burst like a cooked sausage. Amber gills were growing all around this plant, the cap falling away from it like removing a candy wrapper, and to his surprise, he could see and smell something familiar. Not just familiar, but something good, and he knew it immediately to be the crisp scent of paper, and he looked closer at the gills that were growing out of the strange plant. They weren't gills at all but the pages of a book. They sprouted from the top of the stem in an uncountable number like the leaves of a tree, and the branch had now grown so dark it might have been bark. The sound of ruffling paper covered every other sound with its magnitude, it was like invisible rain, and there were moments that he could swear he could feel it landing on his skin.

He didn't know how long the sound went on. It was hard to keep track of time here, but at some point, it stopped, and it was quiet again in his mind, and Taxx was looking up at what he could only describe as a tree made of books. Once he waited long enough that he was pretty sure the thing wasn't about to talk to him, he slowly made his way off the bed and stood under the papers of the book tree. He thought it smelled like old books. The pages were not the off-white he was used to; they were pale green like the underside of a leaf and looked very thick. It could have been vellum for all he knew. The stem did appear to have grown bark now that he was this close, and it was rough under his fingertips. He didn't even remember when he decided to touch it, but he knew it was ok that he did. There is something so familiar about this thing, Taxx thought, but he was sure that he had never seen it in his life because he would have remembered a book tree. He reached up and ran his fingers through the leaves of paper, and they passed all over his hands as silky smooth as bird feathers. When he pulled his hand back, his fingers were covered in tiny lines of red thread, and he pulled it closer to his face to have a look. They weren't threads at all but dozens of small cuts that crisscrossed his hands, he hadn't even felt the cuts, and he still couldn't, even when some of them started to bead up into tiny pools. He looked up at the sheets of paper and saw streaks of red blood all over some of them like red ink splattered as thin as spiderwebs. The threads were moving as well, climbing all over the paper to make shapes and nonsense for a while before the paper absorbed every drop, and then the tree had words with him.

Verdant Blood.

Old Magic.

There were words, and for some reason, Taxx understood them, but to say that they were spoken would be incorrect. It was more like being nudged to share a feeling. In this case, a quick pulse and fast images passed through him until his mind created those four words. It crashed into his mind, warm and heavy but in no way violent. It was more like too many blankets on a warm night, not enough to harm him but enough to make him uncomfortable. The feeling had come from the book tree. Taxx was sure of it, which meant that the book tree drank blood and talked to him. It didn't take a witch's son to figure out he might be in some trouble here, but when he tried to step away, the words came again, like an earthquake inside him. He had to brace his head; he feared it would explode.

We Accept This Gift of Old Magic

"Oh. Thank you," Taxx said.

He wasn't entirely sure who or what he was thanking or what he was thanking 'It' for, but it seemed like common sense to be nice to the blood-drinking book tree right about now. He was running out of time and stuck inside of his mind, which was about to get brushed away like a dust bunny, and for reasons he could not understand at all, he felt the urge to lay down. This was not his will.

"What… What are you doing to me?" Taxx asked.

Receive Us

He couldn't help himself, his body started to move on its one, and he lowered himself to the ground and pressed his back against the trunk of the book tree. He laid his head back against the tree, and he felt something rusting in his hair. He reached up to touch small branches cradling his head. There was something else happening in these branches. He could feel it under his hands like water moving through a pipe. Something was moving. The book tree was pushing something into his head, there was a lot to unpack about all of this, but that seemed like the most important thing. He reached up with one hand and tried to remove the branches from his head, and to his surprise, they did start to move. Unsurprisingly, it hurt like hell. It felt like those branches were attached to his nerves, and he had to release them because his body gave him no choice. They were warm under his hands. With both hands this time, he reached up again, took as firm a hold as possible, and started to pull.

They didn't budge this time, and he felt something in his chest. His heart sank like bad news was coming his way, a shadow on his grave. His arms began to feel heavy as soon as that feeling passed over him, and he was having trouble keeping them up and around the branches. He held on as hard as he could. He leaned his body forward until his weight was also pulled against the branches, the added power started moving the limbs, and the pain smashed into his head like a bullet. He suddenly feared that he might be pulling them out of his skull and was about to damage his brain. He would rather brain himself than just lay here and let some tree suck him up like a juice box. Giving up was not on the table. He fought back as hard as he could, kicking and pulling against the branches.

You Must Dream

"What? I don't care! Let me go!" he said weakly.

He couldn't quite understand, but he could do nothing to fight the compulsion. It crashed through his head just like the pain and the voice of the tree, just like the voice of Te'Amath. It all felt the same, though, sort of fuzzy or muffled, like listening to a conversation and the distracting sound of running water at the same time. This tree had a similar feeling, though it could not have spoken a single word, it was a tree, but even so, he had heard it communicate. He couldn't remember the last time he spoke aloud, so the only sounds now were his breathing and an increasingly loud buzz that had begun to creep in all around him. Death. He opened his eyes sharply at the thought and violently started to fight back against the tree again, hurling himself forward with whatever he had left. It was not enough; more and more branches came out of the tree until he was being held in place with his body tilted at a sharp forward angle. His toes were barely touching the ground now, and the branches continued to grow, encircling him and wrapping around his body, head to toe. He was cocooned in a wicker prison with so many branches that he couldn't see any light. He could no longer struggle, not even to open his jaw.

"This one is surprising," It sang.

This was not obscured. Taxx heard it clear as day, the same odd singing that he and Jackdaw had shared earlier, except the tree's voice was quite different. Jackdaw sounded like a bird, this tree sounded like freestyle jazz, but the instrument changed every few seconds. Compared to birdsong, this was absolute madness.

"It knows the song... how interesting. Perhaps we should kill it?" The tree asked in its song.

Even though it was expressed in tones and beeps and varying frequencies, Taxx still didn't want to acknowledge that he could die, it might seem silly for someone who had recently come back from the dead, but it was also true. He was afraid. The last time he had the impossibly good luck to reach a Goddess or whatever that was who decided to let him live again. He was sure even Te'Amath could not hear him from here. Better men would have been saved if desperate cries could be heard from the Aether. He tried to struggle again, and he felt a pain in his upper thigh and then his lower back and then all over his body as an uncountable amount of branches as small and sharp as needles stabbed into his body from all angles. He went limp in the wicker prison, and he felt his eyes roll into the back of his head. He couldn't help but think about how slow this death was compared to his last one.

"You will not die, Viridescii, only dream," it said.

Taxx didn't even realize he was asleep when the dream started; there were just raindrops on the other side of the window now, and he was watching Sixx run around the courtyard below. The yard was expansive, and the backdrop was a lush forest with bushy green trees that sat like river stones in the murky grey sky. The house was surrounded by a long meadow that seemed to sprout from their backyard and go on into the trees. There was a paved pathway framed by flowers that led to the house. Someone was walking down that path and toward the house, just visible in the distance. Sixx continued to dance his wild dance, scooping up mud and stacking it up by the front gate until he had a pile large enough to hide behind, singing to himself and laughing aloud. Grandma called him 'unique,' but everyone else called him something else. Sixx never seemed to care if it was rain or sunshine. He would do what he liked and ruin clothing and furniture in his quest for a good time. Even now, he was not simply frolicking in the rain. Even though it looked like he was on some innocent boyish lark, he was actually up to no good. He was already a hell-raiser at 13. Taxx knew precisely how old he was down to the day. He and Sixx were born on the same day, down to the breath, his grandmother would say, and their mothers were twins born on the same day. People playfully called them Twin Cousins.

Sixx ceased all of his revelries and began to gather up an enormous pile of soft, muddy earth he could hold and position himself near the gate hiding behind the hill of mud as still as a reed. The person walking down the path reached the gate and knew her on sight; they didn't get many visitors. Offrey was not a visitor. She was their grandma's apprentice and one of the nicest people he had ever met. She was a witch that was special like he and Sixx. She was sweet to everyone except Sixx, who was worse to her than he was to anyone else. They were always picking on each other, fighting with increasing aggression, and only getting worse, which was always how it started. He would ruin her clothes before she met her teacher for the day and immediately draw her into a fight. She always wore delicate black dresses, clean and often lacey, even lace gloves and proper witchy heels with pointy toes. A proper witchy girl. Not to mention one of the only people that ever came to visit that was remotely near their age, she and Taxx got along alright for the most part, but Sixx never seemed to want to get along.

Offrey opened the gates slowly, and with a flick of her wrist, a thread, cable thick and jet black, leaped from her hand and bifurcated the hill of mud instantly. It fell away like cold butter, but Offrey was not content. She lashed out again and cut it into several cubes, never turning her face to look at it, scowling and taking careful breaths. Once the deed was done and Sixx was nowhere to be found, Offrey directed the threads to return, and they did so quickly, spooling themselves back into her outstretched fingers like a spider's spinnerets.

"I ain't with it today. The Lady and I both prefer me to be clean. I won't go easy on you anymore," Offrey said.

Sixx stepped out of a shadow, stepped out of one as though it was a cave with depth and space and not simply a tiny bit of darkness. He was always doing incredible things without regard to how impossible they were. Ever since Taxx could remember, Sixx had been born under more lucky stars than any one person deserved. His twin cousin was born favored by magic and loved by shadows. With the same effort as it would take an average person to walk down a hall, Sixx could step in and out of shadows. As simple as someone might step through a door, that was one of many things he could do that made him stand out from most people, even other witches. Sixx was not just gifted. He was an honest to goodness prodigy, and magic was just one of the things that came easily and early to him. When Taxx was still learning how to speak English properly, Sixx was swearing and casting spells like an adult witch; by the time Taxx had figured out how to concentrate his magic enough to make it visible, Sixx was slipping between dimensions to sneak off into town.

With all of those imposing gifts, he positioned himself until he was standing just behind Offrey, and without blinking, he slammed the ball of filth on top of her head, and he covered her in so much watery mud that it dripped down the brim of her hat and all over her dress. He didn't even laugh or try to run away. He just stood in front of her and bowed, smiling at her as wide as possible when he stood up again.

"Welcome home," Sixx said

She leaped on him and locked her legs around his waist before she started to hit him, and hard. She never held back on him because he was so thick-headed. She smacked and punched and whipped him with her magic objects, but he wouldn't stop smiling at him. This was how they said hello to each other. Then he would make her chase him for about an hour before he apologized and helped her clean up.

"Sixx already knows this. Perhaps you'd like him to try and teach you?" She asked.

His Grandmother was a gentle woman who could change the kind sweetness in her voice into tempered steel when she needed to with nothing more than a tonal shift. Even in this nostalgic memory, he felt a tremble dance up his spine at the sound of the steel in her voice, it brought him back into the room, and he turned from the window to face her. The lesson room had the most windows in all of the house, large rectangular windows with cross panes that were almost floor to ceiling. The room always seemed to have perfect natural light, and somehow the moon was even enough most nights to read without a lamp. Here she kept her things, a desk, and many other things, scrolls in decorative urns, art on paper and cloth and other much stranger canvases, loose bones displayed in between books that lined the walls like a library. There was so much magic in this attic that Taxx often didn't like to be in it alone when he was a child, so whenever he came into this space, he was usually accompanied by his Grandmother, who was sitting behind the desk just now.

Chapter | Seventeen

Maybelline Marigold Meadow Moss was his grandmother's full name, a name of which she was very proud and often said in full. Quite lavishly and over the top when she introduced herself, which was also something that she did often. Those few that came to visit referred to her as Lady M, May, if they were close, Taxx called her grandma, and Sixx called her 'old lady.' Sixx once told him that she was more than one hundred years old and when he asked her to deny it, she said she could not. She did not look to be ancient or powerful. She could have passed for someone in their mid to late thirties here in his memories, and Taxx knew factually that she was several times older, but not how much because only she knew that secret. She kept many secrets, as witches often did, and more than most. Taxx knew that his mother and grandmother were significant in some way. There was something about the way that people treated her. He didn't know any more than that. Maybelline was very careful to keep them away from that.

She was not very short or tall in any remarkable way, her hair was black like his, but her curls were softer, her skin was lighter, and her eyes were like warm honey. She almost always wore dresses and rarely wore shoes. Even then, in their home, she was barefoot and in a simple dress elegantly appointed with simple makeup accentuating the ageless beauty that her magic gifted her. A witch had a strong connection to the Aether. She was a clear vessel of the magic that passed through her, beautiful and timeless, so the witch reflected this in her face. Twisted magic and spells that went against the natural order in exchange for power were often attained through twisted and wrong means, and the user reflected this. The way that Taxx understood it, unbalanced magic was why the form of monsters became so exaggerated and wild. Balanced magic also changed you, but those Others looked closer to humans and animals.

"You ain't speaking to me today, young man?" May asked.

"No, ma'am. I mean, yes, ma'am, I am," Young Taxx said.

He hadn't realized that he wasn't the entity embodying the younger of himself until the boy hopped down from the window seat built into the bay window. His early teenage self carefully made his way across the lesson room and slipped past some of the training equipment he and his grandmother often used to hone his weak magic into something usable. Just looking at the stack made him remember long afternoons in this room toiling over the collection of loose round sticks. The game was simple, use your magic to stack the round dowels one on top of the other. Once you have stacked 24, end to end or side to side, you were the winner, but if you lost focus for even a moment, the dowels would fly in every direction. For years Taxx could only reach halfway before Sixx stacked 24 end to end and then side to side in the same amount of time. His early teen self was careful not to touch them as he passed, settling on a wide pillow in front of her desk and crossing his legs carefully.

"Sit," she said.

His preteen self only nodded and started to center and draw on his magic. Taxx could feel the tiny vein as it blossomed inside the child's chest. Something about it strangely struck him, and he looked away and back out of the window. Offrey and Sixx were standing just to the side of the porch. If Taxx hadn't been so tall, he might not have seen them, but from here, he could see that they were kissing. He took a step back out of shock and stumbled on the stick game. He landed hard on his back, and he found himself lying on the floor next to himself and looking up at his grandmother. She came around the desk with a pile of teacups stacked inside of one another, and then she carefully placed them on the floor one by one until they were all placed. Then she brewed some tea. Not with any kettle, May did not need a kettle to make tea, she waved her hands over the cups, and the tea was simply there, a different color in each cup. The woman settled herself on the floor across from her grandson, and she waved her hands over the collection of teacups. Taxx collected himself and moved away from the display of cups. He remembered this day, and he was afraid of what he was about to see, but still, he moved back to his seat at the window to watch. He glanced out once more to see that Sixx and Offrey had disappeared. He could suddenly remember so many times the two of them shared punishments. He had never dreamed that they were up to that, which is probably why they got away with it. He had more thoughts on the subject, but his grandmother brought him back to her lesson.

"These are simply cups. There is no magic within them. They are lovely things I found at a dollar store a long time ago, so do not fear the cups. It is the Tea that is to be feared. Each of these is a possible future. You must choose one and see your future. Only remember that a choice cannot be unmade once made," she said.

May placed her hands on the floor and closed her eyes, and Taxx slowly stood up from the seat at the window, carefully watching his grandmother. There was something humbling about how little she restrained her power even when he was young. Thankfully, he had been unable to understand its scope then, and he watched his younger self strain physically to call up some part of him that could feel her enormous power. From his current perspective, somehow, he could feel it, and it was like looking into the sun with naked eyes. His heart sank, and the air in the room took on an ominous weight. She said no words to invoke her power, but her hands began to glow with the results. Witches commanded the impossible forces of the Aether by channeling it through their bodies. Just that tiny flash of power had been enough to render his younger self unconscious, and even now, from the window, he had to turn away for a moment. He had come a long way, but May was still the most powerful thing he had ever seen.

When he turned back, he saw his grandmother do something odd. She altered the tea. His grandmother concentrated for a moment, and a sinister dark brew filled up all the cups. The color and viscosity of the fluid were so dark and thick that it could have been oil or pitch. Whatever it was, it was not tea. It bubbled in the cups violently before it settled down to a still glossy black surface. Taxx started to move toward the cups when someone else came into the room, and he froze, standing just over the unconscious form of his younger self.

"Can you please get on with this? You don't need to be so delicate with him," she said.

Her voice was like sweet sadness, and it passed through Taxx like a knife. He would recognize it anywhere because it was a low hum in his mind almost all the time. Her voice. His mother's singing… the sound he could almost hear in his dreams. The sound of it traveled deep and touched some old and painful wound in him, stinging through him all at once like an electric shock.

"Mom," he whispered.

She did not hear him. She could not. She was only a memory of her. Shockingly clear. She stepped into the room with a measured step, pressed slacks and loafers. She had a black lab coat on with the sleeves rolled to her elbow and an oversized sweater. He hated himself for thinking she was beautiful. Her hair was well-manicured like the rest of her. Her eyes were so striking that he couldn't look away. Even when she looked down at his younger self with indifference, she might have been looking at a small animal or an inanimate object. There was no animosity in her eyes. There was no love, no hatred. Her eyes were depthless pools that went on into a mercurial infinity, just like his. Unlike his, there were long pale slits in the center of her dark eyes like a snake's pupil. They made her look cold and critical.

"Hush up 'Cedes. Taxx is so sweet it would rot your teeth.

You might stay and talk to him when he comes back. See for yourself," May said.

Mercy did not blink. She only stared at her mother for a long time without saying anything. Her pupils were the only part of her face that had any animation. They moved strangely.

"What would I say to him? Look how big he is," Mercy said.

Taxx thought she might have been sad, but it was hard to tell.

"Say what you mean," May said.

"Ma, don't you start. I just don't know what I would say," Mercy said.

She knelt next to him, and she reached out to touch his face, gently laying her fingers on the horns on his head and then around his eyes.

"I've been gone for so long. How could he understand? How could he accept what I am… how I am?" she asked.

May sighed slowly.

"What is a child but an apple?" May asked.

"Save your riddles. I won't take this sort of guilt from someone who regularly murders him and calls it training," Mercy said.

Taxx felt the back of his mouth go dry. Murder? Regularly? He turned his eyes back toward the tea, and his heart fell to the floor so quickly that he swore he heard it land. Grandma had been giving him tea every single afternoon since he could remember. Almost every day of his life. Murder. Taxx stepped toward the tea and tried to kick it all over, but his foot passed through them harmlessly. He could not kick them over. He was not even here. He screamed. He cried and tried to throw himself at something, but there was nothing here that reacted to him.

Even the puppets of his family seemed to stop as if giving him time to have his tantrum. He felt heat rise to his cheeks, and he stared at his mother and grandmother, his lip shaking with rage and, worse, embarrassment. How could he feel that when they were doing all of this? He leaned in close to his mother's face and stared into her eyes, he could see himself in her eyes, but she could not. There was nothing different. She never saw him anyway. Knowing she had been there, right there in the house, the whole time but choosing not to see him was worse than any tea. He survived the tea.

"I hate you… and I hate how much I miss you," he said to her face.

Then he moved back to where he had been standing and rubbed the stupid tears from his face. He nodded curtly.

"Whatever, get on with it," he whispered.

They began to move again on command, and his grandmother huffed at her daughter.

"You and I are cut from the same cloth. Let's both of us pray that he will be better than us," May said.

"Better than us both will not be hard. I am your daughter. He is lucky in that way. He is not even my son, is he?" she said.

Taxx shouldered the crush of that wave, and his body rocked just a little from the impact. He stared only at his grandmother for the moment. His eyes were burning, but this was not what he had come here to see, and he had to make sure he saw it all. No matter how much it hurt. His mother stepped out of the room, and May waved her hands, and the black horror in the teacups changed back into the brown fluid he was used to. The tea he drank from her without question every single day. She revived his younger self with a kiss on the forehead, and Taxx looked on as the boy gently came to, looking lost.

"Welcome back, Cally Cal, whatcha say? How was your nap?" May asked cheerfully.

Taxx felt sick to his stomach. His younger self ate it up, and after a brief talk, she booped the young man right on the nose with her finger. A gentle little nothing that always made him smile until right this moment. Then she set him down in front of the teacups. She made him choose which cup of poison to drink the let him take his time as if there was anything different in any of those cups. There was only poison. He gritted his teeth and balled up his fist as he looked on, listened to her humor his foolish questions about the difference. He watched her wait until the young man took a sip from the teacup, smiling at her, right up to when he took even a drop.

Immediately he started to gasp and struggled to breathe. A coughing fit brought black fluid and blood from his mouth. He desperately grabbed his grandmother as blood streamed from his eyes. Thankfully he went still quickly, spilling the tea when his lifeless form slumped on the floor. His grandmother waved her hand, and the tea was gone, even the bit that had soaked into his clothing. Even after all these years, it was still impressive to watch her make magic look simple. His grandmother calmly moved to his sagging body and put her hands on his neck.

"He is gone," May said.

His mother came back into the room with a medical bag. She knelt next to his body and hissed softly. Dozens of pale white snakes slithered from her pockets, from her sleeves, from behind her neck. Each one was as white as milk with bright eyes. They moved with purpose, undulating all over the boy. One took up position over his heart, temples, eyes, and mouth. Snakes were settling all over his body, and once they all stopped moving, Mercy started to hiss again. The snakes went to work, some biting him and extracting blood, their opaque bodies turning pink with the effort. Others gathered fluids from his spine and other parts of his body. Once those snakes were full, they removed themselves and crawled into her medical bag. There were some snakes inside of him, and he could see them wriggling under his clothes. Taxx almost swore he could feel them even now. Mercy pulled some strange tools from her medical bag, a long rod, and a pair of weird glasses. She put them on her face and waved the rod over his body.

"His temperature is still normal for a living being, and his brain is still fully productive, as in all previous tests. You are right that this is a state of catatonic status while he prepares," Mercy said.

"Spare me the details. That is my grandson," May said.

"Oh, you mean this child you just poisoned. Don't play that shit with me, Maybelline," Mercy said.

"Just tell me how many he has now," May said.

Mercy hissed, and one of her snakes wrapped itself around his first finger, and with just a squeeze, the finger was severed with the precision of a scalpel. It was too fast for him to be shocked, but he still didn't believe it. Once the finger was removed, mercy held it in one hand and a snake in the other, holding its glittering eyes toward the bloody end. She squinted into her strange glasses.

"Looks like we broke one thousand. Give or take. I've never seen anything like it," Mercy said.

"I have, which is still not enough," May said calmly.

"Just what do you plan to do when your poison doesn't kill him anymore?" Mercy asked.

"When that happens, blissfully, I can finally be done with all of… this," she said, indicating her lifeless grandson's body.

"What does it feel like?" Mercy asked.

"Guilt? It will cover your mouth and nose when it's heavy like this but never let you die. I deserve to feel exactly that every time, and so do you," she said.

"I can't feel anything," Mercy said.

She looked down at the child and raised the corners of her mouth like a smile. It looked sinister and out of place on her. She stopped and sighed mirthlessly.

"He cannot have a snake for a mother. The work is done," Mercy said.

Her snakes all returned to her body or dutifully crawled into her bag. She closed it and looked down at Taxx again. His horns had started to take on a slight glow, and both women were staring at them.

"Will you tell him?" Mercy asked.

"No, I won't tell him you were here," May said.

"Thank you, but that's not what I meant. Will you tell him what those horns mean?" Mercy asked, turning to her mother.

"I will tell him today, but he won't hear it for a long time," May said.

"You speak in riddles," Mercy said.

"Someday, you may see that I don't, but I hope you never do. I love you, Mercedes," May said.

"Yes. Same," Mercy said.

Then his mother left the room without another word. His horns suddenly came alive with green light, flickering like fire on his forehead. He was shocked, but his grandmother didn't even look up. The flame overtook his whole body, and in a flash, it was gone. In its wake was a perplexed young boy. He was unharmed, with no missing finger, no bite marks. Even the blood that had stained his skin was gone. The fire erased it all, except his filthy clothes.

"Aww, I threw up again," young Taxx said.

"You did. That is so incredible that you only threw up," May said.

"Please don't. Just let me clean myself up," Taxx said.

He wriggled out of her grip and made his way out of the room, stopping at the door.

"I promise I'll do better, Grandma. Just... don't give up on me. I can be special too," young Taxx said.

"You are already special and better than any of us. It's my fault you can't see that," May said.

"I don't know what else I can do, but I will try if you ask me to. I love you," His younger self said.

To the woman who had just poisoned him. He watched his grandmother say goodbye to his younger self, and as the gangly young man left, he turned back to his grandmother only to find her looking squarely at him. He was so startled he nearly leaped out of his skin. He collected himself quickly. There was no way she was looking at him, she must have been looking off into space, and he just happened to be there. Taxx laughed at his stupidity for thinking his grandmother's memory was staring at him. She also almost gave him a heart attack. May kept staring, and in fact, she was starting to look like she had seen a ghost or was worried to see him here, but none of that tracked at all. Everything he was thinking right now was crazy.

"You still ain't learn to speak to me, young man?" May asked.

For a while, Taxx was the one who was staring, his mouth

hanging open.

"If you gonna let it hang open, at least say something, boy. You too grown to talk to your May May?" She asked.

"Yes, ma'am. I mean, no, ma'am, I am not," Taxx said.

"Good. Now come on over here and sit," May said.

Taxx rose from the window seat and followed nearly the same path that his younger self had earlier, removing his shoes and settling down on the wide pillow with his legs crossed. He did not even hesitate, not just because this was part of some magical BS, but because it had been a long time since he and May were able to sit together like this.

"Did you know I was a Godling?" He asked.

She smiled, and that smile evolved into a laugh before she seemed to be able to help herself.

"You still asking a million questions when you should be taking it all in, Cally, just like your grandaddy," She mused.

"Why can you see me? Is this real?" He asked.

"I am more than you know and less than you hope. This means that I cannot, and I will not give you an answer. We just don't have the time, baby boy. You must drink before it's too late," May said.

Taxx looked down at the array of cups, and for the first time, he could see something in them. The liquid was many colors, but all of it was clear enough to see through. The tea leaves gathered at the bottom were moving, and not only that, but they were also moving. The leaves took on shapes and depths to depict sepia-toned images of his life, events that had already happened, and some things he did not recognize. He was going to choose a cup of clear green tea with his image in it. Taxx was sitting on an airplane with Craw and Lyra within the cup, but something stopped him from choosing it. There was a sound. It came from the black teacups. They were hard to see, murky and dark, but there was still motion unfolding, and one of them was gently rippling all by itself. Taxx reached for it, and his grandmother intercepted his hand, lacing her fingers with his.

"You've gotten so tall. Let me look at you once... before you drink," she said.

They sat quietly for a time, holding hands and nothing more, but once she let him go, he felt the corners of his mouth turn down, and she brushed his cheek.

"There is no force powerful enough to take my love away from you boys. Every single thing I have done, I did for your survival. Please remember that if nothing else," May said.

"May, you and me," Taxx said.

"Stop. You must drink. Time is up,"

Taxx took the teacup in his hands and took a long draw of the dark bitter tea, and he balked at the flavor. There was no sweetness here. It tasted like blood and ashes.

"Drink! Hurry!" May shouted.

The world around them began to crumble and fall away, walls first and then chewing up the floor toward them, in its place a swirling black nothing. Death. Taxx took a sip of the tea, and it forced its way into his mind. Once he had finished the last of the tea, he could only stare at the woman in front of him, the woman he thought he knew. He was paralyzed, and he let the cup roll down his fingers until the teacup fell and shattered. May closed her eyes because no matter how hard Taxx tried, he couldn't get the horror off his face.

"Seeing so clearly is a curse. I'm sorry you have to carry it," May said.

She was crying then, and he was not long behind. There was a reason to cry now, partly for the joy of returning his memories to him. Taxx wept for the burden she had to carry all those years since it was now on his shoulders, the weight of the truth. She knew. She knew, and she raised them just the same, kissed his boo-boos, and made him grilled cheeses in the afternoons.

"Same," Taxx said.

The world where she existed cracked and split her into a million pieces until she fell away like a broken mirror. The sky was next and shattered above him until it all fell away like sand, taking the world with it, and he was pulled back into the center of his soul in the blink of an eye. He was no longer in her attic anymore. Taxx was back inside himself. Taxx could feel his arms and legs, but he could not move, no matter what he did. It didn't take him long to realize that it was because of the tree. It was still embedded deep into his body. It was the only thing keeping him from the glittering maw of the door that was drawing everything into it like a collapsing star. It was open full now, or more accurately, the door had been sucked into the Aether, and now a vacuum-like force was drawing everything else in. If not for the tree's branches, he would have already been sucked in. The tree started to force him off the branches, and he felt himself slipping toward the Aether, he tried to hold on to something, but there was nothing to take purchase on. His body flipped horizontally when his legs were free of the branches, and the only thing holding him in this world was a long spike of the tree buried so deep into his forearm that it did not seem to want to come out. He could feel it moving around inside his body, and he screamed, clutching the spike with his free hand to stay free of the Aether.

"You are so much stronger than I anticipated, a boy who lies," Am said.

At first, he thought he had imagined it, but he heard her as clear as day, and after a quick search, he found her form sitting on his bed. She had skin now, impossibly beautiful and as black as the polished night sky. Her eyes were still rings of pure fire inside of her beautiful face. She had human hair and limbs, a dress, and smirking lips, but there was no mistake. It was Te'amath. Over each of her eyes was a horn. Each was as black as a shadow's smile. He couldn't look away from her.

"What? How are you here?" Taxx asked.

The pull of the Aether seemed to get a grip on him, and he started to slip further away.

"Am! Help me!" Taxx shouted.

"Help you? I am the one that trapped you here. If not for this tree, I would have already tossed your useless soul away like rubbish," she said.

Taxx could only stare at her for a long time, and his grandfather's words skittered through his mind. That there was already something inside of him, that is what his grandfather said. Maybe she just thought of the same plan and put it into action before he did. His feet were dangling over the precipice of death, facing down a new horror. He thought about his mother and the sound of her voice. He hated how quickly he knew the sound of it. He knew it so well, better than he should for not having seen her since he was a small child. Why did he know the sound of her singing, the melody but not the words to a song, just on the periphery of his dreams? Every time he was drawn into himself, he was met with another being. First Am, then his grandfather, and honestly, there were other things too. There was always a voice trying to speak to him in his dreams, sing to him. He always thought it was his lost magic calling across his regrets, but now he was afraid it was worse.

"What am I?" He asked.

"Look at you. You were always kind to me, foolish boy. Even now, I can sense your confusion and thousand other things. Do you know what I do not sense? Hatred," Am said.

She stood up from the bed and moved closer, revealing that she was much younger. No older than him. Her face was fresh and pretty, but her eyes were ageless and heavy with madness or genius, he could not tell. She looked so pleased to see him in such peril. She stopped at the base of the tree and placed her hand on it, the tree tried to recoil from her touch, but it could not get away. Where she touched, a blackness started to seep into the tree's trunk, and Taxx was cursed to hear it screaming in a voice of many voices.

"Stop! Please stop!" Taxx shouted.

"You are going to die! Stop worrying about a tree… stop being so sweet when you are nothing more than an evil magic spell brought to life. You are a demigod whose own family hobbled him. Someone hollowed you out and used you as a living curse, a living prison. You were born unlucky, and where there should have been magic, there was only a hungering hole. An unquenchable fire that eats only magic. That grandmother of yours turned you into something impossible and never even let you know it. You still don't. How sad for you," Am said.

"Does that mean that even you don't know?" Taxx shouted.

"How **dare** you! You are not worthy of knowing what you are. What you **were**!" Am shouted.

She stamped her feet and pressed her fingers into the tree,

making it scream even louder in a voice only Taxx seemed to hear.

"You are the center of so much engineering and sacrifice, the nexus of so much hope and hatred that you have been doomed since your conception. You are the vessel for the end of the world, but somehow you are even worse than me. Your grandmother is an admirable woman. On the other side, when her time comes, you tell her I said so," she teased.

"May is alive?" Taxx asked.

"You are in peril! Do you not care about yourself at all? How can you be asking about her when she did what she did to you? She created the most incredibly vile thing I ever saw and trained it to act like a silly child, and that is not even the height of her achievement. A real credit to all witches, she should be studied," Am said.

"I'm not stupid, lady. I don't want to die. I don't want magic. I just want to know why so many people seem to hate me?" Taxx asked.

"It had been so inordinately long since your last visit. I thought she might have changed her mind. Thankfully I was wrong. She knew this would happen. Your grandmother stole her way to The Library. She seized knowledge for herself. She knew we would be here before either of your mothers was born," Am said.

"Why does everyone talk in riddles!" Taxx shouted.

"You only hear riddles when you don't know the truth. Know this. Your time is over," Am said.

The pull of the Aether had him dead to rights now. It was only a matter of moments before he would be sucked in and fizzle away in the core of all magic.

"Am, please! Help me!" Taxx shouted.

"I have always been helping you. Every time you came back from the dead, that was me. Every time you mimicked my thorns or wasted my regenerative power. Me. You are a cheap copy. A doorman borrowing power from your tenants. No longer," she said.

"Why do you have to kill me?" Taxx asked.

"I tried just removing the binding spell your mother left inside you. That was only enough to free the door, not open it. When I thought to, I should have killed you then, but I digress. Once you fall into the infinite, the connection is severed, and Death's Door will be free of the witch at long last. Free of you. All of us! Free!" she shouted with glee.

The tree had a dark line across its trunk, and Am pulled her fingers away. She tilted her head and smiled at him brightly.

"Even you. You'll finally be free of her too. Oh, how she will hate that. Her perfect creation," Am giggled.

"What am I?" Taxx asked.

"Dead. What you were will survive through me," Am said.

She lifted her hand, and it changed into that dangerous blade. It still felt like a coming storm. She hefted it carefully. It was darker now, heavier, and the edge looked even more dangerous, magic crackling along its edge like lightning. She cut through the base of the tree of knowledge in a single blow, and the tree teetered toward the pull of the Aether. The blackness she injected crawled toward him, eating up the tree as it moved. Taxx could feel his legs entering the portal and disintegrating off his body.

"Look how much better your power looks on me," she said.

"You won't get away with this," Taxx said.

She laughed. Not just a titter. A full-on belly laugh that was patronizing and booming in the small room.

"That is the stupidest thing you've said yet. It's done already. You are the only one in the room who doesn't know it, just like always. Goodbye, Taxxis," Am said.

Blood for Blood

The tree spoke inside of him again, and the branch broke itself off while still attached to him, evading the encroaching magic. Once free, Taxx was dragged, untethered, into the wild storm of the Aether. It swallowed him up in one motion. The more he tried to fight it off and will it away, the more it pressed him, dragging him violently downward with crushing force. Thoughts boiled out of his mind and bombarded him with images and sounds and words, ideas, and emotions that were so sudden and varying that he was having difficulty maintaining his consciousness. He saw memories of his childhood. He could smell birch bark and foxglove and hear singing about coincidental things being ironic. He could taste juice boxes from 10 years ago, French bread pizza, and the grape Chapstick of his first kiss. It was overwhelming, like trying to open your eyes in a hurricane. Every time he tried to focus on one thing, it was pulled away as though a harsh wind carried it, he could barely hold onto himself in the storm of it, and it seemed the harder he fought, the faster he was dragged into it. It was all around him and inside him, sending waves of energy coursing through every fiber of his body and inside his mind, filling his lungs with every breath. There were painful moments of clarity, but try as he might, he couldn't find any way out, and the focus he had found was reduced to pine needles in a hurricane.

"Mr. Moss," the voice said.

He heard a voice, sharp and hot, cutting through the low groan and the madness of pain that spread through his body like jolts of spiked electricity. It cut over it all like a loudspeaker. He focused on it instantly, and it helped him gather himself a bit. He was Taxxis Moss, and he focused on that. He could feel that his body was still there, which meant he was at least not dead again, just in pain, searing pain, and his right arm felt like it had been torn off. That was comfort somehow, and he leaned into the memory of the voice and opened his mouth to speak, feeling his lips separate like tape that ripped away flesh with each hair.

"Taxxis," He strained out.

The sound surprised him, and he felt the shock roll through his chest. It was the most fantastic thing he had felt in what could have been days. He could suddenly feel her, a lighthouse in the vortex of depthless magic and sound, so bright and vibrant he couldn't help but gravitate toward it. It wasn't the same movement he was used to, like walking. It was more similar to thinking about someplace you wanted to go and finding that you were suddenly there. It didn't take him very long to reach the flame, and it was much larger up close, as tall as a tree and brighter than a star. Just being this close to it spread warmth all through him.

It melted through the miasma around him, and without really being aware of how he might do it, he reached out to touch it. Once whatever it was that he perceived to be his fingertips contacted the flames, something happened, a sheen of yellow light appeared and started to cover him. Every portion of him that it touched filled up with form, color, orientation, and calm. The madness slowly fell back and away from him like ice melting in the sun, carefully revealing his body and relieving his mind.

The comforting warmth covered him toe to tip until he was

surrounded by it on all sides, and it held him aloft in this mad ocean like an anchor. The music playing so incredibly loudly before started to sink to a much more pleasant level. He could hear the instruments that were at play. The world around him had settled as well, and he could see everything now. It was like he was standing in a painting. There were splotches of color everywhere. All the colors of the rainbow and probably a few more, they were standing alone, bleeding together and shifting into objects that he could understand. Violet watercolor morphed into trees that breathed like the lungs' capillaries, moving in and out in time with the rhythm of his lungs. Everything felt like dancing in this facsimile world, drenched in every color that sat over everything like a crystalline lens. Everything was already dancing. Suddenly he was bobbing his head, and he could feel his entire body again, from his toes to his forehead. He was a person again.

He could see himself, and when he looked at his arm, the long shard of wood was nowhere to be found. He flexed his fingers tentatively, and when he discovered that he was whole again, he also started to dance and bobbed along with the trees. The only thing that did not move and sway and twerk with him was the form of Lyra sitting in front of him with her legs carefully folded beneath her. In front of her was what looked like a glass effigy of his body, lying down on the ground just in front of the warden. The body he was looking at was hollow, like an ice sculpture. It was startling, and he took a few steps backward, but he knew he wasn't a clone or in a new body, not a trick or a spell. He didn't know how he knew it exactly, but he knew. There was just an understanding inside of him that told him it was true.

It wasn't as though he suddenly learned this. It was more like he remembered it like someone had told him the information once before. He knew that he was standing outside of his body in the Aether and this form he had was the magical embodiment of his soul. A formation of his living consciousness wrapped in energy; it was referred to as a Crux.

"Crux, yes, perfect," Lyra said.

Taxx turned to face her, and she smiled at him, he then turned back to look at himself on the ground and her body sitting just above his head. Her body was also an ice sculpture now, but her body's hands were on his glassy face now. He looked back to her crux and nodded slowly.

"As unbelievable as this sounds, I think this is starting to make sense," he said.

"It's a lot to take in all at once. You did very well for someone who cannot enter the magic states. You were already starting to remember yourself before I found you. The Aether is a great power, it grants you knowledge and solace, but it is not without its dangers," she said.

"Yeah, well, if you hadn't found me, I would still be scattered out there, so I'm glad you did," he said.

Lyra was speaking to him, and somewhere in his mind, he heard her, but he was very distracted at the moment by, well... everything. Everything he could see looked so much sharper, and everywhere he could see tiny wisps of magic, vibrant and alive with color, and they danced across his skin and through the air in a kaleidoscope of wonder. That was the source of the watercolors, magic, energies, unseen forces like magnetism and heat, each color of the trillions he could see were different. He just knew it. It came to him like a near memory, as if he had known forever, and if he simply thought about it, he could understand the Aether itself.

It was the clay from which all life was formed, the rippling energy that created the universe to form the planet, the oceans and landmasses, and creatures great and small. They crawled from the seas and carried the same heat, the force that started all life in the universe. The same fire was passed from the smallest mouse in his impossibly long and infinitely vast ancestral line. The power that traveled down that genetic coding for millions and millions of years until it was right here, in this time, in this place, to teach him this lesson. He carried the same fire that stoked the universe. The same warmth his mother held inside her heart was burning and beating still inside his.

That was the Aether. It carried the imprint of every moment from the very beginning and further until the very end. This vastness took benevolence on him and, through the gift of magic, granted him some small insight into the workings of life itself. The Aether was present in all life, energy, and things, even the magic inside and around him. Though he tried to peer into the infinity as hard as possible, he could not see all the answers he wanted. Even the clay of all life could not know the answer to all things. That anyone could understand even a tiny portion of this was humbling.

He lifted his arm, and some of the wisps leaned toward it with just the motion, and he felt something reach out to them. He could feel his own will like a new limb, and it was that limb that he extended. Like a man might gently touch a small pet, but this was not a pet. It was energy and when his fingers touched it smoldered a bright orange. The heat of it warmed him through, and he could see it pass through him in a wave of that bright orange like the embers of a cigarette, and it filled him with strength and calm. He felt like he had a meal or a short but very effective nap, and he had only touched a single wisp for a single instant. Once it passed through his Crux, it slinked out of him and flitted away like a dandelion seed on the breeze.

"Energy is in all things. Animals, plants, and even minerals have some dormant energy inside of them, we call it magic, but it has many names, like chi, power, the gift… but the name speaks of the same thing. This energy is all around us and everywhere in the universe. That little touch you felt was just the smallest possible bit of exchange. You have magic now. You will learn to channel a great deal more," she said.

She seemed happy. Her Crux was illuminated slightly from the inside, like when you hold your hand over a flashlight or something. She glowed, and he could almost see through her. He wondered if that was how he looked, too, and with just a bit of inspection, he discovered that he also glowed. Where hers was a soft yellow and orange, he was lavender light that gently faded through turquoise greens to the bright white center of his being. It was beautiful, and he opened his mouth but was preempted before he could speak.

"Think of it as a magical fingerprint. It's a manifestation that your particular gift develops based on many factors, including your genetics. Each one is unique," she said.

Hers was like fire, it moved like a candle, and the white-orange core that faded to gold made it look like a living flame. The light in him didn't seem to move like that, but it was bright and alive. It danced under his skin in waves and lines.

"The Aether stream is yours to explore at your leisure once you are comfortable stepping out of your body. Time moves differently here, but it does move. The longer you stay here, the more likely you will not be able to enter your body again," she

said.

When she said that, he felt a shudder of fear roll through him and his lavender energy leaped off of his skin into the form of a bubble, and he put his hands up, so it didn't fall on him. It didn't move. However, it hung all around him, over his head, and disappeared. He carefully turned his head to the right, and when he shifted, it moved along with him like it was tethered to his body.

"Good instincts, that is a basic shield. Once you master that spell, it will become something you can perform on instinct," she said.

She held up her hand, and the yellow-orange light solidified like a crystal formation, not in a bubble but covering her close like a second skin. It even flexed with her fingers. As soon as she manifested it, the almost gentle feeling of her magic, which quickly became familiar, erupted to enormous heights. His bubble cracked and shattered under its weight like an eggshell, and he turned his eyes away from it. It was gone as suddenly as it had come, and she was standing next to him now, one of her hands near his shoulder but not touching. She looked concerned and possibly a little amused.

"Forgive me," she said.

Taxx looked down at himself. His body looked tired, and he was so sweaty that he could almost feel it pooling under his arms and around his neck. It made him hesitate.

"Do not fear. It is only difficult this first time. Understand this truth. Magic *is* Magic. Whether you are inside your body or not, you are gifted with the ability to manipulate energy with simple willpower. Magic is the name that we give it, but it has many other names, as all old things do. It is yours to channel and tame, utilize and explore at your whim. It is your right. You are magic. So even here, you can manipulate your Crux in the same way you manifested yourself. All you must do to enter your body again is-" Lyra said.

She was still in her Crux, and in the same breath, her body finished.

"Will it to be so," she said.

In the space between the word "is" and "will," her Crux had disappeared, and her body began to speak. It was so sudden and straightforward that he could only stare.

"I don't know if I can do that," he said.

"Yes, you can, and I do not mean to rush you, but I must ask you to please be quick about it," Lyra said.

He thought about how he had made the bubble appear earlier, and there wasn't much to remember there, he flinched, and it just sort of came out of him. She had startled him, and he reacted. It was as easy as an instinct. As she said, he didn't even know to think of a shield. He didn't even know he could do that; he didn't think he could do anything. It just happened. Could it be that easy for him to get back in his body, he thought? All he had to do was want to be in it as he understood it, so he closed his eyes and took a very deep breath. He knew he wanted to be back in his body, so all he did was accept that he might be able to do it, and it was done.

The others in the conservatory were watching Lyra stare at a space on the floor, and then she started talking to an area on the floor. As soon as Nic opened her mouth to say something cross, Taxx reappeared between her and Lyra, and the younger warden screamed.

"What the hell!" Nic shouted.

"Taxx!" Sixx said.

Sixx crossed the floor and collided with the young man who had just appeared and barely sat up on the checkered floor of the conservatory, touching himself all over. He gratefully accepted when Sixx helped him to his feet and immediately into a hug. He was back in his body now, but it took some adjustment to move it again. He still couldn't believe how fast and easy it had been to change from what was basically a ghost back into a human. It wasn't anything like he expected. He didn't have to crawl into his mouth or lay down on top of himself and sink in like some silent move. Nothing like that at all. It was as easy as taking a breath. He felt a slight tingle inside of him when he decided he wanted to enter his body, and just like that, he felt his Crux begin to break down. He returned to his body like the snap of a spring, and he was there, awake, aware, and feeling not so bad. Maybe that was an understatement. He felt amazing. His head was clear, and his body had never felt more alive or strong, he didn't know what it was, but he felt like he could run a marathon right now. He felt like he could even win it. Ok, at least he would place… ok, fine, he thought, maybe he would finish it somewhere in the middle of the pack. Still, that was an improvement. He tested his feet, and he was surprised to find that his step was light but strong. This was magic. He didn't feel empty anymore. He felt so much more like himself than he had since all of this began. He could feel energy humming through him. If he squinted, he could see the power spreading through his whole body in millions of intricately woven and multicolored threads. He didn't know what it was, but the more he looked at them, the clearer they became, an uncountable number of threads snaking through the whole of his form. He could see them all through his body as though it were a clear container. He could see Lyra's. Hers were strong and steadily racing with bright points he could only assume marked her power. He looked at the center of himself, the bright center of his being, and he could feel the tingle of its intensity. He held up his right hand, and there it was, burned into the back of his hand. The triangle scar from his dreams.

"...Shit," he said.

"Appropriate," Lyra responded.

"Was your grace always there?" Nic asked.

"My what?" He said.

"Grace of the Aether. The mark of magic on your hand," she said.

"No. That came from my dreams, and if that part is real, then that means that everything is too," Taxx said.

"I thought you would be happier to have the blessing of magic," Lyra said.

"I should be, but I know something now. Something that I wish I didn't know," Taxx said.

"What?" Sixx asked.

"All of this. All this crazy stuff, everything that's happened in my whole ass life has been because of grandma. May used me," Taxx said.

Chapter | Eighteen

A heavy knock on the door echoed through the house like a bass drum. Shortly after, there was a second knock and a third in more rapid succession, each booming through the house like a speaker. He placed his hand on the knocker again, but a small hand stopped him before he could lift the large brass ring.

"Calm down, Ronni, they are coming," The young woman said.

She was in full professional stage makeup and still wearing the costume from her farewell show: denim and colored lace, pink and black. Mimi gave the world a farewell show they would very likely never forget. He certainly wouldn't. Ronni was about to say something, but the door swung open, and a young man was there to greet him. The young man sighed with disdain on seeing who had darkened the doorway.

"She won't see you, Byron," he said.

"Who you talkin' to like that? Got me standing out here like this, gone and move out my way," Byron said.

"Don't you think you have caused enough trouble here?" he said.

"Don't act like we are friends, first of all. And B, I ain't think this would happen," Byron said.

"That is exactly the problem," he said.

"Let me in. Tommy... I ain't gonna ask again," Byron said.

Tommy made no motion that said he would move away from the door. Byron took a step toward him but was stopped by the young woman at his side. As soon as Tommy saw her, he bowed his head.

"Maybe," Tommy said.

"It's Mimi. Everybody knows that," Mimi said.

Her voice was positively bubbly by comparison to the two men. She was confident, and she wore it on her face with a bright smile that would light up a shadow. Mimi was standing just under Byron's arm, and she had a small bundle in her arms. Tommy gasped and quickly stepped to the side of the door to let them pass.

"Forgive me, Mimi," Tommy said.

"Tommy boy, you alright," Mimi said.

She and Byron entered, and Tommy carefully closed the door behind them. Byron looked around the atrium before he looked down at Tommy, who had come around and was now standing between them and the house beyond. Byron was much taller than him, where Byron was cocoa brown, Tommy was peach, and Byron's accent was southern American while Tommy spoke the Queen's English. Tommy wasn't just shorter. He was slighter and much more handsome than the other man. His eyes were blue and over-filled with rage as they focused on Byron.

"I ain't never touched that girl," Byron said.

"The evidence tells a different story, you Devil!" Tommy said.

Byron did not move. He only smiled. Tommy had a tirade, and he yelled every word at him, wagging his finger. He paced and slapped his hands together to punctuate his point. His chest heaving from the effort. When he was done, Byron leaned down and jutted out his chin for the shorter man, offering it to him openly.

"You mad, mad?" Byron said.

Tommy lifted his sleeve and exposed an entire arm full of strange tattoos, a large glowing mark that showed overlapping diamonds and nested circles. Many more markings around it seemed to be a random arrangement of dots at first. There was no pattern, but they covered his arm from wrist to elbow, numbering in the thousands.

"I've seen your grace. Am I supposed to be scared?" Byron asked.

Before he finished speaking, the tattoos began to move, and thin black insects started to emerge from them as if they were holes, and in seconds his entire arm was swarming violently with winged insects. They were oil slick black with a high gloss rainbow sheen that made them look like ink as they undulated on his arm. They formed a close layer on his skin, conforming around his limb and obediently waiting for his command. They were constantly in motion, crawling all over and through his fingers but never leaving his skin, awaiting orders. Their steady wing beat created a loud buzz.

"These are black assassin flies. Voracious little beauties that know no fear. They will attack and devour anything I tell them to. Normally, their venom only kills instantly and liquefies the insides, but these lovelies are special. I made them just for you," Tommy said.

"Kinda small ain't they-" Byron started.

"Ronni! Stop it!" Mimi shouted.

Byron visually cooled just from her voice, but he had taken on a stance that said he would not back down. A look on his face seemed only to drive Tommy deeper into anger.

"My name is not 'Tommy,' it's Tomas, and I will show you that size can be deceptive," Tomas said.

"You ain't never gonna get no girlfriend if you tell 'em that," Byron said.

"I have a fiancé!" Tomas shouted.

Byron fell silent instantly and stood up straight. Mimi placed her hand on his shoulder and nodded at him. The larger man sighed and collected himself as best he could.

"You right. I just don't know how to make this better, so I won't stop you, but you ain't gon' like what happens if you hit me," Byron retorted.

"It's just a little early for Tomas to die," she said.

The Lady Moss was simply standing between the two of them as if she had been there the whole time, holding a delicate teacup with just a few fingers. It was white with tiny purple flowers all around it and rimmed with gold, the cup appeared to be empty, but Byron knew better than to believe that. Maybelline was a daunting woman in every respect, she was neither tall nor physically imposing, but her prowess was all too imposing. Magic radiated from her smile with the force of the tide. It lapped up on Byron gently, for now, but he knew at her whim it could drag him under just as easily. He smiled back at her and nodded to acknowledge her warning. Tomas was still seething behind her, and the insects were buzzing louder. She turned and gave him a slight nod.

"That will do, Tomas. Please go and see to her," she said.

"Yes, mum,"

Tomas took one last look at Byron, narrowed his eyes, and then he strolled away, the black flies clinging closely to his arm as he vanished up the stairs. Byron watched him the whole way, a small smile on his face. There was not much ill will between them, just the results of a mistake that neither of them had control over. Forces of nature were like that.

"My daughter," May said, holding out her arms.

"Ma," Mimi said.

The two embraced deeply, and May looked down at the tiny bundle in her arms. A swaddled child was in her arms, shrouded by shadows even with his face exposed.

"I'm so glad he is healthy, considering. What is his name?" May asked.

"Saturday Romaine St. Martin. That's a star's name," Mimi said.

"St. Martin? I knew it, but I still wasn't ready to hear it. This is a Moss boy," May said.

"Half," Byron said

When may turned her eyes to Byron, he held his arms out wide for a hug; she did not return the greeting. She didn't even move. Her lips were pursed, and her hands were on her hips.

"Now that's the woman I remember. How you, Miss May?" Byron asked.

His energy was returned with composure from the elder witch, her careful eyes taking him in slowly and all at once. He did not move or speak until she finished her appraisal.

"I been better. My house is very active because of your poor choices," she said.

"This wasn't how I wanted it to be," Byron started.

"It isn't my fault, you say. She says it wasn't supposed to happen like this, but here you both are, looking guilty," May said.

"Momma!" Mimi shouted.

"Don't you, Momma me. You two have skirted the laws of the Guild for long enough. Not only did you have a forbidden child, but to do it in front of all of those humans? What were you thinking?" May asked.

"We are in love," Mimi said.

"Your love is costly. You have no idea how many lives you have touched," May said.

The young woman pulled the baby back and clutched him close to her chest. The shadows around her grew so deep that she stood out in the room.

"Look at this life and tell me we were wrong," Mimi said.

The ice castle that was Queen May began to melt at the earnest face of her daughter. The sounds of her grandchild. The child, cooing peacefully in his swaddle, was wide awake, and his bright eyes were aware of the heavy shadows surrounding him. He had his mother's eyes.

"Thank the source, he looks like you," May said.

"Come on, Lady M, I'm standing right here," Byron said.

"So, you are. For someone who has risen so high, you sure seem to do your thinking… low," May said.

"Here I am, trying to do what's right. You don't have to

come at me like that, M. I have a crown of my own," Byron said.

"Careful," said mother and daughter at once.

They spoke in perfect unison, looking at Byron with the same eyes on different faces.

"MA! Stop using your foresight on me," Mimi said.

"Nothing but a reflex, little bug," May said, smiling sheepishly.

"That was not a threat. This is just a reminder that I am not just some silly boy in love with your daughter. I am my own man, and we are…" Byron said.

"She knows what we are, Ronni. She knows too much," Mimi said.

"Then I don't have to ask if y'all even tried to…" Byron said.

"This ain't no herb shop down to Bourbon Street. Or don't you know who house you in, Emperor Byron? Crown wearing ruler of what exactly?" May asked.

She asked with an increasingly deep voice that became so low that the ground started to rumble when her tongue moved. Queen May was twenty feet tall and filled up the chamber with her size, larger than a nightmare with crackling eyes to match. There was a teacup in her hands, as large as a loveseat, and it slowly began to lower toward Byron, the walls around her twisting and groaning from the process.

"Wait…" Mimi whispered.

"I am the Emperor of Death. Not even you can kill me, though I am not looking forward to this," Byron said.

The sudden increase in her magic made Byron shudder from head to toe, but he looked up at her with the biggest smile. His pale green eyes suddenly came to life with a flickering green fire.

"You a bad mamma jamma', Miss Moss. But I ain't playin' games no more. You put that teacup away, or I'm gonna cut your goddamn pinky toe off!" Byron said

May, who was towering over him, slowed her teacup's movements and stared at him for a short while. Then she started to cackle, a deep booming sound so rich with magic that it was like a bell radiated from her each time. Its peal could be felt on the skin like a breeze.

"Oh? Now you're gonna cut my pinky toe? Well, here it is," May said.

She lifted her foot, much larger than Byron's whole body, and dropped it toward him with increasing speed. However, before they could continue, a pulse of magic skittered across the room and clattered on the walls. Gently. Like a summer wind, carrying the scent of warm newness. Neither of them moved. Byron had his pale green eyes locked on the child in Mimi's arms. There was a vibration in the shadows, they were the source of his first magic, and he could hear them like the whispers of a friend. They had always spoken to him, always, but never before have they told him to stop. Never had he felt it so clearly from another source other than himself. The shadows sought to protect the boy from the emperor's magic and beckoned to him across the darkness.

Their voice also seemed to reach the Queen because the room had returned to normal in the blink of an eye, as did her relative size. There were still enormous streams of viciously caustic magic boiling off her like liquid nitrogen and dissipating into the air. Byron settled his magic and gave May a stiff nod. She returned the gesture.

"Now that you two are done with y'alls measuring contest

and terrifying my baby, maybe we can act like adults?" Mimi said.

Byron and May both looked at her and raised an eyebrow. Then they looked at each other. The serious demeanors they had taken on made all of this seem too silly. May cracked first, and she laughed, the emperor of death joining her shortly.

"Little old boy," May said.

"You still scary, old May," Byron answered.

May shook her head, and after a deep breath, she approached the child. The angry magic had gone from her, and she stood next to her daughter. She smiled down at the small child and played with him quietly for a moment.

"We tried more things than we should have. Nothing worked," May said.

"How was I supposed to know this would happen? I thought we had protections… provisions," Byron asked.

"What have you done to my daughter?" She asked.

"I never touched her improperly. If that's what you mean, I'm as surprised as you," Byron said.

May would glance down from the baby to look into the teacup after every answer he gave. Whatever she saw in there didn't change the face she showed him one bit. She seemed satisfied, and she lowered the teacup to her side and put it away. On her hip was a leather holster that encircled her waist and thigh with a crisscross strap that held the teacup at the ready like a six-shooter or a sword.

"Be wary of a teacup in the hands of a witch," Byron said.

"Don't flatter me. That is a truth, however slick you may be saying it. Your actions carry weight beyond all of us," May said.

"This wasn't supposed to happen," Mimi said.

"Your sister isn't blameless in all of this. I don't know why she would go along with this fool plan in the first place. She supposed to be the one with brains," May said.

"Damn, May!" Mimi said.

"You ain't disagree," May teased.

"I ain't got a lot of time to stay here. My people have already started asking questions," Byron answered.

"The tea on this will be bitter, Byron. The kind that stays with you," May said.

"I intend to step up," he said.

"If you could control the situation, this wouldn't have happened in the first place," She hissed.

"This ain't **never** happened before to anyone. There ain't no rules about this," he said.

The sound of another baby crying made all of them perk up, and Byron searched the older woman's face frantically, but she didn't look anywhere near as alarmed. She even chuckled a little, crossing her arms over her chest and canting her head in the direction of a door to her right.

"Ironic that that sound should scare you after the spectacle you all put on tonight," May said.

"Momma?" Mimi asked.

"How… what is that?" Byron asked

"You may unclench. That sweet voice belongs to another child. Born long before your mistakes, her father stood right where you are now. He also say that one was not his fault,"

"You know I didn't mean for this to happen, is it…" Byron started.

"'Your it will be a he," May said

"A boy? But is… he... like me?" Byron asked.

"Father will take measures," she said

"Father is here?" Mimi said.

She did not sound happy or sad, but something in her voice said she asked for bleak reasons. May nodded.

"Why?" Mimi asked.

Byron put a hand on her shoulder to stop her. He took her under his arm and sighed long and hard.

"We are grateful for the help. Tell him thank you," he said.

"You can tell him yourself. We are blessed with deep love, but our patience will not last forever," May said.

"You a good woman, May Moss," Byron said.

"It's a curse of good women to carry the weight never meant to be left by bad men," May said.

There was a sudden drop in the air pressure, and the house went black, just for a moment, and the lights came back with the sounds of screaming. Byron looked to Mimi. The shadows were singing again, and their vibrations were visible in the darkness surrounding Byron and the small child.

"Oh no. This is just like the show," Mimi said.

"What do you mean?" May asked.

"When she had the baby," Byron said.

There was a moment when there was no sound

"Mercedes!" Mimi shouted.

May was bounding up the stairs before him, and after exchanging a look with Mimi, Byron took off after her as fast as he could. Somehow, he slipped by Maybelline and arrived at the top of the stairs first. He saw Tomas desperately trying the knob and ramming his body into a door to the left of the landing. May arrived shortly after and gently brushed him aside. Once he was clear, she took a sip from her teacup. Then she spit just a tiny bit on the door, and it swung open so hard it almost came off the hinges. Byron and Tomas rushed toward the door. Mercedes looked so similar to the love of his life that Byron almost fell over himself. Except she had the eyes of a serpent, slitted and calm even now. It was jarring, but this was clearly Mimi's twin. Her eyes were on Byron as soon as he appeared, but they softened not one bit. He slowed, and they looked at each other before the woman tried to speak.

"Stop him!" she shouted.

A man appeared, standing over Mercedes and facing someone else. Father Moss, tall and lean, a hat skewed on top of his fro. He stood between his daughter and the other voice now, a man's voice, speaking in frantic if muffled tones behind the door.

"Who is that? How many people are in that room?" Byron asked.

"It was only supposed to be Mercy and Father," May said.

"No. It's back! It's back for her!" Tomas cried.

"What's here?" Byron asked

"The vampire!" He answered.

The creature in question stepped from behind the door, eyes red and wild, fangs hanging out of his mouth as long as thumbs. The door slammed closed, and Tomas was throwing himself and his flies at the door with everything he had, but it would not budge. Tomas did not seem to be affected by that information. Then the Queen of witches cried out suddenly and drew the teacup from her hip holster. There was a gushing flow of steaming tea pouring over the sides of the cup and spattering all around them. Her leg was drenched, and the floor was wet with the still flowing tea. She and Byron looked at each other warily.

"What does that mean?" Byron asked

"The tea is hot. Something has been changed," May said

"What does-" he started.

She silenced him with a raised hand, and her eyes were dreamy and distant. She watched Tomas struggle against the door, harder and harder, clawing at it to get to his fiancé desperately. Her daughter. The voices turned from muffled talking to unintelligible screaming, and she felt something that would cause a pit in her stomach from this day on. She felt monstrous magic. Fearful magic. Tomas seemed to understand her urgency without saying anything, and he leaped back and away from the door. May opened her mouth to scream, but Mimi beat her to it when she finally arrived at the top of the staircase.

"RONNI!" she screamed.

The young man had already filled the space Tomas vacated, and the attack was over before she finished screaming his name. There was only a flash of green light when Byron unleashed his weapon. The remaining door was still glowing with the green flame of it long afterward, but his weapon was out, employed, and tucked away quick as a whip. The frame was separated almost entirely, but the wide door remained intact. It was Tomas who finally opened it with a timely shoulder. The door fell heavily, but they could not enter because of a thick black cloud that poured out of the room. It was heavy and scented with the sour iron scent of spoiled blood and underworld magic. It was so thick that even Byron had to step back. Tomas was not so fast. The cloud appeared to have simply brushed his exposed arm, but he immediately started to scream. His arm had begun to blacken almost immediately, and in the space between a breath, his hand turned back to the cool gray of spent ash and started to fall away from the rest of his body. The ash continued to eat hungrily up his arm as they all watched in horror. May moved to help him, but Byron held her back. This was magic neither of them had ever seen. He pulled the woman back and away, forcing her and Mimi into the adjacent room. May fought all the way screaming and kicking.

Tomas looked back desperately at them and reached out his insect covered hand as the curse dragged through him like cigarette paper. The black flies all started to take flight. Dozens of them left his arm as the ash closed in and flew toward them. The slowest ones were being turned into ash in midair and falling to the ground like spilled flour. Only a handful of flies made it into the room before Byron shoved them inside and closed the door. He threw himself into it, back first, pouring his magic into his body to reinforce the door. He had to give it everything to keep the tide at bay. It took a moment for the sound to stop and everything to settle. Once it did, the heavy silence said it was over. It was Mimi who spoke first.

"Where is Cedes?!" she asked.

Byron looked up at her. She was sitting on the bed with bewildered eyes, crying heavily and positively glossy with tears. She was wiping at her eyes and trying to keep hold of the baby while struggling toward the door.

"Where is Cedes? Momma?" Mimi asked.

Byron said nothing, and May had settled on the floor with distant eyes. She was slowly gathering the twitching black flies that survived the cloud. They were barely alive, buzzing intermittently, but she collected each one that she could find and placed it into her teacup as gently as she could.

"You did good, Tomas," She whispered to herself.

"Momma, what is happening?!" Mimi shouted.

May perked up and looked at her daughter as if she couldn't understand where she was for a moment, and after she blinked herself back, the old witch rose to her feet. She was careful to store her collected flies in the teacup holster before she took her daughter in her arms and hugged her tightly. She stroked her hair and took her face in both hands, looking at her with wet eyes. Her daughter was confused and exhausted, so she didn't do much more than watch in response. May led her back to the bed and laid her down again, holding her daughter's hand in hers and kissing each finger. When she kissed the delicate ring wrapped around her third finger, it gave her pause, but she did not have time to ask about it. There were things in motion that none of them could control.

"Mercedes is… by now, she and the baby must be…" May said.

She couldn't finish. Mimi started to cry again. A muffled sound made them all catch their breath. May looked to Byron, and without hesitating, he turned and tentatively began to open the door. Ash spilled in at the foot of the door, but it didn't appear to have the same energy as before. He kicked a bit of it with his toe, and when nothing happened, he pulled the door open quickly and ran across the hall. He stopped at the empty clothing in front of the door and cursed under his breath. Byron was no friend to Tomas, but he was not an enemy. He stepped past the ash and into the room. There was a thick circle of ash around the bed, but Mercedes sat up in the center, clutching her swollen belly.

It was so strange to see her like that, she looked so much like her sister, but there was something stately about Mercy, he thought. She was factually as intelligent as most people thought they were and gifted like her sister, a healer and the opposite face of the coin that was Mimi. This was the first that Mercedes had seen him. If she had not just been through something incredible, he was sure he would get an earful from her, but as it stood, she was staring at her belly to avoid looking at the ash. She had ashen lines down both of her cheeks where it stuck to her wet face, and since her crying phase was done, she seemed to be in the quiet section of grief. She hardly even looked up at him.

"What the hell happened here? Where is Father? Where the Vampire at?" Byron asked.

"He tried to take the baby and… then Daddy, he," Mercy said.

She stopped before she could finish to start crying again. The old man was nowhere to be found. There was no one in the room but the pregnant witch and her unborn baby.

"Take him?" He asked.

"Something stopped him. Maybe it was Daddy, but I'm not sure. Whatever it was caused all of this, and they are both… gone…" she said

She waved her hand around at all the ashes, and the dusty tears were washed away with a new set of tears. She put her face in her hands and wept for a moment. Byron didn't have the heart to stop her, so she cried undisturbed until she no longer wanted to, and when she was done, she went quiet again. The next motion she made was to try and look past him. Byron's normally ne'er-do-well smile was replaced with a stern and solemn line. Mercy observed him, but she did not move.

"Why didn't Tomas come?" She asked.

"How did you-" He started to ask.

"I don't care! Where is my fiancé?" She asked.

"I'm sorry to say that whatever took y'all daddy, took him too," he said over her.

She tried to get out of the bed, but the chime of a grandfather clock announced the hour, and just like before, every light in the house winked out at the exact same moment. There was no light coming in through the windows or any other source. It had simply gone in the blink of an eye. Mercedes' breathing became irregular and ragged. Byron could hear her clearly, especially when she started to scream. He tried to move to the bed, but he couldn't make his body move. He could not see. He could only hear the screaming. However, when the Witch Queen spoke, she might as well have been speaking into his ear.

"It is time," The old witch said.

Sometimes her visions would come as unwelcome words in her mouth, and often she had little memory of what she was compelled to say, but this time she knew what was coming. She had spoken these words before. There was a special kind of pain in knowing, seeing what was to come, and the many possible outcomes did not mean that you could be prepared to face them. Often the future is a set line, but every choice is a tributary, and even when you can see it coming, sometimes you still get hit, and it hurts twice as much. Knowing that you could not stop it, or worse, that you could have if not for a single choice, sometimes made for a lonely existence. When his brother was born, Saturday must have known it. He joined the other child, and the two boys simultaneously cried out into the cold world. That song seemed to revive the lights as they all returned at once. When Byron could see again, he looked up to Mercy, who appeared to be unharmed but no longer alone on the bed.

She was now holding a tiny newborn baby in her arms. The two were undoubtedly alive but strangely calm in the center of all the ash and chaos surrounding them. When Byron looked upon his son for the first time, he smiled. Then his face went very still. The baby was dark-skinned like him but had its mother's eyes. There was something else that Byron couldn't take his eyes off of, even as Mercy gently ran a thumb over each of the strange growths coming out of the child.

"It," Byron started.

"He," Mercy said.

"He. Right, of course. He has horns," Byron said.

"He does. They are beautiful," Mercy said.

The child was cooing but quiet, still attached to her as it was. It seemed impossible that the child should be so calm or his mother, for that matter. There they were. However, the two of them were simply watching each other.

"Are you... gonna name him?" Byron asked.

Mercy raised an eyebrow slowly.

"No, that's not what I meant," he said.

They both looked at the ashes in the doorway, and Mercy clutched the still quiet newborn to her chest. The tiny conical horns on his head were barely the size of a cut pinky nail, and they tapered to a point. May entered the room behind Byron, and he stepped aside to let her pass. Once the old witch looked at the child, her eyes showed fear, like she had seen a ghost.

"You had better go, Emperor Samedi," May said.

She said his full title, which made him know better than to ask her any questions. He knew he couldn't leave without saying something to her. So, he turned to the Queen and bowed his head.

"Hey, you know, Maybelline… I never said I'm sorry to nobody for nothing I did. But I wish what happened never happened. You know I appreciate everything you've done for me. For us. And I'm sorry," Byron said.

"Take your sorry ass in there," May said.

"I love you too," he said.

Mercy and Byron looked at each other before Byron ran out of the room, brushing past May on the way. May moved to the bed and sat down next to her daughter, staring at the small child wriggling around in her arms. The boy looked so much like his mother, but it was clear that Byron was his father. May reached out and touched the boy's head, brushing by the set of horns on his head.

"Did you name him?" May asked.

"Crawford wouldn't want any baby to have his name. He hates it…" Mercy said.

"That's not what I meant," May said.

May and her daughter held each other around the newborn child between them, and they wept, Mercy holding her daughter close to her chest and leaning into her grief. It is always unclear how much time has passed when you are in the aftermath of something terrible, but they cried for a good long time. When it was over, Mercy was staring at her now sleeping baby, and May rubbed her back, listening to the sounds of the other room and a much more talkative newborn.

"…I will name him after Father," Mercy said

"Calderhys is a good, strong name. Deep roots. The name of a witch," May said.

"I will call him Taxxis,"

"Your father hated his middle name," May said.

"I know," She answered.

The two of them started to laugh, and it faded as suddenly as it came when the memories came crashing back, and the babies started to cry in unison.

"Are we doing the right thing, Momma? It feels like the wrong choice," Mercy said.

"Sometimes a choice is simply made against us," May said.

"So it is," Mercy said.

"Let's get you cleaned up; your sister has been pretending to be in too good of shape. Her baby is healthy and talkative. I can't wait to let these boys meet each other," May said.

"What did she name him?" Mercy asked.

"After his good for nothing Daddy, just like we knew she would. She also chose to name him after someone and give them a middle name, same as you. Like they were twins, ain't that funny?" May said

"They are twins. If not for the Vampire, she would have given birth to both of them herself," Mercy said.

"Fate is a heavy burden to bear," May said.

"So, what do we tell them? That they are twins and cousins?" Mercy asked.

"They are," May said.

"That will be confusing for them," Mercy said.

"Perhaps they need only know a part of the truth," May said.

"He will never know his truth," Mercy said.

"If only he were so lucky," May whispered.

"You saw it?" Mercy asked.

May looked off into the distance when she whispered those words, but she was not talking to Mercy. Everything seemed to come to a pause. There was no other sound but the queen of witches and the gentle weeping of her grandson. Taxx was watching all of this from the bedroom doorway with his feet carefully placed around the remains of Craw. He could not take his eyes off of his mother. Mercedes Moss was a distant relative to him, but somehow his heart had always instinctively known how to miss her. How to play the song that made him long for the love of someone he had hardly seen before. He reached out to touch her, and the image slipped away under his fingers like a chalk drawing in the rain, bit by bit, until she was gone completely. There was nothing left in the room. It was just a dark space, and even the furniture was gone. There was only Taxx and the image of his grandmother, who was touching his back.

"There is nothing left to show you here," she said

Taxx nodded, and the dark space they occupied began to fill with warm, bitter tea that carried him out of those memories and back into a world made more horrible for them.

***

When Taxx finished speaking, the room was silent. Sixx was looking at him for a long time without saying anything. Taxx felt his bottom lip quiver as he looked over his cousin's face. His **brother's** face. What he saw there was not the thing he wished for. Sixx did not look surprised. He looked relieved.

"You… knew?" Taxx asked.

"Yeah, man, I know lots of shit I wish I didn't know," Sixx said.

"Why didn't you ever tell me?" Taxx asked.

"Cause we were already cousins who acted like brothers,"

Sixx said.

"In what way is that supposed to comfort me?" Taxx asked.

"Knowing who your father was wouldn't have changed anything anyway. It would have just made it weird," Sixx said.

"Does this feel less weird?" Taxx asked.

"Fine. Swing and a miss. Daddy got a goddamn lot of kids. Isn't it time to move on? Brother?" Sixx teased.

"Don't call me that!" Taxx shouted.

"Should I go back to calling you Taxx as if nothing changed? Cause it ain't?" Sixx asked.

"We will have a long talk about this later," Taxx asked.

"Oh, you already know," Sixx said.

"Were you not raised together?" Nic asked,

"Grandma has been taking care of me since our moms took off. She basically raised us both since we were little kids. She was great too. The only thing we were never allowed to do was tell anyone our birthday. She was super serious about that. Guess I know why now," Taxx said.

"You don't. I need to tell you so much more, but there ain't never gonna be enough time. Ol lady said so, and she has so many more tricks than you can think," Sixx said.

"You can tell me now," Taxx said.

Sixx smiled and shook his head.

"Come on. You know it won't be that easy. Never is. Never has been, not since they told me you was dead," Sixx said.

"I'm sorry you had to deal with all of that on your own," Taxx said.

"Don't be like that. I always knew. You are the only brother I like," Sixx said.

The boys hugged each other and lingered for a moment.

When the hug was over, they punctuated it with a fist bump.

"Boom, closure," Sixx said.

"I mean, not really, but sure," Taxx said.

"So why was today different?" Rosen asked.

"What do you mean?" Sixx asked.

"She kept him hidden from everyone, including his twin brother. Successfully. For years. So, what happened today?" Rosen asked.

The question seemed to derail them. Taxx blinked at it and rolled it over in his head a few times. He opened his mouth to say something but had nothing to say. Sixx looked grim for a second before he perked up.

"I got it! Maybe old lady sent the demon after you," Sixx said.

"That's not possible," Taxx said.

"How do you know that?" Sixx asked.

"Because Offrey was the one who gave me to Drip," Taxx said.

Sixx looked like he might have been gut-punched, and Taxx reached out a hand to comfort him. Sixx slapped it away.

"What do you know about Zora anyway?" Sixx asked.

"I saw you," Taxx said.

Sixx blinked slowly, and while he still wore that mischievous smile, he didn't seem to be able to say anything. So, there was a long silence. Lyra and Nic shared a quiet look, the younger warden looking angrier and angrier, but no one interrupted the two of them.

"Taxx, what are you saying, man?" Sixx asked.

"The girl you used to sneak off to make out with hired someone to kill me," Taxx said.

"Taxxy, that ain't what you think. We weren't sneaking off nowhere. May knew the deal," Sixx said.

"I'm sure May knew a lot of deals," Taxx said.

"Wait. I think something is wrong," Sixx said.

"I agree!" Nic said.

"Stop. Do you not feel that?" Rosen asked.

Rosen went distant for a moment, and shortly afterward, the squat orange fairy that had delivered a message to her earlier returned, but this time it looked panicked. It dove for her feet and hid behind her legs; they spoke in fairy song, and Rosen bristled toward the hallway where the small squat thing had come from. The doorframe started to change shape, it widened, and the space on the other side of it changed.

"Someone is invading the transom," Rosen said.

No sooner had she said the words, a body came through the door frame, and a weapon was thrown at Sixx with terrifying accuracy in a fluid motion. It sank into his chest before he had time to make a quip about it and his body started to crumple to the ground. Taxx tried to move, but not a single part of him could seem to do anything but stand still. The only thing he could move was his eyes. There was a prickling heat all through his body.

"Why can't I move," Taxx asked.

"Because I do not allow it," said a deep, menacing voice.

The hooded figure stood in front of him now after very carefully moving toward him in a pattern that was so odd. It took Taxx a moment to figure out that the figure was stepping over things, black objects outside his periphery. No matter how hard he tugged, he could not move, not even his fingers. He had never been so completely paralyzed. He tried to push with all his might and was met with incredible pain and the feeling of his blood dripping down his face.

"Who are you?" Taxx asked.

"I am Kingmaker, and you are all caught in my trap," Kingmaker said.

Under the hood was a hard-to-defined mask, like shadows wrapped around shadows like bandages. The face was so obscured that it was hard to look at. It had too many angles.

"My special threads rode in on your little troll and covered all of you before I entered the room. You may have noticed that you cannot move. I suggest you try to keep still," Kingmaker said.

Kingmaker moved in front of Taxx and reached out to pluck a strand of silk so thin he could still barely see it between the gloved fingers.

"This thread is strong enough to lift a horse and can be sharp enough to butcher it. It will cut you to ribbons if you fight too hard," Kingmaker said.

"What do you want?" Lyra asked.

"Impatient. As always. This is not about what I want. This is not about us. It's about the future," Kingmaker said.

"Oh, spare us your bullshit manifesto and get to the point," Nic said.

"Here, here!" Agreed Grayson.

"Filthy, just like all mistakes. You will be the first to be corrected," Kingmaker said.

Kingmaker removed the cape from her shoulders and let it drop to the floor. She wore a set of armor that was nearly glowing with magic. Life magic. It shouldn't have been possible to infuse metal with life, but it was before them. The sight of it was uncomfortable, it was screaming from the unnatural bonding process, and some of them could hear it. There was also a series of needles and hooks, daggers, and razors hanging around her belt, stained with recent use and almost moving with a current of magical power. A wicked little blade came from that collection and made its way to Nic's cheek, brushing a line into her skin as slender as a hair. It left behind a trail of blood like a red marker, thin and slowly oozing down Nic's face.

"Now, now. There will be time for that later," Drip said.

He entered the room from the same hallway as Offrey and sashayed in a ridiculous dance that made his menacing smile seem all the wilder. FW was standing just behind him, but there was something different about the monstrous albino Other. The arm he lost had been replaced with a golden replica that glittered even in the dark, and there now seemed to be a golden beard on his face. His eyes were the same, though, and they were staring at Taxx.

"Calm yourself, FW," Drip said.

"How did you get here, Demon? What do you want!" Rosen asked.

"Revenge and perhaps just a bit of pleasure. You see… if I had my way, I would kidnap each of you and sell you to the highest bidder. They would harvest and use your little fae body until all that was left to be done was scoop out your brains and use them as a prophylactic," Drip said.

"Drip," Kingmaker said.

"Don't worry. I won't break our deal. Unless it suits me, I never go back on my word," Drip said.

"Once I am free from here, I will kill you," Rosen said.

"You speak out of turn. I am tired of you lower creatures

threatening the eternal genius that is my life," Drip said.

"Let me loose, and I'll show you the limit of genius," Rosen said.

"Whenever someone is helpless, they say the most foolish things," Drip teased.

Then the adjudicator lifted his right hand, and liquid gold crawled out of his sleeves. It made its way up his arm in streams like golden blood and filled his palm until a long, jagged thing was formed. It was a rough hunk of gold with a long straight, cutting edge jutting out of the top like a spike. The demon lifted the knife to Rosen's eye and was about to press its tip into it when Grayson started to laugh. Drip turned to look at him, and then he went back to the business of slashing out her eyeball. Grayson snorted with laughter, this time when the demon positioned the knife for his first cut. Drip sighed with disgust.

"You know there used to be a time where a mother fucka' would be upset when a demon was about to cut on his wife. I will be straight with you. It's killing my buzz. May I ask what is so funny?" Drip asked.

"Yes, I'm so sorry. I am happy to share. I was just laughing because the same old misdirect still works so well," Grayson said.

Drip made a face that clearly expressed his disappointment and resentment toward that answer.

"What misdirect?" Drip asked.

The demon turned toward Grayson and brought the golden blade to his throat, pressing it into the dapper man's skin. Every eye was on the two of them as the man in peril continued to laugh.

"The one where I make you all look at me like I'm going to do something. In reality, I'm just giving Rosie ample time to attack you from behind," Grayson said.

He looked off behind Drip as though she were there, but the demon never looked away from him. Drip smiled, and liquid gold poured out of the corners of his mouth.

"Who would be stupid enough to fall for that?" Drip asked.

"No one. That's why it always works," Rosen said.

Rosen was freed within seconds, and after she flexed her hand just a little bit, the room was instantly filled with pink light. The fairy called up her magic as intensely as she could. The sudden burst changed the temperature in the room with a loud pop. The pressure increased suddenly and swiftly. Her hand held the center of a small sun, and she had it in her mind to drive it into Drip's heart. The Demon was faster. He slipped out of the way before the bright pink fire could touch him, and the air where he had been sizzled from the heat. Drip slashed at Grayson, but the tailor was always just an inch away from the deadly path of the golden blade. Just a hair away when it should have reached his neck. The demon looked perplexed for a moment.

"How did you perform magic with your hands tied?" Drip asked.

The tailor lifted his hands and wiggled his fingers, except the first and thumb of his left hand. Between them was a fabric tape measure. It was hard to say what color it was as it rapidly altered between several shades of gray, but the hash marks were clear no matter what it looked like. His thumb sat at the one-inch spot.

"Metaphysical alteration of the fabric of space-time," The demon said.

"Exactly so," Grayson answered with a nod.

"You must be the Tailor," Drip said.

"You know me?" Grayson asked.

The Tailor seemed genuinely surprised, even as the Demon sneered.

"I know the market value of your blood by the liter," Drip said.

"That's far less exciting," Grayson said.

"It's …low," Drip sneered.

"Now you're just being salty," Grayson said.

Rosen lunged for the Demon again, and he slipped out of the way of her glowing hands. She huffed in frustration.

"Hold him!" She shouted.

She was not speaking to her husband. Instead, vines started to grow from the many potted plants around the house. Each pot popped like a light bulb when the massive growth took hold. As thick as human arms, green vines lashed at the demon, growing thicker by the second. He dipped, ducked, dodged, and cut away the vines with an impossibly speed and agility. All the while, perfectly timing his escapes from the speedy attacks of the fairy, her wings were moving so quickly that she was blinking in and out of the visible spectrum.

"Most people think you are dead, but I always knew you fled the Nexus. Only a fool would stay. I respect that, but to come to the Fae Wilds. That's a clever twist," Drip said.

He spoke between dodging the snapping vines and slicing some of them down with his golden blade, stepping just to the Fairy's left when she came to attack and making her even more furious. Her motions were so sharp that the air around them was starting to fill with electricity as the room began to fill with her magic. Grayson got to his feet and held out his fabric tape measure, sliding his thumb along its hash marks. Taxx was free of the threads when he was done, and he sighed with relief.

"Help the others," The Tailor said.

Then the gray man turned toward the demon and took a deep breath. The fabric tape started to boil with black and white bubbles, like TV snow. The same magic that Rosen had used earlier, but where that was fizzy like a diet soda, this effervesced like acid. The TV snow covered his body like a shell until he was covered in the jagged black and white scatter.

"My turn to ask the questions," The tailor said.

The Demon dodged suddenly when there was no attack to see and sailed across the room until he was standing right next to F.W. Rosen did not give chase for the moment. Instead, she stood between the children and the Demon. Her proximity to her husband had already changed her, and the pink star she was holding was starting to mix with the bubbling static of Grayson's magic. If there was any pink infiltrating the black and white of the Tailor's magic, it was not visible.

"I think I understand your trick, capillary magic. You absorb your husband's bastardized power like a carnation in colored water," Drip said.

"Watch it," Grayson hissed.

The Demon couldn't have looked more delighted with his reaction.

"Did I strike a nerve? You people are always so easy to rile up," Drip teased.

"What the hell does that mean?" Sixx asked.

Taxx was still trying to free Lyra when the temperature in the room rose suddenly. He looked over to find that Nic was on fire. Her body was covered in a pure red fire from toe to tip. It burned so hotly that looking into it nearly blinded him, so he squeezed his eyes shut until it was over. When he looked up again, she was free and walking toward the two of them.

"Sorry," she said.

"Don't be," Taxx answered.

Nic calmed her heat so she could approach them. Nic produced a card and with a flourish of her hand she cut the threads until Lyra was free. The edge had a red fire on it, burning gently. Once Lyra was free, she ran to Sixx who was still lying on the ground. Nic turned toward Drip, her left hand so hot that a haze obscured it.

"Oh, look at you all. So ready to throw it all away, but before that. Let's have a talk," Drip said.

"Why the sudden interest in parlay?" Grayson asked.

"Maybe I know some secrets that you want to know. Secrets like the location of Queen Moss. Or maybe I was doing a bit," Drip said.

"You have violated my home. I'll be the one what decides where your bits end up," Rosen said.

The Fairy was almost filled with static magic and her fierce pink fire burned with its black and white randomness.

"Wait, what bit?" Grayson asked.

"The one where I make you all look at me while my partner attacks you from behind," Drip said.

It all happened in the same moment. Taxx gasped slowly when he felt the blade enter him from behind, and his chest heaved outward. Then Drip's golden knife was flying, and it pierced Rosen's palm with such force that it threw her body through the air. The fairy was pinned to the wall behind her by her hand when she stopped. Instantly all of her magic was drawn into the golden blade, and it started to bleed golden fluid from every surface. Converting her magic into liquid gold and spilling it all over the floor until the knife was a small fountain, spilling in a steady stream. Taxx fell forward, and Kingmaker stood over him. A knife's hilt protruded from his back.

"Taxx!" Lyra screamed.

The knife had a hollow in the center of the grip, and it was starting to fill with blood. Once the blade had done its job, Kingmaker stepped over his body, ripping the knife out on her way by.

"This could have been avoided if you'd all cooperated," Kingmaker said.

Grayson stepped forward, and Drip was there to meet him, faster than he had been before. The tailor opened his mouth, but Drip did that quicker, too, the glittering horror clamping down on Grayson's shoulder. The gold spines sunk into his body, and gray blood spilled out between those teeth. The tailor cried out, and Drip tossed him to the floor like a pet toy that had lost its pizazz.

"You cannot defeat me, only feed me. I grow tired of the taste of weakling," Drip said.

Rosen hadn't made any noise when her hand was pierced. She only watched the demon with intense pink eyes. They were burning like lanterns behind her eyelids. The gold flowed from the puddle on the floor and streamed toward the demon, crawling up his shoe and disappearing into his pant leg. He made the same sound of delight that you might make after the first sip of ice-cold water. His satisfaction only served to infuriate the smoldering fairy even more.

"If they weren't here, I could crush you," Rosen said.

"I do not doubt you. I know well what you are capable of.

You and I come from the same place," Drip said.

He smiled those spiny gold teeth in her face, and Rosen looked deep into his eyes. Something passed between them, and realization slowly twisted her face in horror.

"Impossible, you couldn't be," she said.

"Oh, but I am," Drip answered.

"Mammon!" Rosen shrieked.

"Isn't it funny that they all called me a demon without ever even knowing the truth of it? Life is so bold in its quest for bone-crushing humor," Drip said.

"You are the joke," Grayson said.

"What I am is unkillable by the likes of you," Drip said.

He looked down at Grayson, clutching at the holes in his shoulder. Lyra was standing over Taxx and Sixx, bleeding onto the checkered floor. Nic was stalking toward Drip slowly, every one of her steps melting more of the floor beneath her.

"Drip!" Nic shouted.

"Just one moment, hot stuff. I'll kill you after him," he said, indicating Grayson.

"Like hell, you will!" Rosen shouted.

She tried to dislodge the knife from her hand, but it did not work. The look on her face was hateful enough to kill. Drip was positively glowing with delight.

"Look at you, so sore! Let's make a deal then. You choose one of these useless things, just one, and I'll spare all of the rest of you," Drip said.

The silence over the room was tangible, laying over them all at once. Drip was the only person in the room who was smiling. Whatever Kingmaker felt, the look on her face was indifferent, and F.W. was staring at Taxx as he had been since he arrived. Nic was frozen in her tracks, and Grayson looked at the demon with wide eyes.

"You can't believe she will do that," he said.

Drip did not even acknowledge him. The demon started to laugh, and he moved closer to Rosen, forming another knife in his palm.

"Choose one, or I'll kill your husband right here and now. I'll snap off his head and lick his spinal cord while it's still tingling like a 9 volt," Drip said.

Then the demon leaned forward and a golden tongue, oversaturated with those metallic fluids, smeared over Rosen's cheek, leaving behind a slimy trail.

"Or. You choose one of those riff raffs to add to my collection instead, and your husband lives," Drip said.

Rosen looked up at his face carefully.

"What about me and the others?" she asked.

"Clever girl. Some of you will inevitably die, but on my word, no hard will come to you, and I will spare the Tailor," Drip said.

"She won't choose. You are a fool," Grayson said.

"I choose Taxx," Rosen said.

Rosen spoke without hesitation, and her husband looked up at his wife with a face halfway between confusion and ignorance. The demon could not have looked more pleased with his reaction.

"Decisive. I admire that. Normally I would gripe about how close to death he already is but consider this a professional courtesy," Drip said.

Drip moved so fast again that he left a copy where he was. The other was standing over Taxx's motionless body. The young man groaned and tried to move, even with a large wound in his back that was actively bleeding. The demon reached down and took the young man up, grabbing him by the face with one hand. Taxx grabbed at him weakly, his body trying to fight back with whatever it could move. The demon was openly laughing as he held him aloft and watched his feeble attempt at defense.

"Look how he clings to life," Drip said.

The demon opened his mouth, and a torrent of liquid gold started to pour out of him. It came from his eyes, nose, and mouth in an endless stream that flooded Taxx's face. Taxx screamed, but the sound was quickly stifled, and there was only the sound of his struggle against the invading fluid. In moments, the gold liquid started to leak from Taxx's eyes, streaming down his face until it dripped on the floor. The demon pressed more and more into the boy until his eyes were filled with gold, and his mouth was overflowing. Taxx had gone stiff long before the demon finally stopped his onslaught and stepped back from the young man. Drip held his hand over his shoulder.

"NO!" Nic screamed.

She started to hurl herself at Taxx, but Drip stopped her with a flourish of his golden blade.

"Stay right there, or I'll slit his throat too," Drip said.

Nic froze. This made Drip laugh again, and he shook his head, a look of disgust on his face.

"Pitiful. Your feelings for another are enough to keep you controlled. I would be amused if I wasn't waiting on my god DAMNED handkerchief. FW, would you mind?" Drip said.

As he spoke of his associate, the large man finally hopped to and placed a fine silk square in his master's hand. Drip took it and dabbed at the gold that stained his mouth, just the corners. The rest of his mouth and fingers were always stained and dripping with gold, as were his eyes, and each left a stain.

"Finally. What has you so distracted that you think you can disrespect me?" Drip asked.

He tossed the handkerchief at FW with disdain, and the massive albino took it and carefully folded it with the delicate motions of his remaining hand. The golden hand was clenched in a fist, and FW stared at Taxx even as he worked. FW made gargling scratching noises with his throat and long, sustained noises like gurgling blood. Drip watched him intently and nodded now and again until he was done.

"While I understand your desire for revenge, I will remind you that he is already dead," Drip said.

FW gurgled.

Drip glanced toward Taxx's frozen body. It was still standing where it had been, the gold had completed its work and filled him with luxurious taxidermy.

"Perhaps later," Drip said.

Chapter | Nineteen

"Rosie Dawn, what have you done?" Grayson said.

"What did you do to him!" Lyra shouted.

Drip did not respond. Instead, he was already looking down at the remaining son of Byron, who started to stir again. Sixx gasped back to consciousness on the ground next to his cousin and quickly rose to his feet, unencumbered by the silk. There was a large dagger in his chest to the hilt, and he was looking down at it groggily as blood spouted out of the wound and splattered on the floor. He did not look very familiar with the sight.

"Why am I leaking?" Sixx asked.

"There is a special needle in you. It has been knotted with curses that can eat your healing magic before you can use it. You will continue to die until I remove it," Kingmaker said.

"Damn. That's smart. How the hell you figure that out?" Sixx asked.

He then promptly fell to his knees and then to his face as his body experienced the cycle of death. Again.

"Why did you tell him that?" Drip asked.

Kingmaker examined the boy on the ground for a long moment before she spoke again.

"I cannot lie to him," Kingmaker said.

"What did you do to Sixx! I'm gonna whoop," Nic started.

"Kingmaker, please cut out that racket," Drip said.

He cut her off and threads exploded from Kingmaker and launched themselves at Nic as if their own intelligence drove them. They slammed into her lips and sewed them shut before she could even say her name. The pain was incredible, and she couldn't even part her lips to scream, only moan against the brutal stitchwork that forced her to be silent.

"Zora?" Sixx asked.

Sixx was still lying on the ground and looking up at the violence unfolding. His voice was shaking so hard that it was almost a whisper. Kingmaker turned to face him promptly when he said her childhood nickname, and Sixx looked like he wanted to sink into the floor.

"Take this one," Kingmaker said.

A large figure in a black hooded cloak entered the room behind Kingmaker and moved toward Sixx, grabbing him up in massive hands and throwing him over its shoulder. Sixx tried to fight back, but his movements were sluggish, and he was still bleeding profusely.

"You are killing him!" Rosen shouted.

"Shut your mouth, you filthy creature... if I had my way, I

would kill you myself," Kingmaker said.

"Talk is cheap," Lyra said.

Sixx was still fighting against the people trying to hold him and causing a commotion behind them. Kingmaker looked over her shoulder for a moment and then back to Lyra.

"My words cut deep; you will know this soon. I will take my prize and go," Kingmaker said.

"Some prize," Lyra said.

"He is a promise kept. My prize is something far greater," Kingmaker said.

"Offrey? If that's you, I'll never forgive you for this. NEVER! Grayson, you better take care of my brother!" Sixx shouted.

After being carried off around the corner, the boy was still yelling, but the sound stopped suddenly. Taxx could no longer speak, but he stared at Kingmaker with wide eyes.

"Take the one in the goggles. The digital sorcerer too. It will come along quietly if you take her," Kingmaker said.

"Izzy!!" Lyra screamed.

"You children are far too impulsive, and it's time you learned the consequences," Drip said.

Drip manifested another dagger made of gold in his palm, and he threw it directly at Lyra, the knife planting itself solidly in her chest with a sickening sound. A moment later, steam rose out of Lyra's skin from every pore, silent at first but slowly ramping up to a whistle like a tea kettle.

"This cannot be happening," Grayson said.

"Oh, but it is. You see, you all forgot about the rule of power. You showed too much of your hand, and now someone powerful wants you all dead. It's not even me. Isn't that humorous? I'm afraid we have come to an end. It's time to die," Drip said.

FW gurgled.

Drip turned to look at his larger companion with a calm face, and then he started to laugh.

"Oh, alright, FW. Just one," Drip said.

FW rushed toward Taxx and slammed the golden fist into his face with such force that his head snapped back and was stuck that way. The sound was loud and dense and wet. Taxx did not cry out. His body did not even react, and it was still where Drip had left him. The giant seemed pleased anyway and started to stalk back toward his master.

"There. Is *everyone* all settled up? Good. It's just about time," Drip said.

Then he focused on Taxx's body just a heartbeat before it started to move again. Taxx jerked upward from his middle as though a winch was pulling him up by the hips, but nothing was there. He moved in a way that no creature with bones could carry itself, and then he fell limp. Something was happening inside him, and it was evident on his skin. Things were trying to force themselves out. His arms, chest, and face bulged with movement, but it was centrally at his belly. A large branch suddenly grew out of his chest about the length and width of one of his arms. It was flush with green leaves. Each one had a golden crown in its center glowing with magic. There was a snake wrapped around that branch, the color of cool marble with eyes like molten rock. As it was exposed to the air, it began to absorb magic into every scale.

"What the hell is that?" Grayson asked.

"Not what… who. You are in the presence of the first Viridescii. Te'Amath the wandering forest. Or, I suppose, more specifically, her magic and so much more. The real fun begins once you unite it with the door," Drip said.

"That's impossible. Nothing could bring her back," Rosen said.

"Correct. Nothing that has existed could. Until him," Drip said.

Rosen's eyes went wide with horror. Already she could feel the magic of that creature starting to grow, it was out of place in this world, and its ill weight was apparent. It sat in the space like a stone on a sheet and pulled everything toward it, air, space, and magic. Like a black hole. Kingmaker took a step back from it. Drip didn't seem eager to approach it himself, but he stood his ground.

"You don't know what you are doing," Rosen said.

"Oh, but I do… I know exactly what I am doing. I am taking us back to a world that is long forgotten. The black summer. This world will belong to the strong again. And I hold the keys to that power. I am selling it off to the highest bidder."

"What will you do when they come for you? Once they are done eating the humans and killing us off?" Rosen asked.

"I control the market. Soon, the Nexus will eat itself, and while you are all cowering in fear, I will be reaping only benefits," Drip said.

"How can this be happening?" Grayson asked.

"That boy is half witch and half reaper. Thanks to a power-hungry vampire's revenge plot, his parental blessings were all inverted into curses. Costly for him, but that malice performed a miracle. It destroyed all his gifts and left nothing. Only a hollow where a demigod's magic should reside," Drip said.

"If that were all, this would hardly be worth talking about. It was not just the wandering forest that we found hidden inside him. Hundreds more, and far worse," Kingmaker said.

"No!" Rosen said.

"Yes!" Drip teased.

"How could we have not seen it?" Grayson asked.

"Because you were never meant to," Kingmaker said.

"Collect the key," Drip said.

More cloaked figures swept into the room in all shapes and sizes. One of them carefully collected the strange snake. The others placed it carefully into a special case lined with silks covered with runes. Once they were done, Kingmaker did some strange manipulations of her hand, and the branch began to recede into Taxx's chest. The cloaked figures completed their task by collecting Avogorum and Izzy. They were driven from the room and disappeared around the corner one by one. Izzy locked eyes with Nic as she was dragged from the room, but there was no time to hint at goodbye. Taxx was still hanging limp with a branch sticking out of his chest. Before it could completely reenter his body, the branch sharply snapped and clattered to the ground. As soon as it did, Taxx slipped to the ground.

"This can't be happening. Rosie, sweetheart. What have we done?" Grayson asked.

"Have faith, my dearest love. Have faith and see," Rosen said.

The fairy was staring at Taxx, and Grayson joined her. The young man started to scratch his face. Raking his hands through the gold covering it with so much force that there were deep marks from his effort. He kept screaming something repeatedly and twitching. He wasn't saying words, just some nonsensical things.

"It's time we took our leave. There won't be much of this

place left in a few moments," Drip said.

"There had better not be," Kingmaker said.

"You're bound way too tight. Grab the stick," Drip teased.

One of the cloaked figures reached down to take the strange branch. As soon as fingers made contact, the entire creature was engulfed in green flames, and with a pop like a camera flash, only the cloak remained. The silence in the room was just as sudden.

"What the hell was that?" Drip asked

"Perhaps that object is more powerful than we expected," Kingmaker said.

"No, not that. What kind of pathetic underling did you use that couldn't handle that?" Drip said.

The demon took a few steps toward the branch. His liquid gold eye narrowed as he got closer, moving from the branch to the boy.

"What is he whispering?" Drip asked.

Taxx suddenly sat upright, staring directly at the Demon.

"Lore!" Taxx said.

Taxx held out his hand, and the branch moved into his palm without a sound, it was simply there, and he closed his hand around it. His bandana erupted in green flames and burned right off his head as soon as he did. His horns were dancing with verdant fire. The demon only pointed at the young man, and a torrent of liquid gold rushed out of his eyes, mouth, and nose. The flood ran at Taxx like a gilded tsunami, and he held up the branch from one end like a sword. When the flood met the branch, it was drawn into the wooden limb as though it were only water. It gorged until the branch was dazzling with golden light and not just the branch. The boy too. His horns were glowing with energy as solid gold as Drip, and his eyes took on the same color. The demon stopped his onslaught and stared at the young man in disbelief. Taxx looked just as confused.

"I understand that part, but what is all of this?" Taxx asked.

"Unlikely," Drip said.

"No, sorry, some dude is talking while I'm trying to listen. Say again," Taxx said.

Drip gritted his spiny teeth. Then the demon took a deep breath and snapped his fingers. FW was on the move again, and his massive body moved so quickly that almost no one could follow. Taxx was looking right at him. When the enormous albino appeared to his left and tried to smash his body with a well-placed punch, Taxx met his golden fist with the branch. He swung it like a sword, gently bringing it down on FW's forearm and slipping out of the way. The arm remained while FW continued past, lost his footing, and slammed into a wall. The gilded arm FW left behind was already starting to wither in front of the young man. Its magic was drawn in. Taxx turned to Drip and the golden light from his horns intensified.

"Whatever you believe at this moment is a lie. Not even a reaper can kill me," Drip said.

"I am not a reaper. I don't think," Taxx said.

"You don't know what you are," Drip said.

"I do. I'm the thing that's finally gonna whoop your ass," Taxx said.

"Come on then," Drip said

Taxx lunged at him, holding the branch with two hands. He was chattering something as he ran.

"Can you do all that shit you said?" He asked.

Taxx stopped as if he were listening to something, and he smiled. Drip was watching him with a smile on his face. All of this amused him. The demon lifted his right hand and manifested a golden cable. It spilled from his hands, and on it, there were dozens of golden knives.

"You have no idea what I can do. I wasn't going to spoil the fun, but anyone stabbed by one of these is in for an explosive reaction. This is what whooping looks like," Drip said.

The knives were released all at once, and by manipulating the cord, the demon whipped the knives at him from dangerous angles. Taxx seemed able to keep up with them as he parried with the branch, slashing here and blocking there. Even as the corded knives came from multiple angles. Lore, which was the name of this object in his hands, had been whispering things all the while. It was telling him about the danger he and all of them were in and the things that it could do. It was also informing him where to look. Not with words. No, the branch was a part of him, or at least it had been. There was so much more, but it was too much to wrap his head around. There was something important, though, Taxx thought. The branch said it could change shape.

"Then do it!" Taxx shouted.

The branch did precisely that, growing out of his hands and toward drip suddenly like a spear. Drip was taken by surprise, and the unexpected attack was headed directly for his chest. FW Johnnie took the bulk of the attack, putting his massive form between Drip and the growing spear. The branch passed right through him and merely touched Drip in the center of his chest. The impact was only strong enough to make the Demon take a single step back. Kingmaker drew a bone needle from her bandoleer and held it between two fingers. Drip stopped her with a raised hand.

"That was mildly unpleasant, but I wouldn't call that an ass whooping by any means," Drip said.

FW had not moved since the attack, and the branch returned to its original form. Everyone in the room looked at FW except Drip, who examined his jacket instead.

"No damage. Where is my handkerchief, Fuckwit Johnny?" Drip asked.

By the time the demon looked up, the massive albino had been reduced to spent ashes with a small hole clean through his middle. The edges of the monster were still smoldering with crimson flames like the last pull of a cigarette. His magic was gone, as was his life force. Drip did not change the look on his face when the large man's body fell over and broke apart into a pile of ashes. The demon started to laugh. It intensified until it became a dry and horrible song, like grinding gears. It was slowly apparent that this was not the sound of laughter. This was the sound of a demon weeping.

"Perish," Drip said.

The demon was on top of Taxx so fast that the young man had no time to react. Drip was simply on him, standing on his thighs with both feet, forcing Taxx's body to sit. Drip started to stab him with the blades on the chord as soon as that happened. One after the other. Into his shoulder and then his abdomen, then his thighs and neck, the last one he placed right in the center of him. Exactly where Taxx had struck FW and Drip drove the knife to the hilt. The branch clattered to the ground before Taxx's body joined it, made a pin cushion by the glittering blades, each starting to erupt with a golden liquid. Rosen screamed at the top of her lungs.

"Drip!" Kingmaker shouted.

The demon seemed to exit a trance and looked down at the

boy and the branch. Drip touched the spot on his chest where the branch had touched him and shook his head, smiling at the young man as he gasped and sputtered on the ground before him.

"You were never really very important, you know. The only reason I didn't kill you the last time is because of your grandmother. Her name is the only thing you ever had, and now you ain't got jack shit. Take that with you when you meet your punk ass daddy," Drip said.

The demon nodded and passed by the pile of ashes that was once FW, and he paused for only a moment.

"Shall I have it collected?" Kingmaker asked.

"Why bother. It was just trash. Collect the fairy," Drip said.

"No!" Grayson screamed.

Drip dislodged the knife from Rosen as easily as waving a hand and called it back to his palm.

"Think fast," Drip said.

He threw the knife at Nic with as much speed as he could muster, but she caught the blade in her hand instead of her chest. Unfortunately, she grabbed it with her palm. The sharp tip came out of the back, and when Nic lifted her hand to see it punctured like that, she didn't make a sound. Then screamed, and Drip started to laugh again.

"There. Now I feel better," Drip said.

Kingmaker and more than half a dozen henchmen rushed the Fairy, and even with a wounded hand, she took out a few of them before they descended on her. She swore and screamed the entire time.

"Grayson! I love you! I trust you!" Rosen shouted.

"I will find you! I will! I love you, Rosie Dawn!" Grayson

shouted.

Drip turned to leave the room without even another glance but stopped suddenly. He placed his hand on the center of his chest, in the spot where the bough had only touched him. There was a look on his face that was confused and amused at the same time.

"You know what. I changed my mind. I want the stick, too," Drip said.

He turned toward the young man who was bleeding entirely too much. He smiled, and liquid gold dripped through his teeth heavily, then the drip became a more powerful force. Liquid gold was splashing out of him in thick globs, and he was vomiting in heaping piles on the ground. His mouth was open, and more gold was coming out, some of it stained black. He seemed to have stemmed the leak for the moment and wiped at his face with his sleeve, smearing it gold.

"Take the Fae. It's time to go," Drip said.

Kingmaker stepped toward him, and the demon accepted her help, slipping over her shoulder and allowing her to carry him.

"Shall I kill these remaining fools so that no one can speak of this?" Kingmaker asked.

"It doesn't matter. They won't survive the blowback," Drip gurgled out.

There was only black fluid leaking out of him now, leaving a dark chevron down the front of his suit. Kingmaker was dragging him, the tip of his fine shoes dragging on the ground.

"Take me out of here, Kingmaker," Drip said.

His voice was so quiet that when Grayson began to profess his love, the tailor drowned him out easily.

"I love you!" Grayson said.

"You need to run, Grayson. It would help if you ran away from her, or you will likely die, my sweet," she said.

Kingmaker didn't have time to silence her. Drip was little more than dead weight now, and if she tried to adjust, they would all see the same. When they passed through the door frame, they began to disappear, and they all had left the space in moments. Rosen's voice was barely audible, but she was still screaming his name and swearing her revenge in many languages. Finally, she could be heard no more. As soon as they were gone from sight, the doorframe returned to its original shape. Wasting no time, Grayson raced toward Taxx.

"Demon's kiss, Demon's kiss," He kept repeating.

The tailor adjusted around the knife, using the measuring tape and a small piece of chalk sizzling with his TV snow. After about half a minute, the Tailor cried out in joy.

"Got it!" he said.

Then he removed a knife from Taxx's body, stemming the flow of gold. He removed all of them, one at a time, and then gently laid the boy down on the ground. He was bleeding normal red blood from his wounds, and his horns had lost all of their light. He was dying again, but somehow it felt different this time.

"What can I do? Taxxis? Can you hear me? Tell me what I can do?" Grayson asked.

The young man moved not at all. Grayson wanted to stay, but he had to move on to Lyra. Her body was encased in strange ash. It was so thick that it sank under his hands when he tried to remove the knife. It came out easily and clattered to the floor. The substance was on his hands now, and it did not feel like ash. It was gritty and ground rough like sand but as gray as ash, there was more to this, but he did not know it. He wished they had left Avo or Isabel.

"One of them would surely and excitedly recognize this sort of odd," he said.

Grayson looked up at the gray effigy of Lyra's face, took a deep breath, and pressed his hand into the center of mass. It sank a few inches until he touched something so hot that he had to pull his hand away. A billowing plume of steam came from the hole he made, and his hand took a severe bit of heat.

"Be careful. Her magic can burn you," Nic said.

"I've seen. And felt," Grayson said.

Grayson turned toward Nic as he spoke. She was staring at her hand and the knife that geometrically bisected it. It had pierced the palm of her right hand to the hilt. The blade was exposed and visibly drawing in the fire around it like a black hole. Liquid gold spilled from the handle side, converting the magic into Drips greed laced gold. It splattered on the floor and evaporated instantly, filling the space like dandelion seeds. The air in the room was already full of gold particles. They came from her wound in glittering clouds, forming a slow spinning cyclone around her body. They infected the fire that surrounded her, and it was growing uncontrollably. Larger and hotter by the second. The temperature in the room was already at dangerously high levels, and the gold seemed to compound the heat. Where it was thickest in the air, the floors beneath were ashen. The walls were melting, and the ceiling had a clean hole burned straight up to incalculable heights. The structure of the toadstool might collapse at any moment if everything didn't explode first.

"I won't lie. This one *is* something of a pickle," Grayson said.

"You know what's weird. It doesn't even hurt," she said.

"Nicole. I can help you. I just haven't figured out **how** just yet," Grayson said.

"Am I the thing she was telling you to run away from?" Nic asked.

"I think so," Grayson said.

"Can you take this knife out of me?" Nic asked.

She held her hand forward, and the gold vapor lurched toward Grayson, scorching the space in front of him like a lava flow.

"If I could have moved any closer to you, I would have," Grayson said gently.

Nic looked down at the circle of black around her where her flame and the gold magic turned everything into black glass. Nic frowned but nodded knowingly.

"Can you teleport?" Grayson asked.

Nic shook her head, her cheeks flushing, and her voice broke with tears the next time she spoke.

"Damn. I was hoping you weren't going to ask that. I haven't been able to use my magic since he got me," Nic said.

"I'm afraid I don't know what I can do without getting closer to you. Fret not. There must be a way. We only have to think of it," Grayson said.

"You are a good man," Nic said.

"Don't praise me just yet. Let me save you first. See, what we need here is a miracle," Grayson said.

The tailor nearly leaped out of his skin when he felt a hand on his shoulder. He jumped to the right and wheeled around, screaming in a long-forgotten language.

"Haas! Sai-yah!" He shouted.

"What?" Taxx asked.

Taxx had holes in his clothing but not in his body. He seemed relatively calm while the horns on his head burned intensely. His right eye was also burning with fire, and within it was a second grace, the blessing of the Odo. Grayson took a few steps toward the young man and hugged him tightly around the middle. He stepped back and looked him over.

"How is this possible? You said the wandering forest took your immortality," Grayson said, astonished.

"Lore says it will be hard to kill me now," Taxx said.

"What lore?" Grayson asked.

Taxx held out his hand, and a branch grew out of his palm, splitting the skin and emerging like a seed. It grew to about forty inches in length, about the same as a sword, and he held it like one. Its presence changed the nature of the fire in his horns from calm to roaring.

"What is that?" Grayson asked.

"He says he is a bough of wisdom," Taxx answered.

Grayson stared at him for a moment, his bottom lip working.

"There are so many things that I need to ask you. I don't know what everything you said means yet, but can you help her?" Grayson asked.

"I think I can," Taxx said.

"Then get on with it. If this curse completes, we will all die," he said.

Then he looked between the two of them and the steaming remains of Lyra and sighed.

"Well, I will certainly die, anyway," Grayson said.

Taxx nodded and started to walk toward Nic. As soon as he took one step toward the black circle, Nic screamed.

"No! You all need to stay away from me," she shouted.

Lore touched first, and the sudden rise of heat created a blinding flash of light along its edge. It was on fire and burning fast, Taxx moved to withdraw it, but he stopped suddenly. The end was still scorching in the super-heated zone.

"Are you sure?" Taxx asked.

"Yes!" Nic shouted.

"Not you. It. Him, I think Lore is a him," Taxx said.

He reached out slowly toward Nic with Lore, and the bough began to draw in the fire, gently at first, but soon every place where the heat touched was drawn into the branch. Taxx's horns were glowing brightly on his head, and he smiled as he moved further into the hot zone, drawing up the heat as he came.

"That won't be enough," Nic said.

"Are you always this negative? I'm trying to be heroic," Taxx said.

Taxx reached out his hand to take the knife, and Nic slapped it out of the air before he could reach it. Nic looked as confused as he was.

"That was only a reflex. I'm sorry," Nic said.

"I get it," Taxx said.

He reached out again, but she didn't slap him away this time. She held out her hand like a lion with a thorn, and Taxx took it. He held the blade in his hand and closed his eyes, the golden knife started to waver, and soon it was drawn into his body like water into the soil. His horns flashed gold briefly before returning to the strong green fire.

"How can you do this?" Nic asked.

"No idea, but I know we can help you," Taxx said.

Nic studied his face carefully before she nodded. He took

her hand in his, holding her injured palm over Lore, and closed his eyes. The green flame of his magic came to life along the edges of his blade, and the flame entered the wound left by the golden knife. Instead of burning her, it closed the wound slowly until only the hole in her glove remained. The temperature in the room began to return to normal. The flames around her body subsided, and the pressure of the magical explosion all sank into the dry bark of that strange branch. When it was all over, Taxx opened his hand, and the branch receded into his palm. The hole it came from sealed itself back up with a slight flare of green flame. The tension in the air seemed to give way, and Nic fell forward. Taxx caught her in an awkward hug.

"Sorry," Nic said.

"No. It's Ok. I needed a hug too when I almost died," Taxx said.

Nic nodded, and then they didn't say anything until Grayson came up behind Taxx and clapped him on the shoulder. When he showed up, Nic found the way to her feet and pulled away from the hug. The tailor was too busy giving them praise with animated gestures to notice.

"Good man!" Grayson said.

"Thanks, but Nicole helped. She held out long enough for us to stop it," Taxx said.

Nic rolled her eyes, and Grayson started to laugh. Taxx looked between them with a look on his face.

"Secrets don't make friends," he said.

"They often make family," Grayson said.

Taxx laughed, but he didn't say anything further. Nic and Grayson had a quiet moment before the young woman let out a long, haggard sigh. Once it was over, she started to speak.

"Nicole isn't my name," Nic said.

"What? Why does everyone call you Nic then?" Taxx asked.

"It's a silly nickname. My real name is Fenic, so my friends call me Nic," Nic said.

Grayson nodded knowingly, but Taxx was even more muddled than before, which was very apparent on his face.

"As in, I am a Phoenix," Nic said.

"Oh! Well, that one I have heard of," Taxx said.

"The last firebird, if I remember correctly," Grayson added.

"Not quite, but I am one of them," Nic said.

Taxx opened his mouth to say something, and Nic stopped him.

"Don't. Don't ask me any stupid bird questions right now," she said.

He bit his bottom lip, but his excitement was apparent.

"Seriously? Fine. One. Go," she said.

"Do you have wings?" Taxx blurted out.

Nic scoffed at him, but ultimately, she was smiling beneath the veneer of her apparent annoyance.

"Not that I have ever seen," Nic said.

"Aww," Taxx said.

"I won't take this from a guy with horns," Nic teased.

"Fair," Taxx said.

The two of them smiled at each other. The horns in question had flared out, and the color returned to the strange white they usually were. They were almost translucent up close. Nic looked over to Grayson, standing in front of Lyra and looking very concerned. The ashen form had lost an arm, but there was no Lyra inside it. The smile they shared faded, and Nic made her way toward what was left of Lyra. The corner of her mouth turned down a bit. Grayson stopped Taxx from approaching to give the young woman a moment. Nic lowered her head as though she were about to pray, but instead, Nic kicked Lyra's ashes directly in the chest. The head and remaining arm fell off, and Grayson and Taxx were genuinely horrified and making noises to support that. That is until they noticed the extraordinary thing that Nic seemed to have noticed immediately. The central core of the shell did not fall away. A hill of dark grey mud stood in the center of where Lyra's massive body had once been. It was thin and oblong like a termite mound. The central mass of the pillar gave off gentle steam, and it seemed to be gently and steadily pulsing.

"Wow, I honestly didn't see that coming," Taxx said.

"Don't feel bad. This is some unusual stuff," Grayson said.

"I always knew that overgrown muscle form was good for something," Nic said.

"Are you tough talking your dead boss?" Taxx asked.

"Lyra is **not** my boss, and she isn't dead. Are you Lyra?" Nic asked.

The pillar bulged suddenly, and they all stepped back and away from it at once. Small fissures began to open up at random places all around it, and it only kept growing until it was about to explode.

"Stand back," Nic said.

Nic lifted her hands just as the ash remains burst open. There was a massive explosion, and a wave slammed into the nearly invisible wall of heat Nic had created to protect them. A white ocean of steam filled the space. It even seeped through the firewall Nic still held in place. It was hard to see or breathe.

"What is this?" Taxx hacked out.

Nic was laughing. He knew it was her even though he

couldn't see anything in all this steam. It was so hot he could hardly stand to take a breath. Then, the room started to empty, and it all cleared up in just a few moments. The thick steam was drawn into one of Nic's playing cards like a vacuum and sealed inside with a wrist flick. The young woman slipped the card into her cuff, giving Taxx a slight wink.

"This. Is Lyra… the real one," Nic said.

She looked positively gleeful as she said it, and the horned boy could only stare at her.

"What does that even mean?" Taxx asked.

"It means that she has a big mouth," Lyra said.

At least it sounded like Lyra, but the attitude was an entirely different animal. Lyra was as calm as he had ever seen. This person sounded like they were about to punch someone. Taxx couldn't quite see her just yet as there was still a large amount of steam wafting into the air where she should have been standing.

"Lyra! I'm so glad you are ok. You sound different," Taxx said.

Nic shoved him out of the way and stood closer to Lyra, her eyes sparkling with mischief.

"I do, hot stuff. Whatcha gonna do about it?" Nic teased.

A huff that continued until it turned into a long whistle. It sounded more and more like a tea kettle. The tea kettle sound was slowly intensifying, a whistle growing louder and ascending in pitch every second.

"We had better take cover," Grayson said.

He grabbed Taxx around the torso and physically dragged him out of the room, hiding behind a wall.

"What the hell is going on!?" Taxx shouted.

The kettle whistle was so loud and intense now that it was

all he could hear. It was inside his head. So much so that when he tried to cover his ears, the sound came through just the same. Then it stopped, and the sound of rushing air came next. Dozens of high-pitched whistles came in rapid succession like they were shooting off a chain of bottle rockets. A body came rushing through the steam cloud and slammed into the wall adjacent to them. All three of them turned to look at once. When she stood up at first, Taxx did not recognize her. Her body was several times smaller than it had been, but it was clearly Lyra. She was much smaller now. She couldn't have been standing much taller than 5 feet. There was a smile on her face even though her teeth were bloody, and her eyes were alive with a sort of crazed fire.

"What... the hell?" Taxx said.

Lyra turned her eyes to him, and steam erupted from her skin like an iron, accompanied by the sound of a train whistle. There was a massive plume, and her little body was gone. She was already standing under his chin by the time she was moving slow enough for Taxx to see her, and he was sure he was done for. He flinched and closed his eyes; he could feel the intense heat of her steaming fist near his face, but he never felt the boom. Her fist was hovering in front of his face when he opened his eyes, it was glowing red, and steam was pouring off it like a meteor. The meteor was caught in a trap of thorns that appeared to defend him independently.

"Now **that's** impressive, Kingswood," Lyra said.

She seemed to be calmer now. Much more the Lyra that he knew, and the level of steam coming from her was dramatically dialed back. Nic walked up beside him with an approving, if exaggerated, look on her face. She clapped him on the shoulder.

"You calmed her down in one touch. Even I can't do that,"

Nic said.

"Oh, how did I do that?" Taxx asked.

Dozens of shadowy thorns projected out of his defensively raised hands and forearms. They were long and thin like pencils and surrounded her fist on all sides. They did not hurt. He wasn't even sure if they were piercing his skin or growing on top of it. The thorns receded into his body as he backed away and were gone in moments.

"Well, now we know you can do that defensively," Nic said.

"You took a ton of my magic. You are going to be a terrible fighter," Lyra said.

"I hope not," Taxx said.

He reached up and touched his horns gingerly. They were warm to the touch at the moment, flowing with the steamy magic he just stole from Lyra.

"What am I?" he asked himself.

"I would say it's obvious that you can absorb magic, expel magic and heal yourself beyond any regenerative ability I've ever seen. Suffice it to say that you sure are certainly something. Whatever that is, I get the idea that it will be powerful," Grayson said.

"That's exactly what I am afraid of," Taxx whispered.

Lyra had taken to looking around the room and stopped at a pile of black and gold that remained on the ground. The black inky stuff was eating the gold at an alarming rate, sizzling like soap bubbles. There were little bits of green here and there where the dark material was left to dry. Green plants had aggressively started to grow out of the remains of the demon's magic. The plants grew in rapid succession to peak size. There were long green ferns and small white flowers on thin stalks that reached up toward the sky. The plants then started to die, and they witnessed the entire cycle of life in seconds. All that remained were fragile opaque skeletons.

"What other things you can do remain to be seen. The outlook is quite scary but very much encouraging," Grayson said.

They were all staring at it now as the last bits of gold fizzled away. Then all eyes were on Taxx.

"What?" he asked.

"You hurt him. You hurt a demon with that thing," Nic said,

"His name is Lore," Taxx said.

"Whatever his name, you two are useful," Lyra said.

Taxx made a sour face at her, and she returned one that said she would slap him if he so desired. Medium-sized Lyra was flexing her hand and looking at herself with a massive smile on her face. The tank top and yoga pants she had been wearing fit loosely on this new version of her body. She adjusted the clothing here and there, and it changed shape before his eyes. It seemed to shrink down to a proper fit.

"Ok, how are you a kid now? Is anyone going to explain to me?" Taxx asked.

"I'm not a kid **now**. As you probably guessed, I too am a Viridescii, and I am 16 years old," Lyra said.

"Totally understandable," Taxx said.

Lyra laughed. Taxx looked at her like she had just sprouted a new head.

"My full phase is over," Lyra said.

"Meaning what exactly?" Taxx asked.

"It means that she has physical phases like the moon. A gift from her mom," Nic said.

"Is your mom also some kind of magical beastie?" Taxx

asked.

"Her mother is the Moon," Grayson said.

"Okay. That's kind of on-brand for the present company," Taxx said.

"Izzy too?"

Lyra nodded.

"When will someone tell me who is collecting all these demigod teenagers?" Taxx asked.

"Well. That would be your Grandmother," Grayson said.

"But why?" Taxx asked.

"I suspect she knew all of this or enough to plan ahead. The program. The Guild. Even the house. I think it was all orchestrated to ensure your survival," Grayson said.

Chapter | Twenty

The sun had set on Rozsavad. The Fae planet had more eccentricities in the night, many of the flowers luminesced, and a matched set of bright moons. Each cast a different light down on the planet, like stained glass, bathing everything in slowly drifting rainbows of moonlight. That made it surprisingly easy to see at night. The light was somehow less demanding on the eyes. Half a day had passed since the attack, and though most of the damage had been cleaned up, it was a long way from being repaired. Taxx helped clean up all the burned-up remnants, but Grayson did most of the legwork and did it in a four-button vest. Even now, the gray man was standing on the front steps directing creatures of all shapes and sizes to tasks with a gentle tone. Taxx had figured out that he would rather focus on the work instead of the other thing he could be focusing on. It was sound advice.

The tailor looked up and toward him as if he could hear his thoughts, and he and Taxx met eyes across the yard. Grayson nodded with a small smile, and Taxx returned it, then the tailor looked off into the distance before he disappeared into the house. Grayson had been amazing through all of this. He carefully measured each of them with his tape and furnished them with new clothing in a single hour with the help of the house pixies. The small army of glowing lantern-like fairies that had been giving their praise to Rosen earlier were still about. Their little bits of light hung in the night sky like terrestrial stars.

"They are pretty neat, huh?" Nic asked.

Taxx glanced down and saw her standing below. He was sitting on the thick lower branches of a wide-reaching tree that looked like a hand reaching for the sky. The phoenix joined him on the branch by way of short-range teleportation. She didn't make any sound. The branch simply shifted with her added weight.

"You're pretty casual with the fabric of spacetime," Taxx teased.

"We are old friends," Nic said.

They shared a smile and then fell silent together. Taxx could not take his mind off of Sixx, and it was written all over his face. Nic reached out and touched the top of his hand, squeezing it a little. As soon as she contacted his skin, the horns on his head came alive with green fire, but where they touched, all she could feel was skin. Taxx looked up at her, and the two of them smiled again.

"I still can't get over your eye," Nic said.

"I know. It makes me look even more like him," Taxx said.

His left eye had started to fade from its usual brown after the attack, and it settled into pale green, almost white. On his iris was a visible mark, like a brand.

"You have the grace of the Aether in your eye and your hand. I've never seen anyone with more than one. That's a blessing no matter how you slice it," Nic said.

"So, I've heard. Having it in your hand can't be so bad either," Taxx said.

Their hands were still locked, and he lifted them both together. On the back of Nic's hand was the very same mark.

"I still don't get this," Taxx said.

"The Odo is the mark of magic. If you have magic, you have this. Where it chooses to mark you has some meaning and all that, but that's the basic gist," Nic said.

"I've seen this symbol hundreds of times. It was on my headband, and I didn't even know it. I grew up sheltered by lies. Not like you. You know a lot about a lot," Taxx said.

"I grew up almost alone, so I had plenty of time to read a lot about a lot," Nic said.

"That sounds like the beginning of a good story," Taxx said.

Nic examined his face. His hair seemed to have grown at an alarming rate in the past few hours, and his curls were free on his head. They framed his horns beautifully. The horns themselves seemed a bit longer, if she wasn't mistaken. In fact, Taxx might have been taller all over. It may have just been the way he was carrying himself now, even when he was grief-stricken like they all were. Something was different.

"Maybe I'll tell it to you someday," Nic said.

She punctuated her words with a sly grin, and Taxx shook his head, bumping her playfully with his shoulder.

"You are surprisingly cool for a firebird, Nicole," Taxx teased.

"I told you my name. It's Fenic. Fenic Turul. You can still call me Nic," she said.

"Turul? That sounds cool," Taxx said.

"It's Hungarian. That's about all I know," Nic said.

"Knowing your family history isn't always great," Taxx said.

"You aren't wrong," Nic said.

"But. You never *don't* want to know. That's why it sucks," Taxx said.

Nic smiled, but she didn't say anything, and the two of them sat in comfortable silence for a while. Letting the invisible rain of family drama, mourning, and anger fall on their shoulder while they huddled together in a tree. No one was present to track how long they sat in that silent space before someone spoke again. Eventually, though, someone did.

"We will find him," Nic said.

Then she gave him a playful punch.

"What happened to your glove?" Taxx asked.

Nic flexed her bare hand subconsciously, her Odo taking on the orange glow of her magic with just a thought.

"Beings like us have to regulate the magic in our bodies when we aren't in a protected state. Otherwise, it would overwhelm us and make us explode. Like you did in the quarry," Nic said.

"It did feel like that," Taxx said.

"It was. You overloaded, and you were lucky. Most people just explode and like… well… you know. We have to let off steam and regulate the balance to prevent that. Some people do it literally, like Lyra. Her power builds and normalizes through her phases," Nic teased.

"Right, I get that," Taxx said.

"Some of us grow horns," she said.

"That makes sense," Taxx said.

He touched his horns. Even now, they were gently vibrating with energy.

"I'm always going to have these, huh?" He asked.

"Could be worse. My hand was always on fire," Nic said.

"So what happened?" Taxx asked.

"Actually. It was you," Nic said.

Taxx canted his head a little and turned the corner of his mouth up.

"I am not above flattery, but I like it a little more veiled than that," Taxx said.

"It's not flattery. Something changed. I only need the boots after whatever you did to my hand," Nic said.

She lifted the tip of her boot, and it started to sizzle on command.

"That's convenient," Taxx said.

"Even if you don't remember how. Thank you," Nic said.

"I wish I could tell you how I did it. That might," Taxx started.

"Taxx!" Nic screamed.

She was staring at the rear of the house, and Taxx followed her eyes until he saw an excessive amount of flies. Hundreds of black flies gathered in one place, as slick as oil and shiny with all the rainbow colors. Then there were more. They propagated at an alarming rate, increasing their number by thousands in mere seconds. There were countless flies now, swarming and circling in such controlled patterns. The bugs were arranged into the effigy of a man, the rough shape and parts, the proportions took longer to even out to the correct sizes, but eventually, they did. In a fascinating ballet, the impossible cloud of insects formed together to make themselves appear to be something else. When it was done, there was something that looked like a man standing there before them, composed of a macabre mosaic of insects in various stages of life. It was alarmingly easy to discern a particular face in the constantly moving and undulating web of insects. A face that was looking up at Taxx.

"I bet this is a shock for you. Before we get into the bullshit fighting part, can I say a few things that may help smooth this over?" Craw asked.

Nic stood up on the branch, and her cards manifested on her arms in a mad shuffle. They fluttered as they shuffled, and for the first time, Taxx could see her for the phoenix she was. Nic left the branch before he could stop her and rushed for the insect man.

"Guess not," Craw said

She closed the space between them and superheated the area around her left hand. Craw launched a series of flies at her at the same moment. The air was heavy with volatile magic. Before it could become dangerous, it all started to slip away like the air had been released from a balloon. Taxx stood between them, and his horns were glowing bright orange from the magic he was absorbing from her attack. Lore swept through the cloud of flies, and at once, they all went still and dropped to the ground in its wake. If any of this upset the insect person, it didn't show on his constantly changing face. He seemed pleased. Nic visibly calmed and settled down, but she was still serving some severe looks.

"Stop it. He wouldn't have shown himself to us if he came here to fight," Taxx said.

"Since when do you know that?" Nic asked.

"I don't. Lore told me," Taxx said.

"Damn decent of you," Craw said.

"Don't be cute. I didn't say I wouldn't kill you. I owe you one," Taxx said.

"Too true. First, you need to ask how I got here, and you ain't gonna like that part," Craw said.

"Is this a joke?" Nic hissed.

"Cool it, red boots," Craw teased.

Nic literally and figuratively smoldered simultaneously, the ground under her boots melting like glowing mud. She closed her thumb and fingertip, and one of her cards was simply there between them when she did. Then she took a breath, there was a crackling sound like flint, and the card's edge came to life like lava. She looked poised to throw it in his face, but Taxx's face made her stop. He didn't look upset or bewildered. Instead, the horned boy was smiling at her. Her body clenched, and she gave Craw another look that said she wanted to hit him. Ultimately she put the card away and crossed her arms with authority.

"Fine. How did you get here?" Taxx asked.

"Secondly, you're gonna want to know what I have to offer, and let me tell you that it's **juicy**," Craw said.

"You maggot-infested son of a b-," Nic started.

She was only stopped by the sudden sound of a throat clearing. The curse was still on her lips.

"This is tedious. I suppose he is inelegant, at best, but he is trying to teach you something," Grayson said.

The tailor and Lyra had both been watching from the porch of the toadstool house, hidden away. They stepped out into the light to show themselves. Taxx visibly cooled, and Lore receded into his body. Nic was still looking at him like she might flay him and his little insect bodies at any moment.

"Slick caught me. You look like you're about to go walkin' where you shouldn't be. You don't know a damned thing about talking to villains. To that end, my information is valuable, and as I do love my life, there will be a cost," Craw said,

His accent was slightly English, a bit American and raspy with the sound of beating wings, but it was clear and understandable.

"Crawford-," Lyra started.

"You look shorter, love. My name is Craw. That other thing is a dead man's name. Call me late for dinner instead," Craw said.

"Craw," Taxx said in disgust.

"That's more like it! Say it like you mean it," Craw laughed.

Grayson had pulled out a notebook and was furiously drawing something inside, and after a minute or two, he popped up and lifted a finger to the air.

"Have you found something?" Lyra asked.

"Indeed!" The Tailor said.

Grayson bounded forward and swiped through the air with the nub of chalk in his hand. Two things happened immediately after. Firstly, his hand moved at a speed that none of them could keep up with. He wrote what appeared to be an equation, and it was hanging in the air as though it had been drawn on glass directly in front of Craw. It was made with chalk. Secondly, the complicated mathematics, along with Craw's body and every one of the insects that comprised him vanished in a black and white static flash. Leaving just one tiny maggot. Grayson scooped up the larva into a teacup quickly as a whip and moved back toward Lyra. As soon as they were clear, like the pop of a magnesium flash, Craw's insect body returned. There was something different about them now, as they all seemed confused and disjointed. Then they fell into a massive pile of writhing insects. Most of them did not even move, just wiggled their legs helplessly. It seemed that without a leader, the body simply ceased to function.

"Well, that was easy," Grayson started.

However, he did not get the chance to finish as the teacup soon began to overflow with hundreds of black flies. The room was forced silent under the weight of the deafening beat. Grayson dropped the mug, and it shattered with the sudden increase in occupancy. The formerly helpless throng of bugs reached out like a tendril of magnetic paste and rejoined the hoard. There were three whole bodies now, and one of them was holding the remains of the teacup, looking at it with what might have been disdain on its ever-moving face.

"I hate bloody teacups," All three said in unison.

"What do you want!" Grayson said.

"Don't get loud with me because your plan was piss poor. I'm the first to admit I ain't no saint, but if I were the full-on, cock out, bad guy type, I wouldn't even be here," the Craw bodies said.

The other two copies dispersed back into a cloud of insects and rejoined with the remaining form. As they joined with the body, the definition of his features became more precise. He tossed the teacup aside and held out his hands as if to say, oops. He even laughed, as much as one could laugh with a voice box made of insect wings.

"Why have you come?" Lyra asked.

"To make a deal," Craw said.

"I am not the sort for this kind of showmanship. When there is a deal to be had, it should be clearly made," Grayson said.

"Then let's talk. Tell me what you want to know, and I'll let you know if you can afford it," Craw asked.

"You were there the day I was born. Tell us what we don't know," Taxx said.

"Smart question. Expensive too. I will need some assurances in exchange for that," Craw said.

"You have my word. If this information proves useful and as long as it is within my power," Grayson said.

"I think I would be dead if I trusted someone on their word. I need better than that," Craw said.

"I need my wife," Grayson said.

His voice was low and heavy with an intense and steady hum and hissed like classic broadcast television. TV Snow.

"Calm down, Harlem Nights. I ain't mean nothing by it. Besides, we are all about to become best friends," Craw said.

"Enough, you have his word. We will have yours," Lyra said.

"You all are so touchy. I thought only Taxx was that high strung. Good for a viola but distracting for a man, or whatever our boy is, eh Taxx?" Craw teased.

"Screw you!" Taxx shouted.

"How did you get into my home!?" Grayson asked.

The effigy of a man was wearing a suit made of black wings that fared far better than his face at appearing real. Craw adjusted the jacked and shrugged.

"I slipped into Taxx's clothes after that little accidental murder. A good thing too; turned out to be quite lucrative," Craw said.

"You mean when you killed him?' Lyra asked.

"I ain't meant to do all that," Craw said.

His voice tapered at the end, and he went silent for a

moment.

"Look, you can't know how much I didn't mean to kill that child. More than any. For that mistake. I'll give you this bit for free. Offrey wasn't the one that hired ol' Drip to kidnap Taxx. It was the other way around," Craw said.

"That makes no sense," Lyra said.

Craw smiled, and the buzzing that made up his body calmed to a background sound, like the idling of an engine, his form tightening up a bit, all except his always moving face and eyes.

"It would probably make more sense if I told you that Taxx's birth is why she is blind," Craw said.

"You lie," Grayson said.

"Wrong again," Craw said.

His voice was low, and Craw laughed a little, holding both hands up, palm open, a clear show of peace.

"It's not my fault that you are wrong," Craw said.

"If she hired Drip, why did he pay her for the door? I saw this with my own eyes, a door certainly came out Taxx, and the Demon carried it off," Lyra said.

Lyra nodded, frowning woefully, but then she wrinkled up her eyebrows for a moment and tapped at her chin. Her eyes flashed.

"What is so special about the door? Was it just a distraction?" She asked.

"That door results from a dangerous spell, a door into the soul itself. Death's Door," Craw said.

"That's a lot of work to get into my soul, nothing in there. I saw for myself," Taxx said.

"You couldn't possibly be more wrong when you say that. There's plenty in there. Too damned much," Craw said.

"What do you mean? What's in the door?" Taxx asked.

"Not what. Who," Craw said.

"The Vampire," Nic said.

Grayson seemed unimpressed. Taxx scanned the room, and everyone seemed to understand something he did not. So, he lifted a finger and asked.

"I hate to sound like an idiot here, and I get the dude came for me when I was like preborn, but who exactly is this Vampire we talking about?" Taxx asked.

"A problematic man," Nic said.

"A dangerous one too. He founded the house with Queen May. Roediger Wolfrum, The First Sorcerer," Grayson said.

"He is a sorcerer *and* a vampire?" Taxx asked.

"Indeed. Perhaps even more than that. He was a man when we first met. Ah, Wolfrum, now there is a name I'd hoped to have heard the last of. I thought he died in an accident... Oh, I see," Grayson said.

"How do you know all of this, Craw? You were dead," Lyra said.

"I told you, Tomas Crawford died that night, but he left behind enough life in those few black flies to create something else. Me. I was there, and I know what I saw, and what I saw means everything," Craw said.

"So, get on with it then. The others are headed toward their doom every moment we sit here," Grayson shouted.

"Chin up, ol' boy, just need to haggle about my going rate," Craw said.

Grayson narrowed his eyes.

"What are your terms?" He asked.

He was sure that each of them had theories as to what

he might ask for, some immunity or absolution, perhaps even assist in some sort of escape from justice. They had to have been thinking about it. There was a particular sort of madness in asking anything of the people standing in front of him, but he was a bold collection of insects if Craw was anything. He spoke in plain words when he gave them his price and shattered every one of their expectations. As he had hoped to do, Lyra's face had been the most priceless to him because she did not look angry. She looked pleased in her own way.

"So. You've heard my terms," Craw said.

"I don't get it," Taxx said.

"Bold. I do not like you, Craw, but I now understand why you are considered dangerous," Lyra said.

"You flatter me, but I'm not here to be flattered. I'll tell you all I know, and I know a lot. All you have to do is grant that one little request. I usually charge a much more troublesome fee, so I'll need an answer before speaking another word," Craw said.

"You have some nerve to ask that of us. After everything you've done, I should divide you where you stand," Grayson said.

"The night isn't over, mate. Maybe I'll tack on a few more horrors for ol' time sake," Craw said

"We will not," Nic started.

Grayson stopped her with a hand on her forearm, and Craw smiled. There were times when he looked like a painting come to life and times when he looked like a nightmare. This was a nightmare smile. Nic nodded her head slowly, Taxx and Lyra started to protest in unison, and Grayson silenced them with a hand.

"Is the information you have worth this?" He asked simply.

"Sugar Ray, if you don't think so when I'm done, you can

kill me, and I won't even fight back. Shake on it?" Craw asked.

He solidified his hand into the most human shape and smoothness he could achieve and held it out toward the tailor.

"You scratch my back, and I don't scratch anyone," Craw said.

"I will agree to your request, not because you have forced me, but because you need our help, but I will remind you of who I am. No, there is no time. I will summarize. I am irate and incredibly well-traveled. I know many beautiful and terrible secrets that I will share with you if you betray us. " Grayson said.

Grayson did not hesitate when he took Craw's hand and gave it a good and proper shake, looking him directly in his eyes. Even Craw seemed a little surprised by how quickly he agreed, and it took him a moment to compose himself. When he tried to pull his hand back, he could not, and Grayson squeezed it tightly, drawing him closer.

"With this shake, it is done. I use my position as acting Head of Household to appoint you a member of the House of Wolf and Raven. As you asked, from this point forward," Grayson said.

They shook on it, and Craw smiled again.

"That's good. That's lovely. We are gonna need each other because you have no idea how shit everything is about to become," Craw began.

***

Sixx had been born on stage under dozens of lights, in front of the crowds of adoring fans and event staff of a live concert. He was born with no issues. He had all his fingers and toes and

459

two big brown eyes just like his mother's. He was talkative and active almost from the moment he was born. No slap required. It was clear that he was no ordinary child right from the start, as it was discovered that he was the main cause of several blackouts during the labor process. The shadows had gathered to witness his birth. The birth of a Godling loved by the shadows. The shadows gathered around him even now as Mimi played with the cooing baby on the bed in front of her. Dense darkness collected beneath the child, and it was all but cradling him in his mother's stead, keeping him easily and miraculously aloft as his mother tickled his toes. The child's laughter was beautiful music to the scenery in this room, but May Moss could not enjoy it through to her heart. She had seen too much in a single night to enjoy the laughter of a child, even such a child as this.

"Mimi, don't you think you should hold him yourself?" May asked.

"He is the son of an Emperor, Momma. This is just the sort of thing that happens when you have a blessed child," Mimi said.

She was bubbling so much over her adorable baby with his big wide eyes soaking up the world around him hungrily that she almost didn't see the sour puss on her mother's face. May looked like she had been slapped, and she heavily walked toward her daughter and the child. Mimi pulled her baby close in her arms out of instinct, and the shadows responded. They surrounded the entire bed in a dense dimness, and May stopped walking, gasping at the sudden dark and taking a few steps back. That magic had nearly swallowed up her own shadow, and the room was strangely bright on one side and almost pitch black on the other. The only thing that came through that black dome was the sound of the baby crying.

"Mimi! Enough!" May yelled.

"Whoa… I didn't do that," Mimi said.

"Then we have even more problems to deal with," May said.

"This isn't a problem; this is a miracle! My baby is so strong. This is the best night ever!" Mimi said.

The baby calmed with the sound of his mother's laughter. The shadows around the bed faded away, the shadows moving in three dimensions similarly to smoke as they returned to the objects they had been borrowed from and became regular shadows again. The light normalized in the room, and Mimi was still laughing and holding her baby against her chest until she saw the look of horror on her mother's face.

"What about your other son? Have you already forgotten about him? What about your father?" May snapped

Mimi looked as though she had been slapped this time and her face went still. She nuzzled the baby and buried her face in the soft hair on his head. Guilt flashed in her eyes, and she shook her head, starting to apologize.

"That's not… Mama, I'm sorry, how's the baby?" She asked.

"I know you didn't mean it. I know it," May said.

The two women hugged each other close, and Sixx sat between them quietly cooing and bubbling, May started to cry, and Mimi held her tighter for a moment.

"Tell me what happened?" Mimi asked.

"He is dying, and Mercy can't do anything to help," May said.

"Not even her with **her** magic? She is the best healing witch, like, ever!" Mimi said.

"Not even with her magic. The baby will die tonight, and there is nothing any of us can do to stop it," May said.

"Isn't this... what we all wanted in the first place?" Mercy said.

May and Mimi looked up to the door, and Mercy was there holding an infant with tiny horns on his forehead and a gray pallor on its skin. One of his hands held fast to Mercy's pinky with the blackened tips of little fingers. She looked down on what was supposed to be her child, but there was no joy in her eyes, and her face was as still as ever. Her eyes were the color of honey, but her disposition was as black as pitch.

"This abominable child lives still, and how he suffers. There are no blessings for this one. Only horns and curses," Mercy said.

"You are being too cold again, Mercy," May said.

"I have no cause to be warm toward this thing. I never asked to be a part of this in the first place, and I was made to be. I was told this would not be a child, and it clearly is. I was told he would never survive, yet look how he clings to life. Clings to me," Mercy said.

Her face never changed, but the tears came, all the same. She never even made any noises, just wept silently as she watched this strange being that she gave birth to absorb her magic as though it were nursing.

"Whatever this child may be, he is strong, May. What if we can save him?" Mercy asked.

The tears never stopped coming, but her voice was calm. Even with eyes so red, she maintained an air of control, even when the hands she held him with were trembling. Mimi sat on the bed with her mouth open in a gasp as she watched her sister weep, Mercedes Moss was many things, but she was not often one to cry. May did not speak, but she joined her daughters' silent weeping from the center of the room between her beautiful twin girls and the unlikely twin babies they held in their arms.

"You carried that child to save their lives. Mimi and Saturday would also be dead without you. This child held the weight of other lives," May said.

"But still, he lives. Look at him!" Mercy said.

She shouted, and her face finally cracked with emotion, and she was crying in earnest, holding the child out for them to see him, holding him up and proudly.

"Witness him. His name is Calderhys Taxxis Moss II. He is the curse eater," she said.

He had all his fingers and toes, two eyes, and a regular little mouth and nose, but those parts had been marked black as oil. The iris of his eye was honey-colored like his mother's, but where there should have been whites, they too were as black as pitch. The curse's mark spread through his body as if he had been dipped in ink. Two small horns grew from his forehead, above his eyes, and nearly into his soft baby hairs. They were no bigger around than pennies and about the depth of a small pinky. The child was calm even as his mother fell apart behind him, looking at all the people in the room with the same light as his just born cousin. This, too, was no ordinary birth.

"Mercy, he is beautiful," Mimi said.

She moved from the bed with her infant and toward her sister to take her in her arms, but as soon as she got close, she started to feel that something was wrong. Even before her mother screamed or the energy was ripped away from her, she knew. She knew. Her trick hand twitched.

"Don't let them touch!" May shouted

It was too late. As soon as the two boys came together, something incredible happened. An exchange of energy created something like a well between them. At first, it was a slight crackle of power, but soon it was visible, an arcing electrical line carved into the air between the two babies. It licked wildly in all directions for a moment before it came together into shape. It took the form of two identical rings, one as green as the forest and the other as pale as smoke, side by side for a moment before they formed into a single ring as black as pitch. As soon as the black ring fully developed, they began to draw magic from everyone violently. From everything in the room, even the floors started to blacken under their feet, and the paint dried and crumbled in mere moments. It drew so much power that visible lines of energy came from the inanimate objects, as thin as human hair, and they reached out for the horned child by the dozens. They gently touched him and disappeared into his body, filling him with energy until the horns on his head started to glow. The energy that was feeding him stopped, and the power draw ended, causing all of the women to gasp all at once. The attraction was so strong they could not move. May joined them now that it was gone, pulling Mimi away from Taxx and his mother, separating the black circle back into two rings. The pale ring moved away with Sixx and his mother.

"What is that?" Mimi asked.

They all turned their attention to the perfect energy circles just in time to see them dissipate into the air until they were completely gone.

"That is a problem for later. Tell me how we can stop it now. There must be a way," Mercy said.

"So, that… is how he survived," May said.

"Don't ignore me, Mother!" Mercy shouted.

"There isn't any way to save him. That curse was meant for

much stronger prey," May said.

"He is strong, strong enough to live this long," Mercy said.

"How is he able to absorb energy like that? And, no offense, what's with the horns? Is this because of the curse?" Mimi asked.

"I don't know! This was not supposed to happen. He was never supposed to be alive," May said.

"See how desperately he clings to life despite what is supposed to be," Mercy said.

"Either mother survives, or both die," May said

"Mom. What the actual F word?" Mimi said.

"He was never supposed to live or have to suffer the vampire's curse," May said.

Sixx and Taxx both started to cry and the young women rocked and tended to their infant while their mother stood between them, watching her girls become women right before her eyes. Mimi started to move back toward her sister, and after only a few steps, there was a weight in the air again, which made her stop in her tracks. The two women looked at each other before Mimi took a step back and away from her sister and nephew, holding her child closer to her chest. Something dangerous happened when the two children were that close together. There was no way they could know what would happen.

"That baby is drinking up your magic to stay alive, and it isn't going to stop. That curse cannot be survived. If you let go of him, I am almost certain that he will die, but if you keep him that close there is no doubt that he will kill you and anyone else that he needs to fend off the curse. He won't even mean to, but he won't be able to stop. That ain't no kind of life," May said.

"You," Mercy started.

Her voice caught in her throat, and she collected herself

before she spoke again.

"You are being too cold again, Mother," Mercy finished.

Mercy had not stopped crying since she began an uncountable number of minutes ago, she was starting to get blurry vision, and the child was drawing more and more power from her. She was sustaining both of them and fading quickly. Whatever the origin, she had just given birth, and her body was in a place that was so far beyond tired that the language was different.

"What do I do? There were options when it was just some lifeless nothing, but he grabbed my hand, May, he asked to live," Mercy said.

"Give him to me, Mercedes. Just give him to me, and I'll make sure it gets taken care of," May said.

"You would love to brush this under the rug, wouldn't you? And you would let her, Mercy. I won't let you kill this child, look at him. You can't let him die. There is always another way. There **has** to be! They say we are so powerful, yet there is nothing we three can do?" Mimi asked.

Mercedes gasped, and the other two looked up at her, startled. The woman was staring hopelessly down at the child in her arms and crying uncontrollably, trembling so hard she threatened to drop the baby. May rushed to her side and took her daughter around the waist, and just in time, Mercy seemed to give at the knee, and together they sank to the floor, May supporting the girl.

"Hush now, child. We knew this would happen. He is in a better," May began.

She was interrupted by the look in her daughter's eyes. Mercy looked so angry and delicate that someone as old and wise as May Moss knew to breathe softer so as not to upset the tenuous balance.

"My magic returned so suddenly, I thought… but even now, he fights," Mercy said.

The child was as near death as anything May had ever seen before in a long life that saw many deaths pass through it in more forms than most. There were moments left, if there were moments at all.

"Momma, what the hell is this?" Mimi said from the other side of the room.

Her voice was slightly muffled, and Mercy and May looked up from the child with horns and black dipped fingers to see something stranger. Standing between them and Mimi was a door. A large and heavy wooden door as thick as a fist and carved out of an otherworldly wood colored soft violet. There were elaborate carvings, and the grain was ghostly pale instead of dark, and the handle was as bright and white as starlight with a slender hook at the end like a recurved horn, so bright that it glowed. The handle had the mark of old and powerful magic on it, and that sort of power was alluring to the strongest mind. May stood up slowly and moved toward it.

"My god… I didn't think it would… I'd never dreamed I would see it up close," She whispered.

"Momma, what is it?" Mimi asked.

She poked her head around the other side of the door with Sixx in tow, snuggled into her neck. When she saw how close Mercy was, she gasped, but there was no reaction anymore. Mercy looked up at her and then down to the baby, unable to get up from the floor, and Mimi frowned slowly, moving to her sister's side.

"This is Death's Door. It's only supposed to be visible to…

Why is it here now?" May asked aloud.

"May, the baby is dead," Mercy said.

Her voice was low and emotionless, but she was crying all the same.

"He is not, not completely. This door would be gone if that was the case. This is a door into Cal… no, you said you would call him Taxxis. This door will take us to his center, the place only death can reach, where death comes to claim you when you die. Even this is drawing magic from me just standing here. This boy has power. I bet he could drain us all to empty and probably more. Normally this door only manifests for the space between a breath, but because he has such a strong stream of power, here it is… standing free. Cally, get me," May said.

She had mostly been mindlessly talking to herself as she examined the phenomena, there was certain excitement she and her husband would derive from this sort of work, and she fell back into it so quickly that she had forgotten. She had forgotten that her husband was gone, carried off with the foul homunculus that called himself the Vampire, stripped away in the blink of an eye just like magic does. The most powerful and dangerous force in this or any world, able to see the future but not change it, able to heal slowly but destroy in an instant. Her husband had his secrets and sins, but he deserved better.

"Oh, Momma," Mimi said.

She did not get up from the floor with her daughters. May felt her bottom lip quiver as she looked at them hovering over her tragically lost grandson. Here she was, speaking to the dead and playing old games. She took a single step away from the door when she heard his voice, and the blood in her body froze. It was only a whisper, the slightest little sound, but she knew what she heard, and she turned back toward the freestanding door in the middle of the room, her eyes going to the handle.

"Momma, what are you doing?" Mimi asked.

"Something foolish," May said.

Chapter | Twenty-one

Mimi let go of her sister and slowly rose from the floor, but she was too late. By the time she had only got to her feet, the door was hanging open, and it was May who had done it. As soon as she did, the room was filled with a strange energy that was pulling at her around the ankles like a strong current in a shallow stream. Her magic was being pulled out faster, but it was still gentle by comparison. This child was a vacuum for magic with no end that she could see. This marvelous oddity of nature that he was born into is likely what saved his life. However, as May was starting to see in the dark recesses of the space beyond that open door, he was not the only life saved. A figure gathered in the darkness and moved toward them, walking with a strange gait but bipedal like a man. She was standing face to face with

Roediger Wolfrum, the Vampire himself. He was taller than she thought and younger. His hair was all white on his head, and he had a well-kept beard, but he didn't look older than forty. He was even handsome, perhaps if not for the look in his eyes. They were the color of blood and glowed out of his face. There was nothing there but promises of death and the cold indifference of a predator, the eyes of a vampire.

"I saw this… I saw this door. Just for a moment when Father died," Mercy said.

"If the fly could find a way," May whispered.

The Vampire edged ever closer but was not walking well, his steps were uneven, and he stumbled to his chest before reaching the door, clawing desperately toward it. May could see now what was ailing him. Her grandson was born with a peculiarity that lent itself to sucking up magic like a sponge, and the Vampire was right in the center of him.

"What's wrong with him?" Mimi asked.

"He is in the perfectly worst place to be for a being that exists purely on the magic in the blood he steals. The eater of curses indeed," May said.

"He killed father," Mercy said.

The Vampire lifted his head and started crawling again, getting ever closer to the door and the three of them. He forced himself forward, one hand at a time, whispering the same word repeatedly. Blood.

"Let his ass die in there," Mimi said.

"Wait. Let me speak to him first," Mercy said.

The two girls were together again. Mimi helped Mercy stand to her feet, moving her forward and toward the door until all three women and the infants were standing in front of it. The vampire was shouting the word even more vigorously and crawling faster now, using both hands simultaneously. Mercy held out her baby, blacked fingers, horns, and all his toes. She held him out proudly, and when she spoke, her voice was heavy with power.

"Look at the child you could not kill. The family you could not break. His name is Taxxis Moss, he is my son, and he was born to dig your grave. My child will be your undoing. I curse you, Vampire," Mercy said.

"Ooh. Sexy curse," Mimi said.

The vampire took a long leap and cleared a surprising distance, his long white fingers reaching out for the child and coming so close so quickly that Mercy could not move fast enough. Another form emerged from the shadows beyond the door and intercepted the vampire in midflight with a powerful shoulder, sending the creature tumbling away. Her husband, Calderhys Moss, turned back toward the door, and it was all May could do not to jump in there with him, and if not for her daughters, she might have.

"Don't be so hasty to join me," he said.

"Come on out of there, Cal," May shouted.

"If I could get beyond this door, I would," Cal said.

He was as handsome as ever with his flashing golden eyes that lit up like treasure and his wavy layered hair. He had his own horns, and he was dressed as sharp as a tack even on the other side of Death's door.

"Daddy, just come on through," Mimi said.

The older man smiled and held up his hand to the door, and as soon as it seemed he might pass, his hand only vanished. It was whole again when he pulled it back, but the point was clear.

"Cal, you don't have enough magic to pass," May said.

"Oh my, Mayday, just the smartest witch I ever did see," Cal said.

"Don't you sweet talk me like you ain't gonna see me again, husband," May said.

"The vampire can still pass. Here, he is weak, but he won't be for long, and when he is strong again, he will come through this door and kill you all. I won't let that happen," Cal said.

"Daddy, can't we-" Mimi started.

"There is no time. He crawled inside that baby like a roach skittering from the sun and dragged me along by mistake. I can only stand because my magic was already gone from the fight. What's left is maintaining my form, and soon that won't be here either. The child will take us both with him to death. A fitting place for such a monster. Maybe someone will call me a hero for this," Cal said.

"You are a hero! I love you, Daddy!" Mimi screamed.

Mercy cried and said the same. May cried, the babies and Cal, all of them screaming for something that they could not have, and for a moment, there was only grief in the house of Moss. It was Cal that collected them.

"It's time, he is stirring again, and I'm getting weaker. I love you, ladies, more than anything," Cal said.

"Cally, I surely can't do what you want me to do. I'll find another way," May said.

"Ain't no other way, woman, gone close the door before the flies get in," Cal said.

"You ain't funny, Calderhys Moss," she said.

"Yes, I am," Cal said.

"I love you," May said.

"I love you back. Tell me something, Maybe. Did you see

this coming?" Cal asked.

May only looked at him, and a slow smile spread across his handsome face. He gave her a wink and nodded his head toward the door.

"Go on," Cal said.

It took all three of them to close the door because it was a large, heavy door and because May would never find the strength on her own. Just like that, she had lost her husband twice. Once the door was closed, she and her daughters leaned against it together, and Mercy slowly slid the floor, cradling the weak little infant in her arms as gently as she could. Her mother and sister slid down to join her, Mimi holding Sixx up and near Taxx, the lively baby reaching out for the other. They made sure not to put them too close. The sisters looked at each other, and Mimi started to frown.

"They would have been best friends. Brothers and cousins," Mimi said.

"Twins and cousins," May said.

Mercy could only stare at the baby, who was moving much less and making almost no noise. His honey-colored eyes stood out against the black like wedding rings. The thought flashed through her mind so hard that her body shivered from the effort and Mercy shot her head up suddenly.

"Mercy, are you ok?" May asked.

"Infinite loop… like a wedding ring," Mercy said.

"Ok, yeah, rings are cool, sweetheart," Mimi said.

"No, no, I can save him with an infinite loop," Mercy said

She scooted forward, put Taxx on the floor, and settled on her knees. She lifted her hands slowly on either side of her body and began to speak in another language. The green song, the language of life. Mercedes Moss was born with the ability to speak the language of life and, through it, create wonders. When she spoke, the words came out, but very few could understand the language of life, so the others heard little more than hissing. She held her hands to the floor, and something started to come out of her palms, energy as green as spearmint, and from that light, the body of a snake. It slithered its way out of her hands. Its scales were pitch black and pointed, its head was sharp, and its eyes were brilliant. It was as long as her arm, and each scale and flick of the tongue was edged with the color of her magic. As soon as it was fully formed, it moved toward the baby.

"Mercy, what are you up to?" May asked.

"Something foolish," she said.

"Sister, I love you, but you are starting to sound like your Momma," Mimi said.

"Child," May responded.

"Stop! That snake will attach itself to him and drain all of his magic, all of the time, It took almost all of my magic to make him, but it just might work," Mercy said.

"Doesn't he already do that on his own?" Mimi asked.

"If this works, one will feed the other indefinitely," Mercy said.

"So, he won't die? But wouldn't that seal up his magic?" Mimi asked.

"Yes, but his magic is lethal to him," Mercy said.

"Without the magic in his body, he will immediately succumb to the curse," May said.

The air left the room, but Mercy did not flinch.

"Yes, he will, and he will take the Vampire with him," Mercy said.

"Yes… he will," Mimi said.

The snake finally made its way to the baby and lashed out quickly, touching the baby in the chest, and its entire form disappeared into the child in a matter of moments.

"Did that… work?" Mimi asked.

Mercy started to shake her head but stopped when she noticed the black color on the babies' extremities and eyes began to slowly but surely fade away. His color returned, and his eyes opened fully for the first time since Mercy could remember, then reality came crashing in like gravity. As soon as the child began to improve, the door vanished from behind them, and they all nearly fell to the floor. By the time they got up, Taxx had stopped moving, and all traces of his magic were gone from the room. The baby was still.

"Let me take care of this," May said.

She got to her feet and gathered up the remains of Taxx, covering up his face with the blanket he was wrapped in. She rose slowly and held the little bundle out to Mercy.

"Do you want to say goodbye?" May asked.

Mercy stared at the bundle in her mother's hand for a full minute. She said nothing. It was hard to tell if she was even breathing, but eventually, she shook her head. May nodded and turned to leave the room, her daughters silently crying behind her and her remaining grandchild crying loudly. She had hardly made it beyond the threshold when she felt something strange between her hands, a rushing of energy that nearly made her lose her balance. The teacup on her hip started to buzz as well, and it shattered, hundreds upon hundreds of black flies suddenly bursting forth from it. The flies buzzed around in a strange circle, crawling all over each other, a pillar-like mass of ever-growing flies, born, turned into larvae, and aged into adult flies in seconds. The girls moved to the door behind their mother and looked on in horror as the flies tried to form what could be considered a mouth. A mouth that opened up and screamed with such power and pitch that it sounded like a banshee. Once it roared like that, the mass of flies dispersed all over the room and out of every little place, they could get. Some out of the windows, others up the chimney and down the stairs until the hall was empty of all but a few black flies.

"Craw," Mercy said.

"It never ends," May said.

The infant started to cry, and May turned to Mimi to tell her to soothe her child, but Sixx was babbling and cooing in her arms, oblivious to the recently buzzing flies. The crying was coming from the child in her arms, muffled by the blanket on his face, May moved it aside, and the bright-eyed child was looking back at her. She could have fallen over, but her daughters were right there behind her, looking just as shocked as the rest of them. Mercy scooped up the child and desperately held him in her arms, then pulled him back to look at his face again, her eyes pensive.

"How?" She asked.

"Our babies are not like other babies," Mimi whispered.

"These boys are the children of Death. It will surround them," Mercy said.

"Not if I can help it," May said.

"If the guild hears of this, then this miracle will be for nothing," Mercy said.

The possibilities were more than May could wrap her head around at the moment. She sighed long and slow.

"The guild can't know about them then. Not both of them," May said.

"How do we choose which of them becomes a secret and which does not?" Mercy asked.

"That choice was already made. Long before he was born," May said.

The young woman looked at her mother with clear eyes, the old witch looked back at her, and Mercy saw something like regret for the first time. Neither of them said anything then, not for a long time. No matter how much she tried, every time Mercy opened her mouth to protest, all she could do was cry. All she did was nod, and her mother pulled her close in a hug.

"If we are lucky, he will only judge us by the truth, but witches are rarely so lucky," May said.

"If we are lucky, he will still care enough to judge us," Mercy said.

"Bless your words, daughter," May whispered.

***

Once he was finished speaking, Craw turned to look at Taxx. He had been expecting rage, hatred… something, but the boy only looked confused.

"So, there were three monsters in me," Taxx said.

"Seems like," Nic said.

Grayson was staring at the flyman with a face that gave nothing away to his.

"That's the least of your worries," Craw whispered.

"What do you mean?" Taxx asked.

"May kept that secret for years without any oversight, and

you think she stopped at three? Ain't you a good boy?" Craw asked.

"How many could there have been?" Taxx asked.

"Only she knows and maybe Drip," Craw said.

"That sounds like the end of the world to me. Why hasn't Drip just opened the door and let them all out then?" Lyra asked.

"I have a theory, which is why I come to you lot for help. He must be missing some part of it, which means we have time to take him down and put a stop to all that end of days shite," Craw said.

"You are selling something," Grayson said.

"I'll take you right to him right now," Craw said.

"When a deal sounds too good, it usually is," Grayson said.

"How can we trust that you even know where Drip is?" Taxx asked.

"I've been working for Drip. How do you think he got here so fast?" Craw said.

"You monster, you nearly killed us!" Lyra said.

"You full-on killed me," Taxx said.

"Calm down. Yeah, I did. But I didn't sign up to end the bloody world," Craw said.

"If you are lying, I'll kill you," Grayson said.

"I got no more reason to lie," Craw said.

"What do you mean?" Taxx said.

Craw looked like he took a moment to think, and then he produced a key from within his body which he handed over to Grayson. The tailor took it and quietly examined it. It had a doll face on one side and a black demonic face on the other.

"A key that will take you to the midnight auction," Craw said.

"This key is made of Drips gold. This is a trap," Grayson said.

"God damn old man, you are the real deal. I was just about to get to that part. Yes, this is definitely a trap, but I got a plan. There may be some… improvising needed, but I could have just led you into the trap if that's what I wanted," Craw said.

"Why not just do that then?" Lyra asked.

"When I accidentally killed you, it shook something in me, and I started to remember him. Crawford. Mercedes. I don't know what that all means, but I swore that I would protect you if I got another chance. I swore on your life. So, seeing as how you live, here we are. I'll prove it," Craw said.

"How? What could you do to prove that you aren't just up to something?" Nic asked.

"Wait, I know a way," Taxx said.

He held up his hand, and Lore spouted from his palm and grew to the length of a blade, roughly taking on the curved shape as well. Taxx held it out toward Craw, and the insect man took a few steps back. He seemed to remember what happened the last time.

"You have gotten so strong. I'm glad I killed you when I had a chance," Craw teased.

"Lore says that if you swear on the tree of wisdom, the words become a contract. If you mean it, swear on it," Taxx said.

Craw did not hesitate. He grabbed up the branch and held it tightly. His skin began to move, and a black fly emerged to the surface. It had an almost invisible grace mark on its back, but it was clearly there. None of the other bugs carried any marks. The marked fly crawled onto the bark of the branch and settled down. Taxx found that Craw was looking directly into his eyes.

"I swear on this wooden stick that while I live, you will be protected until every last bit of me is gone. I owe you, Taxxis Moss, and should I ever betray you, may this bough destroy my core. Wherever it shall be," Craw said.

Grayson shook his head in disbelief. Nic and Lyra shared a look, and Taxx couldn't help but blink at the insect man. Craw started to laugh, devouring all of their discomforts gleefully, his body trembling with the effort.

"Well. Go on then, Taxx," Craw said.

"What do you mean?" Taxx asked.

"You got that stupid look on your face that you get when you want to ask a question but don't know how to start. Don't hold back, sweetheart. Ask away," Craw said.

"Screw you and don't call me that… but fine, yes, I have questions. Why did you have a hole in my apartment?" Taxx asked.

"Your Grandma is an old friend. Sometimes I did work for her," Craw said.

"Did you kill her?" Taxx asked.

"Fuck Off,"

"Why did you kill me?" Taxx asked.

"Didn't really mean to do that," Craw said.

"So, you accidentally murdered me?" Taxx asked.

"Is fulfilling your part of a prophecy an accident?" Craw said.

Taxx went silent. His face wanted to say a thousand things, but all it could do was look hurt.

"You knew that didn't you?" Craw asked.

Taxx nodded.

"Don't make that face. Prophecy is bullshit, and the berks

who write it down are worse. No offense to your family, of course. I just mean it's not worth trying to fight against it. You'll do what you are meant to do sooner or later. That's why I say screw it all," Craw said.

Taxx laughed. Then he frowned deeply.

"I'm still mad that you killed me,": Taxx said.

"Course you are. You're just like your ma," Craw teased.

A set of thorns grew out of Taxx's fist like a morning star. Black and sharp, about as long as a porcupine's quills, jutting out from his skin in all directions. Taxx and Craw were both staring at the weapon and then at each other.

"You are much more of a prick than you used to be," Craw said.

"I learned the truth about myself," Taxx said.

The thorns started to recede into his body as he settled down, and he flexed his hand when they were gone. He could feel them in there. Waiting.

"You've only learned enough to see yourself for what you are. That's only some truth," Craw said.

"If you know more, just tell me?" Taxx asked.

"Don't go chasing it too hard. Past hurts can still kill you. Take it from me. It's just a pain in the ass. That's why it starts with a P," Craw said.

The young man smiled and then frowned again, and craw scoffed and rolled his insect eyes.

"Leave it, for the god's sake," Craw said.

"Fine. One last question," Taxx said.

"Shoot," Craw said.

Taxx narrowed his eyes, and Craw smirked at him.

"Just kidding, go on," Craw said.

"If you can make the insects work like that, why do you wear skins?" Taxx asked.

"It ain't easy holding a human form. It's costly and, no offense, limited. But it greases the wheels when it needs to. Case in point. You are talking to me like I'm just a normal pr... I mean, person. How 'bout that?" Craw said.

"Ok. I guess that will do," Taxx said.

"Well then, Bugsy, tell us all about your plan, and don't skimp on the gritty details," Grayson said.

"Wouldn't dream of it. We lot will be pulling your standard double-cross mixed with a little smash and grab. With just a touch of familial revenge. My favorite. Now listen closely bell ends. Cause this is really going to take some imagination," Craw said.

Chapter | Twenty-two

Kingmaker groaned under the stress of Drip's body, the weight continued to increase with every step, and she had reached the limit of her strength. His body had gone from limp to rigid, and his shoes' tips were leaving visible drag marks on the ground.

"Jackdaw!" she screamed.

The massive birdman appeared at her side and attempted to take the weight of the stiff body. At first, even with his massive form, he could not take it on all at once. He had to grow a few sizes larger. Once he did, he carefully slipped the demon onto his back and started to drag him forward.

"What happened?" Jackdaw asked.

His voice was strained with the demon's weight, and Drip

had not moved since they stepped through the portal. It let them out into the main space of a large mansion, the frame of the cased opening still reverted to its original architecture. A key was piercing the door frame that looked like a skeleton key with its many teeth, but all of them were sharp. It required life to use that kind of magic, and one of her own paid the price. He now lay dead on the other side of the door frame. The cursed key stabbed through him. The portal was now closed. The key disintegrated when the curse ended, and his body sagged to the floor. Kingmaker could not look away. Jackdaw laid Drip on the couch, but still, his body did not move.

"He only touched him," Kingmaker said.

"What could do this with a touch?" Serrano asked.

The snake man stepped out of Kingmaker's shadow and bowed his head. The other two bowed in greeting. He had not replaced his human face since Sixx had damaged it. The snake man turned his clever eyes toward the bleeding boy, and he smiled. The girl in goggles was screaming her head off while the digital sorcerer tried to console her.

"I told you I should have killed him in the quarry," Serrano said.

"I told *you* never to sneak up on me like that," Kingmaker said.

"My apologies, Master. I come bearing good news," Serrano said.

Kingmaker nodded. She was watching Izzy weep over Sixx, and she laughed openly.

"Today is a day for good news," she said.

"Craw has succeeded in his part," the snake man said.

"Excellent," Kingmaker said.

"I will inform the emperor that his son is being delivered on schedule," Jackdaw said.

"See that you do," Kingmaker said.

"Shall I send someone to attend to… whatever this is?" Serrano asked.

"No," Kingmaker said.

She spoke too quickly. There was tension in her voice that changed the energy in the room. There were many of her creations in this space, all with bodies of various sizes and shapes hidden under cloaks. Some were human-shaped, but the majority were nothing of the sort, rectangular and bulging shapes draped with darker than black fabric that made them hard to focus on. She could feel them all looking at her.

"Do you know of the miserable creature called a rat king?" Kingmaker said.

She started to remove the complicated mask, it was made of thread, and it unraveled around her face, layer by layer. Even still, her voice never changed. It was deep and terrible. It was still booming with power.

"It is said that one among them demands the throne. A king would sit on a throne of its kin by blood or fear. A throne of rats. The king binds the others to him, tangling their tails so they can never leave him. They only know to do his will and act as the king's glory, a walking crown of lesser beings. A living dominion," Kingmaker said.

Her normal voice replaced the deep demonic voice of the Kingmaker.

"The truth is that they were probably fiction. Until I was born. I command threads that can sew thoughts and cotton. Bind a soul and mend a heart," Kingmaker said.

"Master," one said.

She stopped him with a single finger. At first, it may have seemed innocent, but the violet color of her magic was just barely visible. It bent around her finger like she had taken hold of a beam of sunlight in the early morning. The creature stood straight up like a marionette. The room fell silent. Even the prisoners fell quiet from the look on Offreys face. No, this was not the magistrate. This was the Kingmaker. The witch suddenly burst forward and struck him with terrifying speed. The victim was defenseless, and very quickly, it was over. A quiet assassination, completed in just a moment. Kingmaker raised her first two fingers; she held a long thread glowing like a filament between them. The creature from which she took it seemed to fall apart under its cloak, leaving several chunks behind. They started to move on their own, and dozens of small birds tried to escape the cloak, which had become a cloth prison. The sound of their calls filled the room.

"If I make a crown of lesser beings," Offrey said.

Threads slithered toward the cloak as she was speaking, and like clever snakes, they surrounded the moving mass. Then they struck all at once. The sound of birds suddenly stopped all at once. They slithered back toward their master when the deed was done, dragging crimson patterns behind them like a thread pull painting.

"What am I?" she asked.

All at once, the others kneeled, even Jackdaw, who stood at the door. They kneeled in unison. They bowed their heads and lifted their right arms in the air. No matter how many they had, each wore a single thread. As bright as a filament and glowing purple, the color of her magic. Without her mask, Offrey turned to face her kneeling pets and smiled.

"Hail Kingmaker," They all spoke at once.

"We are your menagerie. We live to serve you," Jackdaw said.

"Leave us and tell no one what you saw here," Offrey said.

"You have fallen so far," Avo said from behind her.

Offrey turned to look at him with genuine surprise on her face. Her eyes were visible for the first time. Where there should have been white, there was nothing but violet planes by the thousands. Like the facets of a jewel. Like the eyes of a spider.

"I honestly had forgotten you were here. I would have lightened up on the melodrama. It doesn't matter. There is no going back now," Offrey said.

"No!" Izzy said.

She pulled away from the odd-shaped being that held her and its many hands, rushing toward Offrey.

"What do you want, *creature*," Offrey said.

"You can come back. It doesn't matter what you did. There is always a way back to good. We are here for you when you want to come back. There will always be room," Izzy said.

"There is no good here, little fool. Kill her," Offrey said.

The cloak opened up behind her, and the creature beneath pounced before Avo could do so much as scream. It was made of hyenas, and there were five heads on long necks as thick around as a human torso. Four of the heads took her shoulders and thighs at once, immobilizing the girl. Izzy started to scream, but she quickly recovered and tried to work her mouth to speak. Before the sounds could become words, the fifth head slammed into her head and rocked her violently. Her goggles were thrown to the ground.

"Damn it, Offrey. You've won! Please! You know you don't

need to do this," Avo pleaded.

"You are absolutely correct," Offrey said.

Izzy shook her head slowly, starting to come around. She was bleeding an alarming amount, making it hard to talk. Her eyes were not eyes at all but puckered holes where eyes should be and an eyeball made of white flame. They had all the details of a normal eye, including an iris that was pale silver and spotted like the moon's surface. The fire danced with her fear.

"**Reflect**," Izzy squeezed out.

That was her final word before the hyena's head came down on her to take her life, striking where the neck met the shoulders. A flash of white light from her body shone between the vicious teeth. The light was gone with a final wink, and Izzy was lying on the ground. Her body was completely free of wounds, and her eyes were forever open. Always on fire. Even when she was no longer conscious. The hyena was howling in pain. It was covered in bite marks and bleeding from the head. Every wound inflicted on her seemed to have been transferred back to the creature that delivered it. The beast cried until it settled onto the floor and went still in a pool of brightly colored innards.

"That was a powerful reflection. Truly you are a formidable speaker. It is a shame. Let us see what happens when she is unconscious. Serrano," Offrey said.

The snake man had already taken two steps before Offrey lifted her hand, and he stopped cold. His haggard human mask was almost invisible around his intense eyes. They had taken on the emptiness of a hunter. His body was shaking with excitement, even in so short a time, but he did not move forward. Not even a step. The witch turned to face them. Avo stood in front of Rosen, who had wilted like a forgotten flower in a vase. Rose petals were gently cascading from her body and wandering to the floor. As they landed, they would flash out of existence. The great Fairy looked so weak now. It seemed that she could barely keep her eyes open.

"You all look pathetic," Offrey teased.

"Haven't you done enough!? She can't even fight back," Avo said.

The digital sorcerer moved to stand over Izzy, holding his arms out to block her with his body.

"You are hilarious. There are more pressing matters. Take them," Offrey said.

Avo tried to protest, but the menagerie fell on him in mass and dragged him out of the room. They took Izzy as well. When one of them tried to take Sixx, Offrey stopped them by approaching the young man and placing a hand on his chest.

"This one belongs to me," she said.

"And the other one?" Serrano asked.

"Don't be rude. Just because he miscalculated and died, he is still the master of this house, Serrano. Be respectful. Leave him. I will deal with this. Tell no one what you saw here. Spread the word," Offrey said.

"It shall be done," he said.

In moments the room was clear of everyone except Sixx and the body of Drip, that had not moved since they arrived. Offrey stood over it for a moment, there were words behind her lips, but her brain was clever enough to let them lie there until she was sure he was dead. Instead, she moved to Sixx and found that he had been left face down on the ground. She carried him to the same couch Drip was on and set him up in a sitting position. Once he was stable, she reached into the hole in Sixx's chest. Her fingers sank in with a wet noise. Then she started to dig around.

"Where have you hidden it?" Offrey asked.

Sixx didn't answer. Nor did he respond while she searched around inside of him. The needled seemed to have traveled quite a bit since she put it in. She found it near his skin on the other side of his chest. She broke it free and removed the needle from him, slipping it into her bandoleer. As soon as she pulled the long, hooked bone needle, he took a long breath. Then he coughed out some fluid that had built up in his lungs while he was dead. Once that was done, his wounds closed up, filling in like expanding foam over his enchanted black bones. He looked happy to see her for exactly one second before he nearly jumped out of his skin.

"Zora? What the hell did you do to me?" He shouted.

"Calm down. I saved your life," Offrey said.

"My beautiful black ass, you did," Sixx said.

"Saturday. Stop. Listen to me. The end of the world can't happen until Drip gets this blood and opens the door," Offrey said.

She reached into her belt and removed the vial of Taxx's blood that she stole when she stabbed him. Sixx covered his mouth as though he was going to be sick.

"Is that? Girl, you musta lost your **damned** mind," Sixx said.

"There isn't anyone else to stop it except us," Offrey said.

"Keep that mess, Zora. You a whole ass lie," Sixx said.

"Don't be like that. I love you," she said.

"Damn you and curse that tongue for repeating it. You don't know how you have vexed me, girl!" Sixx said.

His voice was different. There was less playful nature and

more magic. It was deeper, and its passion sent sparks through the air toward her. He stopped himself and took a deep breath, adjusting his jacket. Offrey approached him and slipped her hand into his coat, brushing his bare chest. He tensed up at first, but he made no move to stop her.

"Why do you stop showing your true self, Prince Death. You have a crown. The power of a god, and you should act as such," Offrey said.

"Speak your words, Delilah, but you will never cut my hair," Sixx said.

"I hate when you talk like an old man," she teased.

"What happened to him?" Sixx asked.

They both looked toward Drip's body and then back at each other.

"Your brother happened," Offrey said.

"She always said that he would show me something worth protecting. I'm sad I didn't see it," Sixx said.

"No one saw it. He barely touched him. Just a tap," Offrey said.

Drip was still frozen on the couch, his arms and leg still posed as if he were draped over Offreys back. All of the gold on him had become black, and there were plants in the last stages of life all over him. Mushrooms, ferns, and grassy weeds. They bloomed, fruited, and then died, just like that.

"Taxx did that?" Sixx asked.

Offrey nodded, and Sixx whistled low. The witch stepped closer and brushed her lips against his chin.

"Don't," Sixx said.

"Can't you see what I have set up for you?" Offrey said.

"This isn't what I wanted. I was never supposed to kill

Drip," Sixx said.

"Then who did your father send you to kill," she asked.

Sixx stepped away from her, ripping her hand from his chest and turning away.

"That's none of your damned business, Zora. Now, what the hell are we going to do?" Sixx asked.

Offrey approached him from behind and put her hands on his shoulders gently. She hugged him to her chest and kissed him on the neck for long slow moments until she felt him lean back into her.

"You have the status to take over the auction, and with my backing, no one could stop you," Offrey said.

She tried to nibble on his ear, but he stepped away from her, raising his hands.

"No! Damn it! I don't want to be some bad guy. That's exactly why I didn't do what he asked. Damn it all, woman," Sixx said.

"Don't fight it," she whispered.

"You confuse me. You are poison," Sixx said.

"Come," Offrey said.

"Wait. Something isn't right," Sixx said.

"Not yet, my prince, but I will make it right," she whispered.

"No, that's not what I mean," Sixx said.

Then she felt it too. There was a sort of heat associated with the energetic intent to kill. It was suddenly heavy in the air and all around them. Kingmaker turned to Drip's corpse. It had been destroyed. The entire chest cavity from the nose to the belly button had been opened up like a mishandled slice of sandwich bread. Something seemed to have forced its way out of him. Kingmaker summoned a threaded knife and searched the room.

"Drip may not be dead. There is something to do first," Offrey said.

There was no answer. She kept searching the room. A gold trail left his body, but it vanished under the furniture. It didn't seem to go toward the door, but she could not find it.

"Sixx. Whatever you are feeling now, you need to put that aside. Demons aren't just powerful. They are deathless. They do not die like things from here because they aren't things from here. If we aren't careful, he can and will kill us both. Probably eat us and worse," she said.

Still, there was no answer.

"Stop being a child!" She shouted.

Offrey wheeled on him. There was liquid gold all over the front of his clothes, narrowing down toward his mouth. She could see the worm-like being that made up the demon's main form crawling into his mouth. Sixx had a hold of it with his hands and with his teeth. He groaned against the monster and started to drag it out of his mouth. Inch by inch, it was being pulled out. Its body was like a salamander with the legs of a millipede, and each of them was a sharp little tack that was digging into his body. Though it seemed like Sixx was winning, he could not seem to pull it fast enough. Offrey didn't have time to think, so she reached out to grab it with both hands, and all of her fingertips sank into the creature's body. She screamed like she had put her hands in acid, and the sound of hissing accompanied the searing pain. When she pulled them back, every one of her fingers was cast in glittering gold to the first knuckle. The witch held back her tears, but her face made it clear that she was in pain. She held her hands up in front of her staring at the ruined tips of her fingers, the source of her magic. Destroyed. She saw the only man she ever loved, clutching at his own throat while liquid gold gushed from his mouth when she looked beyond her wounds. Sixx fell forward on his face and went still. There was only the soft sound of flesh being shifted violently.

"Sixx!" Offrey shouted.

The sound of her voice made his body twitch in reaction. She started to weep. He didn't seem to be dead, and in fact, he began to stir and stumble his way up to his knees. Once there, he looked up at her, and she reached out toward his face, screaming when she tried to move her ruined fingers. He seemed to be in one piece, but there was something wrong. She didn't know what but she was going to find out.

"Sixx. What happened? Where is the demon?" She asked.

He didn't answer. Offrey searched his face carefully, and that is when she noticed what was so off about him. His eyes were gold. Both of them were glittering bright gold behind his skin, and when he opened his mouth to smile, liquid gold poured out of him in a great swell. It leaked down his chin and neck and onto his bare chest. It crawled up his face, over his forehead, and into his hair, staining the white hair on his head with golden accents. Everywhere the gold flow traveled left behind a series of markings on him. Runic symbols in liquid gold now traversed his entire body. Then the gold flow stopped. His body did not leak anymore, and the liquid gold stopped coming. There seemed to be some homogeny inside of him, and whatever this creature was smiled. His mouth was filled with sparkling spiny teeth like an angler fish. They curled in and fit together like a bear trap.

"The demon is right here," Sixx said.

"No!" Offrey said.

"But yes!" Sixx said.

He stood up quickly, his body moving with enormous speed. It even seemed to surprise him. He started to laugh, showing off that horrible smile again.

"This one was holding out on you, homegirl. Such power," Sixx said.

"You can't do this. This wasn't part of the deal," Offrey said.

"Don't you dare try to tell me I broke a deal," Sixx said.

His voice was deep, and it crackled with power like tumbling rock. The reverberation shook the house. Sixx smiled, and then he started to laugh again.

"Excuse me, I still have to get used to all this… pedigree. The deal was that I would not kill him, standard BS. Even though he is now my vessel, that does not make him dead. That makes him useful," Sixx said.

"This is the emperor's son. He won't let this stand," Offrey said.

"So, I start a war. That's always profitable, and thanks to Taxxy, I have a prison full of weapons and the only key," Sixx said.

"I can't let you take him," she whispered.

"Seems to me that your emotions fucked up any chance of you doing shit about it. Unless you'd like to get out of our agreement? I can offer you a way out if you like, right now, in exchange for the boy. Whole new deal, what do ya say?" Sixx asked.

"You know I can't," she said.

"So, the deal stands," Sixx said.

"Drip," Offrey said.

"That's not my name anymore," Sixx said.

"What?" Offrey asked.

There was a soft knock on the door, and shortly after it opened, a man entered the room. He had a baby's face where a man should be, wearing a velour sweatsuit. One of his child-sized eyebrows raised as he looked at Drip's remains. Offrey brightened when she saw him, but the baby-faced young man looked sheepish when they locked eyes.

"Oh," he said.

Then he looked at her injured hands and then to Sixx, who was now covered in golden tattoos from neck to who knows where and smiling at her with those spiny teeth.

"Kiddo. Quickly, use your babble on him so we can get Sixx back," Offrey pleaded.

Kiddo looked back toward Sixx, who now seemed to be inhabited by the demon of greed. Then he glanced back at Offrey, and he smiled with miniature lips.

"Boss, I brought you a change of clothes, but it seems like you don't need that anymore. I think we are gonna need to talk later. Shall I throw out your old… coat?" Kiddo asked.

"Kiddo. You must be joking. You work for me," Offrey said.

"I work for the most powerful person, and that was never you. I was always an agent for Drip. Sorry," Kiddo said.

"I'll kill you!" she hissed.

"Not with those hands. You threw it all away for some boy. How far you have fallen. It's enough to make a baby cry," Kiddo teased.

"Now, now. Kingmaker is a valued associate. It's not her fault that her coup attempt ended in despair. I admire that drive. See that her hands are treated but get her out of my sight," Sixx said.

"Very good, Mr. Drip," Kiddo said.

"No, no, no," Drip said.

Kiddo paused after he slung drips old body over his shoulder and lifted it easily. Sixx started to laugh, flexing his hands, and looking at his body as though he had found money.

"What should I call you now, bruh?" Kiddo asked.

"Call me Mr. Sixx," he said.

"I like that. What's next, Mr. Sixx?" Kiddo asked.

"We have a hundred horrors to unleash. Might as well make it profitable. I think it's time we had an auction," said Mr. Sixx.

To be continued...

Death and Taxxis will return in:

<u>Black Summer</u>

AUTHOR BIO

A lifelong love of mythology, pop culture, and most of all, books are the essential parts of the spell that creates a natural storyteller. Being born in the All-American Naugatuck Valley of southern Connecticut also helps. It is a beautiful place steeped in history, tradition, and more than its share of a supernatural something. The perfect place to nurture and inspire an author. Expect the magical often, the macabre, perhaps, but you'll always find something sensational in the pages of a story told by Chris Graham.

In world where light is magic, two royals from opposite worlds must come together and awaken an ancient hero, or both of thier kingdoms will fall to darkness. Can Baan and Aila learn to get over thier differences in time to save the world?

The Lamplighter
COMING SOON FROM GHI

Chapter One

The sky above went black. The bright light of the Great Lamp was eclipsed by a crack that spread across everything until it was as big as the sky. Darker than black. There was chaos in its wake. The sudden darkness seemed to drive everyone to the ground all around. Only one person was left standing and looking up at the vast black sky. The topsiders panicked, and their cries devolved into wild screaming. They feared the dark. They were not used to their world being closed around them. They were not used to the feeling of weight above their heads. They tried to hide. To deny what they saw. Or rather, what they could not see. Even in the dark, they covered their eyes. Trying to will it away like a bad dream.

Baan could not look away. His eyes were opened to the world above for the first time. The Great Lamp's curse no longer stung his eyes in its light. He could see clearly. There was so much to look at, but the first thing that he saw was something incredible. Someone was flying, riding on a chariot across a bridge of seven colors. It cut across the black sky like a painter's brush. The chariot of light. At its helm was a man. He knew this man. Everyone alive knew this man. His statue watched him grow and fail and flourish all of his life. Baan did not have to see it to know his face. He knew this man. This was his hero. No one else would dash toward an enemy big enough to crack the sky, dark enough to shade the sun. The dark curled back from him in fear of his power. Seven colors of light poured out of his body and billowed out behind him like a cape. The light was the power that sustained this world. The spark that lit the Great Lamp and turned the world. Every shade and tone held the ability to change the heart and mind and affect the elements. The light was in everything.

Most are born with the color **red** in their hearts. It is the most common of the universal three colors, and it speaks of love and fire. Just slightly less are born with **yellow** light, the color of lust and lightning. **Blue** is the last of the universal three, the color of truth and water. **Orange** is one of the peerless three. Few have the color of peace and healing. Less than half that number can make **white** light, the color of hate and time. **Black** is the rarest color that any have been born with, the color of blood and ashes. Then there is **green**, the color of life and knowledge. There has not been anyone born who could make green light since the passing of The High Priest of the Horizon. The keeper of the colors. The only man in history who could hold all seven at once. Callum Alerus. The lamplighter.

Baan felt something stirring inside of him as he watched, and when he looked down at his chest, there was light pouring out of him. He tried to cover it up with his hands, but its energy seeped between his fingers, growing out of him and reaching the sky like a small flame. He felt eyes on him. He had started to close his eyes, but he was startled awake when he felt someone was watching. His body dropped, and his hands moved into the defensive position of his training. There were no eyes here, he could only see the scrambling topsiders, and none stopped to see anything. Baan looked up toward the lamplighter. Callum was staring right at him, and his eyes were so intense and focused that Baan turned away for the first time. He turned sharply, and his head smashed into something firm, and he snapped awake. It took him some time to compose himself, but he calmed down enough to understand that he was awake now. The eyes of the lamplighter were still in his eyes like a bad dream. They dug into his soul, and he could still feel them while they were gone. What was left was worse.

Baan had been down in the darkness of his dreams for so long that he had all but forgotten that he had been arrested. He managed to get one eye open enough to see with some struggle. His eyes were weak here, but still, he could make out shapes. The longer he suffered the light into his eyes, the clearer the shapeless forms became. He could almost make out the digits in the hands that opened the door to his cell and spread that hateful light. Baan turned away. His eyes were squeezed shut now. He did not want the light. The dark was quiet and safe. The Great Lamp brought only crowds of people, noise, and danger. All of the things he hated.

"So, this is one of them, beneath folk?" One of them said.

The voice was fast, like the words all rushed toward the mouth. Baan couldn't tell if it was a man or a woman playing at sounding like a man. Whatever the case, he was sure it belonged to a young one.

"He don't look like much from here. After hearing what happened, I felt he might be taller than this. He don't look so dangerous," the fast talker said.

A finger prodded his unguarded belly, followed by rough little giggles. These were children. Far worse than anything else, some top-side chits probably come to look at the Binethean. See what he was made of. Topsiders were notorious for being curious about Binethean people. They had many banal myths about his people, and the vilest and most dangerous rumor was about their blood. Many of them weren't shy about spilling it to see if it glowed as their lies said. He didn't trust top siders any more than a snake in his boot. He might trust the snake more. The snake could be counted on to be what it appears to be. A man would smile in your face while stabbing you in the backside, topsiders especially. To prove his point, one of them struck him in the stomach, and were he able to, he might have doubled over, but his hands and feet had been chained. He was attached to a rack system and a solid wooden frame to keep him from moving. When he felt the chains loosening and his arms coming down, he might have cried from relief if he didn't know what was coming next. It wasn't like they were going to let him go. The chains slacked enough for him to fall forward and then the manacles were removed entirely, finally freeing him from his bindings. He collapsed forward to the ground for the first time in far too long. He landed hard on his face, but he was so delighted to be connected to the earth again that he could almost feel his color returning.

"On your feet, ya blue bastard, she will be wanting to see you soon." Fast talker said.

The chit then gleaned to give him an offering by way of a warm, encouraging kick to his ribs to make him stand. He did try after a fashion, stretching slowly from the ground with his hands still planted on the mother. He drank of her strength as a topsider might soak up the light of their Great Lamp. He felt it radiate through him.

"I will start by addressing some of your mistakes. My people are called The Bineth. What you see is not my skin, it is a protective suit, and it only looks blue in this poor light," he said.

After hours of almost complete silence. No verbal communication. To hear him speak seemed to have froze them solid. They were just staring at him. His suit was opalescent. It fluctuated through many colors but mainly settled into a cool blue. Baan had his eyes closed tightly, but his accent was well-practiced. As much as he hated them, his father insisted that he learn the language. It had come in handy more times than he was proud to say. Baan found it sharpened up to a useable tool.

"Secondly, I am neither a bastard nor am I blue. My skin is the color you topside mongrels refer to as black," Baan said.

The two men grew increasingly uncomfortable under his condescension and insults. The fast talker was all but rubbing his toe in the dirt.

"Lastly, and this one, you may want to strain to hear topsider. If you try to take me out of these doors without my visor, my eyes will boil out of my head. Did you get all of that?" Baan asked.

The other person with the fast talker finally spoke, though unfortunately for Baan, he was the type to talk with his fist, and as it turned out, he was pretty well spoken indeed. With a **heavy** accent. The blow sent him reeling, and he scampered into a crouch, straining to see where the next attack might come from. His body shifted from toe to toe, turning him almost 180 degrees. Baan lifted his hands to defend himself.

"Come. I don't need eyes to fight you," Bann said in Bin'Eth.

The language of his people was very different from the

topsiders' common tongue. Bineth was music. A portion of it consisted of distinctive clicking sounds articulated in the mouth with precise air control. Baan overused it a bit here, but it was a good distraction. He could produce both sharp pops and smacks between the tongue and the roof of his mouth. Soft clicks between his lips or any other part of his mouth. There were also some whistles and deep throat sounds. He articulated every one of them with joy. It pleased him how much it scared the topsiders. Something hit him, and he recoiled away. The sensation was a soft touch, and it hit his arm and then fell to the floor.

He crouched and felt around with sweeping motions until he felt the familiarity of his visor. Baan snatched it up and slipped it over his face, and immediately the cell stone deadened the light so his eyes could adjust, and he could finally see. Two men were standing in front of him, children more like, no older than him. No more than 18 seasons. Children as prison guards left a lot of questions for him. His visor was clean still, which was a wonder since topsiders always liked to wear confiscated ones. They were crafted of intricately carved cell stone, the only gem that could hold light. His visor was the same ever-changing tone as his suit, as thin as wafers and cut into rectangular shapes. They sat over his ears and circled his head to hold firmly. They were intricately carved to entirely enclose his eyes in the stone and rested on the bridge of his nose like bifocals.

"It was getting embarrassing watching you flounder around like that," the fast talker said.

Bann approached him slowly. He was a hand and a half taller than either of them, and his body was born big. Wide and strong. That was likely where his attitude came from. Baan got as close as he dared and held out his hand, dropping a long shard of rock honed to a wicked point. The makeshift blade landed between them like a stone, and the two men looked down at it and then back up to their prisoner. He was staring at them with no emotions on his face.

"I was not flailing around. I was preparing to kill you both," Baan said.

Fast talker took a step back, and his face involuntarily flinched. The other one didn't move, but his face said he regretted the punches. That was enough for Baan. He looked pleased, but they seemed to take that as a show of force when he smiled. One of them even leaped away like he was an ember that jumped from a hearth. He was willing to let go of some things, but when they treated him like some dangerous animal, that always hurt the most. Some were born with the gift of clever fists. Baan was born with a much more troublesome weapon. A smart mouth.

"Stay away from him, Ed," the fast talker said.

"It's fine, Gon. The Bineth ain't as dangerous as they say," Ed said.

Baan audibly scoffed, and Ed scowled in response. Gon took a step back. Then forward. He looked apprehensive and liable to make some rash decisions. Or worse, act without any decisions at all.

"You may be on to something, topsider. I may be going soft. You win. I will spare your lives," Baan said.

"Cute," Ed sneered.

"Hardly," Baan replied.

Then he held out his hand again. Inside of his palm was another makeshift weapon. It was shaped like a spade, and it bit into the ground when he dropped it. He intended to use it to escape, but he decided not to kill them somewhere along the line. Gon looked like he might faint and froze under the Binethean boy's visor and his condescending smirk. Ed stepped between them and diffused the situation, ruining Baan's version of fun.

"Scaring him won't help you. *She* wants to see you. Whatever plans you have, you'd best change them. No one hates Binny's like she do," Gon said.

"Fracking topsiders," Baan said in Bin'Eth.

The two men forced him out of the cell, and Baan stood and held his head up high as he was escorted from the cell. One of them at his front and the other at his rear. At first, he was grateful for the exercise. He had been there for days, and it was good to walk again. Every step made him feel more vital bit by bit, and he would have plenty of time to gain strength. It seemed they had a long way to go, covering square footage that spoke of a marble palace to his toes. They climbed no less than four sets of stairs and passed more armed men than Baan could have imagined were necessary for all of this. He hadn't even done anything worthy of imprisonment to his eyes. Let alone in a place with so many armed guards. He may have foraged for food in a manner unfit for these people, but scavenging was the order of the day where he was from.

"For the love of ore, it was only one animal," Baan said.

"Is that what you call us?" Gon asked from behind.

"I meant the hoos. Whatever you call the game that I ate," Baan said.

Ed stopped and turned to face him. His face was now red with anger. Baan could not help the sarcastic smirk that took his face. That only seemed to make the young man even angrier. Gon stepped from around the Binethean and tried to hold back his friend, but Ed could not be stopped. He stepped forward and pressed a finger into Baan's chest. The smirk melted into a scowl, and Baan could scowl with the best of them.

"It's pronounced horse!" Ed screamed.

"Your passion for pronunciation is admirable," Baan teased.

"Hey! Don't tease him. That horse belonged to our family," Gon said.

Ed looked like he had been slapped, and the two boys looked at each other for a long pause. It was the first time that Baan noticed that these two beings were relatives.

They both had light hair and eyes, freckles, and round little noses. Their profiles were so similar. Baan lurched like he was going to vomit. Then he started to laugh. Laugh deep and loudly, slapping his knee. Once he had his fill, he settled and lifted his visor to wipe at his eyes. He took a few deep breaths. The boys were silent, staring at him with astonished faces.

"Blood and ashes. You were being serious?" Baan asked.

"Don't you dare laugh!" Gon shouted.

"Her name was Belal! She was not just *some* animal. That horse was to be a gift to the royal family. She was the last in a great line of racers. You **ate** the most famous horse in Lanthorn," Ed said.

His passions were clear, and even though Baan would have loved to push this person to the edge, even he knew when to stop. He lifted his hands. Gon scrambled behind Baan's back and nudged him forward. Baan started walking on, and Ed led the way. His footsteps were more serious now. It had always been his fascination to see the depths that most allowed words to affect them in a world where the color of light could steal your freedom. Take your breath. Baan could not resist his play, but he could be smart about it.

"She tasted like a thoroughbred," Baan said in Bin'Eth.

"What was that?" Ed asked.

"It means I'm sorry about the insult I have caused your

family," Baan said.

He even bowed his head a little to punctuate his lie. Ed nodded and visibly brightened in both color and demeanor. Gon nudged him forward, and on they went in blissful silence. After all that walking, they finally stopped at a wall with no less than a dozen sets of double doors. They moved to the central group and entered the room beyond, which to Baan's dismay, it was an even larger space filled with hundreds of people. All of them topsiders. The scowl on his face must have deepened because the people started to notice. There was collective booing as he was thrust before an empty, well-carved seat he could only assume was a throne. Some seat of power, though the person whose backside it cradled was nowhere to be found. Baan suspected they might have left the sovereign of their tribe mixed in the crowd, so he might not know the face to curse them or whatever nonsense they thought. There was little else for him to do but wait to be judged by these pale, wide-eyed animals. He might have just eaten the farmer if he knew the damned hoos would cause this much trouble.

Time passed, and Baan's knees began to ache. The throne remained empty while the restless crowd continued to grow behind him. People pushed into the room, piling against each other to gawk at the Binetian and scream slurs. *Downworlder* and *Binny,* their offense for his people. Two of them were not so dangerous. There were so many people here that he was effectively surrounded by angry people shouting. For the first time in this ordeal, Baan was genuinely nervous. Calls for vengeance echoed in the hall, and unnatural heat prickled across his skin. A mob of angry men screamed ancient hate and promised bloody revenge through the square. Baan became aware of the faint ringing of bells as armed guards forced him to the throne. Quite suddenly, the room fell silent except for those bells, now ringing so clear and loud and strong he felt them ringing in his skull.

A woman appeared after a moment. Her posture was so straight that it made every back around it seem lopsided. Her energy was not just regal. It was galvanizing. She was beautiful and fierce. Baan had not seen her in so long. Typically, the ceremony doesn't allow for their meeting. Her long body was wrapped in fur, bones, and teeth of unknown creatures. She seemed a feral beast that might gnash her terrible teeth and roar, but she was far more intimidating in her silence. She wore no shoes and made no sound as she walked. Her body seemed to float toward Baan. The unseen bells reached a furious crescendo as she stopped before him. The air in the room sizzled with heat that almost burned his lungs with every inhalation. He struggled to get away from this woman, but she held his body immobile with her gaze. She was the High Priestess of the Horizon.

Her eyes burned hotter than the air, making Baan forget about the ache in his knees. She was an absolute terror to behold. The fear she inspired shook loose the forgotten stories of his childhood. Tales whispered about fearsome topside warrior witches who could break a man's bones and speak light. He never believed those stories until today.

The fire in his lungs and the fear in his belly confirmed it. The Witch Queen had captured him, and he was powerless before her. Her swirling malachite eyes pierced his heart with terrible ease. Still immobile, he watched the bones around her neck scrape against the floor as she crouched down. She was nearly lying on her belly but still agile enough to creep toward him with a powerful show of strength.

The Queen started to sniff him from his foot and up to his scalp. Her body lifted from the ground as she did, her eyes locked on his face the whole time. She sniffed his scalp once more, and the air began to cool. Fear leaked from him as his body became his own once more. There was no curse; this ordeal was merely an appraisal. Her light was powerful. Baan let out a deep sigh of relief, and in a blink, the potentate was seated upright upon her throne. Her gaze weighed heavily upon him, even from afar. None present made a sound until a tottering older man shuffled forward and loudly cleared his throat. There was an atomized cloud of spittle in the air in front of him. Once that was settled, he began to announce his feral Queen proudly.

"It is your privilege to be seen by the blessed High Priestess of the Horizon. Queen Darragh Adair of Lanthorn."

The people howled once to their queen and stomped their feet, then there was silence. The Queen's crisp and clear voice cut through the silence and into Baan's mind.

"I have regarded you," she said.

"If I may," Baan started.

"You may not!" she said.

The crowds howled again. The Binethean only stared at her from behind his visor.

"Remove your Downworlder eyewear in front of 'er grace," the old man said.

"Dear Rohai. Would you dive between this **beast** to protect me? You are the heart of this land," she said.

Rohai blushed, and the crowd began shouting again. Thanks to his suit, Baan could feel his face getting hot, but none of the topsiders would see. The Queen only flexed her hand, and the crowd tapered into a silence.

"I would spare you," she said.

Baan allowed himself a moment of hope. He'd leave these dreadful witches and their delicious game animals far behind. That hope bloomed in his belly for twenty seconds before reality crushed it to a pulp. Rage erupted all around him, and he felt it to his bones. The citizens hurled slurs, spit, and threw trash at Baan between the guards' bodies that now protected him. Desperate hands grasped at his body, scratching him and ripping his clothes before they could be pushed back. These people would surely kill him, and Baan could do nothing to protect himself. He always imagined he'd die old and fat from living too richly. He never wanted to be torn apart by bloodthirsty topsiders.

The guards were barely holding them back now, and

there was nowhere for Baan to go, no way to save himself. Their screams ripped through his mind and threatened to burst his eardrums. Then everyone stopped all at once. The room became unnaturally silent, and the light changed tone all around them like ink in water. Eventually, it all went black. He could see people struggling against her magic, but they were powerless under the Queen's black light. Baan could only stare at her. The Queen whistled long and low, and everyone began to mimic her, even Baan. There was a heavy sense of fear in the hall when she was done. It hung in the air among the chandeliers.

"The fell color can control the blood, and I control the color. Remember that when you choose to defy **my** words," the Queen said.

"Defy **her** words?" Rohai echoed.

"As for you, Binethean. Ignorance is no excuse for breaking the law. I leave it to Lanthornian will," she said.

"What does that mean?" Baan asked.

"Call for th' jars!" Rohai shouted.

There was a flurry of activity, and large jars were being dragged into the room. It took more than a few men to get them moving. There were also dozens of people with baskets handing out rectangular tiles. Black on one side, white on the other. The automation was well-practiced, and each person passed the tile down to the left until everyone had them. Tabled her brought in and long rolls of paper. Quill pens, ink, and fragile older men wearing a sash that marked them as scholars. They wasted no time in starting, and one by one, the Lanthornian people made their way to the tables and slapped down a tile. The tallyman made his mark, and the next stepped up to place their tile. This continued in an orderly fashion until every man, woman, and child had a vote. The count was double-checked and double-counted. Once that was done, the result was presented to Rohai in an envelope. That envelope was delivered to the Queen, who sat on her throne for the hour it took to get the count. She opened the envelope and glanced at the results.

"The people of Lanthorn have spoken. For the murder of our beloved Belal. You owe us a life," The Queen said.

"No!" Baan shouted.

She flicked her hand dismissively, and Baan's whole body rose into the air. He rose as though an invisible rope suddenly yanked him up. Fighting against the power of her light was excruciating. He could see it, a cone of light as black as a shadow coming from the hand she held toward him. It was all around him and inside him, controlling his body by manipulating his blood. The color **black** was rare, and those who could wick it even more. Being born was not enough. There also had to be a knack for making the light show itself. Those who could channel the light from the inside to the outside were called Wickers. The keepers of the light. He groaned against her power. She must have monstrous power to be holding his entire body like this. The Lanthornian Queen was something to behold.

"I will not kill someone who can live in the hold of my black light. Your wick is strong. Perhaps some years in our prisons will prove that your debt is paid," she said.

Baan tried to protest, but he could barely breathe. Then the force that held him aloft was gone, and he fell hard. His body hit the floor with a smack that cracked part of his visor. There was pressure on him from all sides, and he could feel his skull starting to give. He didn't even have time to scream. Blood filled his visor and blurred his vision until everything faded to black. He was only vaguely aware of his legs being dragged along the ground and a dull ache through his whole body. Queen Darragh looked to her left and made a small gesture toward the crowd. The wronged farmer stepped forward as beckoned, eyes respectfully on the floor near the Queen's feet.

"See my stable master and replace what was lost from my private stable. A pale gift in the shadow of the hooves of the Belal line," she said.

"You honor me," he said.

The farmer bowed low, and his anger melted away into gratitude. He waved at his sons, who groaned but blushed with pride. The value of a single animal from the Queen's prized herd was many times more than the horse he had lost. A curse turned into a blessing for their little farm.

"Take him away, and let this matter be done with him. Merry parting," she said.

There was a joyous cry in the hall, and after some time of

respect and reflections, Rohai dutifully dismissed them, and the voting was declared over. The hall was already starting to clear, and many muttered about their disappointments and suspicions on the way out. This had been the most exciting thing to happen since, who even remembers when and it was over before anything good happened. The Queen didn't even show off. The guards filed out of the hearing room behind the townsfolk, and now the space was empty except for the Queen, old Rohai, and a newcomer. There was now a young copy of the queen. A beautiful, severe-looking young woman with bright golden eyes.

"What'll you do with him, dear? Do you need 'is parts?" Rohai asked.

He waggled his eyebrows suggestively.

"I had heard that if you dry and powder some of the good bits, it's good to keep up the libido," Rohai said.

The Queen's eyebrow only raised.

"Inappropriate in front of young priestess Aila, of course. Milady. Forgiveness to an old man," Rohai said.

"She prefers princess," the Queen said.

Aila straightened her back. Rohai looked between the two women, and a slow smile came over his face. There was the warmth of family in that grin, and the girl narrowed her eyes at him.

"I'm sure she does. All the same, what shall I do with the horse eater?" Rohai asked.

"He's just a man as you're a man, and nothing about your bollocks is special. He will remain whole. Besides, it seems a shame to bleed a brilliant man over a horse and bits," the Queen said.

"Brilliant? You mean to say you saw the light in that horse thief, grandmother?" Aila asked.

Her voice was sure and strong like her grandmother but still alive with the aimless mischief of youth. She was dressed in fur and bones and fangs, barefoot and her body was long and robust. There was a ceremonial braid in her dark black hair, but it was unkempt still.

"That is not a horse thief. That was the young Duke Deepstrider, and I've been very rude to him," the queen said.

"That man was Baan? The boy from the march? Oh my. Did you kill a Binethean Duke?" Aila asked.

"Duke, you say. You let one into the castle?" Rohai asked.

"That boy is more than twenty years, same as you," the Queen said.

"Grandmother. Did you kill Baan?" Aila asked again.

"Obviously not. Rohai. Divert our guest to the east tower. Have him treated and keep him well fed and spoiled until Aila arrives to greet him," She commanded.

"That one became a cave spider?" Rohai asked.

"A what?" Aila asked.

"He did. See that he does not hear you call him that," the queen said.

"May I take a few men. In case the young duke is... cross?" Rohai asked.

"I think you had better. His brilliance was remarkable. Be careful," she said.

Old Rohai nodded and shuffled away without further probing. The Queen sighed and a gentle, almost sad expression set on her face. The formality in her manner had disappeared entirely when addressing the younger woman. Her voice softened, and her shoulders relaxed as she motioned for the girl to step closer. The Queen's demeanor snapped back like a rubber band as she approached. The air was heavy, and the room slowly filled with black light.

"Go and prepare for the march," she said.

The Queen spoke slowly and steadily, resting the weight of her words upon her granddaughter's brow. Then the black light left the room. The young woman blanched. She stood in stunned silence for a long moment before crystal clear understanding pierced her heart like a hunter's arrow. She must prove her worthiness to inherit the Queen's mantle. Aila knew the day would come, but it still hit her like a ton of bricks. Aila cared not for power or people. She cared only for life with her animals, preferring the quiet solitude of the forest to life as a priestess, let alone a princess. She had been a recluse for so long that only her family and their longest-lived servants knew what she looked like.

Aila would sleep during the day and spend her nights in a centuries-old castle's gardens, libraries, crypts, and other dark and quiet places. It was a rare occasion anyone saw the princess, and it seemed as though she liked creeping around in the dark, but she didn't want to talk to any humans. The servants who knew her felt she was kind but strange and unruly. They usually only knew when she was home by the faint bog smell that would bloom in her stead where she had lingered. Food would go missing from the kitchen, and mysterious messes would appear.

Filthy laundry had been left under the windows. Plates of bread and cheese are left half-eaten on the floor. Books, papers, or relics are strewn around every flat surface. Dirt and plants, and even wild animals could turn up in the royal halls at any given time. The princess was a whirling dervish. The swirl of emotion passed, and now Aila's thoughts were racing too fast and too loud to hear anything else. The march was nothing new. She had been delegated the duty when she was still a child. A royal from both kingdoms was chosen to ferry Callum Alerus around the world. On the great highway that passed through Lanthorn and ended at the crying caves, the entrance to the Bin'Eth kingdom. It symbolized their alliance and unity in the light.

"Aila!" The Queen barked.

Aila snapped to attention.

"Have ye heard anything I've said? Or did your

imagination run away with you?" she asked.

Heat filled her cheeks, and she looked at her feet.

"Ah, Nan, you know it did," Aila said.

"Go and prepare," the Queen said again.

Aila opened her mouth to protest, but the queen stopped her with a look.

"Are you still having dreams about him?" the Queen asked.

"The Binny?" Aila asked.

"The Lamplighter. A vision of the Great Lamp falling dark?" the queen asked.

"Yes," Aila said.

"I have seen it too. Tell no one," the Queen said.

"Sometimes, he is there too," Aila said.

"The Lamplighter is always in your dreams," the Queen said.

"No. I meant the. I mean, Baan. Sometimes, when I dream of the lamp going dark. Baan is there," Aila said.

"That is a fortunate vision," The Queen said.

"Oh?" Aila asked.

"Or perhaps, quite a grave omen," The Queen said.

"Oh," Aila said.

Then the princess smiled, and she also rolled her eyes. Her grandmother ruffled her already messy hair.

"Prepare like a princess and carry yourself like a priestess," she said.

"Why do we have to do these silly ceremonial trips every seven years? Nobody even cares about the horizon march," Aila whined.

"A priestess does not decry her duty," the Queen chided.

"At least give me some sagely words of encouragement," Aila asked.

The queen thought for a long time. She was tapping her well-manicured finger against her lip. Then she smiled and moved to her granddaughter's side.

"I will tell you something a good friend told me when I was on my Horizon March if you promise to go and prepare," the Queen said.

"I will if the words are sagely enough," Aila teased.

"In the journey, we find our way," the Queen said.

The princess smiled and left the room without another word, leaving the Queen in the great hall, almost entirely alone.

"I wish you luck, Binethean," she said quietly.